NOWHERE CAROLINA

BOOK TWO: SOUTHERN DISCOMFORT SERIES

TAMARA LEIGH

THEY SAY OLD FLAMES DIE HARD.
THEY DON'T KNOW THE HALF OF IT.

Maggie Pickwick is a lifetime away from her days as head cheerleader and the mistakes she made in high school. Twelve years later, this single mom has traded pompoms for an auctioneer's gavel, popularity for peace and quiet, and strives to be a good example for her daughter, Devyn. She's keeping it together just fine, too—until an old flame moves back to her little North Carolina town.

Renowned artist Reece Thorpe wants nothing to do with Maggie—not after what she did in high school—but he might also be Devyn's father. Driven by her own pride and fear for her daughter's happiness, Maggie finds herself on a slippery slope of white lies as she attempts to convince Reece that she's changed. But the truth has a way of making itself known, and now Maggie's past *and* present mistakes could ruin her chance at love.

❧

"Tamara Leigh draws you in with a tale of small-town charm, the pursuit of love, and the life-changing power of letting go. The heart-gripping themes and delightful characters of Nowhere, Carolina *will have you turning the pages."* ~ JENNY B. JONES, award-winning author of *Just Between You and Me* and *So Not Happening*

"Tamara Leigh's Nowhere, Carolina *is just plain fun, Southern style. The characters are quirky and unusual without going overboard, and topping it all off is a sweet, genuine romance. I'm looking forward to reading more."* ~ DEANNA JULIE DODSON, author of *In Honor Bound, By Love Redeemed,* and *To Grace Surrendered*

"Thanks to Nowhere, Carolina, *I'm a Tamara Leigh fan for life! With the perfect blend of humor and heart, Nowhere, Carolina draws back the curtain on the mysterious mix of past mistakes, parental love, and the redemptive hand of God, showing that change is possible and hope is healing."* ~ AMY WALLACE, author of *Enduring Justice*

"Nowhere, Carolina *is a delightful tale that explores the beauty of truth and the freedom found in God's plans for all of us. I always enjoy Tamara Leigh's plucky and down-to-earth heroines, and Maggie Pickwick is no exception. This book was a pleasure to read, and I enjoyed it from beginning to end!"* ~ MARLO SCHALESKY, author of *If Tomorrow Never Comes* and the Christy award-winning *Beyond the Night*

NOWHERE, CAROLINA: Book One in the Southern Discomfort series, Copyright © 2010 by Tammy Schmanski, P.O. Box 1298, Goodlettsville, TN 37070, tamaraleightenn@gmail.com

All rights reserved. This book is a copyrighted work and no part of it may be reproduced, stored, or transmitted in any form or by any means (electronic, mechanical, photographic, audio recording, or any information storage and retrieval system) without permission in writing from the author. The scanning, uploading, and distribution of this book via the Internet or any other means without the author's permission is illegal and punishable by law. Thank you for supporting authors' rights by purchasing only authorized editions.

Print ISBN: 978-1-942326-44-1
Ebook ISBN-13: 978-1-942326-10-6

This novel is a work of fiction. Names, characters, places, incidents, and dialogues are either the product of the author's imagination or are used fictitiously. Any resemblance to actual events, locales, organizations, or persons, living or dead, is entirely coincidental and beyond the intent of the author.

CHAPTER 1

DAILY WORD CALENDAR
for Highly Successful Career Women

[**amal'gamate** *(verb)* to join together; to make as one]

FRIDAY, FEBRUARY 5

Despite the occasional whisper, glower, and slight, I need no one to remind me of my high school days. I was the stereotypical cheerleader—self-centered, superior, and more concerned with hair and makeup than the state of the world. Let alone Nowhere, North Carolina.

Well, not really Nowhere, though that is what I called the town of Pickwick, certain my future lay in some exotic locale like Hollywood. Funny thing is, that's where my introverted cousin, Piper, went when she up and left Pickwick after high school. But that's another story.

Yes, I was the real deal—a pompom-pumping, short-skirt-wearing, belly-button-bearing guy magnet. Not a bad thing. After all, Queen Esther, who in my teenage opinion was the only interesting character in the Bible, made the most of her beauty. And look where it got her. Fortunately for the Israelites, not where it got me.

Once I started acting on the attraction that made guys shove their way to the head of my line, I was all in. Competition for my attention was exhilarating, and though I never planned to *go all the way,* things progressed until...

Well, they progressed. And not just the one time. Which is why, when I ascended the stage over twelve years ago to accept my high school diploma, I did so with a basketball-sized bump that was further proof I was one girl whose vocabulary lacked a two-letter word that my boyfriends said was overrated—*no.*

As for the bump, her name is Devyn, though it wasn't until I delivered my baby that I thought of her as much more than an inconvenience and a threat to my figure. But she soon became everything to me, and I thank God I didn't give her up as planned. Even when she's like this.

I glance at her where she practically melts—

Hmm. Might my daily word fit here? Returning my gaze to the road, I mouth the four syllables: *amalgamate*—to join together; to make as one. This *is* the closest I've come to finding a fit for it today, and research shows that the sooner a person uses a new word, the more likely it will become part of her vocabulary.

Rewind. Devyn practically amalgamates with the passenger door. Uh...no. Makes her attempt to put space between her and her nemesis (that would be me) sound a bit *Terminator 2*-ish. Okay, so she practically *melts* into the door.

Lips pressed together, finger tapping the window, she glares at the passing scenery.

I sigh, wishing she were all bouncy and beaming like when I picked her up from school yesterday. But today, the forecast calls for mopey and morose. Now I know how my mother felt when I displayed teenage angst. Well, how she *should* have felt.

Adele Pickwick was more focused on keeping up appearances that were fast slipping away than on how her children were handling the pangs of adolescence.

The good news is that despite the surge of hormones, Devyn isn't destined to be the barely C-average, promiscuous teen I was. For one thing, I won't allow it. For another, she's not bent that way. Practically all twelve-and-a-half years of her are focused on academics. With me as her mother, I don't know how that happened, but I'm grateful God is answering my prayers the way I want Him to, even though He hasn't always been so accommodating.

Please, God, don't let me be pregnant.

Request denied.

Please, God, don't let my mother find out.

Request denied.

Please, God, don't let anyone try to talk me out of going to the clinic.

Just whom do you think you're praying to?!

Please, God, help me figure out who fathered this baby.

Request denied.

And forgive me for there being any question about it...times three.

Actually, He was very accommodating with forgiveness, approving my request in the person of Skippy Baggett, who should have hated the teenage girl who made her awkward daughter's high school years uncomfortable but who chose to love her instead. The mother I didn't quite have.

This goes to prove that God does know what He's doing. I just wish I knew what *I* was doing. For more than a year now, Devyn has badgered me about the importance of a father in a girl's life, citing articles and psychology journals, but I refuse to marry just to give her a father. That's not to say I discount the importance of one. It's to say I believe it's better to have no father than a bad one.

Slowly, Devyn's chin comes around, and I feel her gaze.

Here it comes again. Three…two…one…

"Did you know that teenage girls deprived of a father are twice as likely to engage in sexual activity early?"

Know it by heart. Just as I know the research she's citing didn't use the word *deprive.*

"And research shows that these poor souls are seven times more likely to become pregnant compared to girls who have a father in their lives."

I'm one of those statistics, as she knows, my daddy having skedaddled when I was fifteen. Of course, it was that or prison. Still, even when he was present, he wasn't always there.

Going for levity, I say, "Why, I think I have heard that."

Her eyes grow big behind her glasses, and then—

Dear Lord! She rolled her eyes. Has she become a disrespectful, button-pushing, mother-hating teenager like the one I became?

I grip the steering wheel hard. Only when my vision wavers, causing the lines on the road to shift dangerously, do I remember to breathe. "Did you just roll—?" My voice breaks, giving me time to reconsider the idiotic question. I look at my daughter, who is definitely amalgamating with the door. "You rolled your eyes, Devyn. I won't stand for that."

Her expression wavers into remorse. "Sorry, Mom. It's just that…" Though her voice is small, I sense a heavy presence behind it.

I brake at a light behind a soccer mom's happily graffitied van and lay a hand on my daughter's knee. "What's wrong, Dev?"

She exhales a breath larger than her small frame should be able to hold. "Do you even know who my father is?"

It's all I can do to keep my head from snapping back. Not that being haunted by my past is anything new, but when it's channeled through my daughter…

Times like this, I wonder why I didn't leave Pickwick as Piper did. Of course, now she's back, not only to aid our uncle with the liquidation of his estate, but to lay claim to his godson and gardener, Axel Smith.

Ah, Axel, previously a top pick on Devyn's list of potential fathers—a spreadsheet-styled sheet of paper I discovered tacked to the back of her closet last spring that identifies each candidate's positive *and* negative attributes. If all I was looking for was a father for her, he would have been a good pick. But I'm selfish. I want someone for me too.

"Well, Mom?"

The light turns green, providing an excuse to avoid her gaze as I accelerate through the intersection. "I'm guessing somethin' happened at school today."

She sighs. "When a person answers a question with an observation, it's often because she's uncomfortable. She doesn't want to answer the question, which answers it, doesn't it?"

When we get home, I am canceling her subscription to that stupid psychology journal she had to have for Christmas. I glance at her, and she raises her eyebrows above her glasses.

Inwardly groaning, I pass the soccer mom's van. "How about this? You spill on what happened at school, and I'll answer your question."

Devyn groans—nothing inward about that. "Parental prerogative?"

I probably invoke it too much, but some of the questions she asks... "That's right." I almost hope she won't spill so I don't have to answer her question, especially since I have no idea how to do it. Why didn't I better prepare for this day?

Devyn pulls away—de-amalgamates?—from the door and crosses her arms over her chest. "All right, I'll go first. Amanda Pigg and I got into it at the lockers today."

Amanda Pigg. Again. That little—

Be Skippy. Be. Skippy.

Oh, but the temptation, especially with a last name like that and a penchant—

Ha! Used one of my daily words!

—for bullying my little girl. "What did the two of you get into?"

"She thinks just because her locker is above mine— And how did that happen? *Pickwick* comes before *Pigg*."

And popular girls come before unpopular girls. That's the way it is in middle school. "Go on."

"She thinks that gives her the right to step on me and my books."

"So you…?"

She hooks a hank of straight brown hair behind an ear. "I told her it gave her no such right."

That's my girl. "And?"

"She put a foot on my books and told me to— I'll spare you the R-rated version. She told me to take my big nose and sorry rear and stick them where somebody cares."

Catching sight of my white knuckles on the steering wheel, I splay my fingers and look at her. I don't expect to see tears, and there aren't. She's that confident, even in the face of bullying. As for her nose, it is *not* big. Okay, a little, but only because the rest of her face is so fine featured. And there's nothing sorry about her rear. She's just small for her age—petite, especially beside me, as it only takes a pair of shoes with a slight heel for me to hit the six-foot mark.

"How did you respond, Dev?"

"I told her to stop bein' a stereotype, and she said, *Stereotype?* So I spelled it for her, defined it, supplied a few synonyms, and said that just because pompoms are her life doesn't mean she has to be plastic like them. Or as skimpy in the brain department as her skirt."

Backlash alert! If someone had had the nerve to say that to me—and there were times I deserved it—I would have reduced her to a convulsing mass of embarrassment. "I'm sure she didn't like that."

Devyn looks ahead. "That's when she said that at least she knows who her father is. That she isn't a..."

A stone drops through me as she sinks her teeth into her bottom lip, doubtless searching for something less R-rated.

"That she isn't the *illegitimate* child of a..."

Another stone.

Devyn's gaze flicks to me, and I think there might be a sheen in her eyes. "...promiscuous, holier-than-thou Pickwick."

Why, that little—

Be. Skippy.

I know, but if that *Pigg-g-g-g* makes my daughter cry...

"She said there were a half-dozen guys who could have fathered me—"

That's a downright lie!

"—and you have no idea which one it is."

Not a lie. Realizing I've exceeded the speed limit, I ease up on the gas and peer sidelong at my daughter. Definitely a sheen. I know God doesn't make children pay for their parents' sins, but it seems Devyn is paying for mine. And Amanda Pigg is the one collecting the back taxes. That...pig!

Oh, Lord, I shouldn't even think it, but You gave me flesh and this flesh is weak—especially when someone hurts my baby. Is there any mother capable of turning the other cheek when her child is being picked on? That is, other than Skippy?

Devyn once more presses herself against the door. "That's what her uncle told her."

Jake *The Bullet* Pigg, running back for the Pickwick Panthers, one year ahead of me, and who had a difficult time comprehending that I no longer cared to date him. Even stalked me for a while.

As Devyn resumes her window tapping and I struggle to untangle my emotions, I nearly miss our turn.

"Is it true what Amanda said? Is that why you won't tell me about my father?"

"No!" *Sorry, Lord, but surely I can be forgiven for a knee-jerk lie, it not being premeditated and all. Too, not all of it is a lie. There were only three who could have fathered Devyn.*

Only *three? Goodness! You were one morally superior young lady.*

"Then?"

I concentrate on the road. After all, it's a rather circuitous route to get home.

"Mom?"

How I miss the days when she called me Mama and I was the answer to all she needed. The heart-tugging word still slips out occasionally, like when she's joyous or sad and seeking comfort, but it's going…going…just about gone.

"Mom?"

I take the next turn. "You know I don't like to talk about your father." True. "It didn't work out between us, so we both moved on." True again. "He is not going to come back into my life and sweep us off our feet." The whole truth and nothing but the truth. No need to mention that last summer the possibility existed—the coming back into my life part—when Piper confided that my uncle wanted to commission Reece Thorpe to sculpt the new statue for the town square.

I was frantic when Uncle Obe refused to budge, but God was watching out for me. Reece's artistic talent is in such high demand that he couldn't be bothered to fit a nowhere place like Pickwick into his schedule. Of course, he probably just didn't want to come back here. But no polish off my nails. It's true that of the three who could have fathered Devyn, I would prefer it was Reece, but the timing of her birth makes it unlikely, so why muddy the water? As for the statue, another sculptor was commissioned, and work is set to begin soon.

I turn one last time into a cul-de-sac and pull onto our cobblestone driveway that, for all its charm, is a bit hard on the well-endowed woman. Cutting the engine, I slip into a smile. "Have we cleared the air?"

Devyn peers at me through a thick fringe of lashes magnified by her lenses. "No."

Too much to hope for. "Let's do it, then."

She pushes back her narrow shoulders. "Setting aside the question of who my father is, the fact remains that I don't have one. And I need one. And you don't seem bothered by that."

She has no idea. I close a hand over her two. "Of course I'm bothered, but finding a father for you and a husband for me is not a mail-order matter."

Her gaze turns so intense it nearly shuts me down for fear of what's about to exit her mouth. "I know, but what if my father isn't married?"

Oh, Lord, this again...

"For the two of you to have... Well, there had to have been somethin' strong between you, right? Some kind of bond?"

That would depend on which of the three we're talking about.

"And what if you were to tell him about me?"

A question first raised a year ago when she asked why she had never met her father, and I had to tell her he didn't know about her. This isn't entirely true, as two of the three were aware of my pregnancy and neither stepped forward to ask if he was responsible. Becoming a teenage father was not in their plans. Thus, I told Devyn what was as close to the truth as I could come without making her feel unwanted. And it might be true—*if* Reece Thorpe fathered her.

She pulls her bottom lip between her teeth. "Maybe we could all be a family."

My face feels as if it might crack. *Lord, I know I'm forgiven, and I will tell her the whole truth one day, but right now she's too young. Please help me give her what she needs without hurting her.*

I sip air, afraid a deep breath will reveal the true state of my emotions. "I wish that were so, Devyn, but it isn't."

Sorrow and disappointment vie for the limited space on her face.

"I love you. You feel that, don't you?"

She nods.

"You are too precious for me to rush into something as important as marriage. If I'm going to give you a father, he has to be the right one." I raise my eyebrows. "Hmm?"

She sighs up her face, fogging her glasses, then turns her hands and squeezes my fingers.

Crisis averted. For now.

"Okay, but do you think you could try a little harder? The longer you wait, the slimmer the chance of giving me a brother or a sister."

I break into a goofy smile. "If we get down to the wire, I could always accept Mr. Peterson's offer of marriage."

She makes a face. "He's a nice guy, but...needy."

"Then I'll have to keep looking, and *you'll* have to be patient."

The genuine smile that appears on her face transforms her from pretty to beyond pretty—even with that little gap between her front teeth. She may not have my fiery red hair, blue eyes, or prominent cheekbones, and it doesn't appear she will have my height, but there is far more to my little girl than the *plain* label others slap on her.

Devyn shows a bit more teeth, proving she does have my smile. "You can count on me to help out however I can."

Ugh. "You just worry about your schoolwork, young lady. I'll take care of the rest."

Shortly, huddled into our jackets against the chill February air, she precedes me up the walkway, and I smile at the bounce in her step.

As we reach the front door, the house phone rings. I turn the key in the lock, and as I push the door inward, the answering machine picks up, plays my snappy outgoing message, and beeps.

"Maggie, it's Piper."

I drop the keys in my purse and head for the kitchen.

"I just found out that Uncle Obe's sculptor pulled out last week."

I halt. What does that mean?

"And I'm only now hearing about it. Can you believe it?"

I feel for my formerly estranged cousin. She couldn't have realized the extent of her commitment to help our uncle put his affairs in order.

"The guy says he can't work with Uncle Obe."

"Miss Piper sounds upset," Devyn calls from the stairs. "Aren't you going to pick up?"

I should, but I'm still angry with Amanda Pigg, and right now I need a few minutes of quiet to put everything in perspective—with my Bible open, as Skippy would advise. "I'll call her back later."

The stairs creak as Devyn resumes her ascent, and a sigh heaves from the answering machine. *"He says Uncle Obe is crazy."*

I wince. Odd by nature, but most recently unbalanced by slowly advancing early dementia, our uncle definitely isn't *all there.* And I wouldn't be surprised if Piper is questioning her decision to sell her partnership in one of the most successful PR firms in Los Angeles to move back to Pickwick.

"I'm still trying to figure out what happened, since Uncle Obe is pretending he doesn't remember the call that caused the guy to back out. I declare"—she groans as she does when the South creeps back into her speech—*"he's using his dementia to his advantage. So now we're in the market for a new sculptor."*

Reece? Surely not. He can't be bothered to fit Pickwick into his schedule, which is one more prayer answered the way I wanted. It's always a relief to discover that God and I are on the same page.

"I just wanted to put you on notice, as it occurs to me that Uncle Obe has someone up his sleeve, and I don't need to tell you who that is."

She's thinking Reece too, but she's wrong. *Right, God? We are on the same page, aren't we?*

"Call me when you get in."

I rush across the kitchen, but when I slap the phone to my ear, the dial tone is on the other end.

Since Southern belles no longer wear corsets, I can't blame my near swoon on a painfully cinched-in waist. It's all me. And my past that may be coming back to haunt me in person.

I place a steadying hand on the writing desk and close my eyes. "I know You know what You're doing, but just for the record, Reece's return to Pickwick would be a very bad idea. You agree, don't You?" I nod. "On the same page."

Oh, Lord, please let us be on the same page, especially where Devyn is concerned.

CHAPTER 2

DAILY WORD CALENDAR
for Highly Successful Career Women

[**bowd'lerize** *(verb)* to remove or change passages, as in a play or novel, due to objectionable or vulgar matter]

THURSDAY, FEBRUARY 11

One thing that should have been established at the outset, and which will doubtless become apparent, is that my mouth is my best asset. Unfortunately, sometimes it lands me in the debit column, which is why I find myself flattened against the outside wall of Fate and Connie's Metalworks, one hand to my mouth for fear of emitting another screech, the other to my heart in an attempt to settle it. But the screech wants out—bad. And once again, that awful feeling that I might swoon can't be blamed on a gut-squeezing contraption. That blame lies with Reece Thorpe. In the flesh.

As I came around the corner, one glimpse of his profile was all it took to transport me back thirteen years. And I let fly a cry as I reversed and slammed back against the wall of the building. But that's not the worst of it. No, that would be too merciful.

Praying my screech wasn't heard over the racket coming from the tin-and-cinder-block building—

You can at least do this for me, can't You, Lord?

—I draw a stiff breath and inch forward to peek around the corner.

That's the worst of it. With his hands in his jacket pockets and face to the sky, Reece stands over my daughter. God and I are definitely not on the same page…chapter…maybe even book.

Lying on her back on the scrubby grass where I left her to make snow angels while I met with Fate to discuss my new signs, she shades her eyes against the sun and swings her hand to the right where the clouds have retreated.

"Those there are stratocumulus," she sweetly drawls. "You see the way they're formed, like pillows stacked on each other?"

"Yes."

With a strangled gasp, I once more apply myself to the wall —not because of the spine-tingling inflection on that single word, but because the voice is almost as familiar now as it was thirteen years ago. As if I never stopped hearing it.

Ridiculous! Fanciful! I silently scold. *You are no Disney princess, and Reece Thorpe is no tights-wearing prince.*

You can say that again. He may have been more interested in art than chest-pounding, bone-crunching football, but he was all guy in a quietly assured way that made a girl take a second look, and a third.

Oh, stop! He's just someone I knew, dated, and…may have conceived a child with.

Lord, what have You done? Piper assured me she had convinced Uncle Obe to go with a female sculptor out of Florida, so what is Reece doing in Pickwick?

I peel myself off the wall and peer around the corner of the building again.

His head is still back, his wavy black hair brushing the collar of the shirt beneath his jacket. “So no more snow, hmm?”

“This is it.” Devyn pats the pitifully thin layer that caused the schools to let out early.

Yes, we do that here—cancel school at the first whisper of snow. People from places like Minnesota, where snow is the status quo and a foot of the white stuff barely registers as a hiccup in their day, can laugh all they like. They’re prepared. We’re not. And so school is canceled and everyone rushes to the grocery store to stock up on milk, bread, and canned goods, just in case more than an inch falls and they find themselves snowed in. Well, snowed in by our standards.

Reece turns his back to me, and I notice that his well-worn jeans fit him even better than they did in high school. He filled out nicely for someone who was already well filled out—just an observation.

And a waste of time that would be better spent extricating myself and Devyn from what threatens to become a mess. I look over my shoulder at the loading dock, which is the only way to get Fate’s and Connie’s attention, since they don’t employ office help and have no time for front door etiquette. As it would seem to be Reece’s destination—most of the manufacturing businesses on High Holler Road having closed long ago—I can’t go back inside.

I consider my SUV parked thirty feet away. It sports a magnetic door sign that advertises Serendipity Auction Services—my business, the one that makes such good use of my mouth. *Hey, bidder, bidder!* Fortunately, the sign is only on the driver’s side, where Reece can’t see it, the passenger-side sign having departed for parts unknown. Unfortunately, I can’t get to the vehicle without being seen. Of course, Reece might not recognize me.

Oh, like you didn't recognize him? Note: you are nearly six feet tall and still an unapologetic redhead.

"What about those clouds?" He nods at the balls of fluff creeping toward Pickwick.

His elongated *O*'s evidence he still possesses some of the midwestern accent that set him apart the one year he lived in Pickwick. I don't know why, but I loved those *O*'s.

Devyn rises onto her elbows, causing her hood to drop to her shoulders and the sunlight to play up the golden hair among the brown. "Just passing through."

"Too bad."

"Yeah, it would be nice to have more snow, but—" She frowns and whips her head around.

I slam back against the wall so hard my head bounces off it. That hurt! But worth the lump if Devyn didn't see me. Did she?

Please, God, this is such an easy prayer to answer. What have You got to lose? Surely not as much as I do.

Above the grind and screech coming from the building, I hear Devyn's voice again...then Reece's...back to Devyn...more Reece. What can they possibly have to talk about?

I peer around the corner. Devyn is standing now, two feet separating her from him. I drop to my haunches behind the straggly hedge that fronts the building and look between the branches. Unfortunately, another of Fate and Connie's whiney, high-pitched machines starts up, and I can't hear what Devyn says. Reece's answer makes her laugh, and then his mouth turns up. Is that my daughter's smile? No, she has mine.

Still, I search for a resemblance between the two that probably doesn't exist. Her hair is brown, his is black. If memory serves me correctly—and does it ever!—his eyes are green, while hers are brown. What about noses? Maybe Devyn's is on the slightly big side because Reece's is? No, his has a bit of a bump halfway down the bridge, whereas Devyn's is smooth. Thankfully! As for their chins—

My daughter extends a hand.

I clench my fingers around handfuls of snow, grass, and dirt. "Don't say it," I whisper. "Do not say it."

But she does, just as the whiney machine quiets. "I should introduce myself."

You should not! Vaguely aware of the chill against my palms, I stare hard at her profile, willing her to be capable of telepathy. *He's a stranger, and you know what I'm always telling you about strangers—*

"I'm Devyn Pickwick."

Obviously, we need to have a talk, young lady!

Were I not watching for the snag between the time Reece's hand comes out of his pocket and the time it closes around my daughter's, I wouldn't have noticed his hesitation. But it's there. In a collective Pickwick sense? Or a Maggie Pickwick sense?

"Reece Thorpe." He returns his hand to his pocket. "I knew some of the Pickwicks when I lived here years ago."

Please, Dev, don't ask which ones.

She pushes her glasses up her nose. "So you've moved back?"

Good girl.

"Actually, I'm here on business."

Uncle Obe and I also need to have a talk, but first I have to get my daughter away from Reece.

It's me again, Dev. Cease and desist! Say you need to...uh...finish reading your psychology journal.

"What kind of business?" she asks.

How about you have to go to the bathroom. Bad!

"I've been commissioned by Obadiah Pickwick, whom I would guess is your great-uncle?"

She dips her chin. So much for telepathy.

"He wants me to sculpt a statue for the town square."

"I thought he was going to hire a lady sculptor."

I press my cold, raw hands together—hands that have grown oddly numb.

Reece shifts his lower jaw, causing something to appear in the left corner of his mouth. A toothpick? He clamps down on it and shrugs. "Must have changed his mind."

Devyn wrinkles her nose. "He does that."

Reece tilts his head to the side, as if sizing up my daughter's face as he once sized up mine before setting it to paper with charcoal. "I'm guessing you're either Luc's—"

Help me out here, Lord!

"—or Bart's."

I can't say where the snowball came from, all compact and reinforced with grass and pebbles, but the moment of contact is etched in my mind—a blur of white striking Reece upside the head, his grunt of surprise, then his chin coming around.

Finding myself on my feet and wondering why my throwing arm feels strained, I run. Down the side of the building. Around the loading dock. Behind the building. Up the other side of the building with its obstacle course of ankle-breaking debris.

When I stick my head around the corner, my daughter is alone with her hands on her hips as she stares at the opposite corner that Reece must have gone around in pursuit of the snowball bandit. Time to go.

"Devyn!"

She turns and startles at the sight of me.

I don't look that bad, do I? Of course, my face feels flushed, moisture dots my upper lip, and if my peripheral vision serves me right, grease graces my pant leg. Great.

Though I control the impulse to run for the SUV, I feel the impatient jerk in my stride as I close the distance between us. "I've okayed the new signs, so we're good to go."

Her lids narrow. "Are you all right?"

I fan my face. "It was hot in there." It really was. All that metalworking generates a lot of heat. Now if only I had the feeling back in my hands. Discreetly wiping my wet palms on my pants, I draw even with Devyn. "Let's go."

"But you look—" As I hurry her forward, she snaps her chin around. "Why did you come around that side of the building?"

"You know that article you were reading about the differences between the brains of happy people and depressed people?"

She gasps. "You haven't been throwin' snowballs, have you?"

"Doing what?" I open my eyes wide and innocent, the art of which I perfected during my elementary years.

Devyn scrunches her nose again and shrugs. "This really weird thing happened."

"Oh?" I give her a little push toward the passenger door.

"I was standing over there talking to this man who, by the way, has been hired by—"

"Get in, Dev." I hurry around the grill of my SUV. "You can tell me on the way home."

"O...kay."

As I yank open the door, I imagine hot breath on my neck and glance around. No Reece. Hopefully, he's caught up in a conversation with Fate and Connie.

"Hurry," I say as Devyn slowly slides in beside me.

"Why?"

I shove the keys in the ignition. "We have lots to do."

"But I thought we were going home." She closes the door.

"We are." I reverse, crank the wheel, and accelerate out of the parking lot.

"Mom!" She clicks the seat belt in place. "What's the hurry?"

I check the rearview mirror. Still no Reece. "Well, there are your chores, and..." I turn onto High Holler Road. If I can just make it around the curve ahead, we'll be out of sight. "...while you're at them, I need to run over to Uncle Obe's." I take the curve fast, and though the wheels stick, it's a close one.

Devyn grips the door handle. "You're acting strange."

Yeah, well, you may have just met your father for the first time, so I'm a little shaken up. Thank goodness she *isn't* telepathic.

"Sorry. It's just that this early school dismissal has thrown my day." I ease up on the gas. "So tell me about the man you were talking to." I slide her a stern look. "You know I don't like you talking to strangers."

She sits back. "His name is Reece Thorpe, and he's the sculptor Unc-Unc hired to make the new statue. Anyway, we were talking when a snowball came from out of nowhere and hit him in the head."

I shift my hands on the steering wheel, glad the feeling has returned to them. "I suppose someone was just having fun with him." I chuckle. "It's not as if he was hurt, right? It *was* just a little snowball." Even if a bit hard and scratchy and pebbly.

"He seemed fine, though annoyed. I told him it was probably Mr. Fate and Mr. Connie messing around. You know how they are."

Fortunately for me, they *are* a bit off the scale. "So he went in search of the perpetrator?"

"Yep."

I shrug. "I'm sure they'll work it out."

"Uh-huh."

Is that it? Did I pull it off? My tension eases when she opens her psychology journal. *Thank You, Lord—*

Do you honestly think He had anything to do with you worming your way out of that one? It's called deception, Maggie. God does not do deception.

The tension returns. Though I'm not perfect and have to ask for forgiveness on a fairly regular basis, I broke myself of the everyday habit of deceit years ago, but I have the feeling it's back. And under the circumstances, I have no idea how to make do without it. I can't tell Devyn the truth, not at her age. And in my defense, it's not as if I came right out and lied. I skirted the issue, cut out the objectionable matter—

Ah! I *bowdlerized.* I sit straighter. Though my daily word calendar defines the word in terms of written work, with a little bending, it fits. And with its high-flying pronunciation—long *O* and all that—it lends an air of legitimacy to my attempt to spare my daughter the truth.

"Here's the article," she says.

"Hmm?"

She nods at the picture that features colorful brain scans. I should have known my earlier attempt to change the subject would come back to bite me. Boring!

"It says there are decided differences between the brain of a person who is not experiencing major strife and the brain of a person who is under great stress—"

That would be me.

"—and has been diagnosed as depressed."

No diagnosis yet. I point to the scan on the right. "That one's kind of pretty."

"It's also kind of depressed."

Figures.

"You want yours to look like this." She taps the left scan.

Does my brain look like that? If so, for how much longer?

Be pro-active.

Right, as in find a way to get Reece Thorpe out of town. And out of my life. Again.

CHAPTER 3

"Got it." Cell phone squeezed between cheek and shoulder, I scribble the phone number called off by my seventy-year-old assistant—a desperate hire until I can replace the traitor my competition enticed away from me.

"And don't forget to pick up toilet paper," Mrs. Templeton says in her crotchety voice as I ascend the steps to the front door of the Pickwick mansion. "Last I was in the bathroom, there was only a few turns of the roll left, and you know how fast it goes with folks who don't know nothin' about storin' up for hard times. Yep, best get you a whole case."

My life is *so* glamorous.

"And don't be wastin' no more money on that fluffy stuff. It's expensive, especially considerin' where it ends up."

I'd rather not. "A case it is." Of the *fluffy* stuff. "Well, I'm at my uncle's—"

"Oh, mercy! He called earlier."

I mute my groan. Since my cousin Piper had to fly to Atlanta three days ago on a consulting job for her old PR firm, I agreed to fill in to ease the burden on the caregiver hired to stay with Uncle Obe. I don't mind. It just would have been nice to know what he wanted me to pick up so I could have made one trip.

"What does he need?"

"Nothin'."

He just wanted to talk? That doesn't sound like him.

"I told him you were off runnin' errands, but when I tried to give him your mo-bile number, he said he didn't need to talk to you after all."

A knob rattles at the back of my mind. "Did you tell him where I was going?"

"I did. Hey, how do the new signs look?"

She told him I was going to Fate and Connie's. That has to be how Reece Thorpe and I ended up at the same place at the same time. "They look good. What time did my uncle call?"

"Two or three hours ago."

That fits. I look at the front door, somewhere behind which lurks my meddlesome kin. Thankfully, Devyn didn't try to talk me into letting her come along (those psychology articles are good for something). "Thank you, Mrs. Templeton. I won't be back in today, so can you lock up?"

"I can. Now don't forget the toilet paper, hear? And would you tell Trinity not to be late for supper?"

Her granddaughter, whose housekeeping services Piper enlists to keep the mansion in shape. "She's not here."

"You sure?"

Who could miss the battered VW Bug painted to look like Cinderella's pumpkin coach? "Positive."

She grunts. "Probably off with that no-good cousin of yours."

Bart, who has been dating Trinity since last year. "I need to get inside, Mrs. Templeton. Bye." I slip the phone into my purse and step forward.

The door is answered almost immediately. "Ms. Pickwick! How nice of you to drop by." Ida Newbottom—retired nurse, once-upon-a-long-time-ago hog wrestler, and twenty years my senior—smiles.

I make a face. "*Ms. Pickwick*? What happened to *Maggie*?" I don't often run into her, but when I do, I'm Maggie to her, and by invitation years back, she's Ida to me.

She smooths her nurse's fatigues. "As I am here in a professional capacity, Ms. Pickwick, I will conduct myself in said manner." She steps aside and grandly pans a hand inside. "Do come in."

Strange. As I cross the threshold, I notice that Piper has once more turned her restless energy on bringing light into the dim corners of what was an impressive showplace in the early 1900s. The grand entryway, dingy and for years in need of a paint job, is freshly cream colored against a gleaming white ceiling and base moldings. The mirrors and side tables shine, the chandelier—formerly a spider refuge—sparkles, and the worn rug that stretches across the hardwood floors somehow made it through a cleaning in one piece.

Ida closes the door. "Mr. Pickwick is takin' his ease in the library."

Ease?

"It's been a busy day for him, and he's tired, but I'm sure he'll be pleased to receive you."

Receive? And what's this about his being busy? "Has he had other visitors today?"

"Only the one." She takes the lead toward the library. "That sculptor."

Another fit. "What time was that?"

"A few hours ago. A nice young man for someone who's not from the South."

No, Reece Thorpe isn't. At the age of seventeen, his family moved to North Carolina when Uncle Bartholomew hired his father to try to save the textile mill from going under. A year later, Reece's father had enough of my uncle's borderline criminal shenanigans and took his family back to Minnesota, never to be heard from again. Or so I thought.

As we near the library, I lay a hand on Ida's arm. "Has my uncle had a good day?"

"He's very here today. I think it's all that talk about the sculpture. It lit him right up."

And you want to take that light from him, Maggie Pickwick.

No, I just want him to find a different sculptor.

"I mixed up a batch of pimento cheese," Ida says. "Would you care for a sandwich?"

"Thank you, but I'm not hungry."

"A cup of hot tea? I took one in to your uncle a while back."

"That would be nice."

As she bustles toward the kitchen on hugely muscled calves, I step beneath the library's arched doorway.

"I knew it was you." Uncle Obe smiles at me from across the desk on the far side of the room. "Come on in, Magdalene."

I falter. *Ms. Pickwick* is one thing, but *Magdalene*? Only my mother calls me that, and only when she's either introducing me to high-society friends or is angry. So why is my uncle taking the long way around my name? Is it the dementia? Of course, it's not always the hard words and names that go missing. More often, it's the easier ones that slip off his radar.

I cross the library and peck his cheek. "How are you feelin'?"

"Good." He reclines in the age-softened leather chair, clasps his hands across his concave abdomen, and nods at the scattered sheets of cream-colored stationery covered with shaky handwriting. "Been workin' on my letter to Antonio and Daisy."

The one he started last summer in hopes of making amends to his estranged illegitimate children. According to Piper, who is itching to take the matter into her own hands, he's on draft number twenty-something.

"It has to be just right." He nods. "Lots of years to cover and..." His jaw opens and closes and his eyes jitter as he engages in the cruel game of hide-and-seek that has become more popular as his dementia progresses. "Apologies!" he exclaims, as if holding up the word by the scruff of the neck. "Yes, lots of apologies to be made." Eyes brightening, he taps his head. "See, all this cogitatin' and ruminatin' is good for the mind."

Don't you dare steal his light!

He clears his throat. "I'm guessin' you ran into an old friend today."

My eyes strain against muscles working hard to keep them in my head. Though my uncle isn't one to sidestep or try to make something ugly pretty, I didn't expect him to be up-front about his interference in my life.

"Don't get yourself in a twist. Just sit yourself down where I can see you proper."

I turn up my hands in an embarrassing display of helplessness. "What's going on?"

He jerks his head toward the chair.

On legs that feel spindly, I walk around the desk. Though I aim for the edge of the chair, my knees fold like oiled hinges, and I sink back into the seriously unsprung seat, giving a little cough as the dusty de-velveted upholstery surrounds me.

"Feel better?"

Actually, in spite of a ticklish dust-sensitive nose, I do. "Talk to me, Uncle Obe."

"You saw Reece, hmm?"

"I did." Considering the slippery slope my emotions are on, I'm surprised at how level my voice sounds. "And you sent him to Fate and Connie's after Mrs. Templeton told you I was on my way there."

He puts his elbows on the chair arms and grips the brass-studded end caps, as if in preparation for take off. "Seemed as good a time as any for him to scout out a place for his...er, studio."

So that's what brought him down High Holler Road—doubtless, unaware he was being maneuvered into my orbit.

"Gotta hand it to me," Uncle Obe says. "My timin' was right on."

"Actually, it was off."

"Oh?"

I defy the seat's gravitational pull and lean toward him. "School let out early because of the snow."

"That must have made a lot of kids happy. Well, not Devyn. That girl does like her schoolin'."

"The point is, she accompanied me on my errands."

"That was nice of her."

Patience. "Meaning she was with me when I stopped to check on my signs."

He stills, then makes a face that rearranges the lines grooving his skin. "Why, that wasn't part of the plan."

I'm supposed to feel better? "The plan being to throw Mr. Thorpe and me together?"

"Exactly!" He jabs a finger in my direction, only to turn it on himself and scratch his head. "I suppose I should have taken it as a sign my train was off track when I called to be certain you were at the theater and that grumpy old woman told me you were off runnin' errands."

I mentally scratch my own head. "You were hoping I was at the theater—er, auction house?" That *is* the function the old building has served since Uncle Obe leased it to me over a year ago. "Why?"

"It's where I originally intended to send Reece."

On the pretext of scouting out studio space. I catch my breath. No, he wouldn't set up his studio at my place of business. Not only would he find the idea of being under my nose unsavory, but every square foot is mine for the duration of the lease. Nothing to worry about. Now I just need to convince my uncle to send him back to his artist's commune or wherever he seeks inspiration and oneness with the world.

"Uncle Obe—"

"Here you are, Ms. Pickwick." Ida appears at my elbow and extends a scalloped saucer, at the center of which perches a delicate china cup, circa late 1800s. Knowing how much the complete set could bring at auction, I glance at the desk. There sits a matching cup and saucer earlier used to serve Uncle Obe his tea. I open my mouth to suggest that Ida use the everyday china, but it isn't my place, and apparently Uncle Obe sees nothing wrong with the casual use of Sotheby's-worthy china.

"Did you change your mind?" Ida rattles the cup in its saucer.

Envisioning chips and cracks, I practically snatch the saucer from her hand, causing hot liquid to slop over the cup's rim.

"My goodness!" She retreats a step.

"Sorry." I sink my nose into the fragrant steam rising from the cup. "I must be thirstier than I thought."

"I'll say."

I'm not an herbal tea person, but the scent of peppermint acts like moisturizer on my dry and cracked nerve endings. "Thank you, Ida. I needed this."

She looks to Uncle Obe. "Anything I can get you, Mr. Pickwick?"

"I'm fine. And stop calling me that. It's Obadiah."

"Yes, Mr. Pickwick." She withdraws, and as her shoes transition from the hardwood floors to the hallway rug, I hear her mutter, "I am his *nurse.* And I will behave accordingly. Humph!"

"Takes her job a tad too serious," Uncle Obe says.

I balance the cup and saucer on my thighs. "Correct me if I'm wrong, but Mr. Thorpe has no idea what you're up to."

He stares at me, and as his smile slips away, a kink appears between his eyebrows. I've seen this more in recent months, and it always strikes me like he's trying to find his place, as if in a book that the wind has whipped closed. I wait for him to locate the page, and eventually the kink resolves.

"Yes, Reece is in the dark. Or he *was*. He might be a wee suspicious after your meeting at Fate and Connie's."

Satisfaction flows over me like hot syrup on pancakes. "We didn't meet."

Uncle Obe cranes his neck forward. "You didn't?"

"No, I saw him before he saw me and ducked out of sight." I bounce twice to free my rear end from the seat, causing the cup and saucer to rattle alarmingly. I perch on the edge of the chair. "Can you guess who Mr. Thorpe was talking to outside the shop?"

"Haven't a clue, my dear."

"Devyn."

He eases back in his chair. "That wasn't part of the p-plan, either. Does he know she's your daughter?"

"No. When she introduced herself, he asked if she was Luc's or Bart's, and that's when I decided it was time for a diversion."

"I'm almost afraid to ask."

I set the cup and saucer on his desk, rise, and walk around to his side. "Send him away, Uncle Obe." I lay a hand on his bony shoulder. "I don't need this complication."

He tips his head back to see to the top of me. "He could be the girl's daddy."

I don't know how he knows that, especially as I had little to do with Uncle Obe during high school, but he probably knows about the other two possibilities as well. "Not likely, and even if he were, it wouldn't change a thing. Send him away."

"Can't."

"It's your money. You're the one who decides which sculptor is best suited to the job."

"But I already decided." He rubs the back of his neck. "And Reece *is* best suited to give our...our...*town*"—he emphasizes the word as if to nail it down—"what I stole from it years ago."

It's still hard to believe he's responsible for the missing statue of Great- Granddad Pickwick that stood in the town square. But according to his public confession at last year's Fourth of July celebration, it was a young and quietly rebellious Obadiah Pickwick who did the deed, and the statue is somewhere at the bottom of Pickwick Lake.

"He does incredible work. Have you visited his website?"

"Uncle Obe—"

"It's mind-boggling what he's capable of. And unlike other sculptors, he's willing to work on site. Of course, it helps that he doesn't have a…that he isn't married or have children to go home to every night." He winks.

Oh!

"So that means I can have an ongoing say in the process." He rubs his neck again.

Realizing my height is responsible for his discomfort, I bend down beside his chair. "You have to tell him you've changed your mind."

"Can't."

"Of course you can."

"Nope, it's all legal."

I stiffen. "Legal?"

"Reece's attorney faxed over a contract a few days ago. I John Hancocked it and sent it back. Legal."

Considering his dementia and that he granted Piper the power to handle his finances months ago, that could be argued—

No! I am *not* going there, even if it means I have to run into Reece Thorpe from time to time. I'm an adult. I can handle this. But if only he hadn't changed his mind about the commission!

"Uncle Obe, last summer Mr. Thorpe declined the commission. What happened between then and now?"

"Budget cuts. He ought to be sculptin' a piece for some

Yankee church up north, but they changed their minds." He gives a satisfied nod. "Their loss, our gain."

Our gain? "So he contacted you."

"No, no, no. I contacted him—well, his agent—same as I've done every month since he turned me down. And this time he agreed, which is why I ceased negotiations with that woman sculptor Piper scrounged up.'" He gives a sour-faced shudder. "She was a persnickety one."

Did Piper know he was keeping after Reece all these months? No, she would have told me. And it's not as if Uncle Obe is under lock and key—yet. Although his dementia is advancing, it's blessedly slow. He credits it to God, the Sudoku that Devyn got him hooked on, and the six-hundred-dollar juicing machine he bought off a home shopping channel. Regardless, he is at a better place than any of us thought he would be last year when he made public his heart-wrenching diagnosis on top of revealing his plans to right family wrongs—

Hold it! Does he regard the question of who fathered Devyn as a wrong that needs righting? If so, he's reaching, as the two others who might have fathered my daughter had every opportunity to step forward. Instead, they ran for cover, and it made sense that if I had to drag them kicking and screaming into the light, they were best left in the dark. As for Reece...

Considering my reputation, he might have ducked out of sight too had his family not pulled out of Pickwick before gossip about my pregnancy became as common as fleas on a dog. So the only one wronged is Devyn, but if Uncle Obe thinks putting a face on her father will right that wrong, he's mistaken. Unfortunately, it appears Reece Thorpe is in Pickwick to stay. But for how long?

"Uncle Obe?"

His whole body startles, as if he dug himself deeper into his thoughts than I did mine. Of course, that's probably a given.

I gently squeeze his forearm. "How long will it take Mr. Thorpe to complete the statue?"

"Oh, he'll be here awhile."

"A month or two?"

"Heavens, no!"

Good. If he's only here for—

"More like six months." He flicks his hands up. "At least, that's the time he's set aside for the project."

Ugh. Pickwick may be growing faster than any other small town in North Carolina, but it's still too small for *six* months.

And there is nothing you can do about it.

I stand. "I'll let you get some rest."

"Thank you. Much as I hate to nap, it's been a busy day for me." He taps the stationery. "And if I'm going to get this letter done, I need all the energy I can muster."

"Can I help you to bed?"

He settles more deeply into the leather. "Best nap is a chair nap—comfortable enough to doze in, but not so comfortable you sleep away the day."

And days, especially good ones, are too precious for him to let slip away.

I peck his cheek again. "If the auction doesn't run too long on Saturday, Devyn and I will drop by for a visit afterward."

"And if it does run long?" He gives me the *knowing* eye.

I feel guilty for the times we haven't made it out to see him, but it's not for want of trying. It's my job to get the seller the best price, and sometimes that requires being more stubborn than those in the audience who are looking for a steal as opposed to a bargain or fair market value. I don't do steals, which is why my competition is wiping my dust out of their pocketbooks.

"In that case, we'll see you at church on Sunday." I step around the desk and retrieve my purse from beside the de-velveted chair. "Piper will be back by then, won't she?"

"Should be."

I give a parting smile and let my long legs loose on the library.

"Are you holding a...what do you call it? When you give people a sneak peek?"

In the doorway I turn. "A viewing. Yes, tomorrow." I don't often display items up for auction a day in advance, since it's easier to allow an hour or so before the auction for buyers to examine them. However, as several high-end items are on Saturday's roster, many of which are from the Pickwick estate and were chosen by Uncle Obe to raise money to right our family's wrongs, an early viewing can create a buzz and bring in more buyers.

"Glad to hear it," my uncle says. "You're doing a fine job."

I hope he really is pleased. Though I'm certain Sotheby's or Christie's could get more, he insists that I handle the sales. "Thank you."

"And Magdalene?" He wags a finger. "Trust me on this Reece Thorpe business. Despite whatever personal issues you have with the man, he will make our town proud with that new statue."

"I'll do my best." And I will—my best to avoid him. I wag a finger back at my uncle. "No more arranging for us to run into each other."

"I shall try to remember that, but, you know..." He taps his temple.

Ah! He's using his mental deterioration to his advantage—again. Fine, I'll just instruct Mrs. Templeton not to divulge my whereabouts should he call. "Have a good day, Uncle Obe."

"I already do."

Lucky him.

CHAPTER 4

DAILY WORD CALENDAR
for Highly Successful Career Women

[**excor'iate** (*verb*) to denounce severely; verbally flay]

FRIDAY, FEBRUARY 12

"Exquisite." The sibilant breath issues from a plump woman who, for twenty minutes, has casually browsed tomorrow's auction items, all the while keeping an eye on two pieces—the English George III period writing table and the nineteenth-century angel wood carving displayed on a stand nearby.

An out-of-town antiques dealer, my senses informed me as I signaled to Mrs. Templeton that I would handle this one and set off to follow the woman at a distance. It often happens when I publish an auction notice in the Asheville and Charlotte newspapers to alert the public to the sale of rare items. The dealers come from all over, among them those who think that because the town of Pickwick is small, its auctioneers are too backward to properly value an item. But not on my watch.

Now Puck & Sons…that's one of the reasons I struck out on my own after three years of slaving under Mr. Puck to learn the auction business. The other reason, the deciding one, is that his undervaluing of items wasn't unintentional. I didn't know what he was up to until I educated myself on how to value items. Anticipating a raise for giving my employer the means to push a buyer to his true limit, I cleverly laid it all out for Mr. Puck. It got ugly from there, but despite evidence that he took kickbacks from buyers, Puck & Sons is still in business and my stiffest competition, not to mention the one that stole my assistant.

The antiques dealer steps closer to the writing table, pauses to glance over her left shoulder to be certain the others attending the viewing aren't paying her notice, then checks her right shoulder. I'm prepared, body angled opposite where I stand twenty feet away, eyes on the binder that details the items up for auction tomorrow.

She turns back to the table. "My oh my. How did you get here, my precious?"

My precious? Sounds like the creepy, big-eyed creature in J. R. R. Tolkien's tale, the one obsessed with the ring. Though the table is beautiful and worth a startling sum, I don't care for the reverence with which it's regarded.

Not that I didn't once regard inanimate objects with awe, and don't sometimes succumb to the pull of an overpriced outfit, but when seen from outside myself, it leaves a bad taste in my mouth. Of course, considering the business I'm in, that can make for a less-than-comfortable day in the life of Maggie Pickwick. But all that misplaced reverence *is* what makes the cash register ring.

The woman glides a hand across the unmarred surface of the inlaid satinwood table. "Perfect. Yes, you are."

She bends and strokes one of four square legs that taper to a delicately arched foot. "Not so much as a scratch." Ignoring the tag that provides details about the piece—she knows what she's looking at—she pinches the dainty knob below the tabletop and gently pulls. "Ooh, look at your sweet little drawer."

Enough! Clasping the binder to my chest, I stride forward. "You certainly have an eye for the exceptional, ma'am."

She whips around and reaches behind to flatten a palm on the table, as if for fear it will sidle away. However, as her eyes survey me up and down, she snatches her hand back and clasps it with the other. "It's a…nice little table."

"Thank you." I halt before her and catch the scent of aged wood, dusty upholstery, and the musty fibers of handworked woolen rugs. Is that how I'll smell thirty years from now? Might I already? I extend a hand. "I'm Maggie Pi—"

"It's quaint." She peers over her shoulder. "Very quaint."

"Actually, *exquisite* better describes this fine piece." Her word, not mine. "Don't you think?"

She hefts her heavily penciled eyebrows. "I don't know about that." She regards the table with the disinterest of one faced with pressboard. "But it's decent enough and for the right price…" She shrugs. "There's a corner in my kitchen that could stand to be filled. You know, to toss the keys on when I come in from the garage."

Stay professional. "Trust me, you wouldn't want to do that with this beauty." I step forward and caress the smooth top. "It's over two hundred years old." As she well knows.

"Two hundred!"

"Eighteenth century. It comes to us from the Pickwick estate."

"The Pickwick estate? Is that how the town came by its name—somebody named Pickwick?"

This is getting old. Though the Pickwicks weren't as prominent as the Vanderbilts were at the turn of the twentieth century (though not for want of trying), most have heard of them—unfortunately, usually in the context of scandalous behavior. "Yes, and the angel carving is also from the estate."

She pats back a yawn as she considers it. "Not bad."

Did someone stamp *stupid* on my forehead? Or is it my hair hanging around my shoulders, a mass of red waves that I didn't have time to tame into my usual chic roll. It could be that I'm without my rectangular burgundy-rimmed glasses. Regardless, I'm no dummy.

"The carving is French. Early nineteenth century."

The woman looks back at me. "It's a bit gauche, but it might work over my garden shed."

I nearly cho—

No, *aspirate.* See, daily words come in handy.

She pulls a checkbook from her purse. "I'll give you eight hundred dollars."

I can't remember the last time my professionalism was so insulted. Actually, I can. Recently, it got back to me that Mr. Puck's sons were putting it around that the only reason widower Warren signed me to auction off his car collection was because I offered *VIP service.* No, indeed, I need no one to remind me of my high school days.

"Eight hundred dollars?" I repeat.

She points to the carving *and* the table. "For both pieces."

If it weren't for the others in attendance, I might shout that this is not a garage sale—

No, I would *excoriate* her. I'd severely denounce her with that highfalutin verb, give her a verbal flaying—

And where would Skippy be in all this?

Right. With her guidance, I've learned to think through my interactions with others, especially about containing the harsh words that tempt me. *Remember Psalm 19:14,* she's always saying. *May the words of my mouth and the meditation of my heart be pleasing in Your sight.*

And don't forget about Devyn.

Right again. As I didn't have time to run her home after school, she's up in the balcony working on a project, and a glance over my shoulder confirms she's still there. Okay, no excoriating.

"I'm sorry, but this is a preview of tomorrow's auction. If you would like to bid, we will entertain an offer then." Providing she goes *much* higher.

"But that's the problem." She *tsks*. "I'm leaving town tonight. And you wouldn't deny your client a guaranteed sale, would you?"

"I appreciate your interest, but it would be unethical for me not to make every effort to obtain a price that reflects the true value of these two pieces."

"I am being more than generous." She wags her checkbook in my face. "Going once...*tick, tick, tick...*going twice...*tick, tick, tick...*"

"Gone." I put a manicured finger on the checkbook and push it away from my face. "Have a good day." As I pivot, I drop my tight smile, but then her hand curls around my arm and pulls me back, nearly knocking me off my heels.

Ooh! What about red hair does this woman not understand? Whether it's responsible for my temper or merely provides an excuse to have one, my anger is surfacing. I twist around. However, the words on my tongue fall back when I hear, *Be Skippy. Be. Skippy.* "Yes?"

"I know how these things work." She winks. "I'll give you fifteen hundred dollars for both pieces—two separate checks, one with your name on it."

She has me confused with Puck & Sons. I draw my arm back, and she releases me. "Since that isn't how I conduct business at Serendipity, I have to ask you to take your business elsewhere."

Her face tightens. "A bit self-righteous, aren't we, dear?"

"The word is *ethical*. And at the moment, I don't feel very *dear*, so please address me by my name—Maggie *Pickwick*."

Her eyes widen. And then she's all smiles. "Naughty you. You should have told me you have a vested interest in these pieces, being a Pickwick yourself."

So much for her ignorance of the Pickwicks. "I have a vested interest in *all* the pieces I handle, Ms...?"

She puts her chin forward. "Turnbridge."

"...Turnbridge, regardless of whether or not a client is kin."

She sweeps her gaze around the theater that still looks very much a theater, though no plays have been enacted or movies shown here for thirty years. I like the nostalgia—the rows of graduated seats that invite auctiongoers to settle in for the duration, the burgundy, gold-tasseled drapes that frame the stage where I take up gavel to pound out the best possible price from buyers, the side balconies—

"So, the Pickwicks have branched out into second-hand goods, have they?"

Her disdain makes my teeth snap.

"Oh, but it's not a first, is it? I believe I heard your family now owns a *used* car lot."

That would be my brother, Luc. Though our mother is less than thrilled with our career choices, I see nothing to be ashamed of. Still, I take offense at this woman's disdain. *Be Skippy.* "The Pickwick family doesn't own Serendipity. I do."

"Semantics, shemantics." She waves her checkbook again. "Now that we both know what we're dealing with, no more games."

As if *I'm* the one playing games. Of course, as an auctioneer, I do have my moments, but for a good cause—getting top dollar, which often is all that's keeping my clients afloat.

Out comes a pen. "I'll give you six thousand dollars for both pieces."

A far cry from fifteen hundred dollars, but not far enough. "That would be an acceptable opening bid, but the pieces will be sold at auction tomorrow."

She gives a gusty sigh and drops her checkbook in her purse. "Very well, I'll see you then."

I tilt my head to the side. "But you're leaving town tonight."

A sly smile transforms her cheeks into puckered apples. "Changed my mind." She bustles past me and around the group before the jewelry display case over which Mrs. Templeton presides. Without a backward glance, she descends the stage steps and hurries up the aisle and out the double doors.

I empty my lungs, only then realizing how shallow my breathing must have been. I may have barely earned Cs in high school, but I'm not stupid, and I hate it when people assume that the bulk of my brain is dedicated to maintaining my looks. Of course, had I taken better care to downplay those looks, what happened might not have.

As Mrs. Templeton describes the jewelry, awkwardly using the words I earlier drilled into her—*classic, carats, cut,* and *certified*—I pass before a nineteenth-century, full-length mirror that has the potential to bring upwards of three thousand dollars for its hopeful owner. One glance at my reflection and I'm scurrying backstage.

"No wonder she didn't take you seriously," I grumble as I halt before another full-length mirror, this one entirely lacking potential to line anyone's pockets—Wal-Mart, $29.95. But it serves its purpose, which is to guide me in reducing the risk of further false impressions.

"*Nice little table.* Ha!" I narrow my eyes on the woman in the mirror who should have chosen her outfit better—a below-knee skirt as opposed to the above-knee one pulled hastily from her closet, a no-frills blouse as opposed to the ruffled one that points up her femininity. And why didn't she wear a low heel? People don't like being looked down on, especially those with a Napoleon complex. "*Quaint*—ha!"

While I can't do anything about my outfit, I can fix my hair.

Full and flouncy and falling in hyper-red waves around my face, it shouts, *Night on the town!*

I drop my binder to the floor, bend at the waist, and whip my hair forward. "*A bit gauche!* As if anyone in her right mind puts a beautiful piece like that *outside.* And over a garden shed!" Scraping back the waves and curls, I twist them up from my nape and into a roll. "*Going once...tick, tick, tick...*" I come to the end of my hair and tuck the ends down. "*Going twice...tick, tick, tick...*" I straighten, and only then realize I don't have clips or bobby pins.

But I have a pencil, which will do me one better by giving me a look of learnedness (is that a word?). I swoop down and snatch No. 2 from my binder. Using the sharpened tip, I weave it through the roll, securing it to the hair at my scalp.

"There." Regarding my reflection and the pert red eraser and half inch of yellow barrel projecting from the top of the roll, I put my hands on my hips. "I believe we understand each other now, don't you, Ms. Turnbridge?" I nod, only to scowl. "*Second hand goods! Eight hundred dollars!* I am *not* a dingle-dangle-wearing, knobby-headed floozy. I am—"

"Maggie Pickwick."

"You got that right!" I lock eyes with my reflection. But the Maggie in the mirror isn't the one who spoke. No, unfortunately that would be the man reflected in the mirror's upper right corner.

CHAPTER 5

Oh, *Lord. Not him. Not now.* But it is. And I know who did this—the one who asked if I was holding a viewing today. *Uncle Obe, you are* so *bad!*

"Why, there she is," says a gravelly voice as a bright yellow blotch appears alongside the man in the mirror.

Speak of the—

No, I will not think it. Even if he is in my bad graces.

"A sight for sore eyes." My uncle moves toward me in his puffy yellow jacket. "My niece Magdalene Pickwick, the owner of Serendipity Auction Services."

Stop staring at your reflection, you mirror monger. Move it! No? Well, at least give me a little air here or, I declare, I'll topple you off those stupid heels.

Hoping Reece hadn't hear all of my mirror talk, I retrieve my binder—and a smile—from the floor. "Uncle Obe, what are you doing here?" And how did he get past me without—

The rear entrance. *Clip, clip, clip* go my heels as I hurry toward where he advances on me with a sturdier stride than I've seen in some time.

As I hug the man beneath the bright jacket, he says, "I rode into town with Ida and had her drop me here while she's running errands." He nods over his shoulder. "This here is Reece Thorpe, our resident..." He blinks. "...artist. I was showin' him around the old theater."

I don't like the sound of that. "Oh?" I drop back and look toward the partially shadowed man who I would have preferred to remain in the mirror.

Having put a shoulder to the wall, he holds my gaze with only a wrinkle of expression. I'd like to believe the wrinkle is curiosity—or something equally benign—but considering the way we left things between us, it's probably disdain.

Uncle Obe turns to Reece. "Our artist is still on the lookout for studio space to sculpt that fine statue for our town."

I tense my facial muscles to hold my smile in place as all of me rails against the unthinkable...the inconceivable...the inevitable...

"We took a look at the east storage room, and Reece here thinks it might be just what he needs." Rocking heel to toe, Uncle Obe gives a satisfied nod.

My laugh is short and sharp. "But that room is part of the auction house."

"It's not being used. Just sitting there—a dusty gaping hole."

"But I have plans for it." Just as soon as business doubles and I need an overflow room to store auction items.

"I wouldn't want to interfere with your plans." Reece pulls a toothpick from his mouth and strides forward.

No! Back! I've seen more than enough of him, have no reason to verify whether his eyes are still the dark green of pine needles or lashes as thick as wild bramble.

"Nonsense," Uncle Obe says. "It's perfect. You said so yourself, Reece. Right here on the town square where the statue will be erected, access to the loading dock, plenty of s-space, ample sunlight, blessed quiet, and—"

"Quiet!" I grab the word and, ignoring Reece where he halts

five feet away, angle nearer my uncle. "Obviously you haven't been here on auction day. Why, the noise the crowd makes!" My attempt to infuse excitement into my voice causes my drawl to kick in full force, and I clear my throat. "You can't hear a thing above the shouting."

Actually, you can, as the auction process is much more civilized than most people realize, but I'm speaking from the artist's perspective. As everyone knows, they're a sensitive and temperamental lot.

Who's stereotyping now?

Oh, shush.

Uncle Obe's brow creases like corrugated cardboard. "That could present a problem."

Yes!

"Of course, aren't your indoor, uh...?" He taps the air as if tapping at a door behind which lies the elusive word. "... auctions! Aren't your indoor auctions held only on Saturdays?"

Reece doesn't work Saturdays? Everyone knows artists work when inspiration strikes, and that could be on a Saturday. "True." I give Reece more of my shoulder. "But business is picking up, and as we move into spring I'll probably start schedulin' auctions mid-week as well. Then there's summer—busy, busy, busy!"

My uncle shrugs. "I'm sure the two of you can work things out."

What?!

"Hold it." Eyebrows flying, he looks from me to Reece. "Didn't you two know each other in high school?"

Ah!

"We did," Reece says, and though I've done my best to keep him outside the circle of my uncle and me, I feel his gaze. "It's nice to see you again, Maggie."

Uncle Obe winks. "Looks like the two of you will get the

chance to become reacquainted and catch up on all the lost years."

I narrow my lids at my uncle. He has to be faking his dementia. Otherwise, how else could he work through that maze of reasoning and come out on this end of shrewd, conniving, and manipulative? Not that he was any of those things before the diagnosis.

"It's settled, hmm?" He nods.

I look to Reece for help, since he can't want to work under my nose any more than I want to work under his. And that's when I get my first eyeful of the man. Above the collar of a dark oilcloth jacket, he wears his age well, evidence of the past thirteen years mostly confined to the deepening lines in a face that is distressingly familiar—and *not* because of any resemblance to my daughter. No, I'm sure he isn't her father.

What I'm not sure of is this tingle of attraction I have no business feeling. It's not that he's particularly handsome. His attraction has always been more in the way he carries his lean, muscular self—shoulders broad and unbending, lower body at ease. It's in the way his careless black hair exerts its will over him, framing his slightly too long face and brushing his brow, ears, and the collar of his shirt any which way. It's in the way his eyes settle on a person as if bracketing them alone. It's in the way his mouth pulls at the corners, emotions differentiated mostly by the degree of the pull, the amount of light let into his eyes, and the flare of his nostrils. The man is enigmatic. Now *that's* a good fit for a daily word.

Yes, you are enigmatic, Reece Thorpe. And you're going to stay that way. I no longer do dark and mysterious. In fact, I don't do anything anymore—menwise.

"Is your hair on too tight?"

I look at my uncle. "What?"

"Your hair." He points to my head. "Is it on too tight?"

Clutching the binder to my chest, I smooth the left, then right side.

"The way you're staring at my artist, I thought maybe your head was bein' squeezed by that fancy bun."

Maybe there is something to his dementia.

"And is that a pencil sticking out of it?" He shakes his head. "Pardon me for being blunt, but that hairstyle doesn't flatter you one bit, Magdalene. You're much prettier with your hair loose. Makes you look softer…more feminine."

And makes the Ms. Turnbridges of the world take me less seriously. "This is work, Uncle Obe, not a date. So, about this studio space." I glance at Reece whose modus operandi—observation at the expense of interaction—doesn't appear to have changed in thirteen years. My awareness of him sharpening, I quickly return my attention to Uncle Obe. "Though locating the studio here would certainly cut down on the expense of hostin' an artist in Pickwick, I'm sure Mr. Thorpe would prefer some place more private, perhaps with living space, so when inspiration strikes he won't have far to go." Who can argue that?

"Actually," Reece says, "this location is ideal, especially since I've taken a room at the Pickwick Arms for the duration."

The old hotel on the opposite side of the town square. Can this get any worse? I finger the delicate cross suspended from my necklace. *God, it's me, Maggie. Are You there?*

"Mom?"

It can *always* get worse. I look from my uncle to Reece, who is staring at my necklace, but neither appears to have heard my daughter's small voice. *Okay, so You are there, God. Just checking.* Now to intercept Devyn before she appears backstage and Reece recognizes her from Fate and Connie's.

"I need to get back to work." As I swing away, I catch Reece's startle and am as surprised by his show of emotion as he is by my socially inept behavior. I cringe at what he must think. And grimace that I should care. So what if he thinks I'm more of an airhead than I was in high school. Or that I still indulge in meaningful relationships with mirrors—

"It's settled?" Uncle Obe calls as I turn the corner.

With Devyn fifteen feet and closing, I pop my head back around. "Settled." Not really, but I can't have Reece and him following me.

Taking the one remaining stride toward my daughter, I flip the emergency switch required to power a smile. "All done with your project?"

"Yeah."

I catch her arm and turn her as I continue across the stage. "I'd say that calls for a hot chocolate at Mr. Copper's."

She frowns up at me. "What about spoiling my dinner?"

One of my regular buyers catches my eye as we near the steps, and I once more flip the emergency switch. When we're past him, I say, "Sometimes you just have to cut loose, you know?"

"No."

How did I end up with a child like this? "Well, give it a try." I hurry her down the steps, release her, and dig in my skirt pocket where I earlier tucked the change from lunch.

"Is that a pencil sticking out of your head?"

I thrust the folded bills at her and glance over my shoulder. No Uncle Obe. No Reece. "It is. Just one more use for your everyday pencil. Clever, hmm?"

"Or desperate." Moving at a turtle's pace when I need her to be a rabbit, she plucks the money from my hand. "You know, Mom, you shouldn't worry about what other people think of you."

She overheard the exchange between Ms. Turnbridge and me.

"At least"—she shrugs—"that's what you're always telling me."

"And I'm right." Another glance over my shoulder verifies all is clear, and I give her a little push. "Get yourself a pastry too."

Her eyelids go to slits.

"Go on."

She looks back at me as she ascends the aisle, and a second time when she pauses to retrieve her jacket from the seat where she earlier tossed her school things. Then she's rummaging in her backpack.

Move it!

Finally, book and binder in hand, she does, and I wave. "Why don't you hang out at Mr. Copper's until I'm done here? It will be a nice change of scenery."

She shakes her head. "You're acting strange again."

Too bad it isn't because my hair is on too tight. "I have lots to do before I leave." Once she passes through the double doors, I trek up the aisle after her to be certain she reaches her destination. I know, she's almost thirteen and ought to be able to walk the short distance without my hovering, but I believe in loosening the apron strings millimeters at a time. And I have begun allowing her to stay home by herself for brief periods of time. Everything in moderation.

From the cover of the old ticket booth at the front of the lobby, which is now used to register auctiongoers and assign paddles for bidding, I watch Devyn pass before the large pane windows that front the theater. When she goes from sight, I scoot forward and lean into the glass to peer up the right side of the sidewalk that she takes at a skip until she reaches Copper's Beanery and Lending Library at the far end of the block.

That was a close one, Reece-wise. Forget that it's only the first of many near encounters, and that eventually he will draw a connection between my daughter and me, but for now I'm living moment to moment.

As I step back from the window, a bright yellow blotch catches my eye. Past the winter-barren park around which the town square was built, my uncle sits on a wrought-iron bench in front of Church on the Square—his church and mine—awaiting Ida's return. Fortunately, he and Reece left the theater the way they came in. More fortunately, there is no sign of Reece, who must have returned to the Pickwick Arms Hotel.

I gulp at the realization that my effort to put distance between my daughter and him could have gone bad had she been the rabbit I pushed her to be and exited the theater as the two men circled around from the back. "Thank You, Lord."

Though I ought to return to the viewing, I can't let Uncle Obe slip away without hearing from me. Determined to make him see sense about this studio-in-an-auction-house business, I pull open the etched-glass door, turn left down the sidewalk, and wish I'd had the good sense my daughter did to retrieve a jacket. It is February, after all.

At the corner, I shoot diagonally across the street that has little traffic to hinder my progress.

My uncle doesn't see me coming, eyes closed and face turned up to the dusky sky, but I know he hears my heels on the pitted concrete.

I halt in front of him. "What are you doing, Uncle Obe?"

He doesn't open his eyes. "Waitin' for Ida. Should be here any minute."

I sink onto the bench beside him. "You know that's not what I'm talkin' about." I look toward the Pickwick Arms on the square opposite the theater. All that can be seen through the arthritic winter branches of the trees thronging the park are bits of gray stone exterior and the glint of windows. "Where did Ree— Mr. Thorpe go?"

He lifts his lids and frowns. "You'll catch your death of cold comin' out dressed like that. Where's the sense God gave you?"

"At the moment, its resources are being pooled to deal with your meddling. Mr. Thorpe cannot set up shop in my auction house."

"I don't reckon why not, seein' as it's the perfect set up."

"Not for me." Man, it's nippy! "What about Fate and Connie's?"

"Too noisy. All the time. And the other buildings around there have been let go too long."

My jaw creaks as I struggle to keep my teeth from chattering. "Uncle Obe, when we talked yesterday, you agreed you wouldn't push Reece and me together—"

"I did?"

Not exactly, but close. "Yes."

He burrows his chin into his puffy collar. "I can't remember much of that conversation. Wish I could, but what with my affliction..."

He's definitely using his dementia to his advantage. Between feeling as tight as an adult-size rear in a child-size chair and as chill as a barefooted chicken on ice, I'm in danger of cracking. I push up off the bench. "I don't like the game you're playing."

His small smile fades. "Give your uncle a break, hmm?" He touches his temple. "This thing has to be good for something."

I bite the inside of my cheek. His ache is real, as is his need to turn bad into good. And when his crazy endeavor fails? I almost hope he will no longer be around—mentally.

Times like these, I miss the self-absorbed cheerleader who rarely cried for anyone other than herself. It hurts to care for others.

I bend down and squeeze his knee. "All right, Mr. Thorpe can set up his studio in the storage room."

"You won't give him a hard time? Run him off?"

There's my old reputation again. "I'll do my best to make him feel at home." And since he's an artist who surely relishes his privacy, that shouldn't be hard. Far be it from me not to allow him the space he needs. In fact, other than the occasional crossing of paths, there's no reason we should do more than exchange greetings. And six months from now when all this is behind me, I'll make a point of laughing about it. Even if it isn't laughable.

"Good girl." Uncle Obe pats my hand. "Now you'd best get back inside before your nose hair freezes."

I do not have nose hair! "I'll wait until Ida—"

"She's here."

I follow his gaze to the retired nurse who is puttering his old Aston Martin past the theater and around the corner. With a whine of brakes, she pulls into the parking space in front of us.

I instinctively reach for Uncle Obe's arm, but he brushes my hand away and, with a grimace, stands. Though last year's knee-replacement surgery was a success, the cold weather aggravates his joints, especially when he rises from sitting.

"I got all of your errands run, Mr. Pickwick." Ida jumps out of the car. "How are you, Ms. Pickwick?"

Shivering, I hug my arms to me. "Good, thank you."

She hustles around the car to open the passenger door. "The only things I couldn't get on the list are those little pecan pies you like. The store is fresh out of them."

"Out of my pies?" Uncle Obe steps past me. "That's unheard of."

"That's what I said to Lolly Madison, who was restocking the bread. *Why that's unheard of, Lolly,* says I. You know what she says? *Bad nuts.*"

"Bad nuts?" My uncle frowns as he eases into the seat.

"Turns out a whole mess of them pies got recalled. Makin' people sick, they were." Ida shoots me a knowing look. "I told him those pies would do him in, and what do you know? Just about did him in."

"I like my pies," Uncle Obe grumbles. "Piper doesn't mind me havin' them."

"Of course she doesn't." Ida tuts. "Bless her heart, she doesn't know any better. But that's what you're paying me for—to know better. *I'm* the professional." She closes the door with her padded hip.

I smile sympathetically at my uncle through the windshield. Though those sickeningly sweet pies can't be good for him, the dementia is likely to take him before the effects of a diet high in sugar and fat. If the pies make him happy…

"Have a nice evening, Ms. Pickwick." Ida heads around to the driver's side.

I step off the curb and tap my uncle's window. As he rolls it down, Ida climbs in beside him.

"Uncle Obe, do you remember Martha's pecan pies?" Martha of Martha's Meat and Three Eatery, which closed its doors when chain restaurants came to Pickwick.

He brightens. "I most certainly do."

"How about I order some from her to hold you over?"

Ida gasps. "Now, Ms. Pickwick—"

"Sounds good." Uncle Obe nods. "Call her tonight."

I step back, and Ida shakes her head at me as she shifts into reverse. Shortly, the car's taillights disappear around the corner.

As I start back for the theater, the last of daylight bids me adieu, and another shudder goes through me. I could use a hot drink, and Mr. Copper serves the best hot apple cider topped with real whipped cream and drizzled with caramel.

I cross at the corner, traverse the long stretch of sidewalk past the theater, and with a grateful sigh, pull open the glass door.

Mr. Copper's bald pate pops up from behind the massive espresso machine he installed a few years back to compete with the chain coffee shop that he claims put a hit out on him. The machine, along with a change of name (previously Copper's Coffee), and the addition of floor-to-ceiling shelves filled with books he lets on loan, was a wise decision. Business has never been so good.

"A cider, Maggie?" he calls.

"A big one." As I scan the tables for Devyn, the shop's warmth wraps around me like a wool coat, and the voices of patrons lingering over drinks and books thread among the strains of classical music.

"Hey, that's my mom!"

And that's my daughter, but who is she talking to?

"*That's* your mom?"

Oh no.

CHAPTER 6

Devyn stands at the back of the shop alongside a bistro table, a steaming mug snuggled to her chest. And seated at the table is Reece Thorpe, whose disbelieving eyes have landed on me.

Hello, God?

"That's her." Devyn waves me forward. "Mom, I want you to meet someone."

It was bound to come to this. Since my long legs have the advantage of quickly transporting me, there's no excuse for my slow advance other than the obvious—I do not share my daughter's enthusiasm. This becomes more evident when Reece rises and my stride shifts to shuffle.

Devyn sets her mug on the table and jumps forward to drag me the last few feet. "Remember I told you about the sculptor I met at Fate and Connie's? This is Reece Thorpe, the one Unc-Unc hired."

Eyes wide—as in *Play along with me!*—I meet his gaze. "Oh?"

The momentary narrowing of his lids may be imagined, but there's nothing imagined about the dismissing blink that turns his gaze from me to my daughter. "Actually, Devyn, your mother and I have met before."

Anger warming me, I feel Devyn's surprise in her hand on my arm.

"We attended high school together the year I lived in Pickwick," Reece adds.

I can't believe I ever thought his elongated Os were cute. They're actually very annoying. I really don't like this man.

Why? Because he refuses to dummy up? To lie by omission as you're so willing to do, Christian!

This is different. This is delicate. This is Devyn. This is *If you can't say anything nice, don't say anything at all,* and as my relationship with Reece ended on a bad note, there is nothing nice to say, so…

Devyn's baby smooth brow wrinkles. "Why didn't you tell me you knew Mr. Thorpe when I said I'd met him?"

Oh, the temptation to lie…the apple extended, turning this way and that to catch the pretty light… Would it really hurt to take a small bite?

What do you think Skippy would say?

Okay, just a nibble. Mouse tiny. I shrug a shoulder. "It's been quite a few years since I last saw Mr. Thorpe. In fact, I think it's been…" *Don't say thirteen, fool!*

Feeling Reece's gaze move between my daughter and me, I sense his attempt to reconcile the Maggie Pickwick he knew with this utterly likable girl. It was the same last year when Piper returned to Pickwick after a twelve-year absence. Until she became reacquainted with the cousin who had to hit a painful low before she could claw her way up and into God's arms, Piper was certain my baby was switched at birth.

Thank You, Lord, for throwing me that rope. Speaking of which…

"You don't remember him?" Devyn asks.

I could use another rope, Lord.

"I must not be very memorable," Reece says.

Don't I wish! And just who is he to throw me a rope? Okay, I'll take it. No use letting a perfectly good rope go to waste.

"Of course, your mother was very popular—"

Did he emphasize *very*? I glare at him, but his let-me-tell-you-a-story expression doesn't falter.

"—whereas I was a bit of a nerd, always putting my art before anything else."

He was not a nerd, at least in the usual sense. It was *his* choice not to be a jock. And that's one of the things that made him so appealing. Then there was his lack of facade, that he saw beyond mine and that he seemed to care more about the Maggie beneath the beauty queen than Maggie *the* beauty queen.

"Hey, I'm a nerd too!"

I hate it when Devyn calls herself that. It reminds me of how smugly I labeled the bookish teens who didn't fit, including Piper. I can even hear my drawl wrap around the word, and though it's just a memory, it feels as if I'm speaking it *against* my own daughter.

"An art nerd?" Reece asks.

She wrinkles her nose. "Nah."

See, not his daughter. I rub the cross at my neck. *Keep the rope coming, Lord!*

"Science is more my thing...and history...and reading. And I'm good at math."

Reece's mild expression turns confused. Doubtless, he's also entertaining the possibility my baby was switched at birth.

"So, were you and my mom in the same grade?"

"We were."

Oh, Lord, next she'll ask if we ever dated.

"Did you—?"

"Hot apple cider on the bar!' " Mr. Copper calls.

Nice rope. Pretty rope. Yes, you are. "Honey, can you get that?" I smile at Devyn. "And pick out a pastry for me. And ask Mr. Copper to give it a shot of heat."

She shakes her head. "You want a pastry?"

Makes it seem as if I never indulge—Maggie Pickwick, who has nearly six feet over which to spread her weight. But I understand her confusion, since my indulgences are usually premeditated. "It sounds good right now. Must be the cold weather."

Scratching her head, she hurries off.

"I'm sorry about the storage room." Reece glances at my neck, which makes me jerk my hand from the cross as if it's garlic to my vampire. "When your uncle offered it, he didn't mention the theater was your place of business." He hooks a thumb in a pant pocket. "Unfortunately, the location really is ideal."

Unfortunately. Not that I don't feel the same way.

"However, if having me there bothers you, I'll find another place."

"Actually—"

Hold it! If you accept his offer, he could take it to mean he's *going to bother you, rather than the situation bothering you.* No, he wouldn't think that.

"Will I bother you?"

"Of course not!" The prideful denial ejects from me like a Pop-Tart from a toaster.

Lord, maybe You should stop feeding me rope, 'cause sure as pigs in the slop, I'm gonna choke myself—and on pride, no less.

Reece tilts his head, causing the ceiling light to skate across his left cheekbone and point up its height. "Are you sure?"

"Yes." *No!* "If the storage room works for you, I can work around you. In fact, providing you use the rear entrance, there's no reason we should disrupt each other's work. Just"—I fish-wiggle a hand—"two ships passing in the night."

He stares at me as I drop my arm to my side. "All right. I'll start setting up my studio on Monday."

What, oh what have you done? "I'll make sure you get a key to the rear door."

"Thank you." He shows a bit of teeth, but it's not exactly a smile. "So Maggie Pickwick is an auctioneer."

And not ashamed of it, though some people look down on the profession. "That's what I do for a living—finally found a good use for my ability to rattle on."

His dark green eyes shift past me as Devyn reappears.

"Just the way you like it." She holds out my drink. "And Mr. Copper is heating up a cherry pastry." As I wrap my fingers around the warm mug, she looks at Reece. "Tell me more about when you and my mom were in high school."

"Oh, not enough whipped cream." I thrust the mug at her. "Could you ask Mr. Copper to add more?"

"But you don't like a lot of whipped cream."

"For some reason it sounds good right now." Ooh, I used that line already.

She gives me a look and takes the mug. "Oookay."

Alone again with my past, I decide it's time to say good-bye. "I guess I'll see you—"

"You were at the metalworks shop yesterday."

Eek! Choke! Gag! "Uh-huh. I was checking on the signs Fate and Connie are making up for me."

"I didn't see you."

"Imagine that, especially with all this red hair. Hard to miss."

"Apparently mine isn't as hard to miss." He runs fingers through the black hair on his brow, briefly revealing surface scratches at his temple.

I did that. Though I may not remember how the snowball ended up in my hand, I remember the feel of it—a compact ball of ice crystals, grass, and the small pebbles upon which the thin layer of snow had fallen. And I remember the moment of impact.

"Sorry about that. My only excuse"—the one I'm willing to give—"is that I don't like my daughter talking to strangers."

I fall under his considering gaze again. "I'm hardly a stranger, at least to you."

Flushing in remembrance of the intimacy we shared that one night, I fight the impulse to cross my arms over my chest. "Aren't you? Thirteen years is a long time. Certainly long enough for people to change. Some for better, some for worse." I long to point out that I fall in the former category, but it's not something you tell. It's something you show. Too, though I believe I'm better for who I've become, I still fall short in many ways.

"Here you go, Mom. Lots of whipped cream, more caramel, and your pastry."

I take the glistening, cherry-topped confection but frown at the mug. "Would you ask Mr. Copper to add some shaved chocolate?"

Her jaw drops. "Chocolate and apple cider?"

I'll take a ruined apple cider over further exposure to Reece Thorpe. "I'm in the mood for chocolate."

Fortunately, Devyn is more respectful than I was at her age and doesn't question me further. She does set her teeth as she turns away, but I can hardly fault her for that.

Back to Reece. "I had better—"

"When I met Devyn yesterday and she said her last name was Pickwick, I assumed she was Luc's or Bart's."

"Nope, mine." *All* mine. Well, God's too, but here on earth—

"No father in the picture?"

What business is it of his? And is that a knowing glint in his eyes? As in, *Surprise, surprise, the Pickwick tramp had an illegitimate child.* Why, I—

Do not get defensive, especially while holding a bright red pastry.

"None needed," I say. Forget that Devyn and her research disagree. "I've done just fine raising her on my own."

"She seems like a nice kid." And now I bet that glint is saying, *How did that happen with a mother like you?* "So Devyn is ten…eleven?"

Oh, God. Help! "Umm…" I shrug. "About that."

His brow furrows. "About?"

Right. That sounds either very detached, very stupid, or very suspicious. Choose one and get thee out of here!

"Got it," Devyn's voice precedes her appearance.

"Wow!" I peer into the mug she hands me. "That's fancy."

"Shaved chocolate on top of caramel on top of whipped cream on top of apple cider," she drones with the weariness of one sent on one too many errands. Just one more…

I check my watch. "Oh, honey, the time. We need to get back. Would you ask Mr. Copper to put our drinks in to-go cups?"

She stares. "Mom?"

"We need to go, Dev."

She looks at the table near the window where she'd set her book and binder. "But you said I could hang out here until you're done."

I know my behavior is over the edge, but does she have to question me? "Since I won't be much longer at the viewing, I'd like you to head back with me now."

She draws a deep breath, retrieves her mug, and steps past me.

"You were never very subtle, Maggie," Reece says in a low voice.

Not something my mother felt the need to teach me. Her lessons were about the right clothes, hairstyle, makeup, posture, and speech. In short, how to leave the other beauty contestants in the dirt. And I did, in not-so-subtle ways and without apology. Thankfully, Skippy showed by example how to deal with difficult matters in a gently honest way. But that won't work with Devyn at stake.

"You couldn't have been more obvious that you don't want me talking to your daughter."

"I'd prefer you don't." Meaning that as long as his studio is in my auction house, I can't bring Devyn there after school as I sometimes do to keep up with business. I'll have to bring work home.

Reece crosses his arms over his chest. "It's been a long time, Maggie, but I don't recall being the bad guy in our break up."

He wasn't, though I wouldn't have admitted it then. But better he believes I still hold a grudge. "Let's just say that thirteen years does a stranger make." Hmm, that sounded like something out of a book of famous quotes.

As Reece's eyebrows slide up into the dark hair on his brow, I nod at the plate. "I'd better ask Mr. Copper to wrap this up. I'll see you Monday." I walk away and shortly turn from Mr. Copper's bewildered expression to usher Devyn toward the door.

She stops to scoop up her binder and book, then swings around. "See you later, Mr. Thorpe."

Not if I can help it.

The cold hits me hard when we step outside, but not as hard as Devyn's question. "Was he one of your boyfriends?"

Recalling Amanda Pigg's taunt that there are a half-dozen guys who could have fathered Devyn, I want to lie so badly that the bitter aftertaste is already in my mouth. But I won't. "Yeah, we went on a few dates." The word *few* is open to interpretation, isn't it?

"And it ended badly, didn't it?"

"What makes you think that?"

"You were both tense, especially you—like you sometimes get around Grandma." As we near the auction house doors, she peers up at me, and her glasses reflect a brightly burning street light. "And you were nervous, and you're not usually nervous around the opposite sex."

Lord, I prayed she would be smart and not struggle as I did in school, but did You have to make her this smart?

"When did you and Mr. Thorpe date?"

Wrapping my fingers around the cold brass handle of the first door, I feel a tremor go through them as I pull it open. "In high school."

"Yeah, but when?" She enters ahead of me.

"My junior year." No need to mention we continued to date through the summer and into the first month of our senior year —right before he moved and six weeks before I suspected I was pregnant.

As we cross the lobby, I fear what's coming, but Devyn doesn't ask any further questions, and not on the way on home either. I hope that means I've thrown her off the scent.

By the time Devyn gets to bed, it's too late to call Skippy. I won't like what she has to say about how I handled the day's events, but I need to talk to her.

There's always God. I hug my body pillow that keeps my bed from being entirely empty outside of me. "Okay," I say, then slide to my knees, where I don't often enough go. "Lord, this could be a real mess—and one I'm responsible for—but please help me keep Devyn out of it."

CHAPTER 7

DAILY WORD CALENDAR
for Highly Successful Career Women

[**misog'amist** (*noun*) one who hates marriage]

SUNDAY, FEBRUARY 14

"Here it's Valentine's Day, and you're havin' lunch with me, a divorced past-her-prime woman." Skippy leans sideways and bumps her shoulder beneath mine. "What's wrong with this here picture?"

As the line inches nearer the hostess's stand, I look down at my fifty-five-year- old friend and mentor who was surely the inspiration for Peg Bundy of the once-popular sitcom, *Married with Children*—bouffant hair, large nose, and a wardrobe right out of the seventies. All that's missing are outlandish high heels, and only because she broke an ankle when she fell off them several years back and her doctor forbade her to wear anything over an inch.

"Why, there's nothin' wrong with this picture." I allow her

drawl to rub off on mine. "I can't think of anyone I'd rather have lunch with today." Especially as Devyn's moodiness hasn't improved much since Friday. Fortunately, my mother offered to take her and me for brunch after church. I took her up on the Devyn part, which freed me to get together with Skippy. Though Skippy and I spoke on the phone yesterday and she was her usual wise self as I filled her in on Reece's return, I need this. I need to see, not just know, I'm loved. I need the warmth of her smile and the cool squeeze of her fingers.

"Seth Peterson didn't look too happy at church today."

I sigh. "I told him last week I couldn't spend Valentine's Day with him. I told him again on Wednesday when he called and yesterday when he turned up after the auction. He's persistent."

"You ain't encouraged him further, have you?" she asks as the couple in front of us is led to the dining room.

"No."

"Good. Stand firm."

She has been after me for years to cut Seth free from his infatuation that began in high school, but he keeps wiggling back into my life. There was a time when I would have put a quick, shrug-able end to his pursuit, but I'm not that Maggie anymore. And so, until last summer when I put my foot down, he continually guilted me into spending time with him—as friends, he'd say, but he always wanted more.

Of course, I'm as much to blame, since loneliness made me say yes when I knew to say no, but this time it's for good, no matter how lonely I get. And if he gets the job in Japan he interviewed for, it will be that much easier.

I inform the hostess there are two in our party, and as she leads us into the dining room, Skippy loops an arm through mine. "How did the auction go yesterday?"

That makes me smile. "We had a great turnout, and most everything sold for what I expected or more. The antiques dealer I told you about, the one who originally offered eight hundred for the two pieces from the Pickwick estate, ended up paying ninety-five hundred for both."

Skippy claps a hand to her chest. "Goodness me! Your uncle must have done real well for his self."

"I think so." Bit by bit, the liquidation of his estate brings him closer to his goal of making restitution to those our family has wronged.

"Here we are." The hostess halts at a square four-person table and sets the two menus opposite each other. However, Skippy and I claim side-by-side chairs.

"When it was all said and done," I say, "we unloaded eighty thousand dollars in merchandise, a third from the Pickwick Estate."

"Well, now, your uncle ought to be mighty pleased."

"I'm sure he will be."

"You didn't talk to him?"

"Devyn and I planned to drop by after the auction, but when we called, Piper said he had gone to bed early."

"Hmm. I hope he's all right. I noticed he weren't at church today."

Weren't. Though my mother would sniff at Skippy's *butcherin'* of the English language, it's one of the things that makes this woman dear to me. As she says time and again, *Whatcha see is whatcha get.* I wish I were as comfortable and accepting of myself, but I wasn't raised that way. I was brought up in beauty pageants, my mother constantly affirming that I was better than others and that the way to prove it was to look it and act it. I've grown deeper in the years since high school, but I'm still too aware of how others perceive me.

"Maggie, darlin', is your uncle all right?"

I blink at Skippy's concerned face. "Piper said he's just tired." I open my menu. "Probably nothin' that a couple of homemade pecan pies can't set right."

"Ooh," Skippy croons. "So you was able to talk Martha into whippin' up some of them fine pies of hers."

Just one of many mouth-watering items served up at Martha's Meat and Three Eatery before the influx of new restaurants drained off her customers, eventually forcing her to close her doors and take a waitressing job at the new Cracker Barrel. "She hemmed and hawed until I said they were for Uncle Obe. She's always liked him."

Decisively, Skippy taps an item on her menu, then sets it aside. "'Course, since she lost her brother to Alzheimer's—What was it? Five years ago?—she understands better 'n most what your uncle is going through."

I pull my gaze from the glossy picture of a Monte Cristo sandwich. "I didn't know Martha lost a brother to Alzheimer's."

"Well, it ain't like she advertised it, and her brother did live in Asheville, so most people don't know. But I'll tell you what, it was her dedication to helping her sister-in-law care for her brother that led to the close of her restaurant."

"Really?"

"Yessiree. One too many times, her regulars came lookin' for a home-cooked meal and there was that Closed sign. So they went elsewhere, and once Martha's brother passed away, her customers' new habits were too hard to break."

That makes me sad, especially since I didn't know about her troubles. Maybe I haven't come as far I'd like to think. Maybe I'm still just as self-centered—

"Now, no frettin'." Skippy pats my hand. "Nothin' you coulda done, and nothin' she woulda wanted you to do. 'Sides, now she doesn't have the stress of runnin' her own business, and she seems happy enough waitressin'."

Enough. And I just had to talk her down from twelve dollars a pie to ten. Well, Martha is going to receive a nice, big tip.

"If you done decided on what you want, Maggie, we can order with our drinks."

I look from Skippy to the waitress who has materialized beside the table. Shortly, the young woman trots off with our orders.

"Any more quarrels with Devyn?" Skippy asks.

I make a face. "I've pointed out that if all she needs is a father, I can accept Seth's proposal, but she's as opposed to him filling her void as I am to him filling mine. We both want more."

"Love."

Yes, *love*—a four-letter word that, in the context of someone with whom to spend the rest of my life, is more alien to me than those four-letter words that call for a mouthful of soap. Hating the lump in my throat, I say, "That would be nice." More than nice—warm and full and forever. "But possible?"

"Well, not if you don't make an effort."

Now she sounds like Devyn. "Are you saying I haven't?"

She puts up her hands. "When's the last time you went on a date?"

I can't answer that, not only because it would be incriminating, but because I don't recall.

"See?"

I shake my head. "It's not that I'm against—" Ah ha! "Though Devyn would probably disagree, I am not a misogamist." Having supplied Skippy with a means to tease me about my vocabulary quest, I smile in anticipation of her reaction.

But her brow rumples. "Well, of course you're a mi...mis... you know. Or will be, once you're married."

"What?"

"A one-man woman."

Oh. "I didn't say *monogamist*. I said *mis*ogamist, as in one who hates marriage."

Her frown dissolves. "Is that today's daily word?"

"It is."

"Well, I'd like to know what kind of person chooses somethin' like that for Valentine's Day. *Mis*ogamist!"

"Pessimistic," I agree.

She laughs. "Well, I'm glad we cleared that up."

I laugh back, liking the sound and wishing I heard it more often...liking the way it unrolls from me like a red carpet rolled out for a visiting dignitary...liking its sweet and airy taste.

"Uh-oh." Skippy touches my hand. "We got us an audience."

I follow her gaze across the dining room to my mother, who glares from Skippy to me, mouth compressed so tightly she's practically lipless. She doesn't care for my friend, and all because Skippy was there for me when she wasn't. Because Skippy has been more of a mother to me than Adele Pickwick. Because, though I love my mother, I don't always like her.

Devyn sits opposite my mother. Spooning up soup that sends tendrils of steam around her small face, she appears oblivious to the emotions that walk the invisible tightrope strung between our tables.

Skippy nudges my elbow. "Go say *hi*."

I'm grateful to turn back to her. "We spoke at church."

"As in *hi/bye*? Come on, Maggie, do it."

"With her glaring at me like that?"

"It's just 'cause she's wishin' she were the one laughing with you."

And, of course, now she knows why I bowed out of brunch, and it doesn't sit well that I chose Skippy over her.

"She's your mother, Maggie."

"I think she needs more reminding of that than me."

She grimaces. "You say you've forgiven her, but have you really?"

How did we get here? It was my dilemma with Reece I wanted to talk through, not my soap-opera relationship with my mother. "Yes, I've forgiven her, but I can't...I..." Oh no. I am not going to cry. I scrunch my nose against the prickling and blink against the stinging.

"Darlin'." Skippy pulls my hands into her lap and squeezes

them. "I know you're no longer big angry with her, but you are holdin' back."

I am, though I tell myself to stop. I can't forget those months leading up to Devyn's birth, when there wasn't a day my mother didn't warn me that if I didn't abort, my life would be ruined. And then the fit she threw at the hospital when I told her I was keeping my baby. She refused to hold her granddaughter and, on the way out the door, said I was on my own. But Skippy took me into her home until I was able to afford my own place. For two years, she sheltered Devyn and me, mothering away the pain and showing me Jesus's love.

I swallow. "Every time I see my mother with her, whether she's being kind or snooty, I can't help but remember that if she'd had her way, there wouldn't be any Devyn."

"But there is, 'cause you made the right choice. And your mother did come around."

Three years after Devyn's birth, and not the way I longed for her to come around. No hugs or tearful reunions, no long unburdening talks, and not a single *I'm sorry.* Just...around.

"She had no idea what a blessing that little girl would be," Skippy continues. "She knows now, even if she ain't too good at showing it. Do you really think she'd prefer to be sittin' over there all by her lonesome?"

I steel myself for more glaring, but when I look around, my mother is leaning toward Devyn, her attention on something my daughter is saying. Thankfully, my mother's mouth has loosened up—not a smile, but her lips are once more visible.

Yes, she cares for Devyn. Though it seems grudgingly so at times, I have caught the tender moment and pride in her eyes when her granddaughter's name appears in the newspaper for straight *A*s or winning an essay contest. But it isn't enough for her. She wants Devyn to be a beauty and often gets on her—and me—for not putting more of an effort into her appearance. She's even said that when Devyn is old enough, a nose job is a must. Thankfully, my little girl wasn't present for that blowup, and I declined to tell her why my mother and I didn't talk for two months.

"All right," Skippy says, "I won't say any more, but you think on it, hear?"

"I hear." I sigh. "So, what am I going to do about Reece Thorpe?"

Her smile is naughty—er, salacious. "Like I said, Maggie, when's the last time you went on a date?"

"Not funny, Skip."

She sobers. "You're right. Serious business is what this is."

I shake my napkin into my lap. "So?"

"So you ain't gonna like what I have to say." She pats her hair, which is so stiff her fussing has little effect. "I know you don't believe Reece is likely to have fathered our little Devyn, but what better time to find out?"

My appetite deserts me. What in the world am I'm doing here?

"Now, Maggie, settle down. I know how much you liked Reece, so much that if he hadn't broke it off and moved away, you might still be on fine terms with him."

Not likely. Regardless, he did break it off—after he saw me at my ugliest, and with Skippy's daughter, no less. I fight the memory that hasn't visited me in its full-length version in so long its pages are dusty and yellowed, but it fans open almost gleefully, causing the memory to flicker to life…

Yule Baggett, a miniature of her mother, has a tardy coming to her. As do I and one of my best friends, Vicky, who couldn't decide which miniskirt best showed off her backside this morning when I swung by to pick her up in my car.

"Man, oh man," Vicky says loud as Yule bypasses our leisurely ascent of the school steps. "What's the hurry, doofus?" Vicky throws me a look that I throw back, as is my duty to a fellow cheerleader. And yet I regret it the moment my eyes return to my head.

Vicky, Bethany, Mimi-Sue, and Cindy have all given me a hard time about my *little guilt trips,* blaming my reluctance and fits of remorse on the influence of Reece Thorpe, whom I've been dating for five months—a record for me.

"A tardy is a tardy," Vicky calls as Yule approaches the glass door on which a sign is taped: *Tardy? Obtain a tardy slip from the office before proceeding to class. No exceptions.*

Actually, there are exceptions—unless you break up with the principal's son as I did last year.

Vicky snorts. "Come to think of it, what are we doing here, Maggie? Why we should have gone all out with our tardies and stopped at Martha's for a muffin."

And a hot chocolate with a splash of coffee. Of course, we could always jump back in the car and—

Yule screeches and, as she falls on the top step, one of her spiky shoes shoots off her foot and hits the glass door.

I mumble something that sounds like *Oh no,* and take the next two steps as one. But that's as far as I get before a clawed hand sinks into my forearm.

"You're kidding, right?" Vicky demands. "You aren't going to rush to the aid of that…reject."

I look at where Yule is scrabbling to get up, her face contorted and brilliant red. I was going to help her, much like I saw Reece do last week when a drunken Elmore Gass stumbled out of the bushes and passed out near the park bench where Reece and I were making fine progress in the *relationship department.* It took five days to get back to where we were—and beyond.

Vicky's nails sink deeper, her pretty face not so pretty anymore. "What in tarnation is wrong with you?"

Is there something wrong with me? There never was before. In fact, you can't get much more popular than me.

Yule is whimpering and, strangely, I hear the pitiful sound all the way through me. There *is* something wrong with me. I think.

"I declare," Vicky spits out, "you either get yourself right or you're gonna be on the outs with your kind."

My kind. I don't know why that doesn't sound right. After all, my mother has always said there's a difference between people like us and people like Yule Baggett. And it's seemed pretty clear to me, but now Vicky is saying my friends might turn on me—friends who've looked up to me and sought my approval and company. Is she right? If so, where would that leave me? At the back of the line?

Suddenly, Yule's whimpers are drowned out by imaginings of my friends' disgust as Vicky tells them—

No! I'm still one of them, the one who says what is and isn't. I will never be the outcast that Yule or my cousin Piper is. Will never suffer the humiliation of being at the back of the line, which my mother and I narrowly avoided when charges were brought against my daddy and Piper's father for illegal activities in their joint bid to be elected mayor of Pickwick. In fact, I'll die before I let Vicky usurp my place as my mother has warned she'll do, given the chance.

I pull my arm free. "There's nothin' wrong with me, Vicky Dixon." I march up the steps to where Yule has made it to her feet. "Quit your snivelin'," I practically shout to be certain Vicky catches every word. "You deserved that, wearin' those tight pants and walkin' around on stilettos that make you look like a hussy on a street corner!"

"At least she isn't one," a steely voice says over my shoulder.

My body jerks, and I look around into Reece's green eyes that bore through me from behind those dark floppy bangs I like to pull my fingers through. The worst of it isn't that he caught me being ugly. It's how I was ugly—making Yule out to be a hussy, as if my walls weren't made of glass that has been shattered time and again. More unfortunately, Reece has firsthand knowledge of this from what happened between us the other night. What I made sure happened.

Movement past his shoulder pulls me back to Vicky. She's watching me, sizing up my crown, itchin' to get her hands on it.

I doll up my face with a smile sure to wipe from memory any picture of my ugliness. "Why, darlin'," I drip honey from every vowel, "you're late again. What was it this time? That scrap metal sculpture of yours? A paintin'?" I gasp. "Or was it that charcoal drawin' of me you've been working so hard on?"

Not a glimmer of softening. But as I stare at him, I notice it isn't just anger he's wearing. There's something else, evidenced by blood-shot eyes and hair that isn't just mussed but messy. Sorrow? Weariness? "Are you all right, Reece?"

He brushes past me, puts an arm around Yule's shoulders, and leads her forward. "Here's your shoe." He picks it up and hands it to her. "You okay?"

She sniffs. "I'm okay. Thanks."

The two disappear inside, and I feel sick at the realization of what I've done. To my detriment—and Yule's—I only know how to apply peer pressure, not deflect it.

"Good for you," Vicky says as I near. "You handled that just fine."

"He hates me," I whisper.

She puts an arm across my shoulders. "I say, good riddance. He wasn't your type."

Or my kind?

"So, Martha's for a muffin?"

I shake off her arm. "I'm going home."

"Whatever for?"

I ignore her question and say over my shoulder, "Tell coach for me, will you?" No after-school pompom pumping for me. Even if my stomach wasn't roiling, I couldn't do it today.

"Okay," Vicky calls. "Love ya."

Five months later, she was the first of my *best friends* to turn her back on me when I could no longer hide my pregnancy. Most of the others followed, and on the day I graduated from high school with a basketball-sized baby bump, I felt even more alone than Yule could have. After all, *her* mother came to her graduation. More, Skippy Baggett, for all of her tight clothes and teetering high heels, was loving and forgiving.

This I learned on the day I skipped school to drive to Asheville for counseling about my unwanted pregnancy. At the outskirts of town, I got a flat and was left at the mercy of the woman who pulled up behind me in a battered convertible. She knew who I was, not only because the town of Pickwick was relatively small then and the Pickwick family prominent despite bouts of scandalous behavior, but because several times over the years, she had complained to school officials about the way my friends and I treated her daughter.

And yet that day, Skippy greeted me kindly and got down on the cold asphalt to change my tire. That should have been the extent of our encounter, but as she bounced a high-heeled foot on the tire iron, she asked why I wasn't in school. For some reason, I told the truth, and instead of going to the clinic in Asheville, I followed her to Martha's, and we talked for hours over muffins. So I guess I wasn't entirely alone the day of graduation. Skippy was there for me too.

I look to the woman beside me, and she grins. "Welcome back."

"Hmm?"

She juts her chin, and I see that our meals have arrived, and Skippy has started in on her French dip.

"Sorry." I pick up one of the quarters of my Monte Cristo. "I was remembering the day at school when Yule fell and Reece—"

"That's what I figured."

I take a bite. The sandwich is a mouth-watering combination of ham, cheese, bread, egg, and powdered sugar, but my taste buds have gone over to the dark side of the moon. I swallow. "I don't know why you have anything to do with me, Skip. Why you give a hoot after what I—"

She shakes her au jus-drenched French dip at me. "Nuh-uh, missy. That's behind us, and it's gonna stay there. Yule'll tell you that herself."

Yes, she forgave me, but that doesn't mean we're friends. Rather, she accepts me, though I don't think she had much choice, seeing as every time she came home from college those first few years, she couldn't get to her mother without going past my baby and me. Too, Yule is a good Christian like Skippy, and while there's no longer a wall between us, I sense the fence and don't begrudge it. I'm just glad that when she leaves her physical therapy practice in Knoxville to visit her mother, she's willing to talk to me over the rails. She really is an incredible woman. Now, if she'd just stop having babies for others, find a nice guy, and give Skippy some grandchildren of her own—

That's another story. I summon an apologetic smile. "I know it's behind us, but I can't help but think of it now that Reece is back and how cool he was toward me."

She waves for me to eat, and I take another bite. "Well..." She dunks her sandwich in au jus. "It seems to me you'll just have to show Reece how the Lord has worked in your life since he left town."

I would protest if my mouth weren't full, which is how she planned it. I chew faster, but in the meantime let my eyes do the talking. I swallow my mouthful. "Listen—"

"It's time you knew who your baby's father is." She sets her sopping sandwich aside. "Even if you're set on keepin' it from Devyn."

"I don't see what difference—"

"Yes, you do. You just don't want to."

We've gone around about this before, beginning with Devyn's birth, when Skippy tried to convince me to seek support for my child, and most recently when Devyn started asking about her father.

I push my plate away. "Things are best the way they are."

"And if you ever need to know her father's medical background?"

That does worry me. Though Reece looks healthy, I haven't seen the other two in years. When Gary Winsome left for college, his parents moved to Florida, and he hasn't been back. As for Chase Elliot, I saw him a few times those first couple of years when he came home from college to visit his mother, but not since.

"I don't know, Skip."

"Well, I say you take the opportunity God has pried open your fingers to put in your hands and ask Reece Thorpe to be tested—"

"No!" The word shoots from me, and I regret it even before hurt flashes across my target's face. Not that it makes me any more receptive to her advice. For one thing, I see no advantage to disproving Reece is Devyn's father. For another, the thought of asking him to submit to testing makes me nauseous. Of course, I doubt he'd be surprised that I lied to him about being sexually active with other guys so soon after our break up, but better suspicion than confirmation of my promiscuity.

"All right." Skippy pulls back. "I shouldn't push so hard." She folds her napkin and sets it on the table. "After all, I ain't your mama."

"No, you *aren't*," says the one who is.

CHAPTER 8

Skippy and I turn to peer up at the bleached-blond woman who has come to stand behind us, purse in one hand, restaurant check in the other. And no sign of Devyn.

"Hello, dear." With a brittle smile, my mother pecks my cheek.

"Why, Adele, it's nice to see you," Skippy says. "Wanna join us?"

I should have extended the invitation, but I know this is as far as my mother will stretch herself with Skippy, not wanting to be associated with her flamboyance beyond the inescapable fact that the woman is my friend.

My mother blinks prettily. "Shame on you, Skippy Baggett!" she says playfully, but there is nothing playful about my mother, who never got down on the floor to play no matter how much I begged. Our interactions were all about curling irons, makeup, and frilly dresses that were never to touch the floor. Ever.

She tuts. "Enticing my daughter away from me, not to mention her own daughter, and on Valentine's Day when we heartbroken Pickwick women ought to be holding one another up. I declare, I have half a mind to be jealous of you and the place you hold in *my* daughter's heart."

"I am certainly grateful for her friendship." Skippy is conciliatory as always. "Especially seein' as I ain't—"

The improper grammar makes my mother's upper lip curl.

"—got my own daughter home with me on this here holiday." Skippy gives my mother's forearm a pat. "I do 'preciate you sharin'."

My mother goes stiff as starch. I know she likes to keep a *public face,* but I sense she's about to make an exception.

"Where's D-Devyn?" My tongue trips in my haste to distract her.

Skippy pulls her hand back, and my mother blinks as if a trance has been broken. "I sent her to the ladies' room to pick the spinach from her teeth. I don't know why she likes that Italian wedding soup. Anyway, seeing as you're here, I'll save myself a trip and let Devyn ride home with you."

As our house is on the way to hers, there is no trip to be saved. This is simply her way of coming between Skippy and me. But on a positive note, her timing is good since I don't care to discuss Reece Thorpe anymore. Too, Devyn adores Skippy. Providing she tempers her enthusiasm, as I've counseled her to do to spare her grandmother's feelings, it's for the best. "Good idea," I say.

"Aunt Skippy!"

Ugh. She called her *aunt* though my mother has forbidden it —especially in public, where others might mistakenly connect the dots from me to Skippy's younger brother, a bachelor who owns the old carwash in town.

"I didn't know you and mom were here." Devyn sidles around my pinch-lipped mother and hugs Skippy from behind.

My friend reaches over her shoulder and pats her arm in an attempt to downplay her own affection. "Why don't you sit beside me where I can see you good?"

Devyn turns to my mother. "Can we visit awhile?"

"*You* can." My mother shakes her shoulders out. "I have lots to do today."

"Oh, stay, Grandma."

"Thank you, but no." She looks to me. "Happy Valentine's Day, *Magdalene*."

Her use of my full name is just further proof of her anger. "You too, Mom."

Back straight, she walks away, and it's a half hour before Skippy and I hug good-bye and Devyn follows me to the car.

A few minutes later, Devyn is tapping at the passenger window as I drive.

"Everything okay?" I ask.

"Just thinking about somethin' Grandma said."

"What's that?"

Her lids narrow as she continues to stare out the window. "I mentioned I'd met the sculptor Uncle Obe hired, and when I told her his name, she said it sounded familiar."

Oh no.

"I told her you were in high school together, and that's when she remembered. She said you and he dated"—the tapping ceases and she cuts her eyes at me—"until he moved away after the start of your senior year."

Double oh no.

"You told me you dated during your junior year."

I return my attention to the road. "That's right, and through the summer. However, we broke up shortly after the start of our senior year and weeks before he moved away."

"Why didn't you tell me that?"

"Come on, Devyn, he's not the only guy I ever dated. There were boyfriends before him and after him." *And that was a careless thing to say.* But if it throws her off the scent…

Silence so completely fills the space between us that it feels as if it's pressing me against the door. Then, in a voice so soft I nearly miss the underlying accusation, she says, "That's what I hear."

From Amanda Pigg. And verified by the perpetrator herself.

"Is he my dad?"

"Reece Thorpe?" His name jumps out of me. After all, I didn't expect her to come right out and ask.

"Is he?"

"No." At least, I'm pretty sure he isn't, so I'm not lying. "What makes you think that?"

"Timing."

Once more, she's staring out the window, and I can almost see the numbers running through her brain—July 1 minus the gestational weeks. Next, she'll ask exactly when Reece moved. Unfortunately, he was still in Pickwick during the conception window, even though he'd broken it off with me weeks before. Of course, if I was off on my calculations (I was never good at keeping track of my periods), or she was one of those babies who lingered past the gestational period, Reece could be her father. But she wasn't a big baby—barely average.

The silence lasts until I pull into the driveway. "Mom, when did—?"

"Devyn, I know you want a father, but Reece Thorpe is not him."

Her jaw juts. "I asked Grandma about when you and Mr. Thorpe broke it off, and she got real quiet. The next thing I knew, she was talking about how pretty I look today." Her eyes flash. "And seeing as I don't look any different from any other day when she's harping about my sorry appearance, it was highly suspicious."

Thank you, Mother. Not that she knows who fathered Devyn, but now I also have to deal with her suspicion. "Regardless, he is not your father."

"Are you positive?"

Close, but I can't tell her that or she won't let go. And I am ninety percent certain she isn't any part of Reece.

Please, God, You know I would prefer he's the one who fathered her, but don't let me be telling a lie.

"Positive."

Her mouth twitches, eyes water, and my heart aches for her disappointment. "Okay." Her shoulders slouch. "Okay."

But it's not okay, especially if it turns out I told a lie. Of course, neither of us will ever know, will we? And that's a good thing. I think.

❧

SURELY I DIDN'T WET the bed! I sit straight up and draw my hands from my hips to my chest and neck—wet, but no pungent odor. Perspiration, then. Why so much? A bad dream? Was something chasing me? Threatening Devyn? I search for images that surely played through my mind, but the film is blank.

I start to lie back down, but as with most of my middle-of-the-night awakenings since Devyn grew too old to sneak into my bed, I'm swept with loneliness. No one to snuggle with... with whom to whisper long into the night...to love.

"Oh, stop!" I toss back the covers and shiver as the sixty-two-degree air latches onto my dampness. Though I know my cousin Bridget is right about the need to conserve energy, especially at night when we're hunkered down beneath the covers, the awakenings tempt me to set my furnace to something more humane—say, sixty-eight.

As I drop my feet to the carpet and push off the bed, I hear a whisper. I look to the doorway, expecting to see Devyn's small shadow, but she isn't there. The whisper sounds again, and I realize it came from within me. The video portion of my dream may be blank, but not the audio.

Liar, it whispers.

I trudge to the bathroom. Fifteen minutes later, the whisper is in stereo—*LIAR-LIAR!* Grudgingly, I accept what I must do. I turn off the shower and, as I towel dry, watch the last of the hot water swirl down the drain. There go my carbon credits, if I had any.

In thick socks, fleece pajamas, and a robe, I ignore the thermostat as I head into my home office. I can generate my own heat. Not only will my effort to conserve make Bridget happy, but I'll be on friendlier terms with my heating bill.

Wishing that were all I had to worry about, I settle into the chair behind my desk and coax my computer out of hibernation. The bear awakens with a whir and a happy twitter reminiscent of a Disney movie.

Shortly, a Google search yields surprising results. I knew paternity testing had come a long way from the cringe-and-wince *who's your daddy* talk shows, but I had no idea that do-it-yourself kits are now available online and at pharmacies for around two hundred dollars and include laboratory analysis with results within five days. I'm relieved, as I was expecting it to be more expensive and extensive.

However, as I read on, my relief deflates. The two hundred dollars is for standard samples obtained from cheek swabs, and there is no way I'm getting inside Devyn's mouth, let alone Reece's. If I'm going to do this, it has to be on the sly, meaning I'll need to order a special kit for non-standard samples (blood stains, hairs with roots attached, licked envelopes, chewed straws, etcetera.). Worse, the cost triples and it takes two weeks for results. Maybe it's not such a good idea after all.

"No, I can do this." And no one need ever know, especially Reece. And why should he? It's just a matter of elimination, of proving to my overworked conscience that I didn't lie to Devyn when I said he isn't her father. But if I'm wrong—

He didn't father her. And I'll prove it, no matter how much it costs.

"It's a good thing I'm saving on my heating bill." Cupping a hand over my cold nose, I blow hot breath over it as I consider the chart that ranks the different types of samples that can be tested and their success rates. For Devyn's sample, a few strands of hair are probably the best bet, but for Reece… Though blood is highly accurate and it might be possible to arrange a deep paper cut, I'll aim for a saliva sample via something like a chewed straw.

Better yet, a toothpick. Surely I can get my hands on one of his discards. I drag my bottom lip through my teeth. I will get it. I will make a silk purse (proof Reece is not Devyn's father) out of a sow's ear (his invasion of my workplace). I log off and return to bed. Unfortunately, all the warmth earlier invested in it is lost, a common affliction of single-person beds.

"Look out, Reece Thorpe," I chatter as I pull the chilled covers over my head. "One way or another, I'll have my pound of flesh—er, DNA."

CHAPTER 9

DAILY WORD CALENDAR
for Highly Successful Career Women

[**delete'rious** (*adjective*) something that is harmful, toxic, even lethal]

THURSDAY, FEBRUARY 18

Three days since Reece appropriated the back room for his studio, and in all that time, I've barely seen hide nor hair of him. But he's in there. I can hear him when I listen at the door. Though I should be grateful he's avoiding me, I need that DNA. Once I get a sample, he can go right back to avoiding me—and vice versa!

I continue to pace the corridor, with each pass pausing to listen at the door behind which Reece is doing whatever artists do behind closed doors.

Knock and he will come. But what do I say? *Er, that toothpick you're chewing looks mighty tasty. Mind if I have a go at it? Why, thank you. But wait, it's almost lunch time. I'll save it for later. And would you look at this! I just happen to have a sterile baggy to put it in for safekeeping.* Courtesy of the laboratory that overnighted the kit to me.

I throw my hands up, then stop to listen again. Silence, paper shuffling, the scrape of a chair, footsteps. I jump back, ready to hightail it. But the footsteps head opposite, and a moment later, I hear the whine of the rear door. Is he leaving? The door closes with another whine, and all is silent. If he left a freshly chewed toothpick behind, this could be good.

I pull keys from my jeans and locate the one for the inside door. It protests a little going in, but gets downright stubborn when I try to turn it. Did I use the wrong key? I pull it out. It's the right one, but two tries later, the door remains locked and my red-headed excuse for anger is surfacing. Reece must have changed the locks—without my permission.

I give the keys a hard shake and the door a kick with a pointed, size nine-and-a-half shoe.

"Goodness me," Mrs. Templeton's creaky voice sneaks up on me, though I have no idea how I missed the creaky joints. "You're actin' like a rooster shut outta the hen house!"

I swing around, and there she stands with her hands on the hips of her elasticized polyester pants, eyes magnified by bifocals, hair poufing like gray cotton candy from beneath an orange and white baseball cap.

I may be acting like a rooster, but I feel like a dog caught with a stolen steak. "He changed the lock."

"I know."

"You do?"

"Um-hmm. Locksmith came yesterday—rekeyed that door and the rear one."

Probably while I was drumming up business with an old tobacco farmer who wants to sell the farm and move to the coast to live out his retirement. Unfortunately, on my way out the door, he told me he was more impressed with Puck & Sons' presentation. His wrinkled little wife had nodded in agreement.

"Why didn't you tell me about the locksmith?"

Mrs. Templeton's wiry eyebrows wiggle together. "Mr. Thorpe said your uncle gave him permission, so I figured you knew."

I can hardly blame her for the assumption, as it would have been proper for Uncle Obe to tell me, and the opportunity was certainly there when he called yesterday morning to thank me for the pecan pies Martha delivered.

"Did he say why it was necessary to change the locks?"

"No, though I'd say it was to keep his project under wraps by keeping uninvited visitors out."

And I have just served up myself as proof of the necessity. I feel guilty, and yet I would hardly be trespassing on square footage I pay for. It isn't fair, especially since I don't care a hoot about his project. All I want is a nasty, chewed-up toothpick. However, I'm grateful Mrs. Templeton believes curiosity over the new statue is what had me acting like a frustrated rooster.

I step forward. "I suppose I'll have to wait and see like everyone else." As I approach, she turns with a crackle of joints.

"So, is there something you need?" I ask as we head toward the stage.

Her mouth tilts as if to smile—a rarity. "I'm the bearer of good news."

I could use some. "Yes?"

"Jenkins called to say he'll be in this afternoon to sign your agreement."

The tobacco farmer who made it clear he'd be signing with Puck & Sons. I halt near the stairs that lead to my office. "You're kidding."

"Sure as shootin', I ain't." She gives in to the smile. "When you told me what he said, I took it on myself to pay Becca and him a visit. Assured 'em you'd get a good sight better for that farm than Puck and his whelps." She chuckles. "'Course, I got some pull with Becca, seein' as we go back a ways to when she frequented my knittin' shop—before it went outta business."

I'm amazed. Though I need to find a real assistant, my desperate arrangement with Mrs. Templeton might not be so—

Deleterious? Tempting, but *bad* is a better fit. I squeeze her shoulder. "Thank you for going above and beyond, Mrs. Templeton."

And there goes her smile. "Just earnin' my pay." She gives my hand on her a hard look that makes it skedaddle back to my side. "No cause for gettin' all friendly. You know how I feel about you Pickwicks."

The way a lot of people feel, which is why Uncle Obe is set on making restitution to those our family has wronged. I respect him for it, but that doesn't mean I like it, especially as the public apologies have made it harder for the Pickwicks to hold up their heads. And it all started with last year's Fourth of July celebration when Piper confessed to the celebrants that it was she, not Trinity Templeton, who many years earlier played Lady Godiva and rode nearly buck naked through town. Bad, especially as her confession was what spurred Uncle Obe to reveal the truth about the statue and his dementia.

Mrs. Templeton brushes off her sleeve where my hand was. "I just hope my Trinity comes to her senses and doesn't run off with that devil's dust–usin' cousin of yours."

I understand her concern, but it does seem that Bart has changed. "He doesn't use drugs anymore."

"Um-hmm." Her mouth crimps. "Looks that way, don't it?"

Best not to argue. I step past her and head for her office. "Why don't we take care of that contract for Mr. and Mrs. Jenkins." It can't be put off until this afternoon since I won't risk further exposing Devyn to Reece.

"It's ready to go." Mrs. Templeton sets her own pace as she follows. "Exceptin' your signature and theirs."

I falter. Considering how disagreeable she can be, I never expected her to be so efficient. And if she has more connections like the one with Mr. and Mrs. Jenkins—

No, I need a real assistant.

Ten minutes later, satisfied the contract is properly completed, I sign and date it. Now all it needs is the sellers' signatures, which should be on the dotted lines by this afternoon. My day is starting to look up.

And it looks up even more when I leave Mrs. Templeton's office and am drawn to the lobby windows that overlook the park at the center of the square. Even dressed in spindly winter finery, it's lovely, but that isn't what grabs my attention. It's the man behind the big granite block that once lifted high a statue of Great-Granddad Pickwick. It's not just the black hair that identifies Reece from this distance. It's the way he carries himself, which is apparent even though I can only see his head and shoulders.

What is he doing?

He lowers his head, and for a moment appears to be praying (his family *were* dedicated churchgoers), but then he springs onto the block, and he's holding a notepad. As he slowly turns, he shifts his jaw. Is he working a toothpick?

He jots something, walks the length of the block, and jots again, obviously trying to incorporate the original granite block into the new sculpture. He carries on for another minute before bounding down as easily as he bounded up. I retreat a step, expecting him to return to his studio, but he strides opposite.

The Grill 'n' Swill is his destination. And mine. Heart racing at the launch of Operation Get Spit, I run to the door, wrench it open, and jump back when the winter chill raises goose bumps across my limbs. Since Reece isn't going anywhere soon, as Duke takes his sweet time serving up his worth-the-wait burgers and wings, I retrieve my coat and exit the auction house.

Thirty seconds later, hailed by Pastor Stanky from Church on the Square and then by Uncle Obe's aged attorney, Artemis Bleeker, I'm back in the lobby. If I'm going to get that DNA, I need to be like smoke—not fire, for which my red hair and height are to blame. One I can't do anything about other than slouch, but the other...

"Oh no, this here's my favorite baseball cap." Mrs. Templeton claps a hand over it. "And how do I know you don't have lice?"

Ew! "I give you my word I don't. And I'll bring it back after lunch."

Her nose twitches. "All right." She pulls the cap off, revealing a helmet of smooshed gray hair. "But next time you leave home, dress warmly. I got my hands full enough with my granddaughter without havin' to worry about you." She thrusts the cap at me. "Kids these days!"

"I'll try to be more responsible in the future."

"Best do more than try."

"Yes, ma'am." There's something not right about that, I realize as I head outside with my hair piled beneath the cap. I'm Mrs. Templeton's employer, and yet I'm calling her *ma'am.* Of course, she is forty years older—definitely my elder—and the loan of her baseball cap isn't in her job description.

Peacoat buttoned to my throat, shoulders rounded, cap tugged low, I cut across the park to the iron bench nestled among the trees. As I lower onto it, I congratulate myself on the vantage point. Whereas the surrounding trees and shrubs offer cover, my view into the Grill 'n' Swill's dining room is nearly unobstructed, thanks to the recent installation of plate-glass windows to update the establishment's look.

Zeroing in on Reece where he sits at a table just back from the left window, I murmur, "Hello there."

Shortly, a waiter appears and Reece sets his menu aside.

"Order a soft drink," I whisper, breath fogging the air.

"Anything that comes with a straw. Go on, indulge that oral fixation of yours—*chomp, chomp.*"

The waiter says something, retrieves the menu, and saunters away.

Bare fingers beginning to ache with the cold, I push my hands into the opposite sleeves of my coat. Unfortunately, unless Reece ordered something easy, this could be a very uncomfortable wait. In fact, my toes are going numb.

Reece's drink arrives—with a straw! Is that root beer? It's what he always ordered when we dated. Not that it matters. What matters is that straw.

As I watch from beneath the bill of the baseball cap, he pulls a toothpick from his mouth and sets it aside. Providing he doesn't recycle them, it's possible I'll have two samples to choose from. This might not be hard after all.

He lifts the glass, and I hold my breath as he puts his lips around the straw. *That's it. Drink it down. And chew, baby, chew!*

After a single pull on the straw, he sets down the glass. This could take a while, but I'm not going anywhere, even if I have to use a blow-dryer to get my toes apart. Sticking my chin into the collar of my coat and panting hot breath down my front, I watch Reece, who's still ignoring his straw, but as I scowl at him, he turns his head in my direction.

I retreat behind the bill of Mrs. Templeton's cap. Did he sense being watched? Does he know it's me? No. Though I can be seen through the leafless branches, I'm fairly nondescript—providing I don't stand to my full height.

I count to thirty, and when I peek at the Grill 'n' Swill, Reece's head is bent toward his notebook. Safe. But cold, my ears as frozen as my toes. I really miss my hair.

Crossing one leg over the other, I bounce them to keep the blood flowing. "Come on, bring the man his food. You're not that busy." In fact, the place is barely a quarter full, and that includes Pastor Stanky ,whose Bible is open on the table where he sits to the right of Reece.

Sadly, for all my muttering and bouncing, it's fifteen minutes until Reece's lunch arrives. If he doesn't start shoveling, drinking, and working over that straw, my frozen corpse might be all that remains of me come nightfall—and my specimen baggy. Forbid!

Reece makes quick work of his steaming bowl of whatever and chases it down with the drink. And then—call me a potato and plant me eyes up!—he picks the straw from the glass, clamps it between his teeth, and returns to his notebook.

Lord, I'm not saying You had anything to do with this, 'cause though this seems the best way to eliminate Reece as Devyn's father, I'm probably going about it wrong. But if You are helping me out, thank You!

After five minutes of watching him shift the straw side to side while moving a pencil over the notebook, I see the waiter deliver the check. Reece doesn't look up.

Move it, artist man, I'm freezing here! I try to wiggle my toes in their pointed confines, but they don't respond. I declare, if I have to undergo amputation—

Reece lowers his pencil. It's time.

Or not. Staring at his handiwork, he shifts the straw to the opposite side of his mouth. After a long moment, he retrieves the check and pushes back his chair.

I hold my breath as I stare at the straw that remains fixed in his mouth. Surely, he isn't going to take it with him. It's one thing to walk around chewing a toothpick, but a straw?

He reaches for his notebook, only to pull back when Pastor Stanky appears. And then—wahoo!— he removes the straw to respond to something the other man says. Then it's in the glass and Reece is shaking hands with the pastor.

Thank you, Stanky. A hundred times thank you.

And now for the next step in Operation Get Spit. I jump up

and wobble as my frozen feet protest. Ha! Protest away. I'm getting that straw and toothpick, and no suddenly efficient busboy is going to stop me. Still, one can't be too stealthy. As Reece and Pastor Stanky move away from the table to square up their checks, I pick my way from tree to tree and am perfectly camouflaged when the two men exit.

Déjà vu hits me hard, but I know the source—Fate and Connie's Metalworks, when I lurked around the corner from Reece and Devyn. And I'm doing it again, further proof I'm going about this wrong. However, asking Reece to submit to a paternity test is unthinkable. The humiliation would be too great to bear. But soon this will be over, and my conscience eased at knowing I didn't lie to Devyn.

I look between Reece's abandoned table and the two men as they cross the street to the sidewalk in front of the church. I strain to hear their conversation, but I only catch a word here and there.

Oh, please don't let Pastor Stanky be inviting him to my *church. Well, Your church, Lord, and I know it's Stanky's calling to fill the pews, but there are other churches around.*

Finally, the way is clear, and I hurry forward and practically throw myself through the doors of the Grill 'n' Swill.

"Hey, Maggie!" Duke lumbers forward, gut straining against his white apron.

Why couldn't he have been busy with another customer? I might actually have to sit down to lunch.

"I almost didn't recognize you with that baseball cap," he says as our combined forward motion draws us nearer. "You tryin' to make a statement?"

Sidestepping, I touch the bill. "It keeps my head warm."

Duke also sidesteps, and I'm forced to halt. Propping his meaty fists on his hips, he frowns me up one side and down the other. "I ain't no fashion expert, but one of them Frenchie head socks you sometimes wear would go better with high heels."

A beret. Unfortunately, vanity got in the way of practicality this morning, as the thought of smooshing my coiffed locks and dealing with the inevitable static made me forego my woolly little friend. And, no, it had nothing to do with the possibility of running into Reece at the auction house.

"By yourself?" Duke asks.

I glance past him and am relieved the busboy is no more timely than usual. "Yes. I, uh, feel like a window table today—that one." I jut my chin, and, when he turns his bulk to look, squeeze past him.

"But it's not cleared."

"No problem. I'm in no hurry." Other than to get my hands on that straw. I'm halfway across the dining room when I realize my mad dash is drawing the attention of the other patrons. Slowing, I unbutton my coat as if in preparation for settling down to a nice hot meal. However, when I reach the table and glance around, I'm still an object of interest. So no snatching the straw and hightailing it.

Since the baseball cap is no longer needed, I pull it off and my hair tumbles down around my face. Reece's chair is still warm, but though there is something uncomfortably intimate about that and I could switch to the chair on the other side of the table, I stay put. After all, there's no need to call more attention to myself. And this chair *is* closer to the straw by a good...inch or so. And after my stint on the park bench, I could use a little heat. In fact, Bridget would be all over me if I let Reece's warmth go to waste, would harp on about the importance of energy conservation.

I set the cap in my lap and lean to the side to retrieve the baggy from the right pocket of my slacks. That's when I catch sight of the toothpick on a beverage napkin. Nicely chewed. Of course, what if it's too dried out to yield viable DNA? Well, I'll just send it with the straw, and between the two, I should have conclusive proof Reece is not my daughter's father.

I pinch the baggy at the bottom of my pocket. Home free. Mission accomplished. Touchdown!

"Well, if it isn't Pickwick's favorite auctioneer."

The voice makes me startle so violently that my knees knock the underside of the table. This is bad—

Make that *deleterious,* as in harmful, toxic, quite possibly lethal.

Easing my hand from my pocket, I look around. "Reece." Goodness, he looks good. No—*bad*ness! B-A-D-ness! I don't like three-day stubble, especially when it's that dark and rough looking. Really, I don't. Nope. Not at all.

I clear my throat. "What are you doing here?"

His lids narrow so slightly that if I weren't looking for suspicion, I might not see it. Then his mouth tilts. "Returning to the scene of the crime."

He knows I came for his straw and toothpick? But is that really a crime? I mean, he abandoned them. And I had yet to touch—

Calm down. All he knows is you're sitting at his table in his toasty chair. He can't know you know this was his table.

I give a little laugh. "Don't you sound dramatic."

"Dramatic is the chili they serve here." He pats his flat abdomen. "I have a feeling it's going to come back to haunt me."

That's what he meant by *scene of the crime*? It would seem so, and yet I suspect a double meaning. Deciding to let his reference to having recently lunched here pass rather than fall deeper into deception by feigning surprise, I raise my eyebrows.

"Actually..." he drawls, though not in any Southern way, and then leans down, causing my olfactory sense to issue a *red alert* as it's assailed by the mingling of his soapy scent with the fibrous scent of his oilcloth jacket. "I came back for this."

This? I catch my breath as his face nears and his fringed, dark green eyes come within inches of mine, and then his mouth is there.

He can't be serious. After all these years and the divide between us, surely he's not going to kiss me.

He pulls back, a notebook in hand.

Where did that come from? Ah. Not a kiss. He was retrieving what I was too intent on the straw to notice.

"I left it behind when the pastor of Church on the Square stopped by to introduce himself."

"Oh." The sound comes out breathy, and it's a struggle to remain upright with my bones threatening to melt. What's wrong with me? Is it his elongated *O*s? Maybe I'm coming down with the flu. Yeah, that must be it. Nothing to do with *O*s or attraction.

A clank and rattle draws my gaze past Reece. On the other side of the dining room, the busboy is loading a deep bin. Unfortunately, there's only one other table that needs clearing between that one and this.

Time for me to secure my samples. I tilt my face toward Reece. "Well, I guess I'll see you later."

"Are you stalking me?" He says it almost teasingly.

I nearly choke. "Stalking you?"

He leans in again, and once more his scent circles me like Indians circling a wagon train. "While I was having lunch, I had this feeling of being watched, and there was someone sitting on a bench in the park—on a *very* cold day. Wearing a baseball cap." He glances at the one in my lap. "And a coat like yours." He reaches with a hand that doesn't look the way one imagines an artist's hand looks. It's large, fingers blunt and graceless, and they brush my collarbone as they slide down the lapel.

Oh no. Let that be fear skittering through me, not something carnal. I don't do that anymore. I'm fixed.

He releases my lapel and straightens. "Now, not five minutes later, I return to find you at my table when there are plenty of clean ones to be had."

It doesn't look good. And neither does the busboy who is carrying his bin to the next table. "Yeah, um…"

"Sorry, Maggie, but until my concept for the new statue is ready to be shared, it stays in here." He raises the notebook, then taps his head. "And in here."

Like Mrs. Templeton, he attributes my suspicious behavior to snooping on his work, meaning he thinks I was after his notebook. I can live with that.

I glance at the busboy. Thankfully, he's taking his time loading the bin. Summoning disappointment, I return my gaze to Reece. "Not even a peek?"

He tucks the notebook in his jacket's inside pocket. "No. Which reminds me, I don't know if Mrs. Templeton mentioned that I changed the locks on my studio."

"I heard about that." I start to say he should have conferred with me, but the busboy is hefting the bin. I tense, but in the next instant, he widens his stance to offset the weight, a sure sign he'll have to return to the kitchen—

Wrong. He's coming this way.

"I'll have them changed back when I leave," Reece says.

"Great. Well, I'm sure you have work to do, so I'll let you go." I glance at the toothpick and struggle against the impulse to snatch it. Maybe I could put a hand over it, casual-like…drum my fingers a little, boredom like.

"Sorry about that." Reece retrieves the toothpick. "Disgusting habit."

"No!" My voice breaks like a youth in puberty.

His hand falters, the toothpick between his fingers taunting me.

"Uh…" I shrug. "…I wouldn't exactly call it disgusting. I mean, at least you don't chew pencils anymore, right?"

"I try not to." He drops the toothpick in his shirt pocket.

So much for that. But I have the straw, and the toothpick probably wouldn't have been of use anyway.

"Excuse me, ma'am." The busboy appears beside Reece, his wiry frame bowed by the bin's weight. "I'll clear your table so's you can enjoy your meal."

"No hurry." I wave him away. "Just get me the next time around."

"Nah, I'd best do it now or Duke'll hang me by my thumbs." He lowers the bin to the corner of the table. "He done told me to clear your table first, and I woulda, but seeing as you and the mister were talkin', I didn't wanna interrupt."

The straw is so close, and yet so far as the young man loads dishes. I have to get rid of Reece. With effort, I turn a dazzling smile on him. "Good luck with the statue." I wave. "'Bye."

He just stands there. And peripherally, I see the busboy remove the bread plate, after which he reaches for the glass. I long to snatch it from him, to run to the restroom, lock myself in, and slip the straw into the baggy. But the only explanation for that behavior, outside of the truth, could mean a trip to the loony bin.

And so I watch helplessly as the busboy shoves the glass into the bin, causing it to tip forward and the straw to disappear beneath the other dishes. Then he lurches away.

If not for Reece, I might cry.

"You look like someone stole your ice-cream cone," he says.

That's one way of putting it. "It's just one of those days."

He frowns. "What are you up to?"

Considering my behavior, his question is legitimate, and yet I long to tell him I'm not that girl anymore—that what I'm *up to* isn't anything that will hurt anyone. It will simply answer a question that proves I didn't lie. "Oh, you know me." I'm surprised at how bitter my smile feels. "Always up to no good."

After a breathless moment, he says, "Have a nice day, Maggie."

I watch him exit the Grill 'n' Swill, watch him cross the

street and cut through the park, watch him step into the narrow alley that leads to the back of the theater.

"So, now what?" I sweep my gaze around the buildings on the town square and over an increasing number of pedestrians, many of whom are answering the call of lunch. Lucky for them, I'm not hungry. Lucky for me, Duke's back is to me when I head for the door.

As I cut through the park, a familiar truck pulls into the town square and brakes in front of the Pickwick Arms. My cousin Bridget jumps out of the cab and slams the door. Blond dreadlocks drape the shoulders of a denim jacket that would be too light for me in this weather, and disproportionately long legs are encased in ratty jeans. She grabs a bag out of the back and hurries into the hotel—doubtless to tend the live plants as her nursery does for various businesses. And, of course, she'll be pushed to the point of rudeness with the day manager whose crush on her is as unwelcome as ticks on a dog. Poor guy. If she'd give him the time of day, he'd probably do anything for her.

But back to my problem. Operation Get Spit having failed, what now?

"Oh!" I move my gaze up the Pickwick Arms. And smile. "*That's* what."

CHAPTER 10

DAILY WORD CALENDAR
for Highly Successful Career Women

[**longanim'ity** (*noun*) patience in adversity]

SUNDAY, FEBRUARY 21

"Whoa." With that single-syllable-turned-double-syllable word, there's no question Bridget's drawl is more pronounced than mine. As she stares at me from where she sits cross-legged on the corner of her desk, I recall the scene she made the first—and last—time she attended Cotillion.

Though my mother went on and on about the importance of girls and boys from good families attending cotillion to learn social graces, my Aunt Belinda should have known better than to try to stuff Bridget into that mold. My cousin came to the gathering with a resentful attitude and unladylike swagger that had Asheville's finest sons and daughters muttering all over themselves.

But that was nothing compared to the appearance of a skunk shortly after Bridget's return from the restroom. Tail plumed, the animal strolled into the ballroom through one set of doors while everyone shrieked and stampeded out the other. They didn't know that Bridget's pet, Stripe, was deskunked. But that was the point. Bridget was told not to come back, and her mother's hopes of transforming her earthy daughter into a true Southern belle were dashed. My mother was humiliated by association, and doubly so when the stunt earned the Pickwicks another unflattering headline: *Pickwicks Raise a Stink at Cotillion.*

Bridget gathers her blond dreadlocks back from her face and pulls the rope-like hair over one shoulder. "That's a pretty risqué plan for a born-again like you." She grins. "Sure you aren't puttin' your salvation on the line?"

I don't like her throwing my Christianity in my face as if it's foreign to her. It isn't. She's just set on keeping her back to God for making her a widow after all the soul-searching she went through to get to Him in the first place.

"Why did I even bother?" she had demanded the day of her husband's funeral. "So I can feel better about Him takin' Easton from me?" She'd jerked free of my hand on her arm, stomped out of the funeral home, and pointed an accusing finger at the sky. "I'm good and mad at You, and I'm gonna stay that way, so just take Your Son and scat!"

Bridget and her penchant for burning bridges. However, I prefer to believe that her bridge to God only suffered smoke damage and that if she would step back onto it, she would find it sturdy enough to hold her weight as when it first spanned the chasm between uncertainty and belief.

"Well, little cuz?"

I don't like being called that, especially as she's only two years older and I'm almost six inches taller. I glance at my watch. I'm going to be late for service if I don't leave now.

"I know it sounds deceitful, but I have to eliminate Reece. I need the peace of mind of knowing I was straight with Devyn."

She snorts, that hair of hers apparently granting her license to do so. "Seems to me if you don't know whether or not you were straight with her, you weren't. Or am I missin' something?"

Since when did Bridget start sounding like Skippy? *This* I would expect from my dear friend. From Bridget, I expected shrugging acceptance and, hopefully, cooperation.

I sigh. "Will you help me or not?"

"Sure, but I'm not goin' through Boone."

The *crushin'* manager at the Pickwick Arms.

She waves a finger. "I won't be owin' him. He may be cute in an Oxford-shirt way, but when guys start droppin' hints about my hair, saying how pretty I'd be if I ditched the dreads..." She wrinkles her small nose. "No."

At least until she stops mourning Easton, who himself wore dreadlocks. Following her husband's death four years ago, she holed herself up with the usual stockpile of funeral casseroles delivered by friends and neighbors. When she finally emerged from seclusion months later, her beautiful blond hair was twisted into dreadlocks.

Some believe she did it in memory of Easton, others that she did it in a *dying wish* way (she had resisted his attempts to convince her to give dreads a try), and still others say it was done to keep *widow sniffers* at bay (her name for men attracted to women who have lost their husbands). Regardless, the closest she has come to having a relationship with another man was with Axel, though she insisted they were only friends. And Piper's return to Pickwick put paid to the possibility of a deeper relationship between Bridget and him.

I'm happy for Piper and Axel, but I wish Bridget wasn't so alone. "So, how are you going to get me into Reece's room?"

"Observation. First, I—" Seeing her opossum stir on the scarf mounded on a corner of the desk, she makes kissing sounds, and the accidentally tailless creature lumbers into her lap.

I don't grimace as I used to when Bridget showed up with Reggie—she of the female persuasion but male name. In fact, I've gotten to like the little creature. However, a lot of people, especially those new to our fast-growing community, think it's wrong for Bridget to keep a wild animal. Even Piper still calls Reggie a *rodent.* Of course, I don't think she's forgiven Reggie for rolling around in her beloved pickled corn.

"While I'm making the rounds of the plants"—Bridget strokes the opossum's head—"I'll find out which room Reece is in and take a peek at the housekeeping schedule. Then, when he's good and gone, you sneak in while the maid is running the vacuum and get your DNA."

I was angling for a key, but this is better. No key means no Boone. Too, if I'm caught *accidentally* wandering into the wrong room, it can hardly be considered illegal entry. And the only thing I'm after is what is found in a comb or brush: a rooted hair or two.

I smile. "Good plan."

Bridget scoops up Reggie and stands. "I'm at the Pickwick Arms tomorrow. As soon as I have the info, I'll call you."

I step toward her. "I appreciate your help."

She backhands the air. Though the gesture appears casual in an *aw, shucks* way, I know it's a reminder of where my personal space ends and hers begins. "You'd best get on to church or you'll be late. And God knows"—light flashes in her eyes—"if the big guy doesn't agree with the way you're goin' about this, you might be needin' some bonus points."

Another deserved rap on the knuckles. She may have turned her back on the *big guy*, but she knows He can't be pleased with how I'm handling this. And so here's a wide-angle view of how shallow my faith must appear to Bridget, who I've begged to join Devyn and me for Sunday services.

Yeah, right, she's probably thinking, *like I wanna come back to* your *God—the one in whom you trust so completely you're sneaking around trying to snag some guy's DNA to prove you didn't lie to your daughter? I'll be sure to get my order in early for some of that faith.*

She circles the desk and settles into a wheeled chair that wimpily protests her hundred and twenty or so pounds with a crackle of cracked vinyl. "Tell Devyn *hi* for me, will ya?"

Devyn, who spent the day with Piper at Uncle Obe's while I was conducting my Saturday auction, and then the night when it became evident my day would run long. Doubtless, she and Piper and Uncle Obe are wondering if I'm going to show for worship.

"I'll tell her." I head for the door of the trailer that serves as the nursery's office.

"And ask her when she's gonna spend a night with me for a change."

That *personal space* thing doesn't apply to Devyn. In fact, if there's one person my cousin truly cares about, it's *Devyn Divine,* as she started calling my toddler the day she took a bad tumble at her feet. Without considering what she was getting herself into, Bridget scooped her up. And Devyn had her *in*—burying her face in my cousin's neck and grabbing fistfuls of her shirt. When she finally calmed, she pulled back and, with runny eyes and nose, said, *Wuv Bij.* And so *Bij* it was, though I tried to correct the pronunciation for all the looks we received from people who thought my little girl was calling her second cousin a very bad name.

I turn in the doorway. "How about next Saturday night?"

Bridget's lids narrow. "And we meet you at church the following morning, right?"

Of all days to try and pull that one on her, this was not it. In fact, after today, I'll probably be too embarrassed to try it again. "No, I can pick her up at your place on the way to church."

Her teeth flash brilliant white, confirming she is the loveliest of the Pickwick women. Even with dreads. "Why, cuz, I can't tell you how glad I am that you came to little ol' me for help."

Right. By involving her in my deception, she has a monkey off her back. But considering the poor example this monkey set, that can't be a bad thing.

❧

Lord, grant me patience—

Hold it! I can do better than that. Rewind. *Lord, grant me longanimity. Lots of it.*

Patience in adversity definitely fits, and not even Devyn, where she sits in the pew beside Reece, could argue it. Not that she'll ever know the context in which it was applied.

I reverse my gaze over the five who have claimed one of the short pews on the left side of the sanctuary: Reece, Devyn, Piper, Axel, Uncle Obe. I linger on the latter's silver-haired head. Is he responsible for Reece's presence at Church on the Square, or do I owe this latest stressor to Pastor Stanky? Regardless, my attempt to maintain distance between my daughter and Reece has failed.

With the pastor expounding on whatever he's expounding on, I stride down the aisle. As I near my destination, Skippy catches my eye with a wave of her hand, pointedly looks from me to Reece, and gestures for me to join her on the front pew.

No can do. Though five is pretty much the maximum for the shorter pews, they *will* make room for me. I shake my head, she grimaces, and I halt alongside Reece.

"Excuse me," I whisper and, without meeting his gaze, turn sideways and slip in. As the back of my knees connect with the front of his, he stiffens.

"Mom!" Devyn rasps, then scoots closer to Piper as I bring my rear in for a landing between Reece and Devyn.

Her movement causes a chain reaction, and when I settle on the bench, I have claimed over a foot of precious space. Still, it makes for a tight fit—on both sides. Feeling the brush of Reece's outer thigh against mine, I nearly groan.

Why didn't I sit with Skippy? It's not as if Devyn and Reece can carry on a conversation in the middle of service.

I look at Devyn and whisper, "Why didn't you save me a seat?"

She's so close that all she has to do is turn her head to put her lips to my ear. "I thought you might have slept in and weren't coming—"

Regrettably, that happens from time to time.

"—or maybe you got sick like Grandma."

Right. We're barely on the backside of February, but twice this year my mother has warned that her days are numbered. In January, she was certain her cough was lung cancer, and this morning when she phoned, her sniffles were symptomatic of meningitis.

I promised that Devyn and I would visit and make her a big pot of soup and—lo and behold!—she asked me to bring an order of Digby Dan's barbecue ribs instead. Though my mother's craving hardly fits the face she presents to the world, it's proof her life is not in jeopardy. Imagine using ribs as the measure of a person's ailments...

"Grandma called you at Uncle Obe's?" I ask.

"Uh-huh. Anyway, when Mr. Thorpe came in late and was lookin' for a place to sit, I invited him to join us."

I'm relieved that Uncle Obe didn't engineer this, but that doesn't alter the fact that I'm sandwiched between a man I once had an intimate relationship with and the child who may have been born of that relationship.

"You slept in?" Devyn asks.

I shake my head. "I stopped by the nursery to visit with Bridget."

"On Sunday morning?"

I shouldn't have volunteered that. I look past her and meet Piper's waiting gaze. She gives me a *what was I supposed to do?* look.

Devyn taps my arm and puts her mouth so near my ear her lips brush the lobe. "You didn't tell me Mr. Thorpe set up his studio in the theater."

I knew she would find out. It won't be long before she becomes suspicious about my new habit of bringing work home. "I didn't think it was important."

She draws back and frowns.

With a shrug, I look to Pastor Stanky who is referencing a verse in Galatians—

Warm breath stirs the hair near my right ear, causing a shiver to shoot to my fingertips. "I would move," Reece whispers, "but that might cause more speculation."

He's right. Some are bound to interpret my behavior in light of my past. *There she goes again, throwing herself at the opposite sex.* But I'm no longer like the adulteress Jesus saved from stoning. He wrote in the dirt for me as well…forgave me…told me to sin no more. And I haven't—well, not in the sexual sense. But as Bridget can testify—

More breath, more shivers to the outer reaches of my person. "It's your call."

I look around. As expected, his face is too close, and I notice he still has the nicest pores I've seen on a guy. I know that's an odd thing to note, but what lies above and below his nose I'd best stay clear of, what with our bodies so close.

"I can handle it," I breathe, only to hear the flustered, snippy side of me add, "Can you?"

Oh, Lord, I issued a challenge. Do over. Take back.

"No problem." Reece shifts nearer me.

Ah! What does he think he's doing? Of course, he is tight against the end of the pew, having moved far right to make room for me. Still, I'm sure it's more a matter of upping the ante.

Feeling like a slingshot drawn taut—make that the stone that's about to be hurled to kingdom come—I turn forward. That's when Seth catches my eye from where he sits across the aisle. He looks from me to Reece with a lowered brow and clenched jaw. If he doesn't get the new job in Japan, maybe one good thing will come of this situation.

I focus on Pastor Stanky, who has segued into the subject of sexual sin.

Rub it in, won't you?

Devyn touches my clenched hands. "You okay, Mom?"

"Um-hmm." I'm healthy, I have feeling in every one of my nerve endings (just ask those in contact with Reece), and I have a wonderful daughter. What's not to be okay about?

Mercy! He moved again. The good news is, in crossing one leg over the other, he broke contact with my thigh. The bad news is, his hip is now against mine—lightly, but there all the same. Thus, we suffer each other's company, and most of our pastor's sermon falls on the infertile, rocky ground of my intense awareness of the man beside me.

"Mom?" Devyn taps my arm. "I'm squished."

If that's her only discomfort, she is one lucky girl. "Only ten minutes to go."

"My legs are falling asleep."

If she were young enough that no one would raise an eyebrow, and if it didn't eliminate the wedge (me) between Reece and her, I'd pull her onto my lap. Instead, I'll have to reclaim the inch Reece took back. I jump my bottom sideways and hear Reece's intake of breath as my hip settles hard against his.

I smile at Devyn. "Better?"

She nods and returns her attention to Pastor Stanky. Surprisingly, I'm not as intensely aware of Reece as I was when more space was between us. Might this have something to do with my mother's advice during my teen years that to get a guy's attention, it's best to leave something to the imagination? If so, it also applies to getting a gal's attention.

How is Reece is holding up? His jaw tenses a moment before his head comes around. Oh no, I am not getting caught up in a game of footsy—er, *eyesy*—like when his face came so near mine at the Grill 'n' Swill I thought he was going to kiss me. I stare at the V-shaped gap between our thighs until the weight of his regard lifts. Close one.

And so is *that.* I blink at the dark hair against the side of his dark slacks. As he's in town alone, it likely belongs to him. But what are the chances the root is attached? That the hair didn't break off? I squint to pick out the translucent bulb, but to no avail. I'll have to get closer.

And how do you propose to do that? "Excuse me, you have a hair on your pant leg. Let me get that for you. Oh, and I'd be happy to save you the trouble of disposing of it."

If that didn't send his suspicion through the roof, he'd think I was making a move on him. Maybe I could just pinch it, but if he catches me…

Though I hate providing evidence I haven't changed in the thirteen years since he left Pickwick—that I'm still a shameless flirt at best, a seductress at worst— if it saves me from sneaking into his hotel room, it's worth the risk.

I slide my right hand to my thigh, bringing it in line with the hair on his left thigh. Just three inches and it's mine. But timing is everything, and so I wait until the right moment, which isn't until Pastor Stanky ends his sermon.

As we pry ourselves out of the packed pew to sing a closing hymn, I make my move in hopes that if Reece feels anything, it can be blamed on the jostling of bodies. But when Devyn stumbles against me, it's Reece's thigh on which my fingers close.

He catches my wrist and presses it against my side as we straighten shoulder to shoulder. "I had hoped," he rasps low as the voices around us rise in song, "you might have grown up some."

He thinks the worst of me. But why is he still holding my wrist? To prevent me from pinching him again? And why does his touch make my insides go all soft and fluttery?

I meet his frowning gaze. "Sorry about that. I..." I moisten my lips, which makes him frown harder and I want to smack myself for adding to his negative perception. "I didn't mean for that to happen."

And he's going to believe you? That was no jostle or bump. You pinched him!

"There was a..." Why not? "...hair on your pant leg." And it's still there, meaning it's back to Plan Bridget.

Reece unclamps my wrist. "I'm here to work, Maggie. That's all."

Though I pretty much handed him the right to interpret my hair quest as a sexual advance, my pride protests. "Believe it or not, Reece Thorpe, I've been over you for a long time."

He lowers those thickly fringed lashes, and when they rise, there's a glint in his eyes. "I didn't realize there was anything to get over."

Which is what I wanted him to believe when he dumped me. Which is why I quickly filled his shoes with someone who didn't fit them...and then someone else. I wanted jealousy to eat at him until he came crawling back. But never did I intend to go as far as I did with those other two, knowing Reece wouldn't tolerate that degree of intimacy. However, I did go that far, and that's why I don't know who fathered Devyn.

Wishing I had focused on God and not Reece, that I had something good to show for my church attendance, I sing the last verses of the hymn. Thankfully, when the final note floats away, Reece steps into the aisle.

"Wait!" Devyn traverses the pew on her knees to get around me. "Do you want to have lunch with us, Mr. Thorpe?"

I nearly shout "No!" but reason prevails. Not only do we have an engagement with my mother, but even if we didn't, there's no way he would accept. Still, I hold my breath as he pauses amid the others in the aisle.

"Thank you, Devyn." He smiles lightly. "But I have other plans."

Plans that do not include suffering the company of a shameless hussy—

No. That is not who I am in Christ. My sins have been washed away. So, why do I feel dirty?

Uh, might that have something to do with your DNA quest?

"Maybe next Sunday," Devyn suggests.

"We'll see." He raises a hand, and as he moves down the aisle, I note that I'm not the only one looking after him. Reece has caught the attention of several of our single ladies, one of whom is pressing hard through the crowd to catch up with him. A moment later, she reaches her objective. A moment after that, Reece is smiling at whatever silliness she is speaking to him.

"You all right?" Piper whispers over my shoulder.

I look around. "That was hard."

"It's over." She squeezes my arm.

She has no idea how comforting that small gesture is. If Piper, who I repeatedly wronged while we were growing up, can forgive me and care about me, I must be doing—or *was*—doing something right.

"Yeah." I nod and meet Axel's gaze over her shoulder. I could hug him for the sympathetic light in his oh-so-blue eyes. And not for the first time, I wish there had been something between us like what he has with my cousin.

Though my mother protested our friendship on the grounds that not only is Axel *blue collar,* but he wears his hair in a ponytail and has a prosthetic leg, he's a good man and would have made Devyn a wonderful father.

Deciding to wait out the exodus, I chat briefly with Piper, Axel, and Uncle Obe, then decline lunch for the sake of Digby Dan's. Oh, joy!

❧

"MIGHT NOT BE MENINGITIS AFTER ALL." My mother dabs the corner of her mouth, though there's no barbecue sauce to be seen. "That or God answered my prayer for healing."

"It was God." Devyn drops the last picked-clean rib to the fine China plate my mother set out for us. Then, forgetting in whose presence she sits, she licks the sauce from her thumb.

"Devyn, stop that!" My mother's head trembles with the passion of her offended sensibilities. "It's one thing to eat with your fingers"—*she* used a fork and knife—"but to *lick* them?! Proper young ladies do *not* lick their fingers."

"Sorry, Grandma." She wipes her hands on the napkin in her lap.

Adele shifts around in her chair at the head of the table. "I declare, Magdalene, after the years and years that went into training you to be a lady, the least you could do is pass some of that learning on to my granddaughter."

I push aside the remains of my barbecued chicken salad. "They're ribs, Mom, and we aren't in public."

She sticks up an index finger. "Manners begin in the home."

I don't want to argue with her, especially with her on the brink of recovery from life-threatening meningitis. "You're right." I slide an apologetic smile from her to Devyn. "Honey, remember to use your napkin."

"Yes, ma'am."

The *ma'am* ought to please my mother, though it always makes me feel old when a remorseful Devyn uses it on me.

"So"—my mother sets her folded napkin on the table—"who's up for a game of Yahtzee?"

"Scrabble?" Devyn says with a hopeful smile.

My mother waves away the suggestion. "Yahtzee."

Two hours' worth. When we finally make it to the door and Devyn bounds past me, my mother grips my arm and pulls me back into the doorway.

"Perhaps we could have lunch one day this week, Maggie. Just the two of us."

Something I try to avoid as we end up arguing or I end up *being Skippy* to the point of exhaustion. "I have a busy schedule, but I'll call if I can work something out."

She stares at me, then shrugs. "So long as it's not Wednesday. Your *brother* is taking me to lunch."

He is? That's not like Luc. Of course, it might just be wishful thinking on her part. Regardless, it's an attempt to guilt me into doing what she wants.

"Poor boy." She shakes her head. "I told him not to marry that woman. And now..." Heavy, heavy sigh. "...he may be on the brink of another divorce."

I know a little about that. Luc tries my patience, most notably last summer when he plotted to have Uncle Obe declared mentally incompetent in order to deny him the right to dispose of his assets as he sees fit, but I make an effort to keep my brother in the family loop. Thus, the lines of communication are open when he avails himself of them, which he did this week.

"He and Tiffany are fine, Mom. Luc bought her roses and apologized for forgetting her birthday." Per my advice.

"That did it—roses and an apology?" Mom's lids narrow. "What else?"

"Er, he also gave her a gift card to her favorite boutique." *That* I did not advise, but Luc knows his wife best.

"Oh, dear." She presses a hand to her chest. "That woman and her designer clothes. When Luc takes me to lunch, I'd better leave my checkbook at home since he probably wants another loan. I'm a bit low on funds, you know."

I didn't know.

"At least until your daddy sends more money."

Which he will, as he's done since he ran off to Mexico to avoid imprisonment. I don't know how he's managed to support himself and my mother all these years, but I am grateful he hasn't stopped loving her. That alone warrants forgiveness of him for leaving us.

"Mom, if you need money—"

"No, no. He'll send it."

"Well, if he's late, let me know." I put my lips to her cheek that is smoother than mine, thanks to a lifelong love affair with moisturizer and, more recently, cosmetic intervention. To my surprise, she leans into the kiss as if to feel it deeper, and my heart stretches as if to ease a tight muscle. Despite past hurts and unresolved differences, she's still my mother.

"I love you, Mama."

Her breath catches, and when I draw back, she's almost smiling. It wasn't just the kiss and profession of love. It was that I called her *Mama,* which she probably longs to hear from me as much as I long to hear it from Devyn.

We stare at each other until a sweet drawl calls, "You comin', Mom?"

"Goodness!" My mother scowls at Devyn, who has stuck her head out of the SUV window. "Do something with that girl's hair. And show her how to use makeup to minimize the size of her nose."

Bite thy tongue! I do, which is only possible since she didn't speak loud enough for Devyn to hear. I hurry to the SUV to find my daughter has turned her attention to a book I haven't seen before: *Steps to a Successful Stepfamily*. Grr!

As I turn the key in the ignition, I catch sight of the daily word taped to my dashboard. Yeah, *longanimity* about sums up this day.

CHAPTER 11

DAILY WORD CALENDAR
for Highly Successful Career Women

[**extrap'olate** (*verb*) to infer from something that is known]

THURSDAY, FEBRUARY 25

Hotel room number #310—check!

Third floor scheduled for 1:00 housekeeping —check!

Subject safely tucked away in studio—check!

Operative (me) in position—check!

Evidence-collection kit present—check!

All that's missing is a trench coat, and though I own one, its bright red color is too loud for the job—as is my hair, which is why it's tucked beneath a brown knit beret despite a good hair day.

As I scan the soda pop machine's offerings for the hundredth time, the housekeeping cart rattles, alerting me to the housekeeper's emergence from Reece's room.

I check my watch. It's now 1:45. Since Bridget delivered the goods three days ago, I've kept watch on Reece's comings and goings. Unfortunately, there isn't much of a pattern, as he breaks for lunch anywhere between noon and two. On the upside, twice he returned to his studio afterward. On the downside, once he returned to his hotel.

I poke my head out of the alcove to peer right down the hallway to where the housekeeper is wheeling the heavy vacuum cleaner into Reece's room. This is it. After waiting through the cleaning of three rooms, the excruciatingly thorough woman will soon be vacuuming her way out of number 310, and I'll be in like—

She halts and looks around.

I press myself flat against the alcove wall, nearly laughing at the thought that if the Pickwick Arms had cameras in the hallways, I would appear as shifty-eyed and suspicious as a comic strip spy—less the trench coat, of course.

The vacuum revs up, and the woman begins to hum over the sound of the motor.

Pulling the baggy from my coat pocket, I look left down the hall at the elevator. Above the doors, the lit number 2 changes to an L as the elevator returns to the lobby. I hold my breath and count to ten, but the L remains as proof no one is traveling between floors. Providing that doesn't change soon, Reece's DNA is as good as mine.

I step out of the alcove. With the sound of the vacuum growing louder in time with the pounding of my heart, I pass rooms 304…306…308…

Ping! goes the elevator for the third time since my vigil began. But this time I no longer have the cover of the soda pop/ice machine alcove.

I consider ducking behind the housekeeping cart, but it's too far away, so I do a one-eighty and stride toward the elevator looking all the while like a guest on her way out. Providing the other guest isn't Reece Thorpe.

I should have guessed—no, *extrapolated!*—this would happen. I halt. He halts. I stare. He stares. I look guilty. He...well, he knows it.

As the elevator doors close behind him, I clench my fingers around the baggy and am grateful the crinkle of plastic can't be heard over the vacuum. Also, I'm grateful I'm not standing in Reece's bathroom. Had he arrived thirty seconds later...

"Maggie." His mouth curves questioningly, the movement emphasized by the toothpick in one corner. "What are you doing here?"

"Er, what are *you* doing here?" The automatic answer-a-question-with-a-question strategy almost makes me groan.

His mouth flattens. "This *is* my home for the duration of my stay in Pickwick."

"Oh. Right." My face feels redder than my hair. "Silly me." I step forward. "Well, I won't keep you—"

"Why are you here?"

No easy way out. Not only do I have to get around him, but there's the wait for the elevator to return to the third floor. I stop before him. "It's personal." And it would be personal for him too if I could only get my hands on his hair!

He looks me up and down, and then to the rooms beyond. "I see."

He says it with such certainty I know I'm found out. But how did he—?

Oh! He thinks I've come from a rendezvous. After all, what else would the Maggie he knew be doing in a hotel in a town where she lives?

Same old Maggie. Still jumping bed to bed, though she does attend church for good measure. Why, all that's missing is a trench coat.

Thankfully! It would have been the polish on the poison apple had I come strolling down the hallway wearing bright red.

Still, even in its absence, the conclusion is the same, and it makes me feel like a tramp. But better that than the truth. Or is it? By not being up-front with Reece, I'm denying him further proof of my promiscuous past, but also providing false proof of my promiscuous present.

Lord, I've dug myself in. With a one-way shovel. That is, unless I own up to my DNA quest.

No. *That* is as much a reflection on my present as being caught in a hotel.

I raise my chin. "It's not what you think. I..."

Reece frowns.

"It's not what you think," I repeat and, feeling the heat rise in my face, step around him. As I punch the Down button, he turns toward me.

"What then, Maggie?"

Does he really want me to dispel his assumption? Is he looking for the good in me as he did years ago when he pushed past my outward beauty in search of the inward glimmer no one else bothered to seek?

Longing for him to put forth the effort just one more time, I turn back.

His dark hair has shifted on his brow, and the impulse to push my fingers through it is so strong, I have to curl them into my palms to stop myself. The baggy protests.

Reece looks down.

Oh no.

Ping! This time I'm thrilled to hear the call of the elevator.

"Believe what you want, Reece." Wincing at how breathless I sound, I slip through the partially parted elevator doors and punch the L button. As the doors start to close, I look up.

He's there, eyebrows gathered, the wheels I set in motion turning. Then he steps forward and puts a shoulder to one of the doors, causing them to retract with a loud thump. Or was that my heart?

"You said it isn't what I think." His voice is frighteningly earnest. "Prove me wrong."

I want to. Badly. I want to ask him to be tested, to let him into our lives if he is the one. But chances are he isn't. Too, the thought of giving him proof that the other guys I flaunted were more than an attempt to hurt him makes me ache. And, really, what gain would there be in letting it all out of the bag? Even if he is Devyn's father, he probably wouldn't want anything to do with us—me!

I draw a deep breath. "You're holding up the elevator, and it's the only one—"

"It's not what I want to believe. You just make it hard to believe otherwise."

The vacuum cuts off, signaling his room is ready for occupancy, but he ignores the cue to retreat.

"First the snowball at the metalworks when I was talking to your daughter. Then the coffee shop when you made it more obvious you don't want me speaking to her. Next"—he gives the persistent door his shoulder again—"the restaurant when I thought you were after my notebook. I got that wrong, didn't I?"

Though years ago, my automatic response would be to affect innocence, I can't stomach it. So I stare at him. And pray. *Oh, God. God. God?*

"And at church you practically sat on my lap to put space between Devyn and me."

And pinched him...

"Now this. What's going on?"

My hard swallow sounds like a suddenly unplugged drain. "You wouldn't understand."

"What makes you think that?"

My laugh sounds bitter. "Because I doubt you've made the mistakes I have or hurt people the way I have." I jab the Close Door button.

This time he doesn't stop the doors from doing their job but steps back and stares at me until they meet in the middle.

Leaning against the elevator wall, I blink at the mirrored ceiling until it comes into focus and reflects my flushed face. I'm making a mess of everything, sowing suspicion in dangerous places—Devyn who has begun to question why I've stopped taking her to the auction house after school and asked this morning if it has anything to do with Reece, and Reece...

"You want me to lay off Reece, Lord? Okay. But how am I supposed to prove he isn't—"

I gasp. Verification, not elimination. Meaning I'm still in the market for DNA, just not Reece's.

My stomach lurches in time with the elevator as it delivers me to the lobby. I hurry through the hotel and outside into the cold, crisp air.

Standing on the sidewalk beneath the canopy, I grip a pole and breathe deep until my stomach settles enough for me to point myself toward the pharmacy. Five minutes later, I exit the store with an economy-sized bottle of antacid less the three chalky chewables I downed. Unfortunately, before this is all over, I may be back for more.

WIN SOME, lose some—Gary's motto. And well deserved, even if it began as a play on his last name: Winsome. He may have been one of the best players on our high school football team, but he wasn't in it for the sport as much as for the girls.

"Win some, lose some," he'd say with a flash of fudge brownie eyes and a swoon-worthy grin when the team lost because he was too distracted by the cheerleaders to catch the football. *I* was one of those distractions, flirting and hanging on him in hopes of making Reece so jealous he would come back to me. He didn't, and my encouragement of Gary, plus a bottle of liquor pulled from beneath his car seat on the way home from a game, is the reason Gary is Candidate Number Two. Of course, he ought to be Candidate Number One since he more likely fathered Devyn—timewise and lookswise—but it only seems right to go in order. Thus, Reece keeps the top spot.

An Internet search having yielded the whereabouts of Gary Winsome, who is in upper-level management for one of the nation's top banks in Charlotte, North Carolina, I close my browser. It's time to pick up Devyn from school.

I scoop my dress watch from the corner of my desk and push its expandable band over my hand. Upon retraction, the springy links catch the fine hairs on my wrist. "Ouch!" Again. If Devyn hadn't given it to me for Christmas, I wouldn't wear it, but she saved and saved for it, so what's a little discomfort?

As I button into my peacoat, I glance through the projection room's windows that overlook the theater. Hundreds of empty seats gape at me, but that will change on Saturday when I bring Mrs. Dudley Tuttle's porcelain doll and perfume bottle collection to auction. Between her items and the vintage women's clothing that was discovered in the attic of the Pickwick mansion, Serendipity Auction Services may be hosting its first full house. Not only will there be the usual antique shop buyers and auction-as-an-outing goers, but also a bevy of women who aren't usually attracted to auctions.

Thanks to PR-savvy Piper, who conceived the idea of a *lady's day at the auction house,* whereby all items appeal to those of the female persuasion, Saturday's event is all the buzz. If it goes well, it should prove highly profitable, especially if the bidding is as fierce as I anticipate. Which could make for a very long day, and perhaps evening.

It's a good thing Devyn is staying overnight with Bridget. And possibly another night next week when I go to Charlotte.

My excitement over Saturday's auction dampened by the

task ahead, I put my shoulders back. Whatever it takes, I will get my hands on Gary's DNA. Now I just have to figure out how.

Reaching up the right sleeve of my coat, I tug the bunched sleeve of my shirt toward my wrist. "Ouch!" Again! I glower at Devyn's temperamental gift that has relieved me of more hairs, but an instant later, I feel a smile coming on. "*That's* how."

CHAPTER 12

DAILY WORD CALENDAR
for Highly Successful Career Women

[**cos'tive** (*adjective*) slow action or speech; tight-fisted; stingy]

SATURDAY, FEBRUARY 27

Reece was warned, but did he listen? No, he just had to set up his studio in my auction house. So he'll either have to work around the noise of the chattering, predominantly female attendees or leave. Hopefully, he'll go with choice B. And soon. I can hardly perform at optimum level with memories of our hotel encounter making me painfully self-conscious.

I glance again at Reece, who appeared at the back of the theater as I finished conducting a mock auction to demonstrate the bidding process to those who have never participated.

Ignore him.

I would if I could.

You can. Just like you do when & Sons *crashes your auctions.*

I *have* learned how to handle Puck's boys, but this is different. For all the nasty rumors they start about me, they're not dark haired, green eyed, and emotionally bothersome. And never have they happened on me looking as if I've come from a hotel room tryst.

Ignore him!

I lift my chin and hold up a hand. "Let's begin."

Though the excited chatter dies down, it transfers its energy to the air, and I draw on it. Tingling from scalp to toes, I smile over the hundreds of auctiongoers who look up at me where I stand behind a podium on stage.

I'm ignoring you, Reece Thorpe. I do not see you there. You're air.

I adjust my headset microphone. "As pictured in your catalog"—a mass rustling of the sixteen-page booklet—"our first item up for auction comes to us from the collection of Mrs. Dudley Tuttle." I look to my left, where the pretty college student I often hire to aid me on stage holds up a doll enclosed in a glass box. "Item number one is a porcelain hand-painted Armand Marseille doll, circa 1890."

A murmur of interest and a craning of necks.

"Our little princess is outfitted in her original blue dress and black lace-up boots. And let me tell you, this baby doll has been babied—not a hair out of place. Let's start the bidding at $200. Who will give me 200?"

A long, breathless silence, and just as I start to think I may have set the opening bid too high, one of three ringmen hired for the day to relay the bids to me from the floor shouts, "I have $200 here!" The ringman—or in this case, ring*woman*—identified by a red Serendipity Auction vest, positions herself closer to the bidder whose paddle is up.

Now if I can just work the buyers to the $600 mark that the doll ought to bring. With a conscious effort not to speak as fast as I do when it's farm equipment at auction, I begin my chant.

"We have a $200 dollar bid, now 300, now 300, who will give me 300?" Not too fast, but not costive either. Nice daily word.

At the back of the theater, near where Reece stands, a paddle shoots into the air.

"We have a $300 dollar bid, now 400, now 400, who will give me 400?" I get it, but a couple minutes later have to back off the $100 increments. With a bit more effort, I get $450, and from there it's a short climb to 500. More resistance, but I'm not done. It's time to connect with and entertain my audience. "Oh, ma'am, if you don't bid on this item again, I just know you and I will regret it come mornin'. Give me 550. Just 550."

Amid chuckles and twitters, the heavy woman flushes, looks to where her husband has nodded off beside her, and raises her paddle.

"Thank you, ma'am. We have a $550 dollar bid, now 600, now 600, who will give me 600?" I look wide-eyed at her rival, a scrawny middle-aged woman on the front row. A ringman is down on his haunches beside her, encouraging her as I pay him well to do.

She bites her lip and taps her bidding paddle on her thigh.

"Ma'am, you don't want to leave here with nonbuyer's remorse." I consider urging her not to be *costive*—the *tight-fisted* meaning of my daily word—but I doubt she'd understand it any more than I did before today. Thus, I could end up offending her with my highfalutin speech and her paddle won't budge. I need it to budge. "Come now, ma'am. For $50 dollars more, this rare doll could be going home with you."

She nods at something the ringman says, then puts her paddle high.

I shoot for $700. However, the heavy woman gets in the last bid at 650.

"Sold to bidder 152! Congratulations, ma'am." One down, many more to go, but by the time I offer item number four, I've found my rhythm and for the last time silently tell Reece I'm ignoring him.

Two hours later, I call a break. Though I'm bound to lose some of the auctiongoers during the twenty minutes I'm off stage, I have to protect my voice and give my jaws and feet a rest. Fortunately, most of the serious buyers will stay. As for the not-so-serious…

I remove my headset and look up the aisle to where the theater doors are open wide to the lobby. At Piper's suggestion, I ordered two dozen assorted pies from Martha to serve with the usual coffee and tea offered during breaks. If her baking doesn't hold a body captive, nothing will. I said as much to Martha, who mused that with a couple more weekly orders like mine, she might consider giving up her waitressing job. I suggested she talk to Mr. Copper who probably sells as many pastries as coffee drinks.

The last time I saw Martha look that excited was when she expanded her meat-and-three eatery from eight tables to twelve. A year later, her doors closed forever. I may have to talk to Mr. Copper myself. And make pies a regular part of my Saturday auctions.

Hoping to snag a slice that I can enjoy once the day's work is behind me, I step from behind the podium. And that momentary feeling of exposure that sometimes hits me after hours behind a wooden stand calls to mind the forgotten Reece. How I miss the adrenaline-inducing act of auctioning that allowed me to skim over his dark, still figure and disturbing gaze.

As I descend the steps, I look past those who are working their way up the aisles to either indulge in Martha's pies or get on with their Saturday.

Did Reece return to his studio? The Pickwick Arms? In this instance, I'm hoping the latter. It took a lot of adrenaline to get past his presence, and once the break is over, it will take a while for me to work myself back into that state.

"Maggie!" Skippy appears in front of me.

I smile. "You came!"

"I done told you I was gonna get me one of them pretty perfume bottles." She slips a hand in her purse and pulls the corner of a one-hundred-dollar bill above the zipper. "Think that'll do it?"

"Providing you don't have your heart set on the Jacinthe bottle. I'm aiming for upwards of three-hundred dollars."

"Gracious, no!" She shakes her bouffant-topped head. "That thing's plum ugly. Looks like a see-through flask, if'n you ask me."

Yes, but rare is rare.

"What I'm anglin' for is item number 82, 101, or 116. Any one of those will look right pretty on my bathroom counter."

I don't remember which bottles correspond to those numbers, but since most are in the $75 to $100 range, I'm sure she'll take one home.

"Oh!" Her hand tightens on my arm. "I got a surprise to share. Come on."

I follow her up the path that her energy blazes for us. The going is slower once we reach the crowded lobby. I couldn't be happier that most of the auctiongoers are staying. Well, at least to enjoy Martha's pies and coffee.

"There she is!" Skippy lifts a hand high above her head to point toward the beverage table.

It's all a sea of heads to me. "Who, Skip?"

"Yule." She beams over her shoulder. "She came to town this mornin'."

I'm happy for my friend, who doesn't see her daughter often enough. Still, I feel the usual kink of discomfort that only Yule can iron out with a smile of acceptance.

"And she's showin'," Skippy tosses back at me.

So what's new? Okay, that's an exaggeration, but this *is* her third pregnancy in five years.

Twenty feet ahead, I catch sight of the back of Yule's head, notable for its abridged version of her mother's bouffant hair. I kink a little more.

Buck up, Maggie. She let it go.

I know, just as I know I should put memories of bullying her behind me—especially the last incident witnessed by Reece.

Try harder. If Maggie Pickwick can turn her life around, go from cursing a god that may or may not be to praising God who is, support herself and her daughter, and command top dollar for secondhand items, she can iron out her own kinks.

Put that way, I *can* do it!

At Skippy's "Yoo-hoo, Yule!" her daughter turns.

But maybe not today...

The man on the other side of Yule makes me kink so hard I nearly trip over my feet, and I kink harder when the smile on Reece's face decreases at the sight of me.

"Mama, look who I found." Yule grabs Skippy's arm and tugs her into the circle of two, shutting me out. "My high school champion, Reece Thorpe."

"Uh, Yule, darlin'..." Skippy glances over her shoulder at where I stand on the precipice of my past.

"Ya remember, don't you, Mama? My senior year when I fell—"

"Join us, won't you, Maggie?" Skippy steps to the side to make room for me.

I'd rather take cover, but Yule has turned her big blue-shadowed eyes on me. And of course, there's Reece who is surely trying to make sense of the unexpected: What is Skippy Baggett doing with the woman who bullied her daughter in school? Or maybe: Will I have to champion her again?

The prettier, softer version of *Married with Children*'s Peg Bundy recovers with a blink. "Hiya, Maggie." Her smile of acceptance is tempered by what is surely a recent trip down memory lane. "Mmm, the pie was awful good." She wags a paper plate that is bare except for a piece of crust and a purple smear of boysenberry.

Feeling Reece's questioning gaze and peripherally seeing him raise his coffee cup, I say, "Martha made it."

"I shoulda known." She smacks her lips. "How's your auction goin'?"

"Well, thanks. We've drawn a good crowd and they haven't been shy about openin' their pocketbooks. It's bound to be a long day." *So you might as well accept you're not going to get any work done and get, Reece Thorpe!* "How have you been, Yule?"

"Good." She pinches the crust between fuchsia fingernails and pops it in her mouth.

"Especially now that she's over the mornin' sickness." As Skippy reaches past me to pat her daughter's tummy, Reece's questioning once more stirs the air.

"Mama!" Yule swats her hand. "There's a gentleman present. Have a care for my modesty."

Reece glances from Yule's softly rounded tummy to her left hand.

No, she's not married, but the pregnancy is intentional. More intentional than he will ever know—until Yule or Skippy clue him in.

"This here's my third grandchild." Skippy jerks her head in the direction of Yule's abdomen. "And no sooner will I lay eyes on the little one than my daughter will give him or her away. Now, I ask you, is that right?"

Confusion creases Reece's face. He probably feels like he's walked onto the set of one of those adult cartoons that feature fat-head people with warped senses of humor. Welcome to Pickwick.

Yule sighs so heavily, the only thing missing is the back of a hand to her forehead. "Now, Mama, you know this is not your grandchild."

"Is so."

"Is not."

Reece looks to me as if I might make sense of the surreal, but it's about to become clear.

"If that child is in you, it's of you," Skippy says firmly, "meaning it's of me—*my* grandchild."

"Mama, you can't be thinkin' or talkin' like that. Yes, it's my body doin' the carrying, but that's all, and I will not become attached to this little one any more than I already am."

Understanding eases the lines of Reece's face.

Yule presses a hand to her belly. "It's hard enough to give up a baby without complicatin' matters further."

"Well, if you'd find yourself a good man and give me my own grandbaby"—Skippy crosses her arms over her chest—"I'd shut up about you borrowin' out your body to make other grandmothers happy."

That drains the argument out of Yule. With a softly apologetic smile, she says, "When I find a good man, you'll have grandbabies. In the meantime, I see no reason to let my childbearing years go to waste when I can help others grow a family."

Though Skippy doesn't deflate as quickly as her daughter did, she does deflate and steps around me to hug Yule. "Of course you will, darlin'. Forgive me. It's just that I ain't gettin' younger."

Yule pats her back. "I'm on the lookout, Mama. Really I am."

They draw apart, but Skippy bumps a place for herself at her daughter's side, forcing me to sidle nearer Reece.

Time to extricate. "Well, I need to get ready—"

"So you're a surrogate." Reece's smile is aimed at Yule.

"Giving-wise," Skippy answers for her daughter who flushes a pretty pink. "Three times now she's helped nice couples whose baby ovens don't work. She has a good heart, my Yule. Refuses to take money for carrying others' children. But now, careerwise, my daughter is a physical therapist. Got her own practice in Knoxville, which is why I don't get to see her near enough."

Reece slings his hands in his pant pockets and rolls back onto his heels. "I'll be in Knoxville next Friday to meet with a group of architects who are interested in incorporating my sculptures into the government buildings they're designing."

Yule gasps. "Maybe we could meet for lunch."

"I'd like that, though since my day is spoken for, we'll have to make it dinner."

Dinner? Reece and Yule? Yule who is on the lookout for a good man—

It's his life, it's her life, and you do not figure into either one. Put your energy into Gary Winsome, not some sad, misplaced, go-nowhere jealousy.

"I'll give you my card." Yule fishes around in her purse. "When you get into town, call me."

The alarm in my friend's eyes goes off. Dear Skippy, worried how I might feel about what could turn out to be a date between Yule and the man who may have fathered my daughter.

I manage a smile that, for as rueful as it feels, is better than the alternative.

Skippy smiles back, nearly as rueful. "Speakin' of dinner"—she wags a finger at me—"on the way here, Yule and I talked about havin' you and Devyn over for pot roast."

Reece is confused again. It's one thing for Skippy and Yule to make polite with me in public, it's another to fraternize on a personal level. Doubtless, Skippy is doing what she advised me to do—showing Reece how the Lord has worked in my life, that I am no longer the Maggie who bullied her daughter, and that I have her forgiveness and Yule's. Clever, but not likely to make him look at me any different, especially considering our recent hotel encounter. I probably should have told Skippy about that.

"So?" Skippy says. "Pot roast?"

I know I'll be tired when the day is done, but I'll also be alone. And without any Devyn-sized distractions, I'll be full up on Reece-sized distractions, even if only in my head. Too, I long for him to know that Skippy and Yule aren't the only ones making an effort to put the past behind us. I really have changed.

And before you ask how much, conscience mine, and point to my little DNA baggy, remember this isn't just about me. It's about protecting Devyn. The mistakes are mine, and she is not going to pay for them by suffering gossips.

I nod. "Devyn is spending the night with Bridget, but I'd love to join you and Yule."

"Great. Will seven o'clock give you enough time to shut this place down?"

"That'll work." A check of my watch shows it's three minutes till show time, and I step back.

"You know," Yule muses, "if you're not doin' anything, you could come too, Reece. Mama makes a mighty good pot roast."

I look to Skippy whose eyes are as wide as mine feel.

"I could use a good home-cooked meal." Reece's smile tucks up a bit more.

Oh! I turn away.

"See you at seven," Skippy calls.

Not if I come down with something—say, lockjaw or laryngitis or gavel-induced carpal tunnel syndrome. Yeah, I can swing one or all of those, and without stretching the symptoms too far. Auctioneering does have its dangers.

"Oh, excuse me!" a dainty older woman exclaims as I almost run her over in my haste to distance myself from Reece and friends.

"My fault." I smile. "Sorry." But as I step around her,

recognition taps my shoulder. That was Chase Elliot's mother. Though I see her around from time to time and she has attended my auctions, I don't think I've ever been so near her.

I'm tempted to look around, but I stay the course. After all, it's unlikely her son is my daughter's father. Goodness, what a day!

CHAPTER 13

What am I doing here? My jaw *is* nearly locked, vocal cords *are* fried, and gavel-wielding hand *does* ache. And yet here I sit at Skippy's kitchen table across from Reece, who is more talkative than I've seen him since his return to Pickwick. Make that *ever*.

When we dated, he never had half as much to say as he does now. Either he's changed, or it has something to do with Yule, who can't keep her hands off him—punctuating tales of the wacky world of physical therapy by tapping his hand, patting his arm, and playfully punching his shoulder. If I didn't know better, I'd say she's flirting—

I don't know better. Considering how much attention Reece is paying her, the smiles he bestows, and eyes so lit that even when Skippy not-so-subtly calls me to his attention they retain their twinkle, that may be exactly what Yule is doing.

"But I do love my work!" She bobs her chin.

Reece grins. "It sounds like life is good."

"Boy, is it! Not that it's a fairy tale, but I'm a good sight happier than when we were in high school."

My past slaps not only me across the face, but Skippy, causing us both to startle.

Yule hoots with laughter. "Talk about an understatement!"

Why did I come? If anyone deserves an early night, it's me. For over six hours, I pushed one-hundred-thousand-dollars' worth of antique dolls, perfume bottles, and clothing. Had I pulled a Puck & Sons, it would have been easier, but Mrs. Dudley Tuttle's heirs are happy, Uncle Obe is happy, my ringmen with their nice bonuses are happy, and my accounts receivables is happy. Me? I could use another antacid.

"Why, I could use some more lemonade." Skippy pushes back her chair. "How about you, Reece? You look to be about out."

"Yes, thank you." He passes his glass to her, and she crosses to the counter.

"Anyway," Yule continues, "like I was sayin'—"

"I apologize for not offerin' you something a bit more lively to drink, Reece," Skippy tries again to change the subject, "but I stopped keepin' that kind of stuff in the house when I come to realize I like it better than I ought to." She tops off the glasses and turns back. "If you know what I mean."

He takes the glass she hands to him. "Actually, I do know."

He does?

"And that's why I no longer drink the stuff myself."

Is he saying he had trouble with alcohol? Reece Thorpe, who always set a good example? Whose only flaw was in liking someone as flawed as me? And what is he doing admitting to it?

"Well, good for you." Skippy gives his shoulder a squeeze before lowering back into her chair.

For several long moments, nothing is said, during which Reece's gaze settles on me, but then Yule picks it up again. "You know, a lot of people would give anything to relive their high school years. Not me."

Why didn't I beg off?

Pride—fear that Reece might attribute your no show *to his* show.

Yule shakes her head. "No way I'd go back to that. I like the *real* world just fine."

I catch the twitch of her lips as she glances my way. Then this isn't merely a bubbly, unthinking Yule? She knows what she's saying and the light in which it casts me? That hurts. What happened to the fence between us? The one over which she willingly talked to me? Is it a wall again, raised by the reappearance of Reece and an opportunity she can't pass up? Revenge? But she's a Christian!

So are you, but that doesn't mean you don't sometimes stray from right to do wrong. For instance—

No! I'm protecting Devyn, and that's that!

Only Devyn?

"Are you all right?"

It's Reece, but not until the kitchen hums with the silence of his unanswered question do I realize he's talking to me. I follow his gaze to where I clench a hand on my middle. "Er, just a bit of an upset stomach."

"My pot roast," Skippy says. "I musta been too free with the pepper."

I appreciate her attempt to help me save face, but I won't pin my discomfort on her. "No, it was delicious as usual. I probably just got too worked up today."

"Poor thing." She pats my hand. "It wore me thin bidding for that there bottle..." She glances at where she set the pink-flowered container on the kitchen counter so she could admire it while preparing our meal. "And I wasn't at the auction but an hour. Why, you're probably about ready to go over the falls."

Without a barrel.

"Can I get you a Tums?"

"Thank you, but I have some in my purse." I push my chair back.

"Enough about me," Yule says as I step past her. "I wanna hear about you being a famous artist and all."

There's my cue. A couple of antacids, a bathroom stop, and this former mean girl is heading home.

I exit the kitchen and cross to where my purse sits on the table near the front door. As I dig through it, I sense Skippy's approach, then her hand is on my shoulder.

"I'm sorry, Maggie. My Yule is in somethin' of a mood. Had I known—"

"It's okay." I continue rooting for the antacid. "Seeing Reece again must have dredged up old memories, good *and* bad."

"Still, that's no cause—"

"Here they are!" I pull out the bottle. "I'll just take a couple of these and head home."

She blinks. "Already?"

I hate how brave my smile feels. "If I don't get to bed soon, I won't be up in time to get Devyn from Bridget's and make it to Sunday service." I head down the hall. "Be right back." Well, not *right* back, as it takes a five-minute *talkin' to* in the mirror to prepare myself to say good-bye to Reece and Yule. When I step out of the bathroom, their voices carry from the living room.

"That's Mama and me on a missions trip into the Appalachians."

"Is that Maggie?" Reece's question makes me falter on the living room threshold. Holding my breath, I focus on the two standing before the wall of pictures on the far side of the room.

Yule laughs. "Why, it is Maggie. I forgot she tagged along. And brought little Devyn too."

They're looking at the picture in which I stand in the background, my drooling baby girl peering over my shoulder from the backpack I toted her in while we ministered to some of the poorest people in the South.

"Why"—Yule cants her head to the side—"that was a long while back."

Oh, Lord, please don't let her clarify how many years a long while *is.*

"Musta been nineteen ninety—"

"Goodness, I don't feel well." As they look around, I grip my stomach. "Not at all." And not a lie, though a hand to my heart would be more fitting,

Yule frowns. "Did you take some Tums?"

"I did. They should be kickin' in soon. Well, I'm going to push off." And hope they don't pick up where they were before my interruption.

"It was nice to see you again." Yule makes no objection to my early departure.

"You too." I consider Reece who is watching me. "'Night."

"Good night, Maggie."

I look around. "Uh, where's Skip?"

"Here!" My friend pushes through the kitchen's swinging doors, cheeks flushed, bouffant leaning to one side. "I was scarin' up some dessert."

It seems like *she's* the one that got scared up.

Skip gives me a hug. "You drive safe now, hear?"

Why is she breathing so hard?

She widens her smile. "See ya at church."

Hmm. "Yes, I'll see you there." I retrieve my purse and slip into my jacket. The chill night air begins to work through the weave of my clothes as I pull the door closed behind me. Picking my way down the walkway, I glance through the big window at where Reece and Yule are talking between themselves again.

Lord, please distract them from those pictures.

I open the door of my SUV, slide in, and once more root through my purse. No keys. Great. I mutter my way back up Skippy's walkway and hear muffled laughter as I knock.

Skippy answers the door. "Changed your mind, did ya?"

"I think I left my keys on the table." As I step inside, I glance at Yule and Reece on the sofa, angled toward one another. At least they're no longer interested in the pictures. *Thank You, Lord.*

"Your keys aren't here, dear," Skippy says.

I pat my pockets. Empty.

"Yule...Reece...have you seen Maggie's keys?"

"I haven't," Reece says.

"Me neither." Yule jumps up. "I'll help her look."

The sooner to get Reece to herself? Or is she once more talking to me over the fence? Regardless, I just want to go home, pull on my pajamas, and fall asleep to the drone of the classic movie channel. But five minutes later, still no keys.

Reece comes back through the swinging doors. "Not in the kitchen."

Skippy straightens from plumping the chair cushions back into place. "They're bound to show up eventually."

And in the meantime? I rise from where I was on my knees searching under the sofa.

"Reece, dear," Skippy says, "I know you and Yule want to visit more, but could I impose on you to drive Maggie home?"

"No!" I look from her to Reece to Yule who has also come up off her knees. "I can call a cab."

Skippy makes a face. "That could take a while, and what with you feelin' poorly, we ought to get you home now."

"You could drive her, Mama." Yule's pitch is on the high side.

"Yes, but I'm as pooped as Maggie looks."

Yule starts forward. "Then you stay here and visit with Reece. I'll take her home."

"In your delicate state? I am not sendin' you out at night, especially when there ain't no call for it, what with Reece goin' Maggie's way anyhow."

"Maamaa," Yule stretches her drawl. "I'm barely six months along, and I did drive all the way from Knoxville—"

"In broad daylight." Skippy tilts her head to the side. "You don't mind, do you, Reece?"

With gritted teeth and mounting suspicion, he considers me where I stand. "Not at all."

What's with the narrowed lids? Does he think I purposely mislaid my keys? I wouldn't do that. But Skippy might.

I look a question at her, and the answer is in the way her gaze slides away from me. The flushed cheeks, skewed bouffant, heavy breathing... She took my keys while I was in the bathroom.

I step toward her. "Can I speak with you, Skip?"

She waves me off. "I'm sure it'll keep 'till tomorrow." She crosses to Yule, who I haven't seen sulk like this since the day she came home from college and found Devyn and me living in her mother's spare bedroom. "Let's get you a good night's sleep, darlin', so you'll be fresh for your drive back to Knoxville tomorrow afternoon."

"All right." Yule turns but comes back around. "See you at church, Reece?"

"I plan on being there."

I am not jealous. He's all hers, especially if their socializing keeps distance between Devyn and him.

Yule beams. "Then I'll save you a piece of our pew." She shifts her attention to me, and her smile tightens. "'Night, Maggie."

Where, oh where, has our little fence gone? "Good night, Yule."

CHAPTER 14

From the passenger seat of Reece's car, I look from my key-forsaken SUV to Skippy on the stoop, her hand waving alongside her lopsided hair. When I get home, she is getting a call. And an earful. *If* she picks up.

She won't. But by morning my keys will have miraculously reappeared, my SUV will likely be in my driveway (dropped off by her and Yule on the way to church), and Reece will be sharing a pew with the Baggett women. Regardless, Skippy will hear about this.

"The case of the missing keys," Reece says as we accelerate down the dark street.

I draw a deep breath. "I assure you, the last thing I want is for you to drive me home. As God is my witness"—thank you, Scarlett O'Hara—"I do not know where my keys are."

He meets my gaze. "Skippy does."

Then he doesn't believe I'm responsible? I'm relieved, but still embarrassed. Leaning back, I vaguely register the houses we pass. "I'm sorry for ruining your evening. Once Skippy sets her mind to something, she's hard to budge."

"What has she set her mind to?"

Stepped smack-dab in that cow pie. Now how do I get it off my shoe? Hold it! There is an alternate explanation for what Skippy did. She did it to push Reece and me together, but… "Skippy is protective of Yule, especially with her at the end of her second trimester."

"I think it's more likely she's trying to push you and me together."

Now, why didn't I think of that? I sink down in my seat and lower my lids in hopes of sending the message that I'm too tired to converse.

A moment later, he brakes, and when I crack open an eye, the stop sign that marks the end of Skippy's subdivision is before us.

"Which way?"

Of course he doesn't know where I live. I straighten. "Left, and then a ways down the road."

He makes the turn, and as we once more pick up speed, I feel his sideways glance. "You and Skippy are close."

"Yes." My monosyllabic response should put an end to his probing, as he's not likely to come right out and ask what hangs in the spaces between his words.

"I wouldn't have expected that."

My, he has become more talkative, but then his success in the art world has made him something of a public figure. Hopefully, this is the extent of it.

"Considering your history with Yule, that is."

Not the extent of it. And no doubt he's remembering the scene on the school steps when he championed Yule against mean-girl Maggie.

I touch the chill window. "Skippy is very forgiving." Unlike some people. I miss the fence between Yule and me. Had I made more of an effort, apologizing to her as I did to Piper, would it still be there? Better yet, would it not be there at all? No fence *or* wall? Just a space crossed by carefully putting one foot in front of the other?

"So she forgave you. How did that happen?"

Why does he care about my relationship with Skippy? Still trying to find some good in me? Regardless, this is a bad direction for our conversation to go since it could lead to Devyn City.

"Is it a secret?"

Getting *way* too close to my daughter. "There's not much to tell. Skippy helped me out of some tight places and showed me what it means to be a Christian." I glance at him and am grateful he's in profile. "She's like a mother to me—the mother my mother has a hard time being."

"What about Yule?"

"If you're asking if she's the sister I never had, the answer is no, but she accepts me." *At least until you plunked yourself down in Pickwick and made her remember the girl I was.* "Not that she had much choice, seeing as I was underfoot every time she came home from…college." Ugh. Took the Devyn exit all on my own.

Seeing Reece's head come around, I avert my eyes.

"You lived with Skippy?"

"For a while."

"Why?"

He wants to know why my mother wasn't there for me, but that street sign reads Devyn Way. "Just one of those tight places I got myself into."

In the ensuing silence, I start to relax, but then Reece says, "Yule showed me a picture of you on a missions trip with Skippy and her."

"I went with them."

"And took your daughter along."

Devyn Way straight ahead. "Yes, and I have to say it was eye-opening."

"An experience not to be repeated?"

I try not to take offense, especially since he posed that as a question rather than a statement. "We return almost every summer."

After a long moment, he says, "Maggie Pickwick, a missionary."

Probably as unbelievable as Reece Thorpe having a drinking problem. I look into eyes that briefly reflect the green of the traffic light beneath which we pass. "The same."

He returns his attention to the road. "Not the same Maggie I knew."

True. But then, an unplanned pregnancy changes a person. And being toppled from one's throne without a friend in sight. And being thrust out of childhood into adulthood. However, more than any of those things, it was unearned forgiveness and the discovery I didn't have to go it alone that turned me around. Okay, I'll go easy on Skippy for the missing keys stunt.

I sigh. "I have my faults, but I've changed."

"I'm starting to realize that."

He is?

"Your uncle thinks highly of you."

Uncle Obe, who is trying to pin down a father for Devyn and no doubt extols my virtues as he did with Piper when he set out to match her with Axel. Yes, his matchmaking worked in that case, but he's going to be sorely disappointed in this case.

"As does Piper," Reece adds.

"You've been talking to—? Oh! Turn right here."

He takes the turn so fast the car careens, causing my shoulder to bump his and the wheels to screech.

"A bit more notice would be nice," he rumbles.

"Sorry. You were saying about Piper?"

He eases back in his seat. "We talked this morning after I met with your uncle to present him with new ideas for the statue."

Then he hasn't decided on a design yet? No real surprise,

just as it won't surprise me if the six months Reece has allotted for the job is insufficient.

"Obadiah had difficulty concentrating on my sketches—"

"It's his dementia." I rush to his defense.

"I know. Fortunately, your cousin sat in on the discussion and directed him back to the topic when he detoured to sing your praises."

I could kiss Piper's feet for not leaving Uncle Obe unchaperoned. Intentional or not, my uncle might have given Reece too much to think about concerning Devyn.

"Afterward, when Piper walked me to my car, I asked her about you."

Why didn't Piper tell me? Oh, wait. After the auction, I saw she had left me a voice mail, likely a heads-up. "Why would you ask her about me?"

His mouth twitches into what might be a smile. "I'm stumped. You look like Maggie…" He leans toward me. "You smell like Maggie…"

That would be the rose perfume I claimed as my signature scent when I was fifteen.

"And you sound like Maggie—voicewise. But less and less you seem like the Maggie who held court at high school and snubbed those beneath her, including Piper. That's why I asked her about you. She knew the Maggie you were and knows the Maggie you are."

"And?"

"She set me straight."

I hold my breath. Though Piper and I have made our peace and it feels as if we've moved toward friendship, I doubt it would have happened if my daughter hadn't drawn us together. Devyn, the very glue of me.

"She told me you're as far removed from the Maggie of thirteen years ago as peanut butter is from pâté and said I shouldn't judge you based on your past. So either you're paying her scads of money to improve your image, or you have a real friend in your cousin."

Feeling a sting of tears, I look away. "I'm glad Piper feels that strongly about our relationship."

After a long moment, Reece says, "I owe you an apology."

"For?"

"Not giving you credit for the past thirteen years…believing you couldn't have changed much from the Maggie I remember."

The mean girl. The one who was free with her body. The one who, despite appreciating that Reece didn't push her to climb in the backseat as her previous boyfriends did, set out to seduce him to stop the speculation about their relationship. The one who proved to her supposed friends that not only was Reece a heterosexual, but she was as desirable as ever. The one who recently gave him reason to believe she is that same Maggie.

"Obviously, you've forgotten about our run-in at the hotel."

His chin comes around. "You could explain that."

And would you like to explain why you brought that up? Hello!

Reece growls and stomps on the brake, causing me to strain against the seat belt, then bounce back as the car screeches to a halt.

He turns to me. "Dead end."

I am? But—

Beyond the windshield illuminated by the car's headlights lies the once-prosperous farm where Bridget's Great Crop Circle hoax played out years ago in her bid to protect her little woodland buddies. It's a literal dead end Reece is referring to, not the figurative one I feared.

"I don't know where you live, Maggie."

"I'm sorry. I wasn't paying attention." I peer over my shoulder at the houses on either side of the street that mark the outer reaches of my development. "We'll have to backtrack."

Reece shifts into reverse, but an instant later, he puts the car in park.

I throw him a frown. "What is it?"

"If we're going to talk, this is as good a time and place as any."

He thinks I want to talk?

"And it's safer since we won't likely end up in a ditch or in the next county." He turns to me and props an arm on the back of his seat. "There's more to this older, kinder Maggie than what I'm hearing and seeing. What am I missing?"

I know what I'm missing—my pajamas. "This is a bad idea, Reece. The residents are bound to get suspicious of a car parked at the end of their street and call the police."

"You're right."

Pajamas, here, I come.

He switches off the headlights, leaving only the dashboard lights to cut the darkness. "Better?"

Not at all, since it seems my pajamas are back in the drawer. Worse, as my past readily testifies, the dark, a guy, and a car, are a dangerous combination. Add to that feelings I've been fighting since Reece's return, and I could be in big trouble.

Lord, keep me out of the backseat. Let Reece be as unswerving as he was before I made him swerve.

I cross my arms over my chest. "There's nothing for us to talk about. You have a job to do, and when you're done, the only evidence you were here will be your name on a hunk of metal in our town square."

And Devyn.

If he's her father, and to prove he isn't, I have Gary Winsome in my sights. I lift a hand, palm up. "Nothing to talk about."

"There's you." His deeply soft voice affects my senses like a long velvet dress floating down over my head, rippling across my torso, and skimming my legs. "The girl who couldn't wait to get out of what she called Nowhere, North Carolina, but never left."

And doesn't regret it, unlike this conversation.

"Piper didn't offer details, and mostly what I get from your uncle is that he's proud of how you're single-handedly raising your daughter and supporting yourself. So, what am I missing, Maggie?" His hand covers mine.

I clench my tingling fingers. "Why does it matter?"

He draws nearer, and I feel a trace of his breath on my lips. "I keep asking myself the same thing."

Danger.

I pull my hand free and draw back until I come up against the door. "I'm just Maggie Pickwick, soon-to-be thirty-one years old, a mother, a friend, and an auctioneer. As for how I got from there to here, I grew up." He doesn't need to know how or how soon after he left Pickwick the transformation began. "Satisfied?"

"No."

I feel the handle in my side. Unfortunately, since amalgamating with the car door didn't work for Devyn, it probably won't work for me.

"What about those tight places you said Skippy got you out of?"

Lord, this is not going well.

"Was Devyn one of them?"

Not well at all. "That was a long time ago." Longer than I want him to know. "Now I can't imagine life without her."

Silence falls, and I assume Reece is mulling over what I said. And how I hope he doesn't ask about—

"Is her father around?"

Is he around? It's possible. Ah! Reece did not father her. It had to have been Gary. "No."

He releases a breath, and I almost feel sorry for the number of teeth I'm making him pull. "Then you're divorced."

Probably what he sees as the best-case scenario, but I'm not going to lie, even if the truth sounds like backseat encouragement. "I've never been married, but I have learned my lesson." *So no hanky-panky for you, mister!*

As he digests that, I search for a change of topic. "What about you? What have you been doing for the last thirteen years?"

He nods as if agreeing with the need to change direction. "Mostly traveling around the country pursuing my art."

And avoiding alcohol, it would seem. "In high demand, I understand."

"When the economy's doing well."

"Er, how are your parents?"

After a moment, he says, "Fine."

"And your brother?"

After *several* moments, he says, "Let's get you home," and once more the headlights brighten the field.

What's with that? Did Reece and his brother have a falling out? Pity. Despite the moodiness of his younger brother, they seemed fairly close.

Shortly, Reece pulls into my driveway. "Nice house."

Determinedly setting aside what became of Reece and his brother, I try to see my home through his eyes. Yes, it is nice—a great starter home for a young couple, though it will suit Devyn and me until she goes off to college. Then I'll probably look for something smaller. And if there's still no one who wants to grow old with me, I might get a dog for company. Or I could borrow Errol, the Great Pyrenees my uncle's lawyer, Artemis, happily loans out when his scattered wife isn't looking. No, the beast piddles, as Piper learned when she first returned to Pickwick and Artemis insisted Errol patrol the mansion to keep my brother, Luc, and Bridget's brother, Bart, from looting Uncle Obe's possessions during his hospital stay.

As I reach for the door handle, I glance into Reece's face to which the accent lighting on my house gives form. "Thank you for the ride." I pull the handle, but he reaches across me and once more covers my hand with his.

"Maggie."

I look around.

He doesn't speak immediately, and I sense he's reconsidering his words, but finally he says, "When I accepted this commission, I thought I had outgrown my infatuation with you, but then I saw you and, more than anything, wanted to draw you again."

More than anything? Then art still comes first for him? Much of the time we spent together as teenagers was devoted to his drawings of me. What happened to them? Did he burn them?

"Still, I thought I was safe, that you were just something pretty to look at." His hand moves up my arm, and I'm grateful for the sleeve of my jacket that prevents him from feeling the bumps he's raising across my skin.

"But you're no longer the girl I decided wasn't worth the effort to drag out of the Maggie who trampled Yule." His hand pauses at my shoulder. "I'm glad you found your way out."

He draws the chain around my neck through his fingers down to the cross, then his face comes nearer to mine. "Maggie," he whispers, eyes bracketing me with such intensity it's as if I'm all there is.

I shouldn't. I know I shouldn't, but I close my eyes to receive his kiss. And there it is.

A strangled sound escapes me as feelings tempt my hands to take hold of his head and push through his careless black hair until all is lost.

Backseat!

It's just a kiss. All hands accounted for.

Really? Last time I counted, you had two. Would you like to guess where one of them is?

It's just hair. And he has such a nice head of it—thick...soft... one day this way, the next day that.

Not until my other hand gets in on the act, sliding around his neck to deepen the kiss, do I come to my senses. "Oh no." I pull free. "I am not crawling in the backseat with you. That is not who I am anymore."

He slowly sits back. "That isn't what I'm after."

"What, then?"

"I was hoping I wouldn't like it—that it would be just a kiss."

Which would be best for both of us, since no good can come of this. I pull the handle, grab my purse, and drop my feet to the driveway. "Thank you for the ride home." I slam the door, and trying not to get tangled in my long legs, hurry up the walkway to the front door.

"Maggie?" His voice is warm on the cold night air.

I stoop, rip the shell off the happy little turtle that lives beneath a shrub by my front door, and pull the spare house key from its hollow resin body.

"It wasn't just a kiss."

I drop the turtle's shell in place. "Oh, yes it was," I call over my shoulder. "Good night."

❧

I DON'T CARE to know why my Internet search for Gary Winsome got sidetracked, because I'd probably lie—call it curiosity, a necessary evil, a missed keystroke, anything but something to do with a kiss that wasn't just a kiss.

"Yes, it was," I hiss as I stare at the photo of a man whose slight smile is emphasized by a toothpick tucked in one corner.

I move my pointer from the About the Artist tab to Sculptures and click, causing the grainy photo of Reece to disappear and a page of sculptures to open. They're also grainy, from the gold-panning forty-niner to the mermaid peering over her shoulder to the biblical Joseph standing with feet apart as his coat of many colors (supposedly, since the statue is bronze) swirls around his calves. However, the lack of professional photographs doesn't detract from the beauty of the sculptures, nor the incredible talent behind them. The Serendipity Web site may have more flash, but it doesn't have much draw compared to what Reece offers. His work speaks for itself: when you're good, you're good.

"And you are good." I touch the blurry image of the artist at work, dark hair sprawled across his brow, fingers caught in the act of forming the immense jaw of a horse.

I snatch my hand back. "Just a kiss, Maggie."

I move the pointer to close the Web page so I can be on my merry way to Gary Winsome, but the tab Other Mediums makes me back up. I click and—voilà!—more grainy photos. These show Reece's work in paint, watercolor, and charcoal, with several of his sketches corresponding to the sculptures. I scroll down. His work was amazing in high school, but this—

"Huh?" I scroll back up until a charcoal sketch of a young woman is centered on my screen. What am I doing there? No, that can't be me. But it is, and I remember the day almost fourteen years ago...

"Don't look here," Reece says from where he sits cross-legged on a big rock by the lake. "Act natural, like you're alone."

"But, darlin'," I put the pedal to the metal of my drawl, knowing it will make it harder for him to keep his distance, "I am not alone. I'm with you." I peer up at him from beneath my long lashes and give my secret smile that few beauty contest judges can resist.

His charcoal pencil, which surely has teeth marks all over it, sticks in the air above his sketchpad.

My, how easily a Yankee boy falls for a Southern belle in full battle armor. "Are you gonna sit there lookin'"—I crook a finger—"or are you gonna get over here and keep me company?"

He starts to rise but shakes his head. "You're alone, Maggie. Not a soul in sight."

I roll my eyes. "All right, but hurry. I can't lie here lookin' natural all day long, especially with it hot as all get out." I wiggle my rear in an attempt to find a softer place on the hard planks of the dock. Failing that, I ease one leg over the edge, dip a toe in the cool water, and wrinkle my nose in anticipation of Reece telling me to resume my pose.

"That's it! Perfect. Don't move."

And I don't until he awakens me an hour later.

"Reece Thorpe! I declare, if I'm all freckled and sunburned, you're gonna get it."

He helps me to my feet. "Sorry, I had to capture you like that."

I slap at the seat of my short shorts to remove whatever debris I picked up from the dock.

"You looked so beautiful."

Of course I did.

"And innocent."

Struck by a longing to be innocent—for him—and not be mired in memories of my not-so-innocent acts, I stop with the slapping. I wish…

No, it can't be undone, and Reece knows it from what my fellow high schoolers say about me. Does it bother him? If it did, surely he wouldn't bother with me. But then, he doesn't bother with me in the sexual sense.

I tip my head to the side. "Do you like me, or is it just that you like to draw me?"

He frowns. "Of course I like you."

Moistening my lips with a slow sweep of my tongue, I step closer. "Prove it."

His gaze lowers to my mouth, and his nostrils flare. We've been here before, proof he is interested in the opposite sex despite what some of my friends and ex-boyfriends suggest.

Now if I can get him to the next step, we can put the whole matter to rest—not to mention the matter of whether or not I'm still the queen of allure.

I take the last step and lean against him. "I don't have to be home for another hour."

He swallows hard, as if he's full up on drool, but he turns away.

"Reece!" I stomp the creaky boards.

He comes back around. "Stop tempting me, Maggie. It's cruel."

I stick my hands on my hips, framing them nicely if I may say so myself. "Cruel only if I don't give you what you want."

He briefly closes his eyes. "We don't have to have sex to be together."

"My other boyfriends did."

"I'm not like them. I respect you even if you don't respect yourself."

I blink at the sudden tears that aren't me at all. I should walk away and not look back. But that would be the end of us, and I really like Reece. My nose tingles, and I have to sniff to keep it from running. Then a tear spills, followed by words. "I don't understand." I hiccup-sob and drop my chin to hide my face. "Why do you like me?"

He pulls my chin up. "I like you because despite that uppity nose of yours, it's all a front. In here"—he taps beneath my collarbone—"there's real beauty."

Is there? I gulp down another sob. "How do you know that?"

"I've seen it." He smiles. "Maybe only glimpses, and only when it's just the two of us and you're not putting on a show for your friends, but it's there."

"Glimpses!" I feel my own mouth tug. "What if that's all it is—little bitty pieces?"

"Then I will be, as you say, sorely disappointed."

I pull my chin from his grasp and swat his arm. "You're incorrigible."

He holds out a hand. "Come on, I'll walk you home."

As I reach for him, I catch sight of his sketchpad under his arm. "Let me see the picture."

"Not yet. It's one of my best, so I want to clean it up and fill in the background before I show it to you."

"Oh, you artists." I slide my hand into his, and he pulls me near and kisses me longer and more deeply than he's ever done...

With a sharp breath, I pull back from the computer screen.

That wasn't just a kiss either. As for the charcoal drawing of a young woman sleeping on a dock, head turned to the side, curls falling over her face, foot trailing the water, it's taken too many years for Reece to show it to me, in a manner of speaking. I did look innocent. However, I was far from it, even though Reece captioned his drawing *The Innocence of Beauty*.

I touch my collarbone where he touched me that day, then work my fingers up to the little cross. While my outward beauty has developed thirteen years' worth of frown and smile lines, greater beauty now exists in me, the spoiled self-centeredness excavated by Skippy and filled by Jesus. And going by Reece's behavior tonight, he's starting to see that too. And willing to give me a chance to—

What? Test his DNA to prove the rumors were true? That not long after your breakup, you crawled into the backseat with a guy who refused to acknowledge the possibility he fathered your baby? Face it, there is no future for you and Reece. If Gary is Devyn's father, it proves you lied to Reece about the rumors. If she's Chase Elliot's...well, that's not much better since that little fling was close on the heels of Gary.

But if she's Reece's—

Come on, you can't base a relationship on deceit. You'd have to tell him it's only by the process of DNA elimination you're able to claim he's Devyn's father. Then he'd be a fool not to demand his own test to confirm it. And what's the chance he'd want anything to do with you after that?

With a click of the mouse, I return *The Innocence of Beauty* to cyberspace and push back from my desk. My Internet search will have to wait.

Shortly, pajama-clad and propped up by pillows, I strain to keep my attention on my parenting Bible study. This unit covers a parent's role during different ages and stages, but it's the teen years I'm concerned about—what the author calls the most challenging stage.

"Like I don't know that."

Of utmost importance is that the parent serve as the child's guide, modeling more than lecturing, living out the life she wants her child to imitate.

"I think I'm doing a pretty good job of that." Mostly. Fortunately, Devyn knows nothing about my sneaky DNA quest.

So, that makes it all right?

I read on. My husband and I—obviously not designed for single parents—are to show by example the following: prayer, praise, service, study of the Bible, and confession when we make mistakes.

Can you say: DNA?

I flip ahead to the next unit, but the title is my cue it's past my bedtime: *The Father's Influence.*

I pop off the light, snuggle in, and close my eyes, but it soon becomes apparent I won't be seeing the backside of my brain anytime soon.

"Okay, Lord..." I drop to the floor, clasp my hands, and knock my knuckles against my teeth. "All I want is to find out who fathered her. Why does it have to be so hard?"

You're the one making it hard.

Was that me? "Uh, was that You, Lord?"

Talk to Reece.

No, not me. I would *not* advise that. "I can't. This whole thing could blow up and send shrapnel straight at Devyn. And what if Reece is her father and tries to take her away?"

Talk to him.

"No. All I can do is find out who fathered her, and one day I'll tell her. If she wants to contact him, she can."

Talk to him.

"Amen."

CHAPTER 15

DAILY WORD CALENDAR
for Highly Successful Career Women

[**auto'nomous** (*adjective*): self-governing, independent]

TUESDAY, MARCH 2

I shouldn't be here, especially considering where I should be—at home putting together an overnight bag and firming up plans that will take me to Charlotte tomorrow morning. But here I am, standing outside Church on the Square at 6:45 at night, and all because Devyn wanted to help a friend research a paper at the library around the corner. I was tempted to discourage her, especially since we were already settled in at home when Bradley called, but the bookishly cute boy whom she's known since kindergarten is probably the closest she has to a friend. Meaning I now have an hour to fill.

I glance over my shoulder at the auction house. Minutes earlier, the paperwork to which there's never an end, seemed the best use of my time, but as I started past the church that should have been closed at this hour, a well-dressed man and woman exited. And I felt the pull of the sanctuary that provided home-cooked solace when I was a teenage mother struggling toward adulthood with a baby under one arm and a full-time job under the other.

The man's and woman's figures retreat. They must have come from one of the community meetings held in the building. Rotary Club? Regardless, the church is open, though probably not for much longer. So maybe I'll spend just a few minutes in the quiet, and then I'll get to that paperwork.

"Here I come, Lord," I murmur as I ascend the steps. "Go easy on me, will You?"

Inside, the sound of voices coming from the corridor on the right tug at my curiosity, and I veer away from the sanctuary to take a peek. At the sight of several adults spilling out of a Sunday school class—yes, must be a Rotary Club meeting or some such—I retreat and cross to the big double doors. I push through, then step into the dimly lit sanctuary. Almost instantly, calm washes over me. I have it all to myself, which is a first in ages.

"Okay, then." I walk the aisle to the front pew that was no stranger to me when Devyn and I lived with Skippy.

"God don't care where you sit," she'd say. "I just like me the front row so's I don't get distracted from the message."

Which sometimes happens to me, especially now that I'm sharing my church with Reece. Of course, this past Sunday, Yule and Skippy sat next to him on this front pew. Unfortunately, it distracted me even more seeing the back of his head between their two and remembering how much nearer I was to him when he gave me what he claimed wasn't just a kiss.

"And, God help me"—I look to the cross behind the pulpit as I sink onto the pew—"it wasn't." I clasp my hands in my lap to keep my fingers from tracing the place where Reece was. I really need to forget that kiss.

"Lord," I whisper, lowering my lids, "I may not be in Your will, but I have to think about what's best for Devyn. This thing..." Emotion rushes up my throat, into my mouth and nose, and heads for my eyes. "This thing with Reece...I don't want to feel this way. I don't want to want him, 'cause when he leaves again..." I pull a tingling breath through my nose. "Too hard."

I drop my chin and shake my head. "Why did he have to come back? Why did You let him? I was on the right track. Yes, sometimes it got a bit crooked and I was a bit too...*autonomous*, but I was heading in a good direction. And now You want me to—"

I am not alone. As the sensation prickles across my shoulders, I open my eyes and follow the feeling around and over my shoulder. But it's not the Lord walking the aisle—silly me. "Reece!"

In the midst of his retreat, he halts with his back to me, then turns and looks past a dark lock of hair that skims his eyebrows. "Sorry, Maggie. I thought you were just sitting there. It wasn't until I got close that I heard you praying."

Praying what? Which of the words weighting my heart made it to my lips? "Wh-what are you doing here?"

He turns to me. "Attending a recovery group."

Recovery? As in—? Oh. That's right. But surely his taste for alcohol isn't serious enough to require a recovery group—Reece Thorpe whose faults were so few that one really couldn't count them against him?

He jerks his head toward the doors. "We just finished up. I was coming out of the classroom when I saw you."

Then that wasn't a Rotary Club gathering. And why is he so willing to expose his weakness? Shouldn't he keep it under wraps?

Like you with your teenage *promiscuity? Maybe you should follow his example and come clean. You couldn't ask for better timing.*

"Again, I apologize for interrupting. I'll let you get back to—"

"No," I say, though I inwardly cringe at the thought of following my own advice. "I'm done. Would you like to join me?"

He hesitates, as if as surprised by the invitation as I am, then strides forward and lowers to the pew. With a respectable foot and a half between us, he stretches an arm across the seat back. "Are you all right, Maggie?"

Which of my words meant only for God's ears did he hear? And is this really the time and place to follow his example? I want to, but…

"Yeah, fine." I peer into his shadowed face, grateful those same shadows fall over mine. "Just everyday problems."

He raises his eyebrows in an invitation for me to elaborate, but I can't. Not yet. "So…recovery, hmm?"

His gaze flickers, but he inclines his head. "Recovery."

"Why?" My smile feels as if pressed into place. "I mean, if you don't have the problem anymore." I blink. "Er, you don't, do you?" If so, it probably *is* better that I keep my DNA quest to myself.

"I've recovered, although it had to have been easier for me than it is for a lot of others."

"How so?"

He eases back a bit, and I'm amazed at how unperturbed he seems talking about something so raw and personal. "I recognized it as a problem before it devastated my relationships and my art. Not that I didn't struggle with denial and suffer the effects, but once I accepted my dependence on alcohol, I got help."

What made him start drinking in the first place?

"And part of staying healthy is regularly attending meetings like the ones held here." No blush, no show of shame whatsoever. "It's a matter of maintenance, accountability, and helping others who are trying to get to the place I'm at."

Just like the Reece I remember—responsible, self-assured, and giving. "That's admirable."

He studies my face, and while my words were sincere, I stiffen at the feeling he can see past the shadows. "I'm glad you think so. Not everyone does. There are those who believe I should bury that piece of my past since it scares some people away."

I can see that. And yet, my emotions aren't running for cover. Rather, they're leaning nearer to him. Yes, if he is Devyn's father, he may have passed on a genetic weakness for alcohol, but that's not something he can control. What he can control, he *has* taken control of.

"In fact, I was able to come to Pickwick because I lost a church commission after I asked one of the committee members if the church offered a recovery program I could attend during my stay in that city."

How bold. More, how wonderful to not worry about what others think…to be that comfortable with who you are…to not allow your past to define you. "I'm sorry he reacted that way."

He chuckles. "I'd like it better if you weren't sorry."

"What?" *It wasn't just a kiss.* "Oh."

Right. He wouldn't be here. With me. But were I as honest as he's been, would he still want to be here? He *was* hoping that kiss was just a kiss, meaning he wants a reason not to be here. And, boy, do I have one that will send him running—that is, unless Devyn is his daughter. In which case, I'm certain he would stick around to some degree, but his relationship with me would surely be based on obligation. And that would hurt too much.

Selfish.

Yes, I know it's not just about what's best for Devyn. I know I'm weak, but I can't tell him. *Forgive me.*

"What is it?" He slides a hand to my shoulder—another reason to remain silent. I like his touch too much to be so near it and never feel it again. Better that when he leaves Pickwick, he stays gone. Then I can get back to… Well, what Devyn and I had before he came was good. Yes, at times lonely, especially when the day is folded away and out comes the night, but I prefer that to lonely *and* achy.

Drawing a deep breath, I shrug. "I appreciate your honesty, Reece. You set a good example."

The curve of his mouth eases, and he releases my shoulder, leans forward, and clasps his hands between his knees "But not good enough that you'll let me in."

I stand. "I think it's for the best."

"All right." He looks up at me, a glint in his eyes. "For now."

I stare at him. "For now?"

"My stay in Pickwick has only just begun."

Meaning he thinks he's going to whittle down my resistance?

A smile returns to his face. "Who knows?"

I know. "Have a nice evening, Reece." I step around him, hurry up the aisle, and blow out a breath when the door swings shut behind me.

I look up. "I thought You were going to go easy on me."

No, you asked *Him to go easy on you.*

True. And He doesn't always answer prayers the way we want Him to. On the upside, that could mean He has something better planned for me. On the downside, there's no guarantee I'll like it.

CHAPTER 16

DAILY WORD CALENDAR
for Highly Successful Career Women

[**legerdemain**' (*noun*): sleight of hand as practiced by magicians; trickery, artful or otherwise; deception]

WEDNESDAY, MARCH 3

If I had to live in a big city, Charlotte could be the one. Like a true Southern belle, she sits pretty as you please near North Carolina's southern border. With her great hoop skirts spread out around her—suburbs, gardens, historic plantations, wildlife sanctuaries—one can easily imagine her coyly smiling over her shoulder at her second-best beau, South Carolina. So close…

"Close doesn't count," my mother would say when I placed as runner-up in a beauty contest. "No tiara, no applause."

Thinking of my mother, she surprised me by offering to stay with Devyn while I'm out of town. Bridget was willing and was Devyn's first choice, but not only have I yet to take my mother to lunch, it's better for my daughter to be in her own home during the school week. My only concern is that in my absence, the distance I'm trying to maintain between Reece and Devyn could be compromised. Maybe I should have let Devyn stay with Bridget—

No, my mother and Devyn aren't likely to run into Reece. In fact, outside of school drop-off and pickup, the two will keep to our home so my mother can make my house look unlived-in with all of her organizing and de-piling.

Ugh. I like my piles. I know what's in them, and with a bit of digging, I can prove it. Speaking of digging...

It took effort, but I dug up enough on Gary to place myself firmly in his orbit. The corporate offices of the bank he works for are located on North Tryon Street in uptown Charlotte, handily down the road from my hotel. As for how to get close to him, that could be easier than expected.

Since his bank is the biggest sponsor of *The Marriage of Figaro,* now appearing at the Blumenthal Performing Arts Center, it's reported that many of those in upper-level management will be in attendance this evening. I'm counting on Gary to be among them. If he isn't, or I'm unable to recognize him from the bank's Web site photo, I'll be out eighty-plus dollars for orchestra-level seating. Worse, I'll have to go to Plan B, and I'm not clear what that is.

I arrived at the theater an hour early to be on the lookout. Now it's only fifteen minutes until curtain time when I'll sit down to an opera—me, Maggie Pickwick, who clicks past the ear-splitting vocal displays that pop up on national public television. Hopefully the experience is better in person. If not, my hope is entirely dependent on getting what I need from Gary.

"Where are you?" I whisper from behind the cup of coffee I hold near my mouth. "Come on, I'm not asking much. And I'm sure your wife would enjoy a night out." Yes, he's married—with one child—which blows Devyn's hope that he and I could be a couple. Not that there was a chance of that on my end, but it's the proof my daughter will need to reset her quest for a live-in father. Providing Gary is the one.

I adjust my shawl and once more scan the immense lobby, searching for a pale and somewhat-pudgy version of the jock I knew. Hundreds of people mill about with wine, coffee, and bottled water. Unfortunately, with each passing minute, the possibility increases that the one I'm looking for has already entered the theater or isn't coming at all.

"Where are you?" I bounce on my two-inch heels, causing my drink to slop near the cup's lip and threaten my cream-colored evening gown.

"Maggie? Is that you?"

"Ah!" Fortunately, my reflexive backward thrust causes the coffee to slop to the floor. Hardly able to believe my luck, I look up into a not-so-pale or pudgy face. So much for luck. "Er...?"

"Gary Winsome."

I wasn't pretending not to recognize him. It was simply a lag between brain and tongue, but who am I to correct him? "Gary! It *is* you."

A grin breaking across his tanned face, he slides a hand down the lapel of his tuxedo jacket, as if to draw attention to his firm chest and abdomen. "It's me."

"Nice to see you again." And it is. Just ask my little baggy.

Gary raises his wine glass as if in toast. "When I saw your red hair from across the lobby, my first thought was of you."

And yet he came all the way over here when I would have expected him to walk wide around me. Has he matured enough to acknowledge Devyn could be his? Does he regret turning his back on us?

Stop it! This only complicates matters, since you're not going to do anything with the DNA results. The testing is to prove Reece isn't

Devyn's father so when she's old enough to know who fathered her, you won't be empty handed.

Which is why I should have confined my hair to a bun, and I would have if the mirror in my hotel room hadn't been so persuasive. In the end, I struck a compromise, pulling my hair back from my face, but allowing it to fall in attractive curls and waves down my back. Unfortunately, though there may be two thousand people in attendance tonight, this much red stands out.

"But then I thought," Gary continues, "it must be someone else, because what would Maggie Pickwick be doing in Charlotte?"

Indeed. His brown hair is nearly the color of Devyn's. I slip a finger inside the springy watchband, tug, and release. *Ouch!* But a good ouch.

"Yet here you are." He lingeringly surveys me. "More beautiful than ever."

I suppress the impulse to cross my arms over my chest. No married man should look at any woman other than his wife like that. I lift my chin. "So, you live here in—?"

"Gary?" a woman's voice approaches and we both look around at a cute twenty-something in a strapless green gown. The woman moves fast for someone with such a short stride and, a moment later, loops her arm through Gary's. "Are you going to introduce me, sweetheart?" Her voice is decidedly un-Southern, her smile big and *don't touch my man* bright.

"Darlin', this is Maggie Pickwick. We went to high school together."

"Is that right?" That last word ends high.

"Maggie, this is Sirena, my date for the evening."

But he's married. I check out his left hand but no wedding band. And his date isn't wearing one either. So, Gary is cheating on his wife? The lowlife!

Lord, please don't let him be Devyn's father.

The woman extends a hand. "Sirena Payton."

I shake her hand, a limp thing that isn't much bigger than Devyn's. "Nice to meet you."

"Um-hmm." She looks up at Gary. "Sweetheart, we ought to—"

"I can't get over this." Gary shakes his head at me. "It's been… what? Thirteen years? Why, the last time I saw you…" His boyish smile sticks, then slides away.

I know what that is. It's realization in the wake of a memory reel that replayed the last time he saw me—a very pregnant Maggie whom he quickly looked away from as she stepped from the stage with diploma in hand.

This hurts. Were I given a choice, he would remain the louse I've imagined him to be all these years—successfully battling his conscience. However, there may not have been a conscience to start with, since he appears to have put *my* daughter from his mind as if she never existed.

Gary clears his throat. "So, what are you doing in Charlotte?"

Haunting you.

Stop it! Be. Skippy. Checking my facial muscles, I meet his gaze. "Taking care of a little business. I head back to Pickwick tomorrow." *If* I get what I came for.

He gives a slow nod, and though I know it's wrong to savor his discomfort, the taste is pleasant.

Sorry, Lord, it's too hard to be Skippy. I really want this all to be over, but not at the expense of this man being Devyn's father. However, if he is, it would sure help if his lack of conscience were a result of the hits he took to the head while playing football. Yes, that would explain it. Some.

My mouth aches with the width of my smile. "What about you, Gary? Do you live in the area?"

"Uh, yeah."

"Oh, wait!" I peer past him to the banner that proclaims the proud sponsor of *The Marriage of Figaro*. "I'll bet you work for the bank sponsoring this event."

"He does." Sirena presses nearer his side. "My Gary is a banker. Upper-level management. And he's in line for a big promotion."

I open my eyes wide. "Congratulations—and on the raise you're bound to get."

His Adam's apple ratchets up, and he looks quickly away like a dog well aware of its place in the pack. I'm guessing his reaction has a lot to do with that raise—fear his date's boasting could result in child support for a daughter he has never acknowledged.

He shakes back his cuff. "Look at the time. We should take our seats."

I check my own watch, ending on a tug and release that results in another satisfying *ouch!* "It was nice seeing you again, Gary, and meeting you, Sirena."

They murmur like words and turn away.

I give them a lead, then follow, the better to see where they're sitting. At the theater doors, the press of people forces me closer to them, and that's when I hear Sirena's reproving voice. "...find you talking to one of your *old* girlfriends—"

I am not old. Just old*er.*

"—and right after I had a run-in with your ex in the ladies' room."

He's divorced? Of course he is, and had I dug deeper, I probably could have unearthed what surely accounts for the demise of pale and pudgy—his return to *bachelor mode.*

"Did you know your ex is sitting right behind us? Not a good start to my evening, Gary." She sniffs, and I feel sorry for whatever hope she's harboring for their relationship, especially after how he looked at me.

Though those behind me won't like it, I slow to put more distance between the unhappy couple and myself. So Gary is single. Not that it makes a difference. Devyn will still have to reset any near-future quest that includes this man who forgot her existence.

I snap the springy watchband again, but no *ouch!* Pushed along by the tide of people, I lift my hand. Whew! It's not the watchband. My wrist is almost bare of the fine hairs that once covered it.

A few minutes later, I suffer a setback when Gary's tickets see him and his date ushered to grand-tier-level seating. I half expected this because of the bank's sponsorship, but hoped he would have orchestra-level seating as it was the best I could secure on short notice. So he'll be overlooking my seat, and somehow I have to find a way to get up there.

As I settle into my seat on the aisle, I look up and over my shoulder. Gary is sitting on the right-hand side of the front row, leaning away from Sirena to converse with a man beside him. I look to the row behind him. *That's* where I need to get. And I will, even if I have to trod his ex's feet.

Hmm. My bet is that the ex-Mrs. Winsome is the sharp-faced blonde staring narrow eyed and thin lipped at the back of Sirena's head.

I open my playbill to the page that outlines the evening. I'll make my move during one of the intermissions, but since the first opportunity is an hour out, it looks as if I'm going to discover what *The Marriage of Figaro* is about.

Or not. Opera is *not* better in person, though it appears I'm the only one with that opinion. Those around me are captivated by the comedy of errors that has me constantly referring to the playbill to make sense of all the characters and their bellowing in an unknown language. It makes me feel uneducated, especially when the young woman beside me starts mouthing the foreign words and sweeping a hand in time with a song sung by the character of…Susanna?

Humph! My neighbor may know her opera, but I'll bet she

doesn't know the word *legerdemain*. Whereas, I…well, I *will* find a way to work it into my day.

Noticing I'm watching her, the young woman leans near, causing me to revise my opinion of her age. She can't be much older than Devyn. "Sorry," she tinkles, "I can't help myself. I just *love* this opera. Don't you?"

"Mozart did a great job of…setting the play to music." Thank goodness for the playbill.

"Oh, yes!" Then she's back to mouthing and sweeping.

Intermission can't come soon enough. Fortunately, when I *accidentally* go the wrong way in returning to my seat, Gary and Sirena are resettling in theirs. Even better, the ex-Mrs. Winsome and those who sat on either side of her are absent, giving me more room to maneuver.

Pausing against the wall of the grand-tier level, I scope out the usher who is helping an elderly man find his seat, then another who is turned sideways and talking into a headset.

I check the shawl I elegantly draped over my red hair (he may not see me coming, but he could see me going), run through my excuse should anyone ask what I'm doing on this level ("Goodness, I shouldn't have had that extra glass of wine."), give the watchband a hairless snap, and enter the second row from the left side. With a *sorry* here and an *excuse me* there, I sidestep those who have resumed their seats. Doubtless, some will start to wonder why I didn't enter on the right side, but that's where Gary is, and only four seats past him is the aisle, and beyond that, the exit.

As I approach my destination, my heart thumps, and I feel my pores open up with the promise of moisture.

Calm down. This isn't Reece. It's Gary, the guy without a conscience. Get what you need and don't look back.

Got it. But I also have the ex-Mrs. Winsome in my sights, moving briskly toward her row. I pick up the pace, dodging feet and knees. Thus, no sooner does she enter the row than I'm upon Gary.

As I pass behind him, I get full extension on the watchband, brush it through the hair at the back of his head, and...*snap!*

"Ow!" His head jerks around, fortunately, in the opposite direction I'm heading. "Did you do that?"

"What?" Sirena squeaks.

I keep going, certain he'll look behind and relieved my hair pinching can't be blamed on his ex. But to be sure...

"Excuse me," I say when we meet, "I need to get to the ladies' room." I lean near her frowning face and lower my voice. "Bad." That last has *female problem* spoken all over it.

She smiles apologetically, as if my *female problem* is her fault. "Certainly." She backs out.

"Thank you." A few moments later, I'm out the exit. A minute after that, I'm in the ladies' room. "Just one root," I beg as I pull the stall door closed behind me.

I lift my wrist toward the overhead light. And smile. There are at least a dozen hairs caught in the links of my watchband. No wonder Gary was so perturbed. That had to have hurt.

"But do we have a root?" I pull my reading glasses from my evening bag and shove them on. "We have root*ssss*." And *that* was a real work of legerdemain.

Shortly, I hail a cab, visions of a good night's sleep dancing in my head. No more operatic yodeling, no more Gary, and no more empty baggy. Closure at last. Maybe.

CHAPTER 17

DAILY WORD CALENDAR
for Highly Successful Career Women

[**clandes'tine** (*adjective*): to act in secrecy, especially for the purpose of subversion or deception]

THURSDAY, MARCH 4

That's one daily word I won't have trouble affixing to my day, starting with reflection on last night's watchband coup that resulted in the drop at the post office (the DNA is in the mail) on my way out of Charlotte this morning, and now this.

My *clandestine* mother glances around the empty theater, then shifts to the edge of her seat, leans close, and taps the spreadsheet. "I told you it was serious."

She did, though she refused to go into it over the phone, and that's why I am the not-so-proud owner of a speeding ticket issued halfway between Charlotte and Pickwick.

I sigh. "I know all about this, Mom." Well, not *all*, since the last time I peeked at the chart tacked to the back of Devyn's closet, Reece Thorpe was not listed as a potential father. He is now candidate Number Eight (as opposed to candidate Number One on my list of potential fathers). And he's chalked up quite a few plus marks in the attributes columns: *Kind, Approachable, Likes Kids, Sense of Humor, Employed, Christian.* He suffers only one negative mark—*Pickwick Resident*—unlike Seth, who refuses to give up on me. In Seth's Comments section, Devyn wrote in small letters: *needy, interacts with me only to look good in front of Mom, too concerned with his looks, dumped Piper in high school.*

"So, what are you going to do about it, Magdalene?"

I sink back in my seat. "Get married."

She doesn't startle. She convulses, which is comical considering the elegance she exudes from her coifed hair to her perfectly polished nails to her scuffless shoes. "Married?" The hope in her voice vies with disbelief.

"*If* I find the right man—for both of us."

Her nostrils flare. "Of course."

But if she had her way, I would have married Seth years ago and be living comfortably enough to join her for weekly outings to the hairdresser, lunch, and shopping. If not him, then Rob Bowie, whose wealth, according to Mom, forgives him for a multitude of sins, starting with the mullet-cut hair worn since grade school and ending with the rumor that his last wife left him when she caught him wearing her pantyhose.

"Maggie." My mother's eyes slide away from mine. "Devyn's daddy…is it Reece Thorpe?"

Her question shoves a cork in my throat. She has never ventured into the mystery of who fathered my daughter. All that mattered was that I get rid of *it*. That I not mess up my life by bringing *it* into the world. And once I did bring *it* into the world, that I give *it* up for adoption. That last option might have worked if not that *it* was, in fact, a baby girl. *My* baby girl.

"Is it Reece?"

The old anger that wants to know what gives her the right to ask is back.

She averts her eyes again, and I know what is reflected in mine isn't pretty. I hear her swallow, a thick, moist sound that ought to prepare me for when she looks up. I'm jolted by the emotion on her face, magnified by tears that appear to be generated by the heart rather than the head.

"I know I don't have the right to ask, and I'm..." She raises her hands as if in surrender. "Well, I'm sorry."

Sorry? Did she really say that?

"Sorry for not giving you"—her mouth and chin pinch —"what that Skippy woman gave you."

Her disdain makes my back stiffen, as if to support the wall between us that developed hairline cracks at *sorry.*

She leans closer. "Though I didn't want you to throw away your life on raising a child on your own, I do love my granddaughter."

Another crack.

"You know that, don't you?"

"I know, Mom."

Relief eases her shoulders only slightly, but I suspect it's due to her love of thick shoulder pads despite the likelihood they may never come back in style.

"And I'm proud of how well you've done for yourself, Maggie. Even though..." She looks around the old theater. "This is hardly what I envisioned for you. But it pays the bills, I suppose."

There goes my back again, holding up the wall. And here comes my mouth—

No! Don't say it. This is progress. She loves you and Devyn, even if it's hard for her to show it.

I close my mouth and then my eyes.

Lord, it's me. I know I haven't been the best at listening lately, but I could use some help with my choice of words and patience.

"I'm sorry," my mother says again.

I flip open my eyes to find her face wrinkled with concern, an emotion she usually avoids for fear of permanent lines.

"I shouldn't have said that. I mean…" She looks at the stage. "I hear you're good at what you do."

Hear, because she has never attended my auctions.

I relax my back muscles as I consider her profile and the years etched alongside sorrow. The life my daddy led her through and left her to hasn't been easy, try as she does to keep up appearances. While I have questioned her love for Luc and me, I've never doubted she loved her husband. He may monetarily support her long distance, but he isn't here for her. He wasn't here to aid in her plans for their children to return the Pickwick name to its former glory, starting with my brother, whose charm and powers of persuasion were to have transported him into the ranks of topnotch lawyers. He sells used cars. With my beauty pageant-refined looks, carriage, and flair for drama, I was to have been a world-famous model-turned-Oscar-worthy actress. I sell people's castoffs.

I lay a hand over my mother's. "One day I hope you'll feel comfortable enough to drop by and see me in action. 'Cause I am pretty good at my job."

She nods, then does something I don't recall her ever doing —drags her teeth across her bottom lip, removing a layer of lipstick. "I would like to come see you sometime."

"I'd like that too."

"Now about Reece Thorpe." She momentarily closes her eyes, as if to block the thought that after all the training to turn her daughter into a lady, I was far from one when out from under my mama's watchful eye. "Is he my granddaughter's daddy?"

I hope that what I'm about to say won't make her react in such a way that we both reinforce the weakening wall. "I don't think so."

She pulls her hand from beneath mine. "What do you mean?"

"I'm sure you remember those rumors about me in high school, the ones you were certain were put out by jealous girls. They weren't all rumors, Mom. My pregnancy was not the result of the first and only time I—"

"All right." She holds up a hand before a suddenly flushed face. "So there was another boy who could have fathered Devyn."

I hate this, and it takes everything I have not to look away. "There are three who could be her father."

Her eyes widen and roll up.

I grip her shoulder. "Mom!"

She slaps her hands to her knees. "I'm just a bit dizzy. It'll pass."

I slide my hand to her back and massage the knots there. "I'm sorry. I didn't want you to know, but—"

"Does that Skippy woman know?"

"Yes."

A sharp breath vibrates through her back. "Of course she does."

"Mom, it's because of her that we have Devyn. You don't have to like Skippy, but I need you to understand what she means to me. She's a good person and—"

"Yes. She was there for you when I wasn't." She stands and hooks her purse over her arm. "Believe me, I understand."

I jump up. "Mom—"

"I have to go." She steps into the aisle but snaps back around. "Does Reece Thorpe know Devyn might he his?"

I shake my head. "His family moved before anyone knew I was pregnant, and he thinks she's ten or eleven. I haven't corrected him."

"Then perhaps he can be forgiven, in time. And the other two?"

I long to look elsewhere. "They knew, Mom, and they walked away."

Her eyes darken, and like a judge who has taken all she's going to take, she pronounces, "Not forgiven."

Not surprised. And not going to mention my DNA quest.

She presses her shoulders back. "I picked up a few groceries for you. There's hot chicken salad in the Crock-Pot for dinner, I folded and put away the laundry—that's how I found Devyn's list—and the dishwasher needs to be emptied."

"Thank you, and thank you for staying with Devyn."

She nods and bustles up the aisle and through the lobby doors.

I stare at the empty doorway until the spreadsheet crinkles in my hand, then collapse into my seat. I should use the two hours until I pick up Devyn from school to prepare for Saturday's auction, but I give in to a baser need—to simply breathe. However, my thoughts are busy little creatures, replaying Reece's kiss, Gary's kiss-off, my mother's hurt and anger, and the list. Oh, the list…

I bend forward, put my head in my hands, and draw comfort from the hair that curtains me, encloses me, conceals me.

"Maggie?"

Why won't he go away? Take his kiss and disappear? I need to breathe.

"Are you all right?"

Whoa! Did a memory just touch my arm? I drop my hands and look around. Reece is down beside my seat, a toothpick in one corner of his mouth.

"Oh!" Like Jack let out of its box, I pop up and back against the seat. "What are you—? I didn't see—"

Did he overhear the conversation with my mother? I search his face. No, he wouldn't look at me with such concern if he had overheard.

He settles his forearms on his thighs. "I called to you, but you didn't seem to hear."

"Uh..." I push a hand through my hair. "Just tired."

"Back from Charlotte, right?"

How did he know where I was?

He shifts the toothpick to the other side of his mouth and smiles. "Your daughter told me."

He was with Devyn? When? Where?

"I ran into her and your mother at the grocery store yesterday."

I wish Mom had mentioned that, and that my face wasn't so vocal. "I got in a little while ago—probably should have gone straight home and taken a nap."

"Did the trip pan out for you?"

In more ways than one, though he has to be referring to the antique pocket watches that were my excuse for going to Charlotte. Happily, the collection was better than pictured and described on Craigslist. I urged the executor of the estate to allow me to sell the watches on consignment, certain that even with my cut, he would get more than what he was asking, but he said the heirs wanted the estate settled yesterday.

"I picked up some nice pieces."

He starts to rise but leans down again and lifts something from the floor. "The Father Quotient?"

"No!" I lurch upright, coming chest to chest with him, and throw out a hand to snatch it away.

He turns his back to me. "What is this?"

"It's not yours." I reach around him. "Give it to me."

Oh, Lord, please don't let him see his name—

"My name's on here."

What is he, a speed-reader? Regardless, what if he thinks the spreadsheet is mine and that *I* put his name on it? That kiss may not have just been a kiss to him, but I doubt he was thinking far enough ahead to fatherhood. I strain to wrest it from him and my chest contacts with his arm.

For goodness' sake, you're practically on top of him!

Face warm, I move to the side and thrust out a hand. "That's my daughter's private—"

His chin comes around, the intensity of his eyes arresting my tongue. "This is Devyn's?"

"Yes."

His lids narrow. "What are you doing with it?"

All I wanted was to breathe. "My mother found it in Devyn's closet and thought I should know how desperate my daughter is for a father." The spoken words do terrible things to my insides, especially those places between my heart and my head. "I knew about it, but I didn't know she had added your name. And for that, I'm sorry." I push my hand nearer. "May I please have it so I can put it back before she suffers the humiliation of knowing her privacy has been pried open?"

There's no mistaking the chagrin in his eyes. "I apologize." He hands me the spreadsheet.

Other than a creased corner, it looks fine.

"Is that why you didn't want me talking to her?" Reece asks. "Afraid she might add me to her list?"

I couldn't be more grateful that Devyn is older than she appears. I compose my face. "She's determined. You wouldn't believe the amount of research she digs up about the importance of a father in a girl's life."

He considers me, but just when I think he's going to press further about my reason for not wanting him to talk to Devyn, he pulls the toothpick from his mouth. "Are you going to give her one?"

I dig into my bag of smiles. "Absolutely. We're heading over to the daddy dealership this weekend to test drive the latest models and choose our options. There's bound to be haggling over price and financing, but I'm confident we'll walk out with my perfect counterpart."

His mouth twitches. "I asked for that."

I almost sigh at having successfully turned the mood. "Um-hmm."

He glances at the spreadsheet. "Again, I apologize for sticking my nose where it doesn't belong. Devyn is a bright, sweet girl, and I'm flattered she considered me worthy of a place on her list."

Though nothing can come of it. Five or so months from now, Reece will be gone again. "So, has my uncle decided on a design?"

His face relaxes. "He has."

"Great. What—?" I roll my eyes. "It's hush-hush, I suppose?"

"Under wraps for the time being." He checks his watch. "And the longer I stand here talking, the longer that will be."

Fine with me. "I'll see you later then."

He raises his left hand to reveal a white rag wrapped around his palm. How did I not notice that?

"I cut myself working on the sculpture's armature."

Armature?

"Do you have a first-aid kit?"

That's why he ventured out of his studio. "In my office." I motion at the projection room overhead.

"Lead the way." He steps into the aisle, and I scoot out of the row and head for the stairs. Shortly, we enter my office, and I flip the light switch.

"This is a good use for the room," Reece says from the doorway.

"I like it, though it's somewhat cramped." I lay Devyn's list on my desk, crouch, and pull the first-aid box from a bottom drawer. "Here you are." I set it on the desk.

As he crosses to where I stand, I sidestep. I should offer to help, but it's better that I keep my distance. And I mean to until he begins unwinding the makeshift bandage and I see red. My heart beats faster. A splotch of red staining stark white material. My breath turns shallow. More than enough red. My mouth goes dry. DNA red. My pores prick with perspiration. Blood—

Ah! Stumbling back into my wheeled chair, I slam my hands to the arms to keep from falling into it. What is wrong with me? Next, I'll be drooling like a B-movie vampire!

"Don't like the sight of blood, hmm?"

I look wide-eyed at Reece, who is peering over his shoulder. Calling on every graceful cell in my body, I straighten from the chair. "Er, I'm just a little on edge." Ooh! Don't want him to think *he's* the one who put me there. "You know, what with the drive from Charlotte and the black ice." The little there was of it.

He drops the rag to my desk, and as he opens the first-aid box, I stare at the baggy-bound DNA sample. I've sent off Gary's DNA, and chances are the results will come back positive, but if not—

"Sorry." Reece sweeps up the rag, and I realize he saw me staring at it with what he probably thinks is horror. He stuffs it in his pant pocket. So close…

Feeling a bit faint, I lower to my chair as he goes to work with an antiseptic wipe.

"Nice picture," Reece says.

"What?" I follow his gaze to the mouse pad I haven't used since I purchased a computer with a built-in mouse a year ago. I would have tossed the pad if it didn't feature a picture of Devyn at her first double-digit birthday—ten years old. And so it still sits on my desk, a gift from Skippy that shows the two of us smiling over my daughter's shoulder as she blows out the candles on her cake.

"Her tenth birthday," he says.

He counted the candles.

"She looks younger than ten there." The used antiseptic pad

joins the rag in his pocket. "In fact, quite a bit younger than she looks now."

Of course she does. The picture was taken almost three years—

Oh! He thinks she's eleven now. That raises the question of how she could have changed so much in a year.

I jump up. "That's hard to do with one hand." I wedge myself between the desk and him, ignore his frown, and take the bandage from him. As I rip open the wrapper, I glance at the cut at the center of his palm. "Are you sure you don't need stitches?"

"I'm sure. How old is Devyn?"

Oh, Lord. "Do you have any kids?" I bend my head to the attention-intensive task of removing the bandage's adhesive tabs.

After a long moment, which reminds me of his reluctance to discuss his brother on the night he kissed me, he says, "No."

"I don't see tan lines on your ring finger, so I assume if you're divorced, it isn't recent."

"I've never been married." His gaze shifts to my mouth.

Is he remembering that kiss like I'm *not* remembering it? I pull his hand closer. The skin beneath my fingers is thicker and rougher than when his hands were those of a teenager—

Get on with it!

I press the bandage into place and release him. "You'll live."

"Thank you."

I close the first-aid box. "I should get going."

"Put Devyn's list back where it belongs, hmm?"

"Definitely." I grab The Father Quotient. "Have a nice evening." I follow him into the corridor.

He looks at me as I draw alongside. "I leave tomorrow for Knoxville, back on Sunday."

I forgot about his business trip. And Yule's offer to get together with him.

Ah! Was that jealousy? Oh no, you don't.

Oh yes, I do, though I wish I didn't. However, beyond jealousy lies something more potent—worry. Yule is a talker, and should the subject of her former tormentor arise, it could lead to Devyn and fill in the missing pieces I've been withholding from Reece. Unlike the other two candidates for fatherhood, I don't believe he would be entirely blind to the possibility he's a father. Thus, if his suspicions are to be raised, and it's foolish to believe they won't considering how long he'll be in Pickwick, I need to have a conclusive answer for him. I need to know the truth. I need to make a phone call.

As we descend the stairs, I look sidelong at Reece. "I hope you have a nice trip."

"I'm sure I will."

At the bottom of the steps, he goes his way toward his studio and I go mine.

SILENCE.

More silence. I probably shouldn't have spilled on everything, but once the ball got rolling, it came out as if the woman on the other end of the line were a giver of absolution. "Yule?"

She draws a noisy breath. "I'm here."

"All I'm asking is that you steer Reece away from any discussion about Devyn—her age and that I was carrying her through my senior year."

"You really don't know which one is her father?"

"I don't, but I should have Gary's DNA results in the next two weeks, and I'm pretty sure he's the one. But until then…"

"Gracious, Maggie, you've got yourself in a real pickle."

A common affliction of the Pickwicks. "Especially with the pressure Devyn is putting on me to give her a father and the kids at school taunting her, telling her I don't know who her father is. And it being true."

"Um-hmm. I know all about those mean girls."

I close my eyes and silently give her permission to say something about the sins of the parent being visited on the child. "I know you know, and no doubt see the irony."

"It is a good sight bigger than a toe stubber."

Here is the opening I should have made years ago. "Yule, I'm sorry about the way I treated you in school." Not long ago, I apologized to Piper for the same thing, and that was the water on the seed of our relationship. "And I'm especially sorry that I never asked for your forgiveness. That I just...took it."

Once more, there is silence, and its weight nearly presses me to my knees there inside Devyn's closet where I returned The Father Quotient to its secret place.

Lord, please let Yule feel how truly sorry I am, and not because I want something from her. Yes, I've asked her to keep quiet about Devyn, but if she doesn't go along with me, that doesn't change my regret over the pain I caused.

"Well, now," Yule finally says, "forgiveness isn't something you can take unless it's given. And much as I hate to admit it, the other night when I was hoggin' Reece and happy to let you stand on the sidelines, I realized I hadn't forgiven you like I told myself I'd done when I realized you cared for my mama and weren't just usin' her. So thank you for that, Maggie. I shouldn't have been waitin' for an apology all these years, but I guess I was."

Thank You, Lord. "Thank you, Yule."

"Um-hmm." She gasps. "Well, shoot! If it turns out Reece is Devyn's daddy, I reckon I'll have to find myself a different fishin' hole."

I can't help the pang of jealousy, but I can correct it. "I'm not asking you to do that. I'd just like you to steer clear of talk about Devyn and my pregnancy. If Reece is her father, that doesn't mean there's a future for us beyond one built on obligation, and that's not what I want for my daughter. So..." Deep breath. "... bait your hook and fish away."

"Hmm."

In spite of my little speech, I wish that didn't sound so non-committal.

"You know," Yule says, "I'll bet Mama advised you to be straight with Reece instead of sneakin' around stealin' DNA from all your candidates."

All. Amazing that a three-letter word should sound so numerous. Of course, considering the context, it is. There never should have been any question as to who fathered my baby. And had I not valued my body so little, there shouldn't have been a baby at all. There goes God again, turning the bad into the beautiful by giving me Devyn.

"Yes, your mother did advise that."

"And you won't listen to me any more than you listened to her?"

I swallow. "It's too late."

"I don't believe that, and since you and I might be friends some day now that we got that apology out of the way, I'm gonna call you on this one. You're ashamed to admit to Reece that you don't know who fathered Devyn."

Called and answered. "Yes, especially since when he confronted me on the rumor that Gary and I had...you know...I lied."

"That was over thirteen years ago."

"Bold-faced lied. No hemming or hawing, just outraged denial. I saw the relief on his face—that he believed me—and if his family hadn't moved, I think he might have taken me back." I laugh brokenly. "Of course, he would have found out how good I was at lying once I started to show, and then..."

Something calls to me, and I step from the closet and follow the feeling to Devyn's white lacquered dresser. I pick up the smallest of the framed photos there, the one that shows a pale-faced red-headed teenage girl, hospital gown slipping off one shoulder, a newborn in her arms. Skippy leans over them wearing a huge smile.

"No"—I touch a finger to Devyn's tiny head—"showing probably wouldn't have been an issue if Reece..." My eyes tear for what would have been the greatest loss of my life. And for the first time, I thank God that Reece left Pickwick.

"You okay, Maggie?"

"I'm just glad I listened to your mother when it counted most."

"Me too." Yule sounds genuine, although the birth of Devyn meant she was forced to share Skippy with my daughter and me.

I return the photo to the dresser and brush the tears from my eyes. Time to change the subject, or I'll be sporting a puffy face when I pick up Devyn from school. "So, how's the baby kicking?"

"Too much. I wouldn't mind poppin' him out a little early, though I do think he's gonna be the hardest of all to give up seein' as hardly a minute goes by that I'm not aware of him." She sighs. "If I don't find myself a good man soon, I may have to content myself with bein' an old maid."

I hope she does find a good man, even if it is Reece. Even if it hurts. I have Devyn, and my little girl is blessing enough.

CHAPTER 18

DAILY WORD CALENDAR
for Highly Successful Career Women

[**flout** (*verb*): to treat with disdain; to scorn, insult, or mock]

TUESDAY, MARCH 16

After picking up Devyn from school, I had no choice but to return to the auction house. Worse, due to the urgent message left on my cell phone by the woman who owns the nearby Ice Creamery, there wasn't time to drop my daughter at home. Thus, as I pulled into the town square, I pressed a five-dollar bill into her hand and told her to wait for me at Mr. Copper's.

I sensed her suspicion, an air that has become commonplace these past weeks, but there was nothing for it. At least, that's what I thought as I ran for the theater to discover the reason for the raised voices that have caused employees and patrons of businesses around the square to tuck into their jackets and venture onto the sidewalks on this not-quite-spring day.

Among those gathered are a group of girls outside of Mr. Copper's, most notably Amanda Pigg.

Lord, please don't let her bother Devyn.

As I bound onto the sidewalk, I wince at the sight of my daughter, whose fully loaded backpack puts a lean in her posture. She eyes the other girls as she nears but doesn't appear worried.

Still, Lord, a wide berth would be nice.

As I reach for the theater's glass door, I catch my first eyeful of what awaits me inside.

"You want my blessin'?" Mrs. Templeton shouts where she stands in front of my cousin Bart, hands on her hips, chin in the air, orange baseball cap smooshing her hair. "I'll give you a blessin'. A blessin' out, you devil's dust-usin'—!"

"Gran!" Trinity hugs Bart's arm against her side as I enter the lobby. "I told you I'm gonna do it, and I'm gonna. With your blessin' or not." She sticks her left hand beneath her grandmother's nose, and light catches the small diamond on her ring finger. "I'm gonna be Mrs. Bart Pickwick."

No surprise, though I don't think Bart's father, my uncle Bartholomew, will be happy about that. Neither am I, but for an entirely different reason. For *this*, I rushed back here? Not for an upset client or a disgruntled heir opposed to the sale of family heirlooms?

Mrs. Templeton grips Trinity's hand and pulls it up to her eye. "Why, that ain't much bigger 'n a grain of salt," she scorns—no, *flouts*, most definitely flouts. "Once he does you wrong like all them Pickwicks do, that there little chip will be as useless as a milk bucket under a bull."

Trinity jerks her hand back and cradles it, as if to comfort the poor offended thing. "There's no call to be ugly."

"Or to carry on like this," I say as I near them. "Half the town square has turned out for your yellin' match."

"Maggie!" Trinity and Bart exclaim in unison, Trinity patting her mouth as if to put the words back and Bart's face reflecting the discomfort of one experiencing intestinal difficulties.

"It's me." I place myself to the left of Trinity and to the right of her grandmother. "And instead of being home where I ought to be, I'm answering a distress call from a neighboring business."

Mrs. Templeton crosses her arms over her chest. "Somebody is stickin' her nose where it don't belong."

I grit my teeth. "Mrs. Templeton, this is a place of business—"

"I am so sorry," Trinity says. "We shoulda known better 'n to spring our good news on Gran, but we were so excited."

I catch movement out of the corner of my eye. I don't have to look close to know Reece has stepped into the doorway between the lobby and the theater, no doubt pried from his studio by the din.

In the week and a half since he had supper with Yule, I haven't been much closer to him than this, though not because anything happened between the two of them. According to Yule, who called the following day, he's to remain her high school champion and a fond acquaintance. He just wasn't *in* to her, she said. As a result, she could hardly be *in* to him. I was relieved, but still have kept my distance. Of course it helps that, since he began the actual work on the statue, he's mostly holed himself up in his studio.

Returning my attention to Trinity and Bart, I smile. "Congratulations. You make a lovely couple."

Trinity blushes, my drug-rehabilitated cousin grins, and Mrs. Templeton mutters, "Mark my words."

I look to Bart. "Have you told Bridget?" In other words, get out before the tide of Mrs. Templeton's displeasure comes back in.

"Oh, Bart!" Trinity bounces. "Sure as shootin', we gotta tell your sister."

He still seems pained, which probably has as much to do with Mrs. Templeton's reaction to their engagement as Bridget's feelings about his *carrying on* with Trinity. It's not that she doesn't like Uncle Obe's Cinderella-inspired housekeeper, it's that she regards their relationship as seriously skewed. They're too similar, too silly, too naive. In this instance, opposites really should attract—for both their sakes, as well as those who will have to stand by them. But though I understand Bridget's concerns, I kind of think this could work.

"I'll see you this evenin', Gran, and don't be frettin' if I'm a tad late. Bart and me, we'll be showin' off this here diamond."

Mrs. Templeton growls at Trinity. "When you see me answer the altar call this Sunday, you'll know what I'm prayin' about. Um-hmm. Don't think I won't tell the Lord what's goin' on down here. Yes, I will."

Time to move. "Have fun, you two." I jerk my chin in the direction of the glass doors, and they march off like good little soldiers.

"I am *not* happy." Mrs. Templeton frowns hard at me. "In fact, I am so unhappy I'd best call it a day 'cause I ain't gonna be worth a dime you pay me." She stomps toward her office, leaving me alone with Reece.

I smile at him. "Sorry about that."

Hands deep in his pockets, denim shirt hanging loose and unbuttoned to reveal a white T-shirt, sleeves pushed up to the elbows, he straightens from the doorway. "I needed the break."

So it appears, his dark hair mussed, eyes shot with red, jaw sporting a double five o'clock shadow. My, he's bristly, but in a roughly appealing way, like he just came down off the mountain and—

Enough! "How's the sculpture coming along?"

"Keeping me up nights." He advances, not with his usual stride, but with shorter reaches, as if those late nights are weighing him down. "But I'm making good progress." He halts before me. "How's the auction business?"

I haven't seen him at the live auction for the past two Saturdays, though I have been on the lookout. Apparently, once he begins work on a sculpture, he's all in. Noticing that in addition to red-shot eyes, he has dark circles beneath them, I fight the impulse to smooth them away. "Going well, thank you. In fact, this past Saturday we broke a record—"

Mrs. Templeton pops up between Reece and me and thrusts a thick envelope in my hand. "Here."

"What's this?"

Oh, please don't let it be a letter of resignation. As difficult as she can be, I've come to depend on her.

"How should I know? It's marked Confidential so I didn't open it."

I flip it over. There's a return address, but no company name.

"I was feelin' particularly helpful today before Trinity and Bart up and ruined everythin', so when you walked out of here grumbling that you didn't have time to pick up the mail, I went to the post office and got it myself."

"Thank you."

"If I recover from my shock of bad news and can summon the strength, I'll see you tomorrow."

"I could really use your help." I give her an encouraging smile.

"I know that." She steps from between Reece and me. "Like I said, *maybe* you'll see me tomorrow."

Reece smiles, and despite the fatigue that prevents his mouth from attaining full smilehood, I want to melt.

I return my attention to the envelope and the word *Confidential* stamped in red in the lower left corner. Hmm. I slip a finger beneath the flap. What—?

Oh! I know what this is. And I could kiss Mrs. Templeton for respecting those red letters.

I snatch my finger from the flap and blink at Reece. "I guess I'll see you later."

He frowns, but with the envelope burning a hole in my hand, I slip past him and hurry toward Mrs. Templeton's office.

"I was going to ask you to join me for coffee."

"Raincheck," I call over my shoulder. A moment later, I close the door behind me and lift the envelope with both hands. Deep breath. "This is it." In all likelihood, the end of the trail, proving Reece is not Devyn's father.

Ignoring a stab of regret, I open the flap, pull out the pages, and unfold them. "Okay," I whisper at every period I come to as I read the polite letter that surely includes the word *positive*. It's not on the first page that goes on and on about it being an honor to be entrusted with something so personal and important, followed by an explanation of the procedure carried out to determine the existence of a genetic relationship between the samples. "Okay." Next page...

Of all the words in all the little boxes stuffed with data, the one that stands out is printed in red like the one on the front of the envelope. I read it again and drop my arm to my side.

"Okay." I sag against the door. "That's that." I slide down, drop the lab report, and gather my knees to my chest. "Negative."

Gary will never have to face an illegitimate child on his doorstep—at least, not mine. Though I'm relieved by the elimination of Candidate Number Two, anxiety sticks its head around the corner, the intensity of its gaze making me hug my knees tighter.

I'm not done. Miles to go before I sleep, or in this case, before I obtain another sample. I consider Devyn's date of birth and what she weighed—seven pounds on the dot. If Reece is her father, she came into the world a couple of weeks late. Shouldn't she have weighed more? If Chase is her father, she came into the world a couple of weeks early. Shouldn't she have weighed less? Of course, if I factor in how petite she is... Maybe God kept her in the womb a bit longer to get her up to a healthy seven pounds.

Or let her out early since she had attained a healthy weight. Just because she's petite now doesn't mean she wouldn't have been a big baby had she stayed in the womb a couple more weeks.

True, but there seems a better chance that Reece is Devyn's daddy. Tentative relief unfurling, I unhug my knees. Even if it means I lied to Devyn, I'd rather that than have her father be someone who shunned her all these years.

"Reece," I whisper to the ceiling, the sky above, the heavens over all, God everywhere. "Please let it be Reece. I don't know how and when I'm going to work this out, but I need it to be him. And so does Devyn."

And the only way to know for certain is to resume my DNA quest.

Or face this head-on by having a talk with Reece.

I clasp my head between my hands. "I can't." And this angst would be entirely unnecessary had I not been so certain Gary was the one, had I rooted through the Dumpster to search out the rag Reece bled onto, had I accepted his invitation and set my mind to snagging a chewed stirrer or toothpick over coffee—

Mr. Copper's Beanery and Lending Library! Devyn's destination.

"Stupid, stupid!" I snatch up the lab results and stuff them in my purse. "Not good, Maggie," I *flout* for all the word's worth. "How could you?"

CHAPTER 19

Reece is at the far end of the counter where customers claim their drinks. However, my relief fizzles when I follow his gaze to the back of the shop. Against the backdrop of crowded bookshelves, Devyn is there with Amanda Pigg and her friends, all of whom stand over my daughter by inches and then some. Whatever is going on, it isn't friendly, as evidenced by Devyn's defiant stance and the other girls' thinly sarcastic smiles.

While all of me tenses in preparation to rescue my daughter, I hesitate, afraid my interference will embarrass her and make matters worse.

Reece has no such inhibitions, and I catch my breath when he strides from the counter toward the girls. "What's going on?"

Amanda and her friends look around.

"What concern is it of yours?" Amanda tosses her hair back.

"It sounds like you're bothering Devyn." Reece to the rescue of a damsel-in-bullying. Again.

Move it, Maggie!

Amanda slides her gaze over him. "What? Are you her dad?" She drops her mouth open and looks to Devyn. "Oh, wait! You don't have a dad. Or should I say, you have no idea who he is."As I weave between the tables and sidestep errant chairs, Reece says, "You girls need to leave."

"*We* need to leave?" Amanda puts her hands on her hips.

"Hey, aren't you that famous artist guy that who was in the paper last week?" another girl says. "The one makin' a new statue for the square?"

Amanda Pigg's eyes widen, and in the next instant, she's boldly appraising him.

"Reece Thorpe," he says, and though his back is mostly to me, there's no mistaking his anger. It's in his voice and the span of his shoulders. "I don't like seeing kids bully other kids, especially younger ones."

I suck air so hard that were my tongue not attached, I might swallow it.

"She's not younger than us." Amanda flashes a coy smile. "She's just a runt."

I practically leap the last few steps to Reece's side. "There you are, Devyn."

Her eyes go big, the kind of big that says, *Not my mother!*

I don't look at Reece, afraid of what might be playing across his face. I don't look at the other girls, afraid I might say or do something stereotypical of a redhead. Instead, I jut my chin at the table where Devyn set her backpack and hot chocolate—fortunately. "Grab your stuff. We need to go."

She opens her mouth. I stare deep into her eyes. She opens it wider. I raise my eyebrows. She eases it closed. I breathe again.

"Oh, right!" She beams at Reece. "I forgot that you're going to show Mom and me how work is progressing on the statue."

She's saving face, and I can't begrudge her, but why did she have to pull Reece further into this?

Amanda stands straighter and flutters her lashes at Reece. "Ooh, can we come?"

His fatigue is still there, but anger and annoyance are firmly alongside it. "I'm sorry, but I prefer to keep my projects under wraps until they're ready for public display."

She sticks out her full bottom lip and says in a baby-doll voice, "Why does Devyn get to see it?"

"Rules are meant to be bent—for friends."

The slate of Amanda's face wipes clean, but in the next instant, she's clenching her jaw.

Reece turns to Devyn. "Ready?"

She grabs her backpack and drink, and I stand back to let her past.

A narrow-eyed glance is all Reece affords me as he turns. He crosses to the pickup counter, retrieves his coffee, and follows Devyn from the shop. I bring up the rear, and as I head outside, Devyn falls into step with Reece.

"I respect your need for privacy," she says, "so you don't have to show me the statue. I just said that so it didn't seem like I was running away from Amanda and her cronies—a dangerous precedent to set."

"I know." He slows to accommodate her shorter stride. "But I don't mind if you have a look."

"Really?"

He nods.

Though I feel like a second-class citizen as I follow behind, I hang back, afraid of another of his narrow-eyed looks—or worse.

I told you to talk to him. He's no dummy, knows Devyn is older than you led him to believe, might even be entertaining the possibility he's the father she doesn't know.

Lord, are You listening? It's me, Maggie Pickwick. Help!

Reece holds open the theater's door for Devyn, and I half expect him to let it swing closed in my face, but he remains the gentleman.

I have every intention of meeting his gaze as I pass through but make it only as far as his unmoving mouth before I'm overwhelmed by the need to avert.

Inside the lobby, I drop back and fumble for an excuse to deny Devyn a peek at what's happening behind Reece's closed doors. But there's nothing for it unless I want to look like a highly suspect kill-joy. I lower my eyes as I step ahead of Reece into the storage room-turned-studio.

"Hey!" Devyn drops her backpack and turns full circle. "You cleaned up the place and painted it and everything."

He certainly did. As he brushes past me, I stare at the formerly dingy and disorderly room. The discolored cinderblock walls have been painted white, the rotting indoor-outdoor carpeting torn out and the cement floors stained in earth- tone colors, the blown-out bulbs replaced with new bulbs that shine light in every corner, the ceiling-level windows scraped clean to allow sunlight to mix with electric light. As for the mildewed boxes and broken and rusty film equipment, the piles have been replaced with a drafting table, chair, a set of cabinets, and two tables. And here I thought Reece was drawing away during those first few weeks.

"It's back here." He heads toward a multi-paneled room divider at the rear of the studio. Where did that come from?

Devyn turns to me. "Come on."

I hesitate to follow. After all, she's the one to whom Reece directed the invitation.

She waves me forward, and my feet drag as I close the distance between us.

"Are you all right?" I ask as we walk side by side.

She looks up. "In the words of Jesus, there will always be the poor among us. I submit this is also true of the mean, but"—she shrugs—"sticks and stones." Then she frowns. "Do you think Amanda and her friends will ever change? You know, once they mature and discover it's not all about them?"

I feel suddenly caught in her sights. How much does she know about my past?

"You did."

That much. Doubtless, also courtesy of Amanda.

"Anyone can change if they he or she really wants to and has enough faith." Reece stands beside the room divider, eyes on Devyn, words on me. "But those are the keys, *want* and *faith.* How much you have will determine the degree of change."

I had both, thanks to Skippy. Unfortunately, since Reece's return to Pickwick, I haven't much exercised the faith element, which is the reason I find myself in this predicament.

"So yes," he says, still looking at Devyn as we halt before him, "those girls can change. How old are they?"

Oh, Lord!

"Around thirteen."

I drive my nails deeper into my palms as the tension increases around Reece's mouth, revealing his struggle to keep his smile in place.

"And you?" he asks with a subtle deepening of the voice.

Devyn tilts her chin up. "Most everyone mistakes me for being years younger and assumes I must have skipped a couple of grades, but I'll be thirteen on July 1." She grins. "A teenager at last!"

"July 1..." He still doesn't look at me. "Just think, if you'd been born late, you could have been a Fourth of July baby."

I swallow the last of the moisture in my mouth. With that seemingly innocent comment, he's gone fishing, probably in hopes Devyn will volunteer she was born on time or premature. Were she, it could disqualify him from fatherhood. And he could rest easy.

I feel for him. This is not how a man should learn he's a father. I had the chance to do it right, albeit painfully humiliating to me. Now not only do I get my just desserts, but he gets his *un*just desserts.

I'm sorry, Reece. Please look at me.

He continues to wait on Devyn, whose thoughtful face he's likely searching for resemblance to his own.

"Yeah." She nods. "But since my mom chose natural childbirth, I don't think she wanted me any bigger than I was."

That pretty much nixes the possibility she was significantly premature, might even be assumed she was late. But does Reece remember the exact day I seduced him?

"I wouldn't think so." He turns away. "Let me show you what I have so far."

Devyn hurries after him, but I don't move, even when they go around the screen and out of sight.

She gasps. "What is that?"

"The armature, the structure that supports the sculpture and on which I'll apply clay to build the form."

"Cool!"

I remain rooted to the spot, my world too shaken to satisfy my curiosity over what she applied that particular word to—a word I don't know I've ever heard her use.

"All these pieces," she marvels, "they look like..."

"They're mostly plumbing parts and wire."

"*Plumbing* parts?"

He chuckles, and the sound gives me a measure of comfort that whatever he's thinking can't be too bad if he can still laugh. Right?

"That's right," he says, "believe it or not."

Too bad he isn't talking to me. But how could he, seeing as I'm cowering on this side of the divider? Since Devyn's bound to question my reason for hanging back, I step around the corner and do a double take at the sight of what rises from a three-by-two-foot pedestal.

Goodness! What is that skeletal jumble of plumbing parts supposed to be? Has Reece gone all modern-slash-abstract-slash-junk?

Devyn walks around the metal monstrosity. "I can't tell what it is."

"That's because the armature isn't complete."

That's a relief. Still, it's hard to believe all that metal will look like anything I've ever seen. And isn't it a bit small? Something three times that size could easily fit on the granite block.

"Look over here." Reece turns toward the numerous sketches taped to the wall behind them.

As Devyn follows, she flashes me a lively smile that wouldn't have been possible when she stood before Amanda and her friends. If not for what that encounter cost me and that I might never be able to pay the bill, I would be grateful to Reece for this gift. If, if, if.

The two stand side by side, backs to me as I cling to the furthermost reaches of their realm, Reece with his hands in his pockets, Devyn looking from sketch to sketch.

"I see it!" She pivots and sweeps a hand to indicate the right side of the tangled pile of plumbing parts. "That's the loom."

Really?

She points to the left. "And that's the guy working the loom."

"The master weaver," Reece says.

I don't see either one.

Devyn gasps. "Wait! This commemorates the old textile mill."

Of course. The one my great-grandfather founded and around which the town of Pickwick grew. The one Reece's father tried to save from going the way of so many old textile mills in the South. The one that forever closed its doors under Uncle Bartholomew's *mis*management. Fortunately, from the proceeds of items sold at auction, Uncle Obe recently made restitution to all those who had lost their jobs and were owed their last month's wages—plus interest and a bonus as way of apology.

"A good choice?" Reece asks, and I notice he doesn't appear

as tired as he did earlier, as if reenergized by Devyn's enthusiasm.

"Excellent." She nods. "But it's kind of small, isn't it?"

"It's a maquette—a working model. Once the sculpture is complete and your great uncle approves it, I'll take it to a foundry in Knoxville for enlarging and casting. Trust me, not an inch of that granite block will go to waste."

"What do you think about the statue, Mom—the master weaver?"

That it's a far better choice than the statue of the beneficent-looking Gentry Pickwick that Uncle Obe dropped in Pickwick Lake.

I smile at her and offer the slightly used smile to Reece, but he still doesn't look at me. "It certainly represents our town's heritage. I'm sure Uncle Obe is pleased."

Devyn returns to the platform and runs a hand over what seems to be the master weaver's arm—providing I squint. "This almost makes me want to be a sculptor."

Uh…

Reece's jaw shifts. "I didn't think you had an interest in art."

"I don't." She reaches higher to something that isn't quite a head but maybe will be once he attaches more plumbing. "However, this is amazing." She pivots so suddenly her glasses go askew. "You get to create beautiful things out of practically nothing. Why, you're a creator. I don't mean like God, but here on earth." She pushes her glasses up her nose. "It's inspiring."

Reece's smile is wry. "Maybe you have a bit of an artist in you, after all, Devyn *Pickwick*."

If ever there was a good excuse for swooning, this is it. But I won't. I will keep my balance. I will not sweat, perspire, or remotely glow.

Devyn laughs. "You know, I just might."

Swoonsville. I widen my stance. "Devyn, we should let Mr. Thorpe get back to work. He has lots to do and we don't want to overstay our welcome." Just watch, he'll contradict me, thereby prolonging my agony.

"Your mother is right."

Mercy, thank you!

"If I'm going to complete this statue on schedule, I need to apply myself."

"I understand. But can I come again?"

Say no—gently, but no.

"Certainly. I'll let you know when I begin forming the clay on the armature, and you can watch."

"Can I, Mom?" Devyn's eyes are luminous.

"We'll see. School comes first."

She grins at Reece. "In that case, yes, since other than the extracurricular projects I assign myself, school rarely figures into my after-school hours."

She's right, and I am stupid. "Let's go, honey."

"Bye, Mr. Thorpe." She waves as she starts toward me. "And thank you for letting us see your work in progress."

"You're welcome."

I venture one more look at him where he stands before the wall ignoring me.

Please stay there. Don't see us to the door.

I turn away as Devyn steps past me. A few moments later, I reach to pull the door closed.

A hand grasps my wrist, and I pivot to find Reece before me. *Now* he looks at me, eyes cold. "Devyn, do you mind if I borrow your mother a moment? We have a little business to discuss."

She adjusts her backpack. "Okay."

Not okay, but what choice do I have? "I won't be long, Dev. I'll meet you at the car."

"All right." She heads around the corner.

Reece pulls me back into the studio, closes the door, and drops my wrist. "She's mine, isn't she?"

I swallow. Why is he so quick to take responsibility? Though

I lied to him about the extent of my involvement with other guys after our break up, shouldn't he be scrambling for that lie? Demanding a DNA test so he won't be stuck supporting someone else's child?

He makes a harsh sound, thrusts a hand through his hair, and turns his back to me.

What do I say? Yes, I think you're her father. And that *think* part? That's because I need one more DNA test to be certain. Got blood?

Don't be so dramatic. Tell him the truth.

But all I need is one more sample, and then we don't have to go there. He doesn't ever have to know—

What if Chase is Devyn's father? You'll have dug yourself in deeper by allowing Reece to believe she's his.

Chances are he is!

I thought you were done with deception. What happened to Be Skippy?

What's wrong with *Be Maggie?*

Well, that's a new concept and a good one, providing you're ready to listen to God directly rather than filtering everything through how Skippy would behave. And *act on what He says.*

Am I? I think so.

Prove it.

For all my height and bluster, I suddenly feel small as I glance from Reece's tense shoulders to his hand gripping the back of his head. "I need to tell you something."

He whips around. "No, you *needed* to tell me something. I had to figure it out—would never have known I had a daughter if I hadn't come back."

I take a step toward him, though he hardly looks receptive to closing the distance between us. "I didn't contact you about Devyn because..." Oh, I'm glowing—no, perspiring. That's definitely a trickle at the back of my neck. "...I didn't know for certain you were her father."

His lids snap nearly closed, leaving only a sharp light visible between the slits.

"And I still don't know." *Though I have eliminated one candidate —say it!* "You see—"

"So, the rumors that you denied *weren't* rumors after all?"

The temptation to clasp my hands and knock knees is almost too great to resist. "Yes."

The anger that came off him when Devyn was under bully attack is back. "Then one of my classmates may have fathered her?"

Two, actually, but how important is it? He already knows I'm guilty as charged, so why throw in unnecessary details, especially since Gary came back negative?

You're going to regret this. For goodness' sake, Be Maggie *who listens and responds to God!*

If he weren't so angry…

"That's what you're saying," he presses.

Thumbs cramping, I realize my hands have joined forces and drop them to my sides. "Yes, I lied to you that day."

His lids lift just enough to reveal how dark his green eyes have turned. "And you're not lying now."

"No."

Uh, doesn't omission qualify as lying—at the very least, deceit?

I try to stare him square in the eye but fall short. "Why would I lie?" I throw my hands out, hoping to distract him from my indirect gaze. "I've admitted to being a…tramp. That's nothing to be proud of."

He lets me feel the weight of his scrutiny. "No, but it's useful to keep Devyn from me like you've been trying to do since I came to town."

Then he'd prefer to believe I'm a liar now than a liar then? "You're wrong. I mean, yes, I tried to keep you apart, but it was to prevent this from happening—baring my past…my lies… having you look at me the way you're looking at me now."

He peers down his nose at me, which is something of a feat considering he's not much taller. "If that's true, it's selfish. Your daughter wants a father, and to save you embarrassment, you deny her."

But I was getting there, untangling my mess one strand at a time. Just one more sample, then I would know, and when Devyn was ready, she could make the decision about contacting her father.

"No, Maggie. I don't believe you. And as uncomfortable as it is for you, I will not allow you to shut me out of Devyn's life. I didn't come to Pickwick in search of fatherhood, but I accept the responsibility."

Why does he have to be so honorable?

And what happens if he has no reason to be?

"Why do you care so much? You barely know my daughter."

"*Our* daughter. I may hardly know her, but that isn't by choice, and she has the right to know me just as I have the right to know her."

"But—"

"No, I won't let you deny Devyn anymore."

He makes it sound as if I've intentionally harmed my child. But to defend myself would only lead to further argument. I sigh. "All right, but know this, I am not lyin' about the possibility you aren't her father."

His gaze doesn't waver. "The timing is about right."

"*About*. Before you claim her, Reece, you should have a DNA test."

His color deepens. "No."

"No?"

"Unless it comes to that."

"Comes to what?"

"I don't want to fight you for the right to spend time with her."

Lord, help!

"Don't worry, I won't say anything to her—yet."

I swallow hard. "Is that a threat?"

"Mom?"

The door muffles the voice, then Devyn sticks her head inside. "The car is locked, and I started getting cold."

I thrust a hand into my purse in hopes the keys are somewhere at the bottom.

"Sorry, Devyn, I didn't mean to keep your mother so long." Reece looks to me. "I appreciate your input, Maggie." His mouth tilts, enough to pass for friendly. "I'll see you at your uncle's home for dinner this Friday."

I freeze. What is he talking about?

"And you, Devyn."

Oh, *that*. Piper warned me to expect an invitation to join the family for a dinner that Uncle Obe is hosting for Reece. Of course, I was going to be too busy preparing for Saturday's auction to attend, but now…

That *was* a threat.

"I didn't know we were having dinner at Unc-Unc's." Devyn beams. "That'll be fun."

Since my back is turned to her, I make no pretense of a smile. "Then we'll see you there, Reece."

He pulls a toothpick from his shirt pocket, clenches it between his teeth, and says around it, "Definitely."

Frustration wells inside me. I hate the feeling of being cornered. And with no antacid at hand. I turn away. "Time to go."

Devyn pushes the door wider and, as I step past her, waves at Reece. "Bye again."

"Good-bye, Devyn."

He said her name differently—a bit softer and slower, as if it held meaning for him.

Devyn catches up with me in the corridor. "Who all do you think is comin' to dinner at Unc-Unc's?"

"The entire family is invited—a belated welcoming party for Mr. Thorpe."

"Awesome!"

Another word I'm unaccustomed to hearing from her, at least, in this context.

"We, um, probably won't stay long, what with my auction on Saturday."

"Then I'll spend the night with Miss Piper."

And have her keep company with Reece without me present? On second thought, even if it means my auctioneer's chant is off the next day, I'm not going anywhere before Reece calls it a night.

Lord, help me.

CHAPTER 20

DAILY WORD CALENDAR
for Highly Successful Career Women

[**zaf'tig** (*adjective*): plump, pleasingly so; often relative to a woman's figure]

FRIDAY, MARCH 19

He might not be coming at all.

Answered prayer, Lord?

Not that I prayed Reece wouldn't put in an appearance tonight, but I did pray for a way through this evening, especially after what I've had to endure these past few days.

Though I've avoided Reece like a bad banana, Devyn is determined to match us. If she's not pressing me to put in after-school hours at the auction house ("You don't want to get behind in your work"), she's not-so-subtly dropping Candidate Number Eight's positive attributes ("How often does a single mother come across a single guy who knows how to talk to kids

—and not in a condescending way?"). Doubtless, Reece has garnered more positive marks on her spreadsheet.

I glance at the front door beyond the pillars that separate the mansion's entryway from the great hallway where most of us are gathered. Unfortunately, even if Reece doesn't show, it could still be a long night. After all, where two or more Pickwicks are gathered—well, in *Uncle Obe's* name—it can get choppy.

Devyn's moodiness is in remission, as evidenced by her smiles and animated conversation with Piper and Bridget, but Uncle Bartholomew is unhappy. Standing alongside the banister of the grand staircase, a plate of stuffed eggs in one hand, his other hand splayed over his rounded stomach, he glares at Trinity where she hangs on his son's arm in the library's arched doorway.

Then there's Luc and his overly made-up wife who have been arguing since their arrival. Thankfully, they stepped into the library and are carrying on against the backdrop of ceiling-high bookshelves.

As for my mother, she has practically pinned Uncle Obe to the wall and keeps interrupting Aunt Belinda's attempts to get a word in edgewise.

Yes, unless I find a way to pry Devyn free, it's going to be a long night. And I'm only fifteen minutes into it, meaning it's more likely Reece is fashionably late.

Lord, I don't want anything to happen to him, but it's fine with me if he's so caught up in his art—You could send a little inspiration his way—that he forgot about the dinner party. He does have the excuse of being an artist, so You might as well put it to good use. I mean, if You want.

I raise my glass of Coke, only to pause at the sound of crackling paper as my arm brushes the breast pocket of my silk wrap-around dress. I tug the scalloped edge forward and peer at the folded paper I belatedly pulled from the little block calendar as Devyn dragged me toward the door so we wouldn't be any more late than I'd already made us.

Though I usually start my day with a daily word, my routine has been off for the past three days, thanks to Reece's revelation —one I'm sorely tempted to accept since I'm almost certain now he is Devyn's father, and it's not as if he's demanding a DNA test. If he's willing to believe she's his sight—er, DNA —unseen…

I turn my attention to the daily word for which I have fewer hours than usual to speak or think into my vocabulary. "*Zaftig*. Plump. Pleasingly."

"Who's plump pleasingly?"

I jump at the appearance of my uncle's ponytailed godson/gardener. Despite Axel's prosthetic leg and the accompanying hitch, he's stealthy. "No one." I smile and am rewarded with a twinkle in eyes Piper calls *capital-B blue*. "At least not in this family. You know how body conscious we are." In fact, the only one who comes remotely close to pleasingly plump is Aunt Belinda. As for Uncle Bartholomew, he's past pleasingly plump and defends his right to be now that he's retired.

Axel nods. "Before Thorpe arrives, I thought I'd ask how it's going with him working out of the auction house."

He knows Reece may be Devyn's father, since I gave Piper permission to share this with him in hopes he could use his influence with Uncle Obe to convince him to go with a different sculptor. Plus, Axel was my friend before he was Piper's, and I trust him, even though I didn't care for his advice that I be up-front with Reece. Advice I should have listened to.

I shrug. "It's uncomfortable." I'm tempted to confide the most recent development, but I resist. This is not the time or the place. I sweep waves off my brow and tuck them behind an ear. "So, how are things between you and my cousin?"

Were I not watching closely, I might have missed his momentary smile. "What are you hiding, Obadiah Axel Smith?"

He clears his throat. "Nothing I can talk about."

In the next instant, the weight of my worries eases. "Hold up!" I step closer to him to prevent others from hearing. "You did it, didn't you? Asked her to marry you."

He glances at where Piper is leaning forward to capture something my daughter is saying. "I'm not supposed to say."

That means yes! "Why?"

"It turns out Bart and I proposed on the same day."

Meaning Axel and Piper don't want to steal the spotlight from Bart and Trinity. I pat his arm. "I'm happy for you."

He raises his eyebrows. "I didn't say she accepted."

I snort. "Of course she did."

A broad grin rises above his goatee. "Just remember, I didn't volunteer the good news."

"Okay. What about the ring?"

He whispers, "She's wearing it as a necklace."

As I shoot my gaze to Piper, I register the beep of the front door that alerts Uncle Obe's caregivers that he may be wandering. Unfortunately, my cousin has buttoned her blouse all the way up, meaning I won't be getting a look at her diamond anytime soon. Might it be *zaftig*?

"Brace yourself"—Axel settles back on his heels—"the guest of honor is here."

My joy over the pending nuptials pours out the hole Reece's arrival opens in me as I look down the hallway to where Martha, hired to cater the dinner, ushers him toward us.

I have never seen this side of Reece. His usually mussed hair is almost tamed. Gone is his everyday attire, and in its place is a sports jacket, the dark color of which contrasts nicely with a white button-down shirt. Thankfully, he didn't throw in a tie, as it would have looked pretentious on an artist whose hands shape clay into metal. His slacks...well, they're *slacks,* aren't they?

I look back at his face. I expect him to avoid eye contact as he did while showing Devyn his sculpture, but he smiles. Then—?

"Mr. Reece!" Devyn runs to him. *She's* the one who put the curve in his mouth. "I was afraid you weren't going to make it." She tugs his shirt-sleeve. "Come on."

Their first stop is Uncle Obe, who sidesteps my mother too quickly for her not to notice his eagerness to escape.

Reece extends his hand. "I apologize for being late, Obadiah. A family emergency needed to be handled."

Uncle Obe's shake is two-handed. "I'm just glad you could make it for..." His lids flutter. "Yes, glad you could make it. And I'm certainly familiar with emergencies of the f-family sort."

And increasingly familiar with dementia. Recently, Piper vowed that if he doesn't finish his umpteenth draft of the letter to his estranged children, she will take it on herself—and hand deliver it if need be since time is running thin for any possibility of reconciliation. After all, though his children might forgive him for choosing his inheritance over them, it will eventually reach the point that he's entirely unaware of any peace they might offer. And, of course, they need to know about the early onset dementia they may carry in their genes.

"Let me introduce you around." Uncle Obe pulls back from the handshake. "This here is my sister-in-law, Belinda. She's married to...my brother over there. You may have met him when your father worked at the textile mill."

"I did."

My throat tightens at how happy Devyn seems standing beside Reece. It's as if she senses he's more than an acquaintance.

"Thorpe has stopped by several times to see your uncle,"

Axel says near my ear, "and we talked some. Seems decent enough."

"Yes, well..." I shrug.

"Devyn likes him."

There's no getting around that. "I think I'll check in on Martha. She might need help."

"Time to regroup?"

I nod and, shortly, enter the cavernous kitchen that was put to good use this past December when Uncle Obe stepped outside of his reclusive nature to host a Christmas Eve dinner for the Pickwicks. It nearly proved a disaster. Most notable was Uncle Bartholomew getting into it with Luc, whom he accused of selling him a lemon at *that slimy, lowdown, no-good used-car lot.* Then Bridget sniping at Luc's wife for double flushing the toilet when one bowl of water was wasteful enough, and my mom's table-pounding attempt to convince Devyn to be fit for contacts so she wouldn't look so plain. Oh, and mustn't forget the argument Uncle Obe had with his long-dead father over how best to slice the ham.

That shut us up. From what we can tell, it was the first and last hallucinatory conversation he's had, which made me wonder if it was an act. After all, he's always on the lookout for a silver lining to his dementia, and we did behave after that. For the most part.

Martha looks up from where she stands at the island before crystal bowls filled with frilly salad greens and sliced tomatoes. "Everyone gettin' along out there?"

"As well as can be expected."

"Well, that's somethin' better 'n nothin'." She claps her palms together and rolls her eyes up. "Lord, let peace reign in this big ol' house." She parts her hands and flashes a mouthful of yellowed teeth. "That there girl of yours looks to have taken a shine to your uncle's artist."

I know there's more to her words than meet the ear.

However, seeing no reason to probe, I pan a hand at the platters of food that will feed the Pickwicks. "This looks wonderful."

She gets back to work, sprinkling each salad with sliced green onions. "I like doin' this. In fact, what with your weekly pie orders, Mr. Copper's daily orders, caterin' jobs, and only so many hours in a day, I might have to hang up my Cracker Barrel name tag."

I was hoping it might come to this. "You can count on me to keep the pie orders coming. They've given my auctiongoers more staying power."

"Glad to hear it."

As Martha checks on the entrée in the oven, I deliver a salad to each place setting in the formal dining room, then fill the water glasses with iced tea. That's when I notice the place cards and read around the table to discover I've been assigned the seat between Devyn and Reece. Surely the work of Uncle Obe.

Ten minutes later, everyone enters the dining room, and Uncle Obe tells us to join hands where we stand for the blessing of the meal. We spread out a little, reaching for the hand of the nearest person, in my case Devyn's and Trinity's. In Devyn's case, Reece's and mine. And so here we are with our daugh—*my* daughter!—between us. But as soon as we take our seats, this threesome is over.

"Lord God," Uncle Obe says, and we all bow our heads, "bless this food that it be nourishing to our minds, b...bodies, and souls. Bless this gatherin' of Pickwicks and not-so-Pickwicks, and thank You for that. We could use some dilutin'."

I look up, but if he's funning with us, I can't tell from his deeply bowed head. As I start to resume the position, a toe-tapping Bridget catches my eye where she stands between Uncle Obe and her mother. Mouth turned down, my cousin's gaze lazily flits from bowed head to bowed head.

"I pray You will watch over each of us," Uncle Obe continues, "and draw us nearer one another as we draw nearer to You."

Bridget raises her eyebrows at me. Caught. I shrug. She shrugs back, causing the dreadlocks on her shoulders to shift. Well, at least she didn't scoot off to the garden for this part of the evening. Progress?

"And, Lord, You know our..." A long pause as he searches for the word. "...sins better than we do. Please help us to overcome those things that stand between us and You that we may walk strong in Your merciful shadow. It is in Jesus's name I pray. Amen and amen."

Amens buzz around the gathering like flies around a watermelon, then we move toward our assigned seats.

"Well, look at that!" Uncle Obe says as Bridget starts to lower into the chair beside Reece. "Someone up and changed my seatin' arrangement."

He's not going to make a scene is he?

"Bridget, you switch places with Maggie. Devyn, you switch with your Aunt Belinda."

I long to snatch Devyn back as she eagerly moves toward the head of the table, but it would only make matters worse. And so, avoiding Uncle Obe's narrow-eyed gaze, I follow my daughter, sidestep Bridget who grins knowingly, and slide into the chair she vacated without protest.

For all my dread over sitting beside Reece, Uncle Obe pretty much monopolizes him throughout the meal. The only real source of discomfort—besides the occasional bumping of elbows—is when Devyn talks to him around me. That's when the contents of my plate become something to behold.

At last, dessert arrives, and Aunt Belinda chirps with delight. "Martha, no one does red velvet cake like you." Her eyes devour the elegantly tall slice set in front of my mother. "It looks ever so moist. I can practically taste it. Of course, perhaps I ought to decline." She turns to her husband. "What do you think, Bartholomew?"

So he's minding her calorie intake again—my uncle who could stand to lose quite a few more pounds than his wife.

"Well, now, a woman must watch her figure, Belinda dear, and you have been indulgin' of late." He leans near her as if to continue in privacy. "Got yourself a bit of a paunch there."

So much for privacy.

"Daddy!" Bridget bites. However, in the next instant, she draws a deep breath. "Perhaps you and Mama can share a piece."

He raises his eyebrows. "Perhaps not. Seein' as you haven't been around much lately, you couldn't have noticed your mother's weight problem."

Embarrassed color flushes my aunt's face. Angry color sweeps her daughter's. But it's Trinity's voice that rings out. "Oh, she doesn't have a weight problem!"

Gulps go around the table, Bart's being the loudest.

"You're"—Trinity considers her future (maybe) mother-in-law—"zaftig."

Did I hear right? Did Trinity Templeton, better known in high school as Trinity *Simpleton,* use my daily word for highly successful career women? A word that, if I'd heard it before today, I would not have known the meaning? Does *she* know the meaning? For her sake, I hope not.

"Zaftig?" Uncle Bartholomew grunts. "What in blazes is that?"

"Why, it means *pleasingly plump.*" Trinity nods. "Looked it up myself when that lady on HGTV was talkin' about fluffy pillows—the kind with big buttons in the middle that pinch and poof up the stuffin' all around."

Bad visual.

Uncle Bartholomew juts his chin forward. "Are you implyin', Miss Templeton, my wife is fat?"

Her eyes widen. "Why, no! She's zaftig. That's the desirable end of fat. Like I said, *pleasingly* plump."

Mercy! I clear my throat. "It's a compliment, Aunt Belinda… Uncle Bartholomew."

The latter scrapes his chair back, stands, and points a finger at Trinity. "There is nothin' pleasin' about fat, Miss Templeton, especially used in reference to my wife."

Bart puts an arm around his fiancée's shoulder. "Trinity didn't mean any harm, Daddy." He looks to his mother. "You know that, don't you, Mama?"

Confusion pinches her face as she peers down her front, as if in search of that big button in the middle. "Well, it is a pretty word, *zaftig*. Sounds like somethin' a New York City person would say."

"See?" Bart looks hopefully at his father.

"I do not see. Just like I don't see why you had to go get yourself engaged."

"I wouldn't mind being zaftig myself," Uncle Obe says with more volume than I've heard in a long time, causing all of us to shift our attention to the man at the head of the table. He pats his concave chest. "Too much bone on me. Makes me seem sickly." He smiles at Trinity. "Thank you for introducing that artsy word to us." He moves on to his sister-in-law. "*Zaftig* sounds healthy, don't you think, Belinda?"

She looks up at her husband, who remains standing. "Bartholomew?"

"Yep, healthy," Uncle Obe overrides him, "somethin' we could all stand to be—in body, mind, *and* spirit. I'm sure my brother agrees."

Uncle Bartholomew drops his pointing finger, which somehow unbalances him and causes him to teeter. With even less grace than usual, he plops down in his chair.

"See there!" Uncle Obe smiles at Martha where she hovers behind his brother and sister-in-law, a cake plate in each hand. "No need to skimp on that c-c-…er, sweet bread you're so famous for. We'll each take a big slice."

Uncle Bartholomew's eyes widen as Martha sets her generous creation in front of his wife. "Well, now, maybe we *could* share a piece, Belinda."

To my surprise, she pulls the plate closer. "Actually, I think Obe is right. A little *zaftig* never hurt anyone." She lifts her fork. "And if I can't finish it, I'll take it home."

Martha slides a slice in front of my uncle, and thus ends what could have been an unpleasant scene.

"Close one," Devyn murmurs.

Before I can respond, warm breath fills my ear. "Welcome to the family, hmm?"

I gaze at the man who isn't supposed to be talking to me. Or breathing in my ear. Or alluding to being part of my family, even if he is.

I glance at Uncle Obe. Though his face is turned to my mother where she sits on his other side, I know he's listening.

I lean toward Reece and whisper, "I wouldn't blame you if you ran for the hills."

His smile isn't nearly as forced as mine. "That sounds like advice disguised as comment."

It is. And selfish, but I don't want him taking any part of Devyn from me, especially considering what he thinks of me. If only—

"I said," my mother hisses, "Bart is makin' a mistake." She scoots nearer Uncle Obe, and my quick glance around brings comfort that only Reece and I heard. Everyone else is too busy with their own buzzing. And cuddling. Luc and his wife have made up, her head on his shoulder as he slides a forkful of cake into her mouth.

Returning my attention to the latest drama to hit the Pickwick table, I cringe to see my uncle's brow pucker hard. *Please, Mom, don't be judgmental...pull back...stop!*

She nods. "Big mistake."

"Trinity is a fine young woman," Uncle Obe rasps. "Just look at the change in my nephew since they started seein' each other. She's kept Bart honest and outta jail, so you and my brother had best get used to the idea that she's gonna be one of us—"

"Ha!" My mother scoffs. "If a cat had kittens in the doghouse, would that make them puppies, Obadiah Pickwick?"

I nearly drop my face in my cake. Antacid. Need it now.

Not daring to look at Reece for the distaste surely on his face, I push my chair back. "Excuse me."

No one questions me or seems to notice, thankfully. As I step from the dining room, I hear Devyn exclaim, "Really?"

I glance around. Obviously, *she* noticed my exit, having claimed my chair the better to converse with Reece. I nearly turn back, but I need an antacid.

Shortly, I stand alongside the enormous telescope Uncle Obe had mounted on the rooftop observation deck when Devyn first became interested in astronomy. I prop my elbows on the railing and take in the cool breeze on which a Carolina spring snow travels, big flat flakes angling left to right, then right to left, as they take the long way to the ground where tomorrow's sunshine will begin to dry them out.

Yes, *dry*. These are no ordinary flakes. Though at first glance, they appear to be of the shivering *snow* variety, they're actually the delicate petals shed by the Bradford pear trees on the property. Pretty, soft little things, but smelly—like dirty socks.

I flick them from my shoulders and sleeves, but it's futile since the shedding is in full swing. Working my tongue over my teeth to dissolve the last of the antacid, I step to the telescope and put my eye to it. With a little adjusting, the unclouded night sky is crisply magnified, revealing thousands and thousands of stars. Slowly I pan the heavens until something like a wispy cloud fills the lens. Hmm. Devyn could tell me what it is—probably some far-off galaxy—but I think…

"Hello, God. I see You. Well, not *see* see You, but I know You're there. And that You're listening and wondering why I'm not listening." Sigh. "I know I should get off this train, even if I land on the tracks and the next train runs right over me. But I'm scared. I've messed up, and I don't know how to fix this without getting my mess on Devyn. Would it be so bad if I let Reece believe what he wants to believe, which is probably true? And why is he so eager, anyway? A deep sense of responsibility? Or does he really want Devyn to be his?"

I lift my face to the sky. "We're a package. If he wants to be her father, he'll have to deal with me, and I don't think..." I shake my head. "He won't like that, even if he still likes kissing me."

"Is that right?" someone drawls in the night.

I know the voice, but still I screech.

CHAPTER 21

Mercy! A body would think I'd attacked you." My blond-even-in-the-night cousin steps from the top of the stairs that ascend from a third-floor balcony on the backside of the mansion.

"Bridget!" I choke. "You could have let me know you were there."

"I just did." She steps forward, her rubbery shoes making squishing sounds as she crosses the observation deck to where I stand. "So, you and Reece Thorpe are becomin' intimately reacquainted, are you?"

Though I know she will keep my confidence, there's still cause for discomfort. After all, she isn't Skippy. "I don't know why it happened."

"Uh-huh. Maybe the two of you were alone, and just maybe it was...daaark." She puts every bit of the South into that last word.

"Oh, stop!" I return to the eyepiece.

"Tell me, did this nose rubbin'—I am givin' you the benefit of the doubt here—occur before or after you told him he's Devyn's daddy?"

So much for stargazing. And talking at God. And getting myself out of this mess. "I didn't tell Reece. He—"

"Is this a Maggie-Bridget thing, or can anyone join?"Am I really so out of it that I didn't hear Piper either? Bridget may be wearing Crocs or Dawgs or whatever those fat, ugly things on her feet are, but Piper is wearing noisy heels.

"Apparently, I'm havin' an open house," I call. "Come on over."

With her shoulder-length red hair, Piper isn't as visible across the rooftop, but as she nears, I make out her petite figure in the taupe pantsuit she wore this evening. Oh, to be so small and feminine. Hard to believe she envies my height.

"Things appear to be a bit strained between you and Reece." Amid the drifting petals, Piper comes alongside Bridget, and I feel as though I'm standing before a united front.

Did they plan this? No, they may have started coming around to each other, but I can't see them being in cahoots —yet. "I—"

"They kissed," Bridget says, "so how strained can it be?"

I growl. "That was before all the clues added up and he figured out that Devyn is"—another growl—"or thinks Devyn is—"

"He knows?" Piper gasps. "And she *is*?"

Bridget harrumphs. "So the DNA test came back positive. I suppose that's good news considerin' the alternatives."

"DNA test?" Piper sounds confused.

I considered telling her, but I knew she would try to talk me out of it. "Yes, a DNA test, but the result was negative."

"Say wh-at?" Bridget's voice cracks.

"And the test was for Gary."

My dreadlocked cousin steps closer. "It was Reece's DNA you were after."

"Yes, but he came this close to catching me in his hotel room pickin' at his hairbrush. When he was suspicious about why I was in the hotel, I knew it best not to push my luck. Rather than try to verify that he's Devyn's father, I decided to use the process of elimination by getting a DNA sample from Gary. That's why I went to Charlotte."

"I thought you were there on business," Piper says.

"Gary agreed to be tested?" Bridget asks.

"Er, no. I..." Grateful for the night that conceals my heated embarrassment, I square my shoulders. "I arranged an accidental meeting. At the opera."

Bridget snorts. "You went to an opera?"

"I did. Unfortunately, Gary saw me before I saw him. But when he wasn't looking, I swiped a few hairs from his head."

"How?" Piper holds up a hand. "Never mind, I don't want to know."

Good. "Anyway, the test came back negative. Thankfully."

"What about Chase?" Bridget asks.

"I still need a sample from him, but first I have to find him. *If* I decide to eliminate him."

Piper takes a step toward me. "What do you mean?"

"Since Reece is certain Devyn is his, and there seems a greater chance she's his than Chase's, I'm thinkin', why muddy the water? Why spit in the wind? Why rock the boat?"

Piper makes a snorty sound I doubt she ever let slip when she was working her fancy PR job in Los Angeles. "Well, at least you and I have one cliché in common."

"What's that?"

"The rockin' of the boat. About this time last year, that was my excuse for not owning up to my Lady Godiva ride. But think about this: If I hadn't, everyone would still be pointing fingers at Trinity, and I don't know if Bart could have held up under the pressure. Trinity might not be at Bart's side now, a ring on her finger. And who knows what Bart would be up to?"

I sigh. "You did the right thing, but this is more complicated than riding nearly naked down Main Street as a teenager."

Piper lays a hand on my forearm. "I know, but I also know you're no longer the seventeen-year-old girl who got pregnant our senior year. You made a mistake, but you took responsibility for it. You had Devyn, found a way to support yourself and her, and you're a great mom."

My throat tightens. "I appreciate that, but you're forgetting that when Reece confronted me back in high school about sleepin' around, I lied to him in hopes he would take me back. It turns out, he believed me, 'cause when I admitted there's a possibility he isn't Devyn's daddy and suggested he be tested, he preferred to believe I'm lying now in order to keep her from him."

"You could show him Gary's test results."

"I could, but then I'd have to tell him about Chase and I—" I shake my head. "It's bad enough it could have been Gary, but Chase too? It about makes me sick to think how Reece will look at me...how he'll judge me even though I'm no longer the girl who made those bad choices."

"Maybe it'll be like that in the beginning, but in time he'll come around, and the two of you will work out a satisfactory arrangement with Devyn."

How cold that sounds. And far away. I shouldn't admit this, but out it comes. "I don't just want a *satisfactory* arrangement with Reece. I want more."

Silence, only to be torn top to bottom by Bridget's low whistle. "Well, howdy, our cousin is still in love with her artist."

Is that what this is? This ache to be with Reece, to have him think well of me, to want him to want to be with me? Love?

Piper's grip on my arm tightens. "If that's true, Maggie, you'd better get off the ride you're on or—"

I pull away from her. "I already blew my chance. I should have told him on Tuesday when he found out how old Devyn is, but I let him believe what he wanted."

"Okay, just don't blow it again. Tell him the truth now."

Piper makes it sound easy. I turn from her to the telescope, but Bridget gets there first, bends over the eyepiece, and begins *hmm-ing* as if this was her reason for coming up to the observation deck. And maybe it was, although I'd like to think she was concerned about me.

"If you let Reece go on believing Devyn is his," Piper continues, "and it turns out she isn't—say, she needs a blood transfusion or a genetic blueprint or some such—he may never forgive you."

I grit my teeth. "That's why I need Chase's DNA. If she's Reece's, I can leave it be. If she's Chase's, I'll show Reece the test results, and he can go his way and Devyn and I can go ours."

She groans. "Tangled web, Maggie, tangled web."

I know, Piper, I know.

"Bridget," she says, "you think she should be straight with Reece, don't you?"

Though my back is turned to my stargazing cousin, I feel her shrug. "Sure. Of course, I'm not in her shoes, am I?"

I almost smile at Piper's grumbling. Nobody pins Bridget down—at least, not for very long. Just when you start getting smug sitting there on her chest, she twists everything around and leaves you thrashing like a turtle on its back.

"Maggie," Piper says, "you know I'm not much for quoting Scripture—"

"Then don't," Bridget says.

"Hush, you," Piper hisses, and I can't help but smile at how much the South has crept back into her speech and vocabulary. "Here's somethin' to think on: *For whoever would love life and see good days must keep his tongue from evil and his lips from deceitful speech.* Uh…First or Second Peter. I don't remember which."

Neither do I. "Thank you."

"Would you like me to pray with you? I'm not very good at it, but—"

"Ick! Nasty!"

I swing around. "Bridget!"

She peers over her shoulder and grins white in the night. "Oh, just inhaled some petals. They taste about as bad as they smell, you know."

I don't know. What I do know is that she'd as soon listen to a person pray over another as lop off her dreads, those constant companions of hers since her husband up and died—and I do mean *up* and died.

Speaking of those ropey locks, she swipes at them. "Ants pants! Those petals are all over me. I probably smell like an old dishrag." She gives her head a hard shake, causing several dreads to thump my shoulder. And then with a yelp like a pup whose tail has been trodden, she stumbles against the telescope. "It's got me!"

"What?" Piper and I ask in unison.

"My dreads!" She whacks the side of the telescope that, if it weren't bolted to the deck, would crash over. "The contraption's got hold of my dreads."

Five minutes later, Piper and I are still struggling to free the hair that is wound and wedged between two knobs.

"Well..." Piper says with a sigh. "...we could cut it."

Bridget jerks where she's bent over the telescope. "You are *not* cuttin' my hair." As if in fear one of us has a pocketknife, she yanks hard at the dread only to yelp again.

"It would be just a little shorter than the others," I say. "No one would notice."

"*I* would notice, and Easton—" She draws a sharp breath.

I understand, as I haven't heard her speak her husband's name since... Is it possible that the last time I heard it pass her lips was the day of his funeral when she told God and His Son to scat?

"Bridget." I relax into my drawl, all the more to soothe. "I am sorry about Easton, but I don't know how else we're gonna get you loose."

"Axel." Piper starts for the stairs. "He might have to take the telescope apart, but if anyone—"

"Don't you dare!" Bridget gives the dread another yank that makes her whimper. "I'm not a freak show." More tugging, grunting, and whimpering while Piper and I stand by, as if our shoes are nailed down.

"All right," Bridget finally croaks, "but I'll do it." Bent over the telescope, she digs in her jeans pocket. A moment later, moonlight slides across the blade she unhinges. "*I'll* cut it loose."

But she doesn't. Despite the dimness, I can see her shoulders rise wide and fall deep as if she's steeling herself. And anyone who believes as I do the reason she wears dreadlocks knows that's exactly what she's doing. Easton is in every breath, and when she finally grasps the lock and puts the blade near the knobs, I have the sense she's about to cut him loose. Only the one lock, but surely it's a start.

Regaining her full height, she jumps back as if afraid the telescope will reach out and grab another dread. "All right, then." She peers at the severed end, then gently smoothes it amongst its dread-ful companions. "I do believe I've had enough of this foolishness." She tosses her head to the side. "Maggie, you just do what you gotta do to protect our Devyn."

I warm at her genuine affection for my daughter.

"If that means marching downstairs and confessin' your promiscuity to Reece Thorpe, so be it."

I cool at her choice of words. Not that there's a syllable of untruth in *promiscuity*.

"If it means huntin' down that other knockhead—Chase whatever his name is—for his DNA, so be it."

I quietly groan at the thought of rooting him out.

"Even if it means yakkin' at the big guy up there and asking Him to fix up everything nice and tidy, so be *that*." She turns her head aside and says as if under her breath, "As if He cares one whit about us mere mortals."

"He *does* care," Piper inserts.

An unladylike sound issues from Bridget's nose. "I've seen how much He cares, thank you very much, little cuz." Back to me. "Just know I'm behind you, Maggie."

"*Little*? You're not much taller than I am, Bridget."

She angles toward Piper. "A good three inches taller. By my measure, that's plenty much."

Piper doesn't immediately retort, and my guess is that she's shifted into PR mode. "Not by Maggie's measure," she finally says.

Ooh, decided not to take the advice of her *inner image consultant.*

"Okay." I lay a hand on each of their shoulders, a friendly gesture with the added benefit of keeping space between them. My cousins may be moving in the direction of the friendship I enjoy with each of them, but they still rub each other wrong. "Thank you both. Though I'm not sure what I'm going to do, I appreciate your concern and advice. Now let's rejoin the party before we're missed."

Shortly, we approach the library. Devyn is sitting across the chessboard table from Reece. My first instinct is to rush in and break up their game. But not only would it cause a scene, but Reece has a right to know his daughter—

Ah! Why am I so willing to accept she *is* his daughter?

Because that's what you want him to be...and you did say you want more from him.

Yes, but it's a dangerous mind-set without conclusive proof. Thus, as much as I long to blindly accept as Reece accepts, I can't risk being mistaken. Truth is truth, and though I know I'm getting at it wrong, it has to be found out. And once it is, I'll decide what to do with it.

As Bridget enters the library ahead of Piper and me, I see my *little* cousin finger the chain at her neck.

I touch her arm, and Piper looks up. "Hmm?"

"Congratulations."

She halts, blinks away her surprise, and whispers, "How did you know?"

"Axel's smile."

Her face brightens, and then she's pulling me from the library doorway and around the corner toward the grand staircase. Once we're out of earshot, she lifts the chain from beneath her blouse. "Isn't it beautiful?"

The light tickles the gold prongs and jumps diamond facet to diamond facet. Her engagement ring isn't anything fancy like I expect U.S. Congressman Grant Spangler would have put on her finger if they had ever gotten past the *engaged to be engaged* stage. In fact, its simplicity seems to make the point *I am only a symbol of something bigger, brighter, and more intricate.*

"Yes, it's beautiful." I hug her. "I'm happy for you."

She returns the hug without hesitation, which makes me thank God we have each found the cousin—and friend—we never had growing up. Piper has put my past behind me. Now if only I could. But soon...

She pulls back. "Thank you, Maggie."

I smile. "So, when will a wedding band be taking up residence alongside that lovely engagement ring?"

"We haven't set a date, but within a year. We'd like to marry before Uncle Obe..." She sighs. "Well, while he can still revel in his role as matchmaker. His lapses are becoming more frequent, he's wandering some, and he's had a few anxiety attacks."

I squeeze her shoulder. "Thank you for being here for him and sorting out his estate so he can stay in his home."

She averts her gaze.

"What is it, Piper?"

Her top lip worries her bottom lip. "There's something we need to discuss. Could we have lunch together next week?"

Dread drops through me. Considering what caused this about-face, I can guess what the discussion is about. I stand taller, the better to support the weight of worry. "The theater has to be sold."

She closes her eyes, and when she opens them, they're full of apology. "It looks that way, and still Uncle Obe will fall short of making restitution. But if we can find a buyer for the theater, it may be possible to hold on to the mansion until"—she draws a deep breath—"he doesn't know any different."

I nod. "It's the Calhoun land, isn't it?" The land he believes our great- grandfather underhandedly won in a poker game, which he probably did. His son, Uncle Obe's father and my grandfather, may have been deeply committed to his faith, but he didn't get it from his daddy.

"That's a big part of it." Piper tucks the ring back inside her blouse. "Since Pickwick became so desirable, the land around here has appreciated dramatically, especially large tracts with the potential for single-family developments. We discussed the possibility of deedin' the land back to the Calhoun heirs, but since the last of the family left the area over twenty-five years ago, monetary restitution will likely be better received. Too, since the Calhoun land is situated near the middle of the estate, if it was broken off, it would almost guarantee the rest would have to be divided. Not that it isn't an option, but a buyer might find the intact estate more attractive. Say, for the development of a golf course—"

"A golf course?" Bridget's voice makes us both jump.

Why, oh why couldn't I wait to discuss this over lunch?

She steps nearer, and we quickly pull apart like a couple of gossips. "The Pickwick estate is going to be turned into a golf course?"

For all of her diminutive size, Piper squares up nicely to face our tree-huggin', animal-lovin', ever-grievin' cousin. "That's just one possibility, and not a bad one, believe me. A couple months ago, I was approached by a theme park developer—"

"Theme park!"

Piper's gaze slides past Bridget toward the library. "Nobody wants that, but if Uncle Obe is to make restitution and provide an inheritance for his kin, the estate will have to be sold."

Bridget snaps her fingers inches from Piper's face. "Just like that, hmm?"

"No, not *just like that.*" Piper's jaw shifts. "A lot of work has gone into liquidating the estate, and there's plenty more to do, but it's my responsibility to obtain the highest possible price—"

"A theme park!"

Piper draws a deep breath. "Theme park, golf course, housing development. With rezoning, the Pickwick estate could become any of those." She turns her palms up. "Yes, if I had my druthers, some wealthy person would swoop in and buy the entire estate for his personal home, but it's not for me to say. It's for me to follow Uncle Obe's instructions and liquidate."

Bridget's flushed face tightens. She was among Uncle Obe's earliest supporters, believing that regardless of his early onset dementia, he ought to be able to dispense with his assets however he saw fit, but I doubt she foresaw the loss of the estate to commercial development. Thus, though I regret that the relationship between Bridget and Piper is floundering, I'm grateful I'm not being dragged into the middle of—

"You're okay with this, Maggie?"

Grateful too soon. "Uh…" Movement in the library doorway draws my attention to where Reece has settled into our little scene by putting his shoulder to the doorjamb.

"After all," Bridget says, "with all this liquidation, you're bound to lose your auction house."

She's right, and having momentarily forgotten about that, I was kiss-the-ground grateful not to be in the middle of this mess. "I know." Just as I know that even though my lease is good for another eight months, I'd give it up to accommodate a buyer if it keeps Uncle Obe in his home a while longer. And then…

There are some good buys on High Holler Road where Fate

and Connie's Metalworks is among the last holdouts, but the location is hardly ideal, not to mention the money required to renovate one of those dilapidated buildings.

I shrug. "I suppose that means Serendipity will once more conduct business entirely on site." Ouch. Not that I didn't make a decent living before I took over the old theater, but I'll surely lose ground to Puck & Sons.

Pride, Maggie. Let it go, or it'll bite you.

"So"—Bridget cants her head to the side and narrows her lids —"it's okay with you that our family estate—?"

"What's up?" Devyn asks, and I peer past Bridget to where my daughter now stands alongside Reece. And coming up behind them is…

"Uncle Obe," I whisper, which makes Bridget blink and Piper suck air.

I summon a smile to put Devyn and my uncle off the scent. "Girl chat." I check my watch. "Unfortunately, Dev, I have an early morning, so we'd better—"

"But I'm going to show Mr. Reece how to work a Sudoku puzzle. He tried it once but got frustrated, so I promised to explain the strategy to him." She steps forward. "Would it be all right if I spend the night?"

I feel Reece's stare and know he expects me to refuse her—to continue to block the path between them—and I probably should in light of Chase Elliot, but I hesitate.

"That is," Devyn adds, "if it's okay with you, Miss Piper?"

"I'd love to have you stay the night, but it's up to your mom."

"Please, Mom?"

"All right." I look at Reece and am strangely satisfied with the surprise in his eyes. *There. Happy?*

Devyn smiles up at him. "I hope you're not an early bird like my mom."

"Not tonight," he says as she leads him back into the library.

I'm not the only one watching them. So are Piper and Bridget and Uncle Obe. Pajama time.

❧

THE FATHER QUOTIENT stares back at me with its pluses and minuses, including those littering Reece's row. Although in addition to not being a Pickwick resident, he has added another minus under *Mom's Interest* (she has no idea), his plus tally is impressive, and goodness knows how many more he'll rack up after tonight.

I scan the column headings. *Intellectual Games* and *Table Manners* will certainly earn him more plus marks, and I wouldn't be surprised if, surrounded by the books in Uncle Obe's library, Devyn undertakes to discover his status as a *Reader*. The next heading makes me step back. Not that it's a new addition. It just never before stared me down.

Forgiving. I shake my head. Now *that* might earn Reece a minus. Well, if Devyn knew the situation. I pray she never will, that she won't know the worst of me, that her quest for a father will be rewarded, that she will be as unscathed as possible. Which reminds me, I need to get on the whereabouts of Chase Elliot.

As I turn out of the closet, a stuffed animal on the shelf above Devyn's hanging clothes catches my eye. The Easter bunny is adorably disproportionate, his little head barely visible above an enormous tummy tightly wedged between huge paddlelike feet.

"Zaftig." I smile. "Definitely zaftig."

Buoyed by satisfaction at my efforts to increase my vocabulary, I'm unprepared for Piper's voice that memory whispers into my ear. *For whoever would love life and see good days must keep his tongue from evil and his lips from deceitful speech.*

With a sinking feeling, I exit Devyn's closet and close the

door. Piper is right, but knowing it and that my time would be better spent in *the* Word as opposed to my daily words, doesn't change the fact that, like the bunny's tummy, I'm tightly wedged. But I do have a pry bar, and its name is Chase Elliot. Now I just have to find him.

CHAPTER 22

DAILY WORD CALENDAR
for Highly Successful Career Women

[**loqua'cious** (*adjective*): talkative, wordy, long-winded]

SATURDAY, MARCH 20

Why do I have this feeling it's going to be a bad day? For one, when I peeked between the curtains, who should be among the auction goers but one of *& Sons*, the eldest of Puck & Sons? For two, Seth was out there—recently returned from Japan—and had claimed a front-row seat. For three…

I hold Mrs. Templeton's bristling gaze. "You did what?"

She props her fists on her hips. "She sassed me, so I sent her sorry little behind packin'. Yes, I did."

So ten minutes before the first opening bid, I'm out one attractive college student whose job is to present the items so I can concentrate on the bidding—bad. But even worse with *&*

Sons (a.k.a. Macon Puck) in the crowd and Seth, who left a voice message last night saying he's back and has good news and *really* needs to talk to me.

Lord, grant me a heaping helping of peace. Please.

"What?" Mrs. Templeton's posture is rigidly defensive. "You think I ought to have let her bruise me up one side and down the other with her disrespect? Oh no. It was her or me, and since you have a mighty need for my services, *she* had to go. And good riddance. Um-hmm. If the Lord don't get ahold of that one soon, she's goin'"—she hikes her eyebrows out of sight beneath her poufy bangs—"you know where."

Let's see your daily word get you out of this one. I know. I should have spent time in God's Word this morning, but I was running late, and then there was the excitement over today's daily word —a perfect fit for auction day—and the next thing I knew, I was pulling out the dictionary to further explore the meaning of *loquacious*.

I clear my throat. "So, who am I going to get on short notice —make that *no* notice—to present my items?"

Mrs. Templeton grabs the lapels of her lavender, lace-trimmed jacket that made me do a double take minutes earlier. "That would be me. I scooted over to Betty Sorgham's antique shop, and she loaned me this here jacket right off her body."

But that woman doesn't like me, believing as she does that my business has hurt hers. I beg to differ, since she always gets busy after my auctions when unsuccessful bidders go looking for something similar at her shop. Apparently, Mrs. Templeton has an *in* with cranky Betty.

"Well?" She flaps the lapels, which draws attention to the worn button-up man's shirt beneath.

As upset as I am with her, I hold it in. It won't do any good to remind her who's boss, and besides, I actually like her a little and have reason to appreciate her a lot, so much that I haven't tried to replace her. However, the thought of having her up on stage, especially with Macon wearing a smirk as broad as a smooshed Little Debbie cake—

"I know what you're thinkin', Missy Pickwick, who believes I'm too old." She wags a stubby finger. "But I'm the one who catalogued the merchandise, so I know it about as well as you—and certainly better than that disrespectful floozy."

I have no choice. "Okay, let's do it."

For the first hour, all goes well despite the confusion on the faces of my regular attendees as they watch Mrs. Templeton do her thing, the smirk I knew to expect, and Seth's stream of thumbs-ups. Mrs. Templeton holds up each auction item, slowly turns it front to back, and points to the features I call out. But then comes the potato masher.

"Early twentieth century," I say into my headset. "The shaft is made of fruitwood, as is the circular wooden base."

Most everyone appears bored with this domestic, low-end offering. However, that doesn't mean a battle won't be fought. A half-dozen women, nearly all over the age of sixty, eye the kitchen tool that resembles an *Alice-in-Wonderland*-sized mushroom. Well, not that big, but big. And upside-down.

"Let's start the bidding at 20 dollars. Who will give me 20?"

Four paddles shoot into the air, a good sign, since it's not worth much more than that. Now 30. Now 35. 40? Yes! Now 45. And there the bidding stalls, but just as I'm about to bang the gavel, one of my ringmen squeezes the extra 5 dollars out of a beetle-browed eighty-year-old spinster.

I smile. "Thank you, ma'am. Who will give me 50?"

Another stall, though the ringmen work it for all they're worth. I raise the gavel.

"Why, Ginny Jean," Mrs. Templeton exclaims, "why are you holdin' tight to your pocketbook?" Her polyester-covered legs make *whooshy* sounds as she scoots to the edge of the stage. "You know you want this here tater masher. It wasn't but last month you were sayin' they don't make mashers the way they used to—said you'd give an arm and a leg for a real one."

The seventy-something Ginny Jean stares open mouthed at Mrs. Templeton. And all the while, Macon smirks.

This is not how I run my auctions. I clear my throat. "I appreciate your enthusiasm, Mrs. Templeton, but—"

She tosses up a hand to silence me, then *whooshes* to the steps and descends them.

Oh no. "Mrs. Templeton—"

"Hold your horses, Missy Pickwick, I'm workin' the crowd."

Macon guffaws.

The ringman near Ginny Jean looks askance at me.

Mrs. Templeton halts before the other woman, grabs her hand, and sets it on the circular wooden base. "Fruitwood that is, and smooth as a baby's bottom. Ain't never mashed nothin' but soft taters. Feel good, don't it?"

Ginny Jean's smile rises as if from the dead. "Why, yes, it is smooth."

"Yup. Now you gonna give another five dollars, or you gonna regret to your dyin' day that you didn't have this beauty in your kitchen?"

"Well, I don't cook much nowadays."

"But you still like mashed taters, don't you? What with your dentures and all?"

Frowning, Ginny Jean takes the masher from Mrs. Templeton and examines it. "Maybe I'd cook more if I had this."

"Fifty?" Mrs. Templeton asks.

Ginny Jean nods, then peers at the eighty-year-old spinster. "And higher, so don't waste your time or my money, Erlinda."

Erlinda goes *humph* and we're off again. Five minutes later, Ginny Jean is the proud owner of a potato masher. Wow, seventy dollars for something Betty Sorgham would probably sell for thirty.

I call a break, during which Mrs. Templeton and I are going to have a little talk.

As the attendees head for the lobby, I remove the headset and turn from the podium.

"How're you, Mag?"

"Hey, Maggie."

The voice that slides in first belongs to Macon. The second belongs to Seth. I look at Mrs. Templeton's retreating back, but I can't pretend I didn't hear the men.

I turn to where they stand below the stage. Macon's grin is self-satisfied. Seth's is hopeful. Mine is forced. "Yes?"

"You know," Macon says, "you might be onto somethin', Mag."

I *hate* being called that, and he knows it, since I took issue with it when I worked for his father and he started calling me that after I politely declined several dinner invitations. I knew he wanted what I'd denied him when we were in high school, but he refused to believe those days were behind me.

"I might be onto what?"

"The old lady thing. Get a bunch of biddies fightin' over a bone and"—he claps his hands—"money!"

And people say my brother, Luc, is oily. "I suppose this means you intend to hire Mrs. Templeton out from under me like you did my former assistant."

He chuckles. "That would be an act of desperation, which Puck & Sons has no need to resort to, unlike a certain competitor." He wiggles his eyebrow—and I *do* mean that in the singular sense.

Resisting the temptation to further the advantage of the three feet I stand over him from atop the stage, I glance at Seth. Hands in pockets, chin down, he appears to be examining his shoes.

I sigh. If he were Reece, this exchange would have been over long ago.

"No, Mag, I was just bein' sarcastic in a pals-y way." Putting on that smooshed smirk, Macon draws a thumb and forefinger down either side of his scraggly attempt at a goatee.

"Sarcastic?" I frown. "Why? The fighting over one bone worked just fine. In fact, that potato masher pulled in double what I expected. The law of supply and demand at work."

Good-bye Little Debbie cake. And look at that—his unibrow is attempting to shorten itself right in the middle.

I shift my gaze to Seth. "Is there something—?"

"Yeah, well," Macon says, "it's a pity that law is gonna be workin' against you before too long."

I sense a red flag. "How's that?"

He looks around. "This theater—er, auction house. I hear it's gonna be on the block soon so's your uncle can square up them family debts y'all accumulated."

Once again, the imaginary corset cinches.

Macon resettles his vile attention on me. "Leastwise, that's what your brother told me when I took a test drive in one of them fancy sports cars on his lot."

Thanks, Luc. Not that I believe his slip was intentional. I am his sister, after all. No, more than likely, he wasn't thinking, set as he was on making a sale. Searching for a clever response to hide my alarm, I glance at Seth, but his cuticles are now the height of interest.

"Yep," Macon says, "my daddy's lookin' forward to taking this dump in hand."

Cinch, cinch.

He throws his arms wide. "Puck & Sons Auction World. Can you see it?" He grins. "Maybe you could come work for us again."

Though I manage to squeeze in one more *Lord, grant me peace,* out of my mouth comes, "Work for Puck & Sons? Why, I'd—"

"That's assuming Serendipity is going out of business," says a voice from behind.

Lord, I said peace, *not* Reece. *But okay.*

While I know I should resent his interference, I'm grateful, since it gives me time to whip my temper into shape.

"I wouldn't count on it, Macon," Reece continues.

"Why, if it isn't Reece Thorpe." Macon smiles. "I heard you're gonna sculpt us a new statue to replace the one crazy Obadiah Pickwick dumped in the lake."

"He's not crazy," I snap.

Up goes that unibrow again. "Um-hmm."

Hearing Reece's advance, I glance at Seth, for some reason expecting him to spring into action now that an example has been set. Although he is no longer absorbed in his body parts, neither does he appear inclined to defend my family or me. He stands there, looking from Point A (Macon) to Point B (me) to Point C (Reece).

Reece halts alongside me, and though pride tempts me to refuse his assistance, I stand taller and steal a glance at him.

"The auction is about to resume, Macon," he says around the toothpick.

The other man peers over his shoulder at those beginning to trickle in. "Yeah?"

"That's your cue to report to your daddy."

Macon narrows his lids at Reece, but as I tense in anticipation of a scene, he shrugs. "I'll do that. Have a nice day, Mag. Oh, and you too, Seth."

"Why, thank you, Macon." As the other man turns away, Seth looks to Reece. "It's been a while."

Reece nods. "It has."

"Well, good luck on that statue." Seth's dismissal is obvious, but Reece doesn't move from my side, causing annoyance to take over Seth's face. "You got my message last night, Maggie?"

"I did."

"How about an early supper, then? Like I said, there's something I need to discuss with you."

Please, not another offer of marriage. "I—"

"Sorry, Seth," Reece says, "Maggie and Devyn are having dinner with me. Or, rather, I'm having dinner with them."

As I stare at him, it strikes me that he may simply be rescuing me from Seth as he rescued me from Macon—that my daughter didn't, in fact, issue an invitation.

Reece looks at me with a seemingly genuine smile. "Devyn tells me your macaroni bake is the best."

Mrs. Templeton isn't the only one with whom I need to have a talk.

"I see." Seth's face tightens. "Then we'll have to make it for later. I'll call you, Maggie."

"All right."

He heads up the aisle toward the lobby. Once he's out of earshot, I turn to Reece. "Devyn shouldn't have invited you to dinner without first speaking with me."

He studies my face. "You're welcome."

Embarrassment softening my tense shoulders, I lift my hands in surrender. "I'm sorry. It's not that I—" At the realization we're drawing attention, I motion for him to follow me backstage. Once behind the curtains, I say, "It's not that I don't appreciate your helping me with Seth and Macon, but the auction is bound to run late and I won't have time to make macaroni bake. I'm sorry that Devyn—"

"She didn't." He removes the toothpick from his mouth. "She only broached the possibility, said she had to discuss it with you first."

That's my girl. Of course, I would have preferred she hadn't *broached* at all. "Good." I check my watch. Show time.

"I'll bring dinner," Reece says as I part the curtains. "Seven late enough for you?"

I snatch my hand back. "Reece..." What do I say?

His eyebrows lower. “Don’t make this any harder for me than you already have, Maggie. I’m not certain what the future holds or how I’m going to fit a child into it, but I want to know my daughter, and right now my time in Pickwick is limited.”

Right *now*? Meaning that could change?

“Dinner,” he says.

I sigh. “Make it seven thirty.”

He starts to turn away, but pauses. “Devyn told me she’s never had sushi. Are you okay with that?”

I frown. “Raw fish?”

“Not all of it’s raw. I’ll bring a variety to ease you into it.”

I didn’t even know you could get that stuff in Pickwick. My, we’ve come a long way. “Whatever you want, but don’t worry about me. I’ll make soup for myself.”

He nods and heads toward his studio.

I touch my cross necklace. “Raw fish.” I straighten my blouse’s collar. “Slimy.” I smooth my navy blazer. “No way.”

“You ain’t old enough to be conversin’ with yourself,” Mrs. Templeton’s crotchety voice falls around me like a spray of gravel.

I pivot, ready to unload the talk I need to have with her but am surprised by her smile that makes her appear years younger.

“We done good, hmm?” She halts before me. “If we can get seventy dollars for a tater masher, just think what we’ll get for that old washboard and Miss Jean’s miniature bottle collection and those leather steamer trunks from your uncle’s estate.” Her eyes twinkle. “And here you thought I was too old. I done proved you wrong. Go ahead, admit it.”

As I stare at the transformed woman, the talk sticks in my throat. Though I need to lay down some rules, it can wait. “We make a good team, Mrs. Templeton.” I nod toward the stage. “Ready?”

“Just try and put a bit in my mouth.” She hurries past me.

Four hours later, my nerves dangerously unpluckable, the receipts from today's auction prove that Mrs. Templeton is as big a hit as Martha's pies. Maybe it won't be such a bad day after all.

CHAPTER 23

"According to statistics, the average age of marriage for men in the U.S. is 26.8 years. That means you're not average, Mr. Reece."

I nearly choke on the sushi I had no intention of sampling. Working my throat muscles to keep the soy sauce-steeped tuna, rice, and seaweed from heading toward my lungs, I look at Reece.

Seemingly unperturbed by Devyn's conclusion, he reaches his chopsticks to the tray of sushi and pinches an ultra-raw salmon. "That's not a bad thing, not to be average."

"True." She snags a piece of spicy shrimp. "But you don't want to be an outlier—in your case, getting too far right of the bell curve. If so, you could end up a lonely old man."

Why couldn't they have stayed on the topic of bronze casting? I may not have found the method of producing a sculpture fascinating, but it was safe.

Fortunately, Reece laughs, and I'm grateful he knows about her Father Quotient so he won't think I had anything to do with this discussion.

"You're right." He smiles at her. "So, I'd better get a move on, hmm?"

She nods. "God Himself says it's not good for man to be alone."

I lower my chopsticks to my plate. "I'm full."

"I'm not." Devyn pops the piece in her mouth.

Reece meets my gaze, shakes his head, and inserts salmon.

I check my watch. 8:45. Though we didn't sit down to eat until 8:00, we should be finished. And would be if not for all this lingering over raw fish. Is this how sushi's done? A precaution against food poisoning—see how it settles before getting in over one's head, er, stomach? Or is conversation the culprit? Although I'm all for mixing meals with talk, this is extreme. Especially under the circumstances.

I stand. "How about I make some tea while you finish up here?"

"None for me, thanks," Reece says. "Perhaps later."

"Me neither." Devyn returns her attention to Reece. "Want to hear some other interesting statistics?"

I sit back down. Fortunately, the next round of statistics focuses on admission to Ivy League schools. Unfortunately, our evening continues with a game of Scrabble that does little to showcase my improved vocabulary and much to make me ache over the banter between Devyn and Reece that often ends in laughter—Devyn's sweet and high, Reece's rumbly and low. And then *Les Misérables* is in the DVD player despite my reminder of church tomorrow.

Halfway through Liam Neeson's amazing performance, my stomach orders up two antacids. "Tea anybody?" I try again.

"Sounds good," Reece says.

Devyn shakes her head and refocuses on the movie.

Five minutes later, as I stand in the kitchen chewing the chalk and scrolling through the memories made this night, the phone rings, and I don't know why I pick it up without checking caller ID. As I press the receiver to my ear, I realize where I might have just landed and hold my breath.

"Maggie?"

Yep, hot water.

"You there?" Concern quickens Seth's words.

The temptation to press the Off button is overwhelming, but more overwhelming is the possibility that it would bring Seth to my door. "What's up?"

He sighs. "You had me worried there a minute."

"Sorry. Um, everything all right?"

"Is he still there?"

"Yes, Reece is here. Why don't we talk tomorrow?"

"I'd like to get this over with. Can we talk in private—away from him?"

I look around. "Actually, I'm alone in the kitchen."

"Well, then, all right." He draws a noisy breath. "I've decided to take the job in Japan."

There's relief in that, not only because he won't be able to pressure me into spending time with him, but because it's what he needs—a new beginning away from Pickwick and me. "Congratulations. You must be excited."

"I am, but that brings me to you."

Oh dear.

"And Devyn, of course."

"Of course." I wish there were some way to apply brakes to where this car is heading, but it's best to let it reach its destination so I can get out in one piece.

"What I want to say would be better in person, but since he's there, I'm reduced to doing it over the phone." Seth clears his throat. "The reason I came to see you at the auction house was to ask you to come with me. And Devyn, of course."

"Of course." If my daughter hasn't always been just that to him—an *of course*—I might have accepted him years ago, but nothing doing.

"I was pretty sure what your answer would be, but the news that your auction house is going under gave me hope."

Should I be offended? No, though he sees what he perceives to be the end of my business as an advantage to be used in his favor, I know he doesn't wish me ill. Still, a little concern and regret would be nice.

"So I'm going out on a limb here and praying it doesn't snap back and whack me in the face. I'm asking you to marry me, Maggie."

And I have to turn him down. Again. While it seems wrong to do it over the phone, if I postpone it until we get together, it will only lead him on. Thus, after a long pause meant to convey thoughtful consideration, I say, "I'm honored, Seth, but you deserve someone who loves you as much as you love her. And as fond as I am of you, I am not that woman."

He blows out a breath, and I'm panged that he was holding it. "You're sure? 'Cause I'm not going to ask again."

That's what I'm aiming for. "I'm sure."

He blows some more. "Then I'm off to Japan alone."

"Maybe you'll meet someone over there."

"Someone who'll appreciate me, hmm?"

"That's what I wish for you."

"Thanks. Well, I'll let you go."

"Good-bye, Seth." I return the receiver to its base and my mind to the memories made tonight—the sound of a father delighting in his daughter and a daughter delighting in her father. That is, if…

Yes, *if.*

I don't know how long that word echoes through me, and my distorted reflection stares at me from the stainless-steel kettle I set on the back burner, but I don't move until I hear a groan. Compressing my lips to keep the sound from escaping again, I grip the kitchen counter with both hands and lower my forehead to its cool surface.

Lord, I have to know. And so does Reece. No matter what he thinks of me, I can't let this continue. Can't let him eek out a relationship with Devyn if she isn't his. If I do and it proves a waste of his time, the more hurt Devyn will be when he pulls back. And surely he will if he isn't her father. It's all good and noble to take responsibility for your own child, but another's? Sure, Seth would, but only because he wants me, and Devyn and I are not *labeled for individual retail sale.*

"Oh, God," I whisper, "forgive me for trying to take the easy way out. I should never have turned this into deception."

"Are you sick?"

I flip around to find Reece in the doorway. Though moisture blurs my vision, I can see his brow is furrowed.

"No, I...Devyn?"

"Asleep on the sofa." He steps farther into the kitchen. "Are you sure you're all right?"

His concern causes a fresh well of tears. I drop my chin. "Yes, I just..." I breathe deep, and the silence between us stretches like so many years—thirteen going on fourteen. That's a long time. Despite my moist eyes, I look up at where he stands tensely on the other side of the kitchen, as if struggling against an unseen hand.

"We were doing just fine without you. Not perfect, some bumps and detours and sharp turns along the way, but fine. Why...?" I shake my head. "Why does she matter to you? Why do you care? Is this like a new puppy, loved for its novelty but soon reduced to an inconvenience that needs to be cleaned up after?" I lower my chin. "I don't understand."

I hear his footsteps, and then he's in front of me, his hand gently lifting my chin. "I'm sorry." His green eyes search mine. "Maybe I shouldn't have pushed this on you, but thirteen years... There's so much catching up to do and not just with Devyn, but you."

"Me?"

He looks toward the French doors that lead onto the back patio. “Let’s take this outside.” He releases my chin, and as I start to follow him, I remember my reason for being in the kitchen. “Let me get your—” The glow beneath the kettle is nonexistent, the knob in the Off position. “I forgot to turn on the stove.”

“Don’t worry about it.” He motions me forward, and shortly I switch on the patio light and step past him into the chilly night. He joins me at the small café table that overlooks our pretty little backyard, and I startle when he takes the chair beside mine.

He clasps his hands on the table. “I’ve been thinking. The day I ran into you at my hotel, I asked why you were so set on keeping Devyn away from me.”

I close my eyes for a moment. “Yes.”

“You said I wouldn’t understand, that you doubted I’d made the mistakes you had made or hurt people the way you had.”

“Yes.” It’s all I can say.

“You were wrong, Maggie. That day at school when Yule fell on the steps—”

I cringe.

“—there was something I wanted to share with you.”

My behavior made certain he never did.

He angles nearer, and the patio light fingers his dark hair. “I want to tell you now so you’ll understand why I’m here and why I was so angry when I learned Devyn is mine.”

I should stop him right now and tell him—

“When I drove you home from Skippy’s, you asked about my brother.”

A memory of the boy who was three years younger than Reece rises—a fair-headed, sharp-faced youth who was not happy at being uprooted and moved to Pickwick. “Yes.”

“I didn’t answer you because other than secondhand accounts, I don’t know how he is.” Reece’s jaw shifts. “I haven’t spoken with him in years.”

The strain in his voice tempts me to reach to him, but I clasp my hands in my lap. "You had a falling out?"

"We did. I don't know if you remember, but my brother resented leaving his friends when we moved here, and Jacob and my father started butting heads."

"Teenage rebellion."

"Yes, but the night before you got on Yule, it became something else. My dad wanted to free up room in the garage for his car and asked Jacob and me to finish unpacking the boxes from our move. Jacob was in one of his moods, boiling with resentment as he tossed around books and pictures and cursed. And because I was so tired of constantly prying him out of his moods and walking around under the cloud he cast over our family, I started to boil too."

Reece boil? I'd seen him simmer but never boil.

"I struggled to get the job done so I could put distance between us, but then he thrust a picture in my face. It was one of Dad standing between the two of us when we were in grade school, an arm around our shoulders."

Reece swallows loud, and I long to squeeze his arm, but something tells me that would make it hard for him to continue.

"Jacob said, *I hate him* and dropped the picture. The glass shattered, and I wanted to hit him. He knew it—I could see it in his eyes—but he didn't pull back. He laughed and stomped on the picture, and I lost it. I grabbed him by the collar and said, *Then it's a good thing he's not your father.*"

Not his—? Oh.

After a long moment, Reece continues. "Ironically, it wasn't until our family was packing to move to Pickwick that I learned Jacob and I didn't share a biological father. One day I got home from school ahead of Jacob and heard an argument between my parents. It was about some love letters my father had found while packing. I knew my parents had separated when I was two, but what I didn't know was that my mother met someone."

He draws a deep breath. "My father knew about the other man, but he chose to raise Jacob as his own, and my brother and I probably would never have known any different if I hadn't overheard their argument and acted out of anger."

I lay a hand over his.

He allows it, his only acknowledgment a slight pause. "Jacob ran into the house and told Mom and Dad what I'd told him. He accused our father of favoring me over him, said that was the reason their relationship had gone bad." Reece looks hard at me. "If there was favoritism, I never saw it, and I don't believe Jacob did either. Our father loved both of us, but nothing he said would change my brother's mind. It got uglier—Jacob raging, my mother crying, my father shaking, and me standing there, hating myself for betraying a confidence my parents didn't know they had entrusted to me, feeling the wounds I had caused."

Now I understand the reason he looked the way he did that morning on the school steps—eyes bloodshot, hair a mess.

"Jacob demanded to know the identity of his biological father, but my parents refused to tell him. They said when he was older and more mature, they would, and he could decide then whether to contact him.

Devyn...

"It wasn't just the trouble at the textile mill that made us leave Pickwick. It was Jacob. He made life miserable until my parents relented in hopes that once he was back among his friends, he would settle down."

"Did he?"

"Some. My father tried, but Jacob didn't want much to do with him beyond his wallet. I tried, but things were never the same between us. When he turned eighteen, my parents told him who his father was." Reece's hand beneath mine tenses. "But it was too late."

"What do you mean?"

"His father had passed away a year earlier. Jacob vowed he would never forgive my parents for denying him the chance to know him, and in all the years since, he's kept alive his fantasy of the perfect father. He slips in and out of my parents' lives when he needs something, and each time he leaves them scarred by more guilt. And for years I took that guilt onto myself, beating myself up for my betrayal, taking the blame for the state of our family."

I know where this is going. "That's why you started drinking."

"Mostly." There's a rough edge to his voice. "A heavy burden of guilt and being alone too much with one's self is a bad combination."

"Your parents are still together?"

"They are, though after one of Jacob's visits—like the night I was late for your uncle's dinner party—the strain returns. Fortunately, their faith always puts them back together."

And Reece, it would seem. "I see."

"Maybe now you can understand why I acted the way I did when I found out I have a daughter."

"Yes."

"I don't know when the timing will be right for her to know the truth, but you can't put her off forever, Maggie. She's mature, especially for her age, and you need to start making plans."

"I am."

He stares at me, and something swells between us that makes it hard to breathe. Pulling his hand from beneath mine, he reaches up and runs his thumb across my bottom lip. "Maybe we can make this work."

Harder yet to breathe. *This?*

A moment later, *this* becomes a kiss, and I lean in and let myself feel it, not as a teenager heady with her ability to make a guy so crazy he'll forget his values and his faith, but as a woman who longs to be loved. Still, I shouldn't let this happen, not with what stands large between us even if he can't see it.

Please be Devyn's father. I slide my hands over his chest and curl them around his shoulders. *Be the one.*

And if he isn't? What will you do with what's happening between you now? What about when he finds out?

I told him there were others, and he chose not to believe me. He had his chance—

So speaks the old Maggie.

But I want this.

Temporary happiness followed by acres of hurt for everyone, especially Devyn.

"Maggie?"

I open my eyes to find Reece has pulled back.

"What is it?" he asks.

Show him.

I'll lose him.

Better now than later.

"Is it my drinking problem?"

I blink. "What?"

"The night I attended the recovery group and sat with you in the sanctuary, I sensed there was something you wanted to say. But then you ran off. Were you going to tell me about Devyn?"

"I wanted to, but..." Pulling my hands away, I shake my head. "It wasn't your drinking. I was just scared. Like I'm scared now."

"Why?"

"Because of what I need to show you."

Wariness enters his eyes, and I feel bad that he has no idea how wary he ought to be. "What?"

Is this how Marie Antoinette felt when told it was time to keep her date with the guillotine? Setting my teeth, I push back my chair, and Reece follows me inside and into the living room, where I pause at the sight of Devyn. I meant to cover her with a throw, but Reece beat me to it, and the fatherly gesture deepens my conviction that this can't go on.

I enter my office and flip on the light. "Close the door."

I hear the soft click as I go around my desk, and when I look up, Reece is standing on the other side, eyebrows raised.

Knees weakening, I lower to my chair. "I'm sorry."

He frowns.

"More sorry than you can know."

His lids narrow, and though I can barely see his eyes, I feel the sharp edge of his gaze.

"I was straight with you." I open the bottom desk drawer and reach to the back. "Or nearly so."

"What are you talking about?"

Closing my hand over the envelope, I nod at the chair in front of my desk. "Would you sit down?"

"That bad?"

Worse. "Please."

His suspicion is so thick, it's as if the pressure has changed in the room. However, he finally lowers into the chair.

Hands in my lap, I press the envelope between my palms. "Promise me you'll finish the statue for Uncle Obe."

"I always honor my commitments."

"Thank you." I rub the envelope between my hands, trying to warm my cooling self with the heat generated by friction.

"What is it?" Reece prompts.

"I…"

"Yes?"

"Well…" So much for my mouth being my best asset. The loquacious one is loquacious no more. "I wasn't lying when I said you may not have fathered Devyn."

His jaw hardens.

"The lying was done when we were seventeen and I so wanted you to take me back that I denied the rumors about Gary Winsome." I swallow. "One night after a game, he offered to take me home. We got to drinking and…as you know, drinking and being lonely—wanting to be with someone who isn't there—is a bad combination."

Reece doesn't say anything for a long time, but when his lids lift, his eyes are like cold dark pools. "All right, so Devyn could be Gary's."

Hands beginning to shake, I slide the envelope across my desk. "Please look at that."

"What is it?"

"I received it the day you found out Devyn's age and jumped to the conclusion you're her father."

"The letter Mrs. Templeton gave you?"

"Yes."

He pulls out the pages and unfolds them. With a last glance my way, he gives his attention to the lab report. I know the moment he reads the results, because he stiffens. "Negative." He looks up.

I nod. "For Gary." I see the startle in his eyes and wish this were the end of it. "That's why I went to Charlotte—to get a sample of his DNA, like I was trying to get from you the day you found me outside your hotel room. I was only moments from slipping into your bathroom to get a few stray hairs when I heard the elevator."

"*That's* why you were there?"

I clasp my hands hard. "And why a week earlier I slipped into the Grill 'n' Swill after you lunched there in hopes of snagging a chewed toothpick or straw. But after the hotel incident, you were so suspicious I decided to go after Gary's DNA instead."

His nostrils flare. "Why didn't you come right out and ask me to be tested?"

Lord help me. "That would have required an explanation."

"And confession."

Of my high school lies. "Yes, but since I was fairly certain

Gary was Devyn's father, it didn't seem necessary, and I didn't want you to... I couldn't stand the thought of you knowing what I was all those years ago and seeing me that way still." I shake my head. "I'm not. I've changed."

Reece pushes a hand through his hair. "Have you?"

That hurts.

He sits forward. "Explain the sudden interest in who fathered Devyn. Is it child support you're after? I have done well for myself."

"Money?" It comes out shrill, and I clamp my lips for fear of awakening Devyn. When I speak again, it's on a whisper. "All I wanted was to prove you aren't Devyn's father so that I..."

"What?"

"When she found out you and I dated in high school, she asked if you were her father, so I set out to prove to myself I hadn't lied."

"You told her I wasn't."

I start to raise my hands in the universal sign of pleading, but that's so pitiful. "I didn't think. I reacted."

He slowly nods. "All right, but now that we know she is mine, how are you going to explain it to her?"

I feel sick. "We still don't know that you're her father."

His brow slams down. "You aren't making sense." He shakes the lab report. "If she isn't Gary's—"

"Chase Elliot." Really sick. "Devyn might be his."

Reece stares at me, saying more with his eyes than words could ever express.

And all I can do is repeat, "I'm sorry," and catch my breath at how husky my emotionally cramped drawl sounds.

Reece rises and drops the lab report on my desk. "Anyone else I should know about?"

I tip my head back. "No, it's you or Chase."

His stare makes me feel like an ugly stain. "You haven't changed, Maggie Pickwick."

That sends me to my feet. "How dare you!"

Be Skippy—

No! I don't want to be Skippy! I want…

I squeeze my eyes closed. I want to be Maggie. Maggie who kept her baby. Maggie who was saved. Maggie who *is* saved. Yes, she messes up big, but all who say *I do* to their Savior still make mistakes.

Okay, Lord, I'm ready to be me. All I ask is that Your patience continue to outweigh my weaknesses.

I open my eyes to find Reece tensed for what brews beneath my angry words. "You're wrong. I'm no longer that spoiled teenage girl who seduced you to prove I was desirable, who trampled other girls' feelings, who let anger and pride and alcohol land her in the backseat with Gary and then Chase, who nearly aborted her baby."

He flinches.

"I'm Maggie Pickwick, a grown woman who left that other life to make a new life for her and her daughter." My eyes sting. "And I did, and I believe I did it well, but you came back and I set myself up for another big mistake. Pride again—wantin' you to see only the new Maggie, not the old."

"Why?"

His question is unexpected, but this time, pride is not getting a hold of me. "I stopped obsessing over what other people thought of me a long time ago and started focusing on how God sees me. But it turns out your opinion matters more than anyone else's."

His mouth softens slightly.

"Even God's apparently, since I knew He wanted me to be honest with you and I ignored His nudges and the advice of those He used to try to reach me. Though I have changed, there's obviously some of the old Maggie in the new, and I'm sorry she showed up."

He doesn't say anything.

Wet eyes, tight throat, a chest full of sorrow, I'd say we're about done here. "You'll be tested?" I ask, only to add, "Not that I want anything from you. It just would be good to know for Devyn's sake so when she's old enough..." Like when Jacob was old enough. He's thinking it too, I know he is, though I can no longer look him in the eye.

"I should leave." He turns away.

"Reece?"

At the door, he looks around.

"This is my fault, not Devyn's."

"I know she isn't to blame." He twists the knob. "Good night."

A minute later, the front door closes. I drop into my chair, and all that stuff in my eyes, throat, and chest takes it as a cue to pour forth. I hug my arms on the desk, then bury my face in them as hurt squeezes out of all my tight places. I thought I knew what sorrow was, but this is worse. This goes deep, and all because I don't just care what Reece thinks of me. I care *for* him. This is no teenage infatuation. And this is no ordinary bad day.

CHAPTER 24

DAILY WORD CALENDAR
for Highly Successful Career Women

[**insip'id** (*adjective*): dull, unexciting, lacking stimulating qualities]

MONDAY, MARCH 29

"Hey! What happened to your routine?"

"Hmm?" I stick my head back inside the house and grimace at the sight of my backpacked daughter flipping through my daily word calendar. I forgot about that.

"You've missed eight days." She looks up. "Not that it's a loss. I mean, come on—fustigate, lubricious, abnegation?" She shakes her head. "*Highfalutin words* is what Aunt Skippy would say."

And does. I may find ways to incorporate them, but they're nearly always substitutions for more common and easily understood words.

"Of course"—the teasing goes out of her voice—"I did recently hear someone use today's word." She pulls it off the pad. "*Insipid.* It's what Bradley called me when he was assigned to be my lab partner."

Bradley, who she's always going out of her way to help, even if it means interrupting our evening to meet him at the library and help him research a paper. "Oh, yeah? When was that?"

She looks away. "Last Friday."

Friday… She was moody when I picked her up from school and turned moodier when I wiggled my way out of her suggestion that we stop by the auction house so she could see how the statue is progressing. Then came the silent treatment, and there was nothing I could do short of telling her I doubted Reece would be receptive to her company, which would have raised questions I'm not prepared to deal with just yet.

Devyn gives a short laugh, but I feel her hurt, even without knowing what *insipid* means. "You know," she says, "what's wrong with simply saying, *Ugh, I have to partner with Devyn Pickwick. She's so dull.*"

I feel my mommy claws come out. Obviously, Bradley is moving up in the world, and Devyn doesn't fit the new parameters. "Oh, Dev." I step back inside and wrap my arms around her before the teenager she will soon officially become realizes what's happening.

"I'm okay, Mom," she muffles into my arm.

I ease back. "You are not insip—" I grunt. "You are not dull. You're amazing." I sweep her brown hair out of her eyes and loop it behind an ear. "And beautiful."

Eyes slightly distorted by her lenses, she sighs. "Thanks. I just wish I had a…" She closes her mouth and steps back. "I'm going to be late for school."

She wishes she had a father. That's probably what she was going to say. What she doesn't know is that today, after waiting over a week for Reece to let me know if he'll submit to paternity testing, I'm taking the matter into my own hands. But this time, I'm doing it right.

"I've been praying for this day." Chase's sixty-some-year-old mother stares up at me as she grips the door as if for fear of toppling over.

I frown. "I'm sorry?"

She nods vigorously, causing her cap of silver-streaked brown hair to swing. "If you wait long enough and your prayer is in His will, the good Lord will answer it the way you want."

Is she off a little? Maybe a lot? "Um..." I smile. "I'm Maggie Pick—"

"I know who you are."

She should. After all, not only has she lived in Pickwick for as far back as I can remember, but she occasionally attends my auctions, the last time being when I nearly ran her over in my haste to get away from Reece and Yule.

Her lightly lipsticked mouth curves. "I've been waiting for you a long time."

She has?

"Mercy! Where are my manners?" She swings the door wide open. "Come in."

I'm no longer certain of the wisdom of that, and so I stick to the stoop.

"Please. I know what you need. And I have it."

Something turns inside my mind, searching for focus, and when my mind finds it, spins out of focus again as if to look too closely on her words would transform me into a pillar of salt like Lot's wife.

"Maggie?" She says with more familiarity than there should be between us. "You are here about Chase, aren't you?"

Another brief moment of focus that makes me swallow hard. "I need to get in contact with him."

"Yes. You should come in."

Feeling like Gretel should have felt when she entered the

witch's house, I assure myself that not only am I half her age but nearly a foot taller, and I cross the threshold.

She closes the door behind me. "We can talk in the parlor."

Didn't the spider say something like that to the fly?

With a spry stride, she leads me to the rear of the little house. "Here we are." She enters a bright room, the large windows of which overlook a wooded area that borders the Pickwick lands. "I was fixing to have me some coffee. Join me?"

"Yes, thank you."

"Make yourself at home. I won't be long." She starts past me, but pauses. "I am so glad you came." Then she leaves me to once more try to bring everything into focus. She's been expecting me, knew I was here about Chase—

"Pecan sandies?" she calls from beyond.

"Not for me, thank you." As I move farther into the room, I take in the dark plank flooring, plump sofa, vibrantly colored chairs reminiscent of little girls' summer dresses, an antique writing desk that would make many an auctiongoer raise the paddle, and family pictures around the walls.

As I start to lower into a daffodil-print armchair, Chase's senior picture grabs my attention. But it's the picture of a spectacled, gap-toothed girl beside it that makes me hover inches from the seat. No, that can't be.

I blink. It can be. I cross the room, and as I draw near the picture of the girl as she appeared two years ago, goose bumps break across my skin.

I stop before the side-by-side pictures. That's my child hanging on this woman's wall. And that's creepy. I *am* Gretel! This woman has no connection to Devyn, and yet she's stuck her on her wall as if *my* daughter is her—

Focus. Sharp Focus. I clap a hand to my mouth. This is why Mrs. Elliot has been waiting for me. She thinks Devyn is her granddaughter.

I turn and move from picture to picture around the room.

There are two more of Devyn. In one, she's leaning against a low wall outside the front entrance of her school and reading a book (probably waiting for me to pick her up). In the other, her slight figure is partly enveloped by a beanbag in the school library, a book clasped to her chest, eyes closed. There's also a framed newspaper clipping of the two of us standing outside the auction house on the day of its grand opening.

"I imagine you understand now," Mrs. Elliot says.

I turn to where she stands in the doorway holding a tray. She gives what seems a hopeful smile, and I feel horrible for what I have to ask of her that could reveal this all to be an illusion.

"Yes."

Smile brightening, she hurries to the coffee table and sets the tray down. "I've worked hard at being patient." She lifts the coffee. "Waiting and waiting." She pours a steaming stream of brown into one cup, then the other. "Hoping for a space to open up where I could squeeze myself into my granddaughter's life." She sets the pot down. "Just a little space, mind you. It gets mighty lonely here in Pickwick, what with being a widow and my Chase long gone."

"Gone where?"

She settles on the edge of the sofa and waves me over. "Sit down."

Discomfort crawls all over me, and I'm tempted to ask outright if she has a lock of her son's hair and, if not, where I can find him. Instead, I return to the daffodil-print armchair opposite the sofa.

"I suppose you're curious as to how I got hold of the pictures of Devyn."

As I reach for my coffee, I glance at the picture alongside Chase's. "Yes."

"I took them myself when I substitute taught at her school." Her narrow shoulders puff with pride. "Was very discreet about it."

"I didn't know you were a substitute teacher."

"For more than two years now—ever since I decided to find out if that girl is mine, like I always wondered when you turned up pregnant. Chase denied he was the daddy, but the older she got, the more I saw him in her. She's mine all right."

Her claim makes me stiffen.

"I even had her in my class twice." She flashes two fingers. "And let me tell you, those were the best days."

Working over how to tell *her* she's jumped the gun, I sip at the coffee.

"So, Maggie, how do you propose we tell Devyn?"

With a clink just shy of chipping china, I return the cup to its saucer.

"Should we do it together?" she presses on.

"Mrs. Elliot—"

"Call me Corinne. We *are* family."

Maybe. "Corinne, I don't know how to tell you this, but..." I draw a deep breath. "I don't know if Chase is Devyn's father, and that's why I came. I need—"

"But *I* know."

She *thinks* she knows. "Chase isn't the only guy I was with—"

"I know that too."

My breath deserts me.

"That's why when that mean boy at school stuck gum in Devyn's hair a couple years back—and earned himself a hefty detention, I might add—I offered to cut it out for her."

Someone stuck gum in Devyn's hair? She never told me.

"It was an opportunity I couldn't pass up." Mrs. Elliot rises to her feet. "And that's how I know our girl is an Elliot."

Then she...?

"Let me show you." She crosses to the antique writing desk and opens it out. Shortly, she hands me an envelope. "It's the proof you're looking for."

Oh, Lord. I know what this is. With trembling fingers, I pull out the lab report. The samples submitted by Corinne Elliot are a positive match. Her son is Devyn's father.

Not Reece. Not. Reece. What remains of my hope flickers at the end of its wick.

"I'm a grandmother, and since that's all that's left to me, with your permission, I'd like to enjoy it."

I look up at her where she stands beside me, clasping and unclasping her hands as if for fear I'll refuse her.

I want to. I want to reject that her son, who didn't step forward and share in my responsibility, is my daughter's father. I want to say the lab is mistaken. I want to rip up this stupid report and get as far from here as possible. But she *is* Devyn's grandmother.

One more flicker, then the hope goes out. I set the report on the coffee table and clear my thick throat. "You said being a grandmother is all that's left to you. What about Chase? I tried to trace him over the Internet but couldn't find anything. Is he…?"

She shakes her head. "As far as I know, he's alive."

"As far as you know?"

Regret seams her mouth, but then she breathes deep. "Second year of college, he went to Brazil for spring break. Got caught up in drinking and women and decided to stay. I was angry with him for throwing away his scholarship but kept thinking he'd get some sense and come on home. But not even when his daddy died. Last I heard from Chase was three years ago when he needed money to"—she leans forward and whispers—"pay his way out of prison for dealing drugs."

My daughter's father is a drug dealer.

"I would have had to sell my house. I would have lost everything, and he probably would have gone back to dealing. So I told him no." Tears trembles on her lashes. "I haven't heard from him since."

I breathe in, breathe out, then rise and lay a hand on her shoulder. "I'm sorry. I didn't know."

She grabs a napkin from the tray and pats her eyes. "Nobody does. People ask after him sometimes, but I tell them he's doing fine, and I pray he is. Lord willing, one day he'll show up on my step like you did." Her smile is weak. "One answered prayer at a time."

Am I really an answered prayer? It's selfish of me considering how lonely this woman is, but I can't help but wish God had answered *my* prayer that Reece would be in my daughter's life, and therefore mine, even if only a little bit.

"We'll work it out, Mrs. Elliot. All I ask is that you let me determine when and how to tell Devyn."

She nods. "I've waited this long."

"Thank you." I square my shoulders in preparation to leave.

"Maggie?" She hands the report to me. "Now that you know, I won't be needing this."

I hesitate before taking it.

"One more thing," she says.

"Yes?"

"I'm awful sorry about your artist."

"Excuse me?"

"I'm guessing you were hoping he was Devyn's daddy. Everyone knows how much you liked him—even my Chase, who you wouldn't have looked twice at if that Thorpe boy hadn't broken up with you."

Feeling as if my soft underbelly is exposed, I grip my arms against my sides. "I'd better get to work."

"You will call me, won't you?"

"Of course. I just need time to digest this." I stick a hand out. "Thank you, Mrs. Elliot."

"Oh no." She stands and hugs me as best she can with the considerable discrepancy in our heights. "We're family."

I tentatively pat her back, but though I command myself to

verbally acknowledge our newfound connection, I can't. Not yet. But maybe in time.

❧

I STARE at the empty balcony where I left Devyn to do research for a school project a half hour ago. I know where she's gone. She's where I firmly told her not to go so she wouldn't disturb his work—or my day any more than it's already been disturbed right off its axis.

I hurry across the stage. I shouldn't have trusted her, should have known she would defy me. If only I had dropped her at home. And I would have if Mrs. Templeton hadn't whispered into the phone that Mr. Orley was threatening to take his business to Puck & Sons if I didn't immediately meet him at the auction house to discuss the sale of his one-hundred-unit storage facility.

"Teenage rebellion," I grumble as I thrust aside the curtains and stomp backstage. I don't stop stomping until partway down the corridor when I catch the sound of music and see the light cutting across the floor that reveals Reece's studio door is open. I approach with less fervor, and as I near, I hear Reece's voice above some sleepy jazzlike crooning.

"Insipid?"

"That's right—insipid."

She's telling *him*? The temptation to stand outside the door and eavesdrop is strong, but I enter.

"I can see why that bothers you," Reece says from behind the screen, "but as my mother is fond of saying, consider the source."

Devyn sighs. "I know, but...I kind of like him—as far as an almost thirteen-year-old girl can like a guy—and I thought he liked me. But then for him to call me that..."

"Are you? Insipid, I mean."

I falter, outraged he would ask.

To my relief, Devyn gives a resounding, "No!"

"That's my girl."

His girl? I stop dead.

"Er, could you…hand me the one…with the curved blade?" His stop-and-go speech evidences I'm not the only one who realizes he said that. He clears his throat. "So, if you aren't insipid—and I can vouch that you aren't—why do you think he said that?"

"Probably because Amanda was there."

She didn't tell *me* Amanda was present.

"Then he was playing to an audience."

"That's how it looked."

"Peer pressure."

Devyn sighs again. "So now he wants me to forgive him—"

She didn't tell me that either.

"—and I'm not sure I can."

"Was his apology genuine?"

"Seemed like."

"That one," Reece says, "the one with the looped blade."

Metal clatters on metal, then Devyn says, "Here you are."

"In my experience," Reece says, "people do foolish things when they worry too much about what others think of them."

I'm one of those experiences—on the schools steps that morning, feeling for Yule when she fell, doing an about-face in hopes of returning Vicky to her proper place and ensuring my leadership, then Reece…

"That doesn't mean they aren't good people," he continues. "It means they have a weakness you need to be aware of, especially if you want to continue to pursue a relationship with them."

He didn't want to continue pursuing anything with me. Well, not exactly. It may have taken him thirteen years, but he did kiss me again. And I blew it.

"You're right. I guess I just need to proceed with caution where Bradley's concerned, especially when Amanda is around." Devyn harrumphs. "Honestly, sometimes it's hard to believe she's human, she can be so mean, but I try to pray for her like Jesus says to pray for those who persecute us. I ask God to grow her up for the better, just like He did my mom."

As I near the partition, I brake hard.

"She's changed, you know, not anything like the way she was in high school."

Oh no. Amanda has been instrumental in educating my daughter about my past, but exactly how far past Maggie Pickwick 101 has her education progressed?

"Of course, you've probably noticed."

Reece doesn't respond, and my guess is he's searching for a change of subject.

"Want to see how I do this?" he asks.

"Oh." Her voice sags. "Okay." I hear her footsteps on the cement floor.

"You need to work the clay before you form it over the armature. Warm it between your hands like this. And then press it in place."

"It's hard to believe that's going to be a face."

"The details come later. Now try it. Give me some clay right here where his ear will be."

In the silence, I imagine my daughter kneading the clay between her small palms. Shortly, she says, "Here?"

"Yes."

"Hmm. It's even harder to believe that's going to be an ear."

"Trust me, Devyn."

Trust Reece. All well and good providing you don't trust him with your heart. Not that it's his fault mine feels as if it's been put through a juicer.

"You know what?" Devyn sounds triumphant. "I do trust you."

I hold my breath through the silence, expecting it to end with Reece changing the subject again, but he says, "I appreciate that, Devyn." And the gentle, yet weary way he says it makes it sound like surrender, as if he's done with the fight he's been fighting this past week, as if he accepts she's his.

Not good. I step around the screen. "Devyn."

She swings around where she stands alongside the pedestal on which sits the crude figure of Uncle Obe's statue, a jumble of plumbing parts, wire, mesh, foil, and now clay.

I don't mean to look at Reece, but I do, and his smile runs away without a backward glance.

I turn to my daughter. "I've been looking for you. It's time to go."

"Now?" She shows me her hands that evidence the gray of the clay she was kneading. "I'm helping Mr. Reece."

"I'm sure he appreciates it, but we need to get home."

"But I've finished my homework." There's a whiff of a whine in her voice.

Angst, moodiness, and now whining.

"Actually," Reece says, "I'm pretty much done for the day. But you're welcome to stop by another time, Devyn."

Disappointment tugs at her mouth as she looks at Reece, but when she shifts to me, her mouth lowers even more.

I nod at the sink across the room. "Wash your hands and we'll go."

She walks stiffly past me.

I follow her with my eyes. Why does it have to be so hard?

"I want to talk to you," Reece says in my ear.

I turn and am surprised by a softening around his eyes. Not that he's anywhere near smiling, but the anger I'm owed appears to have mellowed.

I wait until Devyn turns on the water. "I want to talk to you too." I have to tell him.

His pine green eyes hold mine hostage. "Tonight."

So soon? I want to get it over with, but I need some time to process what has happened. "I can't."

"Tomorrow then."

"How about Wednesday morning?"

"I'll be on a plane to D.C. to discuss a museum project and won't be back until the weekend."

Too much breathing room…not enough breathing room. "All right, tomorrow. My office?"

"What about the dock at Pickwick Lake, if it's still there?"

In all its shabby glory, though who knows for how much longer. With the revitalized Pickwick putting its best face forward, the dock may soon have an entirely new face. Even so, it's not the place to tell him what needs to be told. I live here, and the last thing I want is for a memory we made there years ago to be overwritten by what will send him away from Devyn and me forever.

"I'd prefer my office."

He opens his mouth but closes it when Devyn shuts off the water.

"Ten?" I suggest.

"Ten it is."

Devyn ignores me all the way across his studio, pausing only to retrieve her backpack from beside the door. A moment later, I step into the corridor and pull the door closed. And tomorrow, I will close yet another door. For good. And bad.

CHAPTER 25

As far as the east is from the west, so far has He removed our transgressions from us. (Psalm 103:12)

So do not fear, for I am with you; do not be dismayed, for I am your God. I will strengthen you and help you; I will uphold you with my righteous right hand. (Isaiah 41:10)

Peace I leave with you; my peace I give you. I do not give to you as the world gives. Do not let your hearts be troubled and do not be afraid. (John 14:27)

MARCH 30

"Do not be afraid." Head bent to the Post-it note on which I wrote the Scriptures that Skippy said would help me through what lies ahead, I read them again. The first is assurance of forgiveness for my past. I know He forgave me long ago and continues to forgive me for my stumbling and bumbling, but knowing it and feeling it aren't always the same, especially where an unresolved piece of my past is concerned.

"But soon to be resolved." I glance at my watch. Ten till ten.

The second and third Scriptures are the Super Glue of the words of God and Jesus, not only to help me overcome fear when I reveal Mrs. Elliot's proof of paternity, but to strengthen me with the expectation of peace afterward.

I close my eyes and silently run through the Scriptures, having determined to memorize them and put more of an effort into *God's* daily word. As for my Daily Word Calendar for Highly Successful Career Women, I gave it to Devyn as we were going out the door this morning and told her to dispose of it as she saw fit.

She smiled before remembering she doesn't feel like smiling, then tossed it in the trash. As hard as it will be to get through this with Reece, it will be harder to reveal the truth to her. Unfortunately, it looks like I'm on my own. More unfortunately, I'm no nearer to giving her a father. And the right man isn't going to magically appear. But maybe with lots of prayer.

The door opens, and I'm surprised that Reece didn't knock.

"There you are." My mother bustles in.

I stand quickly from behind my desk. "Mom, what are you doing here?"

She halts so abruptly that she sways like a sprung doorstop. "What?" Her thinly arched eyebrows take to her brow. "I can't drop by to visit my daughter? I have to make an appointment?"

"Er, no." I hurry forward. "Of course you can drop by." Though I'd love it if she dropped by just to drop by, not to drop bombs like when she showed up with Devyn's Father Quotient. I give her stiff figure a hug. "It's just that I have a meeting in a few minutes."

"So you don't have time for your mother."

"Of course I do, but could we...?" Jolted by her suddenly moist eyes, I roll up my tongue and gently draw her to the chair before my desk.

She drops into it like a skinny sack of potatoes and grasps my hand with what seems like desperation.

I bend down. "What's wrong?"

"Your father." She squeezes my fingers so hard, I would whimper if I wasn't afraid of the news she's about to deliver.

"He sent the money and wrote that he'll continue to do so, but…"

Then he hasn't passed away. I let my shoulders slump. Though my relationship with him was off and on depending on his mood, which was dependent on the state of our finances, he afforded more affection than my mother, who mostly saw me as a reflection of her dreams. And he did give wonderful piggyback rides when I was little.

My mother sniffles. "He says if I won't come to him, he wants a divorce. He's tired of waitin' and says my job of raisin' you and Luc is long past. He's ready to move on and spend the rest of his life with someone." Her grip tightens, causing the tips of my fingers to purple. "If not me, then someone else."

"Mom, do you still love Daddy?"

"Of course I do! Jonah *is* the man I chose to spend my life with." Her indignation turns to anger. "Then he had to mess it up by getting in trouble with the law and runnin' off to Mexico —and it's all your Uncle Jeremiah's fault."

Piper's father.

"If he hadn't run a dirty campaign, your father wouldn't have felt obliged to do the same."

And the mayoral campaign wouldn't have earned the Pickwicks more scandalous headlines.

My mother releases me and puts her face in her hands. "Divorce. What is he thinking? He still loves me. I know he does."

Fingers tingling to life, I touch her shoulder. That's when I hear footsteps. Ten o'clock.

Do not fear. Do not be afraid.

"I think you should go to Mexico."

My mother peeks above her fingertips. "You do?"

"Yes, Luc and I will be fine."

She sits straight up. "What are you sayin'? That you don't need me?"

"I'm saying Daddy needs you more. And you need him. It's time."

"What about Devyn? I am her grandmother. The only one she has, mind you."

Past her shoulder, Reece halts in the doorway. Bad timing. Or could it be God's timing? As Reece starts to withdraw, I act on impulse to hold him there. This *is* what I need to discuss with him. "No, Mom, you aren't Devyn's only grandmother."

Reece hesitates and I momentarily meet his gaze.

My mother makes a sound of disgust. "That Skippy woman—"

"I'm not talking about her."

"Then"—she swallows loudly—"who?"

Peripherally, I see Reece shift in the doorway. "Corinne Elliot."

"Elliot?" My mother's voice pitches high. "You're saying that you and that maladjusted son of hers—"

"Chase is Devyn's father."

She searches my face, and when she looks away, I peer past her shoulder.

Reece's lids are narrowed. Does he think I'm lying again?

"But I thought Reece Thorpe might be her father," my mother says almost mournfully.

I know how she feels—times one hundred. "I hoped he was, but he isn't."

"How do you know?"

I turn to my desk and retrieve the envelope meant for Reece. "I went to see Mrs. Elliot yesterday to try to track down Chase for DNA testing." She doesn't need to know he's in prison. "She gave me this." I hold up the envelope. "For a long time, she suspected Devyn was her granddaughter, so she paid for a paternity test a couple years ago."

She jerks as if struck. "How would she do that without your knowledge?"

"She substitute taught at Devyn's school. Apparently, Devyn got gum in her hair one day, and Mrs. Elliot helped her get it out."

My mother's eyes widen, causing her lashes to splay beneath her eyebrows. "Why, that sneaky—!"

"No." I lay a hand on her shoulder. "She didn't want to cause trouble. She's lonely, what with her husband having passed on and a rift between her and her son. I think she just needed to know she still has ties to someone in this town."

My mother opens her mouth, closes it, and eases back in the chair. "Well, it's not like I don't know where she's coming from. It hasn't been easy all these years without Jonah, especially since..." She sighs. "Well, mothering was always difficult for me, and it's not as if my children are clamoring to be with me now that they're all grown up."

The tug in her voice and the defeated slope of her back shows this isn't all *woe is me*. She feels it—deeply.

I look to the doorway, but all that remains of Reece is his retreating back. And I feel the loss of him—deeply.

Putting my arms around my mother, I close my eyes. "It's been ages since you came to our house for dinner. How about this Saturday night?"

She draws a quick breath. "Why, yes. I...I would like that."

"Me too. I love you, Mom."

She nods into my shoulder. "I know you do, Maggie."

IT WOULD BE easy to pretend I don't see him sitting on the bench near the block of granite that patiently awaits his masterpiece, but cowardly. Deciding the errands I was going to run can wait, I cross the street on shaky legs. Thus, I'm almost grateful to lower to the bench. Almost. I angle toward Reece where he reclines two feet away with his hands clasped behind his head.

"I'm sorry." Nothing new. I hug my sweater to me, though it's actually pretty warm for early spring. "I know I went about that wrong."

He continues to direct his sunglassed gaze at the block. "It wouldn't have changed the outcome."

"That you're not Devyn's father." It doesn't need to be clarified, but just in case he needs an opening...

He unclasps his hands, and when he turns to me, the afternoon sun flashes off his dark lenses. "Do you know why I wanted to talk to you?"

I think I do, and that makes it hurt even more.

Do not let your heart be trampled—er, troubled.

"About tryin' to make it work between us?"

He nods. "For Devyn's sake."

I appreciate the sacrifice he was prepared to make, but I long for it to have been, even just a little bit, for his sake and mine. "For Devyn. Right. And now, look"—I toss up my hands—"all that worry for nothing."

He blows out a breath and sits forward. "You didn't have to tell me about Gary or Chase. You could have let me go on believing the rumors were just that."

"I could have, and as ashamed as I am to admit it, I considered it."

He removes his sunglasses and those green eyes pierce me. "Why?"

Oh, to be coy, but he doesn't deserve that. I rise from the bench, the better to make my exit. "Because you fit the The Father Quotient perfectly." A furrow appears between his eyebrows, but I plow through my pride. "Not only do I agree with Devyn that you would make a wonderful father, but there would have been something in it for me as well." I avert my eyes. "But now...well, all I ask is that you keep your commitment to my uncle and put something on that block of granite before he no longer cares."

"That's all you want from me?" Reece says in an uncharacteristically coarse voice.

Is this an opening? No, just wishful thinking. "That's it." I turn and walk away. And he lets me.

❧

I RAISE my hand and tap, something that's hard to get used to in my own home.

"Come in," Devyn calls.

I enter her room, and she half smiles at me where she sits in the middle of her bed with books spread around her.

Grateful she still appears to be in the good mood she treated me to when I picked her up from school, I smile back. "It's nine. Ready for bed?"

"Yep."

Bedtime has rarely been an issue for her, since she's the one who keeps current on the amount of sleep necessary for someone her age to lead a healthy, productive life.

She starts stacking the books, and I help her gather them until one of the titles catches my eye—*Immerse Yourself in Sculpture*. Oh, dread.

"The process is fascinating. Did you know—?"

"Devyn." I sink to the mattress beside her. "I know you like Reece Thorpe and...I do too, but once the statue is raised in the town square, that's the end. Reece will leave and there isn't any reason for him to come back."

Her expression wavers, but she bolsters it with a full-on smile. "There's you. If you and Mr. Reece decide to do something about all that silent stuff that goes on between you, then he has a reason to return. And stay."

The depth of her hope makes me want to cry.

"So I've decided to educate myself about sculpture, which will allow me to more easily converse with him—one of the keys to a successful stepfamily." The mischievous glint in her eyes barely registers as my dread gains momentum.

Swept by the feeling of falling, I reach for her hand and am grateful when she lets me take it, since this moment may not come again for a long time.

"You okay, Mom?"

I will strengthen you. I will uphold you with my righteous right hand.

"I will be, but I think it's time I told you a story—about who I was before you were born and before I knew Jesus. About what I did and how it changed my life in ways that seemed harsh, but...were actually blessings. Do you know why?"

She rolls her eyes, but in a playful way. "Does this have something to do with me?"

I hate that my smile feels sad, but it's that kind of day. "*Everything* to do with you. So, are you ready to know who Maggie Pickwick was before Devyn Pickwick came into her life?"

As she studies my face, worry creeps across her brow. "This isn't going to be a fairy tale kind of story, is it?"

"No, but despite the hard things I need to tell you"—my throat convulses—"it is the most wonderful story I have ever lived."

Devyn considers me, then scoots near as if to prop me up. And it's all I can do not to gather her tightly to my side. "Okay. I'm ready."

Please, Lord, let her really be ready for this. And ready to forgive.

"You remember that day on the way home from school when you told me Amanda said I didn't know who your father was?"

She stiffens. "Yeah."

Uphold me, Lord.

"She was right, Dev. I didn't know."

She looks away for a moment but doesn't make for the other side of the bed.

"Though not to the extent she believes. Let me tell you what happened."

And I do, as gently as possible, while taking my cues from her lowering brow and the tension in her slight frame that flicks on and off like a lightning bug. I tell her about Reece and the peer pressure to which I succumbed that day when Yule fell. I tell her about the bad choices I made after Reece broke up with me and the drinking that coaxed me into compromising positions with two other boys. I tell her about finding out I was pregnant and how scared I was. I gloss over my mother's reaction and focus on Skippy's championing of my pregnancy.

"You could have aborted me," Devyn speaks for the first time since I began.

It tears at me just to think about it. "Yes, but Skippy knew how badly I would miss you and that I would never be whole without you. She helped me see that."

"You could have given me up for adoption."

"That too. But then I held you and fell in love—real love. I couldn't let you go, and Skippy made sure I didn't have to."

Please don't ask about your grandmother.

"Grandma was scared for you." Devyn stares at me from behind her lenses, reminding me of a wise old owl.

"She was, but you have to know she loves you."

Devyn sighs. "She just has a harder time showing it than Aunt Skippy, but I think a lot of that's because of Grandpa. She's really lonely without him."

Yep, wise old owl. I apologize for telling her Reece couldn't be her father when it was still a possibility, then tentatively reveal the results of Gary's DNA sample and Chase's, and how I came by both.

"Oh." She lowers her chin, pulls her feet in, and stares at her toes. "I have another grandmother."

"You do, and while I don't know her well, she seems nice."

"She is." Devyn gives a little laugh. "The gum in my hair incident, right?"

"That's how she found out."

"And she waited this long—waited for you to come to her?"

"Uh-huh."

She shakes her head. "That's sad, especially since she's probably lonelier than Grandma."

"I think so. Though she doesn't want to do anything that would make you uncomfortable—won't rush it—she longs to know you better."

Devyn nods. "We'll go slow. But what about…?" She looks away. "Do you think I'll ever meet my real father, seeing as he's in prison?"

I hate that I had to tell her, but she asked where Chase is and I couldn't put her off. "Do you want to meet him?"

"Eventually, but only if he straightens himself out."

"He might."

She mulls that over, then lays a hand on my knee. "Okay, so not a fairy tale, but that doesn't mean there can't be a happy ending. You and Mr. Reece could still get together."

I nearly tell her how impossible that is, but there's been enough reality for one day.

"I may not be his daughter, but he likes me, I like him, and more important, you two like each other. So you never know."

I know. "Now that everything's out in the open, are you okay, Dev?"

When she doesn't immediately answer, nausea stirs my stomach, but finally she says, "Yeah, and I suppose I ought to be grateful to Amanda. Though she was being a bully by telling me all that junk, I guessed there was some truth to it, so this wasn't the shock it could have been." She frowns. "You know, I feel bad for her, especially if she doesn't turn out like you did."

A warm shiver goes through me. "You think I turned out okay?"

She slides her small hand from my knee to my fingers. "Better than okay."

Moisture fills my eyes. "I'm sorry I wasn't straight with you sooner." I sniff. "I was just so ashamed that I didn't know who your father was, and I couldn't stand the thought of burdening you with a past like mine. You were so young, and maybe you still are—"

"No." She squeezes my hand. "The timing's good, Mama."

Did she just call me Mama? It's been so long. I swallow, swallow, swallow, but the sob pushes through.

Devyn puts her arms around me. "Everything's goin' to be all right."

I turn my face into my little girl's hair and breathe in God's gift. "I love you, Dev."

She pats my back. "I love you too, Mama."

Thank You, Lord. "And I'll try to give you a father."

"I'd like that, but only if he's a keeper. For both of us."

I'm relieved she didn't try to push Reece on me again. But then, we Pickwick women must be realistic. "Yes," I whisper, "for both of us."

CHAPTER 26

"For I know the plans I have for you," declares the Lord, "plans to prosper you and not to harm you, plans to give you hope and a future.
(Jeremiah 29:11)

APRIL 29

Nothing hope-shattering happened between Reece and me. At least, that's the way it might appear from the outside.

Work continues on the statue, and I have it on good authority that Reece's master weaver will do this town proud. Though he and I politely avoid each other, Devyn refuses to be affected by what I revealed a month ago, continuing to seek out Reece when she accompanies me to the auction house. To his credit, his behavior toward her doesn't appear to have changed.

To my relief, Devyn and Corinne are easing into one another with weekly after-church visits. My mother is another matter, but she tries to keep her jealousy in check. And she is going to Mexico—only for a visit, she says, but she sparkles when she talks about seeing Daddy again, so maybe longer.

I crumple the aluminum foil that wrapped the chicken salad sandwich I made this morning, then push open a lobby door and brake at the sight of three men on the sidewalk outside the theater —Macon times two and their unshaved, tobacco-chewing father.

"Sizin' it up, they are." Mrs. Templeton pokes her baseball cap-covered head out of her office.

"They can size all they want. We're not closin' up shop."

"They seem to think so." She raises her eyebrows. "You want that I should go get Reece Thorpe? He'll send them slitherin' back down their snaky holes."

"No! I mean, I can handle them." I set my shoulders and stride forward on unfortunately low heels (just had to be practical today).

"Gentlemen." I step onto the sidewalk. "What can I do for you?"

Puck pushes his tongue into his tobacco-stuffed lip, causing it to bulge larger. As for Macon, his choice of mouth fixation is a toothpick he works awkwardly from one corner to the other as he leers me up and down.

Ugh. I would never have guessed there was an art to toothpick chewing, but Reece has it down in a nonoffensive way. Hmm. Was he working on one the day he intervened when Macon showed up at my auction? I believe so.

"Hey, Mag," Macon mumbles around the toothpick.

Macon's younger brother gives an appreciative sigh. "Maggie."

I really wish he'd get over his crush. Compared to his brother, he's not so bad, but he really isn't a nice person. I tilt my head to the side. "I presume you're standing out here for a reason."

"Yep," Puck says.

"Mighty fine buildin', this," Macon muses, causing the toothpick to waggle alarmingly. "Lots of potential."

I start to cross my arms over my chest but remember Piper's admonition that the defensive posture weakens my presence. "I'm very happy with it."

"Pity," Macon says. "You see, we've"—the toothpick flops onto the sidewalk—"we've—"

"You are going to pick that up, aren't you?" I glare at him.

"Uh...sure." He bends and pinches the object of what I'm certain is a newly acquired fixation. "Like I said, we've put in an offer on this buildin'."

I feel a chill, though I shouldn't, since I have the situation under control. Or nearly so. I glance at the bank across the square where I've been spending quite a bit of time. "You don't say."

"Yep." Puck again, showing no evidence of his ability to yammer up a storm at auction. "Sent our offer over to Artemis Bleeker yesterday."

My uncle's aged attorney who must not have alerted Piper. But then, his mental faculties aren't much better than Uncle Obe's.

Macon takes a step back. Still pinching the toothpick, he frames his hands overhead. "*Puck & Sons Auction World*. That'll look nice, won't it, Pa?"

"Is everything all right?" a painfully familiar voice asks.

I swing around and there he is, closer than I've been to him in weeks.

"*You* again," Macon grumbles.

Yes, once more showing up when the question arises of whether or not I'll hang on to the auction house.

Thank you very much, Mrs. Templeton.

Catching sight of her on the other side of the glass door, I give her a *look*. She raises an eyebrow, flaps a hand as if to shoo a fly, and ambles toward her office.

When I look back at Reece, I nearly smile at the ease with

which he clenches a toothpick. "Yes, everything's fine. Puck & Sons and I were just discussing—"

"Our ac-qui-si-tion of this here theater." Puck enunciates each syllable.

"That's right." Macon clamps down on the dirty toothpick, as if issuing a challenge to Reece.

Oh, dear, it's the battle of the toothpicks. Who will prove himself the master of the manly art of toothpick chewing, and who will cry wee wee wee *all the way home?*

As Reece draws alongside me, I look sidelong at him. No contest.

"My understanding," he says, "is that Obadiah Pickwick wants to keep the theater in the family."

How did he come by that? Or is he bluffing?

"Well, now"—Macon's toothpick waggles, and he bites down with a *crunch*— "we'll see about that."

I press my lips hard. No matter how ridiculous, obnoxious, or mean some people are, I don't laugh at them anymore. It's cruel. Reece doesn't either, though a glance his way confirms the muscles of his mouth are taut.

Macon rubs a thumb across his fingers. "Money talks, you know."

True. I consider the bank again. *Come on, big shot loan officer. Get it approved.*

"Have a good day, Mr. Puck…& Sons." Reece puts a hand on my elbow and turns me toward the door.

I'm too breathless to protest. *It's just a hand on your arm,* I tell myself. *And it's just for show.*

Reece pushes the door inward and guides me inside.

"Thank you." I walk beside him across the lobby, certain we're being watched. "Not that I needed your help, but…" I look across at him. "Thanks."

Green eyes on mine, he removes the toothpick and drops it in his shirt pocket. "You're welcome."

"Oh, and thank you for letting Devyn continue to visit your studio. She enjoys watching you work and, I'm sure, talkin' your ear off."

"She's good company." He releases my elbow, pushes open one of the doors that lead into the theater, and nods me through. "Would you like to see how the statue is coming along?"

As the door swings shut behind us, I face him. Is this an olive branch? Maybe. I disregard the hope that searches for a spark to return it to life. He's just trying to make the best of the time he has to spend in my presence.

"I think I'll wait for the official unveiling. After all, good things are worth waiting for."

He considers me, and it may be my imagination, but I sense he's gearing up to say something profound, but all that comes out is, "True."

Yes, just my imagination. "I almost forgot that I need to talk to Mrs. Templeton. Have a good day." Averting my gaze, I back my way through the door. Once it's between us, I peer at the sidewalk outside. Puck & Sons have cleared out, and from the sound of it, Mrs. Templeton is on the phone. No problem. I need to make a phone call myself.

"Haven't heard anything about it," Piper says a couple minutes later, "but Artemis did take Uncle Obe to breakfast this morning, so..."

"You don't think Uncle Obe would sell to them, do you?"

"Of course not."

"I need to talk to him, Piper. Can I come over?"

"Sure. Hey, Bridget's delivering a load of fertilizer around noon. Why don't you come a little early, and after you and Uncle Obe talk, we can all sit down to lunch."

"I'll be there."

"I DO THAT TOO," my uncle's voice scores the book-scented silence.

I pull my shoulder from alongside the window and turn from the view outside to where Uncle Obe advances across the library with Piper shadowing his measured stride. "You do what?"

He pauses halfway across the room and grips the back of a sofa, as if to catch his breath, and my chest grows heavy at the noticeable decline from this past Sunday when I sat beside him in church. Maybe he's just having a bad day.

"Daydream," he says, "though my version is surely less..."

I glance at Piper who presses her lips as if to keep from supplying the word and earning his wrath.

"...less...without thinkin'..." He wags the fingers of one hand before him as if flicking through file folders. "Deliberate! Yes, my daydreams are less deliberate than yours. Obviously." With a sad chuckle, he continues forward, and Piper drops back when he settles in the chair behind his desk.

"Come 'round here where I can see you, Magdalene."

I cross to the chair before his desk and lower into it. "I need to talk to you about—"

"Did you know I sent my letter to...?" His eyes grow large. "...to..." He blinks. "...my children?"

Antonio and Daisy, whose names have left him. Hopefully, only temporarily.

I start to rise. "You know, maybe we should talk later."

"No!" he practically shouts, then more quietly, "Later doesn't work for me anymore."

I glance at Piper. She smiles sadly.

"Now..." He sits forward and clasps his hands on the desk. "You want to talk to me about the theater, hmm?"

"I understand you've had an offer on it."

"Two, actually."

My heart beats faster. The more people there are who want one thing, the more it costs. I know it by heart.

"I heard Puck & Sons put in an offer, but who was—?"

"Is that you, Bridget?" He peers past me. "Well, this is good timin'. Come on in."

My cousin considers us as she pulls at the fingers of her striped work gloves and steps into the room on legs encased in worn, dirt-smudged jeans. She looks out of place in the elegant library, but more out of place is what's probably in her fanny pack—Reggie, the opossum.

She halts alongside me. "What's this about?"

The slight movement of her fanny pack draws my gaze. Yep, Reggie. Since normally she would pop her nose from beneath the flap, she must be sleeping.

"It's about the theater," Uncle Obe says, "and the Pickwick estate. I'm sorry to have to be the…the…" He grunts. "…the you-know-what of bad news, but I'm gonna have to sell the estate."

Bridget's hands at her sides snap into fists.

"'Course we knew I'd have to, but it seems like sooner rather than later." Another chuckle, though this is tinged with bitterness. "You see, I've decided to give the th-theater to Maggie and Devyn as their inheritance."

As all of me breaks out in chill bumps, I look to Piper.

She shakes her head, obviously just as much in the dark.

Joy starts to bubble to my surface, but then I see Bridget's fists go white.

"Sell the estate." There's a tremor in her voice.

"Yes. Were I to sell the theater, I could hold out awhile longer, but the end would be the same. So, sooner rather than later."

"Meaning the Pickwick Estate is destined to become a theme park," Bridget says with her own brand of bitterness. "Or a bunch of tightly packed single-family homes. Or both. Or worse!"

He sighs. "I don't know, but I've been thinkin' on this a while, and it's the right thing to do for all my kin, including you."

"Me?" Her laugh is not pretty. "Me?"

"I'm gonna break off... What was it? Uh, I think I told Artemis thirty acres. Anyway, I'll break off some acreage nearest town for you so you can expand your...plant business like you been wantin' to do."

Her face is a struggle between gratitude and desperation. It's a beautiful gift, so perfectly *Bridget* just as the theater is so perfectly *Maggie*. Still, she loves this land, its heritage, and its wildlife.

She steps to the desk. "Maybe I can find someone to buy the estate who won't bury it. I've been lookin' into organizations that finance private wildlife preserves. They're hard to crack, but if I could just have some more time—"

"Time I do not have, Bridget. I gotta set things right now."

"But—"

"It's gonna be hard for me too, especially if this"—he taps his head so hard I hear the knock on bone—"doesn't take me sooner. I love this place, and I don't want to be lookin' out the back window of a...thing with wheels and knowin' that what I'm seeing is for the last time."

My throat tightens, Piper's chin quivers, and Bridget whispers, "I understand."

He jerks his chin around. "You did mail that letter to my children, didn't you, Piper?"

Her eyes brim with tears. "I did."

"Good, good." He reaches across his desk and pats one of my dreadlocked cousin's hands. "It's the only solution."

Not true. It's the only way to give me what I want—

No, that's not true either. There is another way, one I was working out for myself. And still could. It would require sacrifice, but I was willing to make it. And still am.

I sit up straight. "You should sell the theater, Uncle Obe."

He leans to the side to peer around Bridget. "You are going to have that building, Magdalene."

"Yes, I am." I rise and step alongside Bridget. "But I'm going to *buy* it."

"What?"

I laugh. "I've been working with the bank for the past few weeks to get a loan for the fair market value. And I have a good chance of being approved, especially considering how much my business is growing. Though the estate will still have to be sold, it will give Bridget more time to find the right buyer."

I look from Piper, who is staring big-eyed at me, to Bridget, whose mouth is hanging open so unbecomingly I'm tempted to pop her chin into place. But despite my height, I'd probably end up flat on the floor, my smaller cousin straddling me, dreadlocks thwacking me in my face.

"I may need a cosigner and may have to rent out a portion of the theater to cover the mortgage payments, but I know I can do it."

Slowly, my uncle eases back in his chair. "I suppose that could work."

"It will."

Piper raises a hand, as if requesting permission to speak. The band that appeared on her ring finger two weeks ago, causing a stir in Pickwick, glints. "If you do need a cosigner, I'm in."

"And me," Bridget says. "My nursery's doin' all right for itself."

I could hug them both. "Thank you."

"Pickled corn," my uncle murmurs, eyes suddenly unfocused.

My cousins and I exchange glances.

I sigh. "Goodness, who would have thought, hmm? I came here worried about Puck & Sons and—" I frown. "Uncle Obe?"

He blinks back to us, and I'm struck by the urge to put an arm around him to hold him here. "M-Magdalene?"

"You said you had two offers for the theater. Who else?"

He scratches his forehead. "Oh, yes." He smiles, and the dry skin at the corners of his mouth ripple like disturbed water. "The artist."

I teeter on my low heels. "Reece?"

"That would be him—offered to buy it when I visited his studio last week." His eyes brighten. "That statue is going to be a beautiful thing. *The Master Weaver*—that's what he's titled it." He turns to Piper. "It ought to have a Scripture inscribed on a plaque. Piper, I'm going to need the family Bible."

If the heart truly has strings, mine are about to snap. "Why would Reece want to buy the theater? He's here for only a while longer."

"Maybe."

Oh, Lord.

Uncle Obe puts an elbow on the chair arm and cups his chin in his hand. "I asked him, *Why do you want that old theater? You don't have any ties to Pickwick, not a one.*"

I recall the pained disappointment on my uncle's face when I revealed who fathered Devyn. Piper said that day was among his worst.

"Then I said…what did I say? Oh! *Nothin' holding you here.* I let that sit, then asked the big one. *Or is there?*"

I hold my breath.

He grins.

"And?" I croak.

"He loves you, Maggie."

I feel a flicker of hope, and it frightens me. "No, he doesn't." The words are shrill but followed by softly spoken words. "He said that?"

"No."

Of course not.

"I saw it in his eyes—realization, panic, d-denial, the need to pretend I was a crazy old fool. Of course, that last part didn't require much pretendin'. But the man does love you."

"Or just wants to control her," Bridget suggests.

"Oh!" I throw my hands up. "He doesn't love me, and he isn't trying to control me."

Uncle Obe pushes out his lower lip. "Then you probably should find out for yourself what is what."

"I will." I consider Piper. "I know we were going to have lunch, but I need to get back to town." To find out what is what. Nothing more. Of course, something more *would* be nice, but I'm not holding out hope. Not much.

CHAPTER 27

I almost walk past him, focused as I am on reaching his studio, but the feeling of being watched makes me glance across the street to the grassy square that spring has lovingly turned green.

Reece is sitting on the granite block, legs hanging over the side, hand in a bag of something. And he *is* watching me.

I hesitate to change course. After all, I thought I had a couple more minutes to work through what I want to say. Maybe this isn't such a good idea.

For I know the plans I have for you...

"But I don't, Lord," I whisper. *Is Reece part of Your plan, or has what Uncle Obe said gone to my heart?*

Uncertainty makes me want to walk on, but then I might never know. Might never ask the question, and an unasked question might never be answered. And then Reece will be gone. I step from the sidewalk and cross the sleepy street.

"Hi," I say as I near.

"Hi."

Shortly, my heels sink into the damp ground from this

morning's light rain. In this instance, I'm grateful I eschewed (yes, a daily word throwback) high heels.

I halt before the granite block and look up at where he sits above me. Only then do I become aware of the slight breeze as it runs its fingers through his black hair, shifting strands in and out of his eyes.

"I…um…" How do I say this? And what if his answer hurts?

...plans to prosper you and not to harm you...

"Boiled peanuts?"

I blink at the bag Reece offers. "Why?"

He shrugs. "Because they taste good?"

"No, why did you make an offer on the theater?"

He looks away, paying too much mind to where he sets the bag beside him. "Why do you think?"

"I…" So much for my mouth being my best asset. "I don't know."

He clasps his hands between his knees. "Neither did I. That is, until your uncle stuck his nose where it wasn't welcome."

I'm flickering again, though I shouldn't. Humiliation of Pickwick proportions could lie in that direction. I don't dare, but… "Do you love me, Reece?"

Oh. My. Lord.

He pulls back slightly, but after a moment, a smile appears. "Good question."

...plans to give you hope...

I moisten my lips. "But is the answer good?"

He reaches a hand to me. "Let's find out."

I stare at his calloused fingers, afraid to believe what this could mean. If I do, what if this moment is the height of the memory of this day? It's a long way down from here.

"Maggie?"

...plans to give you hope...

I consider his mouth out of which he softly spoke my name.

Lord, just help me to receive as You would have me receive. I put my hand in his.

Reece helps me up onto the granite block, but even after I've settled beside him, he doesn't release my hand. That has to be a good thing.

"You have to know"—he lifts his gaze to mine—"that the last thing I wanted when I came back here was to have anything to do with Maggie Pickwick."

Not good. Can't be. But he is still holding on. "I know."

"But I've come to realize I had nothing to worry about."

Not good at all.

"Because that Maggie isn't here. You are."

...plans to give you hope...

"I told myself it was teenage infatuation all over again, that the bits of you I was drawn to years ago were just that. Bits. That the bigger part of you was the girl on the school steps with Yule, and you had simply become more sophisticated in dealing with others. I struggled with evidence to the contrary, but after I kissed you that night..."

Yes, *that* night.

"...it became harder to look back. I wanted to know you from that point forward. That's why when I thought Devyn was mine..." He closes his eyes for a moment. "...I was angry. Yes, for the years when I should have been a father to her, but also for letting myself believe you had changed. You should have told me."

"I was ashamed and afraid you would judge me by my past and my lies."

He sighs. "I would have. And I did. Then, just as I settled into the idea of being Devyn's father and started to think we could give her a real family, I found out she isn't mine. And I was angry all over again, mostly because I should have been relieved. I'd convinced myself the plans I was making were out of obligation, but all I felt was disappointment over the loss of

Devyn *and* you." He turns my palm up and stares at it. "You asked if I love you."

...plans to give you hope...

He gazes into my eyes, and it's as if he's holding open a door to allow me to see into him. "I feel strongly for you, and I want to feel more, but we need to take our time getting there."

No declaration of love, but there's something oddly comforting in that. No rush. Time to allow our relationship to root deep and wide so that when adversity comes, what lies below holds firm. Though I long to hear *I love you,* it means more that he wants to do it right.

His mouth tilts. "That is, providing you feel what I think you feel for me."

"I do."

"So, you'll give me a chance to know you and Devyn better?"

Hope. "And for us to know you." I smile, but only for a moment. "You'll be leaving in a few months." How much of a chance is that?

Reece holds my stare with a confidence I want to believe. "When I approached your uncle about buying the theater, I did so to help you keep it out of the clutches of Puck & Sons. However, there was the added benefit of giving me a reason to stay in Pickwick—that I could make my studio here permanent."

Then he wants to greatly improve our odds—here, in little old Nowhere, North Carolina. "You still can. I've been working on a loan to buy the theater, and today my uncle agreed to sell it to me. So once you finish *The Master Weaver,* I could rent the space to you. That is, if you still want to know my daughter and me better."

His gaze moves all over my face, and I feel it almost as strongly as if it were the brush of his fingers. Then he leans toward me. "Put me down for a thousand square feet." And his mouth touches mine.

...plans to give you hope and a—

—future," I whisper against his lips.

True, in the end, my future and Devyn's may not include Reece, but I believe God is at work here. In fact, if I let Him, my faith, rather than my mouth, could become my best asset.

Dear Reader,
I hope you enjoyed Maggie and Reece's love story. If you would consider posting a review of Nowhere, Carolina *at your online retailer—even if only a sentence or two--I would appreciate it. Wishing you many more hours of inspiring, happily-ever-after reading.*

READERS GUIDE

1) In high school, Maggie was a stereotypical cheerleader—self-centered, superior, and more concerned with hair and makeup than the state of the world. What are your experiences with this type? Do you believe the stereotype is justified? Why or why not?

2) The painful irony of Maggie's adult life is that her daughter is an outcast like those Maggie looked down on throughout high school. Thus, her proud behavior haunts her. What in your teenage past has haunted you?

3) Skippy has every reason to dislike Maggie, but she heaps grace on the young woman and offers encouragement on her journey toward salvation. Has anyone heaped grace on you? Do you feel you deserved it? Have you ever heaped grace on another person?

4) When Devyn asks if Reece is her father, Maggie's quest to discover who fathered her daughter begins with a lie. As with so many lies, it backs Maggie into a corner out of which she can

escape only by coming clean. However, Maggie chooses instead to add to her lie. When has a lie backed you into a corner? What choice(s) did you make?

5) Reece lost a church commission when he was open about his recovery from alcohol dependence. Have you ever been penalized for being honest about your struggles? What did you need that you were denied?

6) We are called to forgive, even if a person doesn't acknowledge an offense. Though Yule is outwardly accepting of Maggie, it isn't until Maggie asks for forgiveness that Yule is able to truly forgive her. Why is it so hard to forgive a person who doesn't seem repentant? How does forgiveness benefit the forgiver?

7) When Maggie finally owns up to her DNA quest, Reece is angered by her deception and initially is unwilling to offer forgiveness. When have you struggled to forgive another person? Were you able to overcome your struggle? If so, what steps did you take to extend forgiveness?

8) Maggie's relationship with her mother is strained by past offenses. Thus, they miss out on the blessings of a loving mother-daughter relationship. How strong is your relationship with your mother? Are there issues you need to address to receive the blessings that Maggie and her mother begin to enjoy once they pack away the past?

9) Maggie corrects her thoughts and behavior with a reminder to *Be Skippy.* However, she finally realizes she needs to be herself—the Maggie who kept her baby, was saved, and made a good life for herself and her daughter. A mentor who sets a

godly example is a blessing, but as we grow as Christians, we need to move toward reliance on our own faith. Do you agree?

10) Uncle Obe's early onset dementia first appeared in Piper's story, *Leaving Carolina*. His deterioration continues in Maggie's story. How close have you come to someone with dementia? A parent? Spouse? Relative? Friend? How has this heartbreaking disease affected you?

RESTLESS IN CAROLINA EXCERPT

BOOK THREE: SOUTHERN DISCOMFORT SERIES

SHE'S ALL ABOUT GOING GREEN. COULD HE BE HER WHITE KNIGHT—OR WILL HE MAKE HER SEE RED?

Tree-huggin', animal-lovin' Bridget Pickwick-Buchanan is on a mission. Well, two. First she has to come to terms with being a widow at thirty-three. After all, it's been four years and even her five-year-old niece and nephew think it's time she sheds her widow's weeds. Second, she needs to find a buyer for her family's estate—a Biltmore-inspired mansion surrounded by hundreds of acres of unspoiled forestland. With family obligations forcing the sale, Bridget is determined to find an eco-friendly developer to buy the land, someone who won't turn it into single-family homes or a cheesy theme park.

Enter J.C. Dirk, a high-energy developer from Atlanta whose green property developments have earned him national acclaim. When he doesn't return her calls, Bridget decides a personal visit is in order. Unfortunately, J.C. Dirk is neither amused nor interested when she interrupts his meeting—until she mentions her family name. In short order, he finds himself in North

Carolina, and Bridget has her white knight—in more ways than one. But the things Bridget doesn't know about J.C. could mean the end of everything she's worked for…and break her heart.

❧

CHAPTER ONE

Your presence is eagerly anticipated
at the wedding of
Ms. Trinity Templeton to Mr. Bart Pickwick
on Saturday, July 24, 10:00 a.m.
at the Pickwick Mansion
1001 Pickwick Pike
Pickwick, North Carolina
Reception to immediately follow
Regrets Only

Deep breath. "…and they lived…"

I can do this. It's not as if I didn't sense it coming. After all, I can smell an *H.E.A.* (Happily Ever After) a mile away—or, in this case, twenty-four pages glued between cardboard covers that feature the requisite princess surrounded by cute woodland creatures. And there are the words, right where I knew the cliché of an author would slap them, on the last page in the same font as those preceding them. Deceptively nondescript. Recklessly hopeful. Heartbreakingly false.

"Aunt Bridge," Birdie chirps, "finish it."

I look up from the once-upon-a-time crisp page that has been softened, creased, and stained by the obsessive readings in which her mother indulges her.

Eyes wide, cheeks flushed, my niece nods. "Say the magic words."

Magic?

More nodding, and is she quivering? Oh no, I refuse to be a party to this. I smile big, say, "The end," and close the book. "So, how about another piece of weddin' cake?"

"No!" She jumps off the footstool she earlier dubbed her *princess throne*, snatches the book from my hand, and opens it to the back. "Wight here!"

I almost correct her initial *r*-turned-*w*, but according to my sister, it's developmental and the sound is coming in fine on its own, just as her other *r*'s did.

Birdie jabs the *H, E,* and *A*. "It's not the end until you say the magic words."

And I thought this the lesser of two evils—entertaining my niece and nephew as opposed to standing around the reception as the bride and groom are toasted by all the happy couples, among them, cousin Piper, soon to be wed to my friend Axel, and cousin Maggie, maybe soon to be engaged to her sculptor man, what's-his-name.

"Yeah," Birdie's twin, Miles, calls from where he's once more hanging upside down on the rolling ladder I've pulled him off twice. "You gotta say the magic words."

Outrageous! Even my dirt-between-the-toes, scab-ridden, snot-on-the-sleeve nephew is buying into the fantasy.

I spring from the armchair, cross the library, and unhook his ankles from the rung. "You keep doin' that and you will bust your head wide open." I set him on his feet. "And your mama will—"

No, Bonnie won't.

"Well, she'll be tempted to give you a whoopin'."

Face bright with upside-down color, he glowers.

I'd glower back if I weren't so grateful for the distraction he provided. "All right, then." I slap at the ridiculously stiff skirt of the dress Maggie loaned me for my brother's wedding. "Let's rejoin the party—"

"You don't wanna say it." Miles sets his little legs wide apart. "Do ya?"

So much for my distraction.

"You don't like Birdie's stories 'cause they have happy endings. And you don't."

I clench my toes in the painfully snug high heels on loan from Piper.

"Yep." Miles punches his fists to his hips. "Even Mama says so."

My own sister? I shake my head, causing the blond dreads Maggie pulled away from my face with a headband to sweep my back. "That's not true."

"Then say it wight now!" Birdie demands.

I peer over my shoulder at where she stands like an angry tin soldier, an arm outthrust, the book extended.

"Admit it," Miles singsongs.

I snap around and catch my breath at the superior, knowing look on his *five*-year-old face. He's his father's son, all right, a miniature Professor Claude de Feuilles, child development expert.

"You're not happy." The professor in training, who looks anything but with his spiked hair, nods.

I know better than to bristle with two cranky, nap-deprived children, but that's what I'm doing. Feeling as if I'm watching myself from the other side of the room, I cross my arms over my chest. "I'll admit no such thing."

"That's 'cause you're afraid. Mama said so." Miles peers past me. "Didn't she, Birdie?"

Why is Bonnie discussing my personal life with her barely-out-of-diapers kids?

"Uh-huh. She said so."

Miles's smile is smug. "On the drive here, Mama told Daddy this day would be hard on you. That you wouldn't be happy for Uncle Bart 'cause you're not happy."

Not true! Not that I'm thrilled with our brother's choice of bride, but...come on! *Trinity Templeton?* Nice enough, but she isn't operating on a full charge, which wouldn't be so bad if Bart made up for the difference. Far from it, his past history with illegal stimulants having stripped him of a few billion brain cells.

"She said your heart is"—Miles scrunches his nose, as if assailed by a terrible odor—"constipated."

What?!

"That you need an M&M, and I don't think she meant the chocolate kind you eat. Probably one of those—"

"I am *not* constipated."

Pull back. Nice and easy.

I try to heed my inner voice but find myself leaning down and saying, "I'm realistic."

Birdie stomps the hardwood floor. "Say the magic words!"

"Nope." Miles shakes his head. "Constipated."

I shift my cramped jaw. "Re-al-is-tic."

"Con-sti-pa-ted."

Pull back, I tell you! He's five years old.

"Just because I don't believe in fooling a naive little girl into thinkin' a prince is waiting for her at the other end of childhood and will save her from a fate worse than death and take her to his castle and they'll live..." I flap a hand. "...you know, doesn't mean there's anything wrong with me."

Isn't there?

"It means I know better. There may be a prince, and he may have a castle, and they may be happy, but don't count on it lasting. Oh no. He'll get bored or caught up in work or start cheatin'—you know, decide to put that glass slipper on some other damsel's foot or kiss another sleeping beauty—or he'll just up and die like Easton—"

No, nothing at all wrong with you, Bridget Pickwick Buchanan, whose ugly widow's weeds are showing.

"See!" Miles wags a finger.

Unfortunately, I do. And as I straighten, I hear sniffles.

"Now you done it!" Miles hustles past me. "Got Birdie upset."

Sure enough, she's staring at me with flooded eyes. "The prince dies? He dies and leaves the princess all alone?" The book falls from her hand, its meeting with the floor echoing around the library. Then she squeaks out a sob.

"No!" I spring forward, grimacing at the raspy sound the skirt makes as I attempt to reach Birdie before Miles.

He gets there first and puts an arm around her. A meltable moment, my mother would call it. *After* she gave me a dressing down. And I deserve one. My niece may be on the spoiled side and she may work my nerves, but I love her—even *like* her when that sweet streak of hers comes through.

"It's okay, Birdie," Miles soothes. "The prince doesn't die."

Yes, he does, but what possessed me to say so? And what if I've scarred her for life?

Miles pats her head onto his shoulder. "Aunt Bridge is just"—he gives me the evil eye—"constipated."

"Yes, Birdie." I drop to my knees. "I am. My heart, that is. Constipated. I'm so sorry."

She turns her head and, upper lip shiny with the stuff running out of her nose, says in a hiccupy voice, "The prince doesn't die?"

I grab the book from the floor and turn to the back. "Look. There they are, riding off into the sunset—er, to his castle. Happy. See, it says so." I tap the *H, E,* and *A*.

She sniffs hard, causing that stuff to whoosh up her nose and my gag reflex to go on alert. "Weally happy, Aunt Bridge?"

"Yes."

"Nope." Barely-there eyebrows bunching, she lifts her head from Miles's shoulder. "Not unless you say it."

Oh dear Go—

No, He and I are not talking. Well, He may be talking, but I'm not listening.

"I think you'd better." Miles punctuates his advice with a sharp nod.

"Okay." I look down at the page. "...and they lived..."

It's just a fairy tale—highly inflated, overstated fiction for tikes.

"...they lived happily...ever...after."

Birdie blinks in slow motion. "Happily...ever...after. That's a nice way to say it, like you wanna hold on to it for always."

Or unstick it from the roof of your mouth. "The end." I close the book, and it's all I can do not to toss it over my shoulder. "Here you go."

She clasps it to her chest. "Happily...ever...after."

Peachy. But I'll take her dreamy murmuring over tears any day. Goodness, I can't believe I made her cry. I stand and pat the skirt back down into its stand-alone shape. "More cake?"

"Yay!" Miles charges past me.

Next time—

No, there won't be a next time. I'm done with Little Golden Books.

Birdie hurries to catch up with her brother. "I want a piece of chocolate cake."

I want to go home. And curl up in my hammock. And listen for the hot air to stir up a breeze and creak the leaves. And try not to think about my lost happily ever after.

I set my shoulders and thoughts against memories and check my watch. I've been in this dress and these shoes for four hours. It's time.

Outside the library, I pause at the grand staircase, step out of the heels, and try to flex my toes. They're numb. I declare, if I have to have anything amputated, someone will hear about it. I retrieve the shoes and hobble into the hallway, through the kitchen, and outside into a bright day abuzz with wedding revelry.

No matter the season, the beauty of Uncle Obe's garden always gets to me, especially now that it and the entire Pickwick estate will be passing out of Pickwick hands. For months I've about killed myself trying to find a way around the sale that will provide restitution to those our family has wronged as well as something of an inheritance to kin, but everywhere I turn, I find walls.

"Hey, babies," my sister's voice rings out, "did you have fun with Aunt Bridge?"

I halt and look toward the linen-covered table where a large three-tiered wedding cake was the centerpiece earlier. Only one tier remains, and it's had its share of knifings.

"Yeah, it was okay." Miles holds out a plate for his mother to fill. "Until she made Birdie cry."

My little sister's gasp shoots around those standing in the twenty feet between us. "What happened?"

"Aunt Bridge didn't want to finish the book. Did she, Birdie?"

Hugging it to her, she shakes her head.

"Well," Bonnie slides a piece of cake onto each of their plates, "maybe she's tired."

"Nuh-uh." Miles leans his face into the cake, takes a bite, and with crumbs spilling and frosting flecking, says, "She told us the prince gave the glass slipper to another girl and kissed Sleeping Beauty and then died."

"Oh." Bonnie's lids flutter. "Huh." Sunlight glints off the knife in her hand as she meets my gaze. "Well." She forces a smile. "Hmm." Back to her daughter. "We know that's not true, don't we, Roberta baby?"

Birdie bounces her head. "They lived happily... ever...after."

Time to go. But as much as I long to run, I'm civilized, despite rumors to the contrary. I search out my brother where he stands with his bride, Trinity, my mother and father, and

Uncle Obe in the gazebo built for the reception. A quick congratulations and I'm out of here.

"Bridget!"

I hurry past Maggie's brother and his latest wife, around Uncle Obe's attorney, between—

"Don't think I don't know you can hear me, Bridget."

And so can everyone else. I swing around. "Bonbon!"

Bonnie rushes the last few feet. "I know we're mostly family here, but I'll do you the kindness of talking to you in private." She points to the mansion.

I don't care to accompany her, but neither do I want to throw a shadow over Bart's special day. And going by the eyes turning our way, it's fast approaching. "Of course." I set off ahead of her, raise my eyebrows at Maggie when she turns a worried face to me, and give Piper a shrug.

In the kitchen, I cross to the pantry and raise my hands in surrender. "I didn't mean to say what I did. I certainly didn't mean to make Birdie cry."

Bonnie steps near, causing my hackles to rise. I don't like sharing my personal space, even with my own sister. My *hotheaded* sister. And then she goes and puts a finger in my face, and I have the urge to bite it. But I won't. That would end badly.

"I trust you with my most precious possessions," Mama Bear growls, "and what do you do? Try to steal my babies' sweetness and innocence with that *life is dark* outlook of yours."

"I'm sorry. I'm just on edge, what with tryin' to find a buyer for the estate who won't turn it into a crowded development or a nasty theme park. And now Uncle Obe has listed it, and the real estate agents are swarmin'. It's too much, Bonbon."

She narrows her lids. "Don't you Bonbon me!"

Though she's five foot two, one hundred ten pounds to my five foot six, one hundred twenty pounds, I know she could take me down if I riled her enough to forget we're grown women. But that's not the reason I pull back on my emotions. I do it because I'm the one who lost control in front of her twins. I clear my throat. "I didn't mean to—"

"Yes, you did!" The finger again. "You can't stand for anybody to be happy if you aren't happy."

Ignore the finger. "That's not true." My throat strains from the effort to keep my voice level. "I—"

"Woe is me. My husband's dead, and I refuse to get over it. Even though he's *four* years gone!"

I suck breath. *Oh, God. I mean, no! I'm not talking to You. Of course, I could use a little self-control if You've got some lying around. But that doesn't mean I'm talking to You.*

"Have mercy on us, Bridget, 'cause you know what? Grief is contagious. And I don't want my babies catchin' it."

A chill goes through me. I never thought of grief as contagious, but I suppose it could be.

"So stop casting your widowhood like a net, catching others in it and saying stuff like that just because Easton is dead."

Just because? I feel warm again. "Maybe…" My voice sounds all wet and booggered up with that stuff that booggered Birdie's nose. "Maybe I said it because my *constipated* heart needs an M&M."

Bonnie startles so hard I find myself checking the whereabouts of my hands to be certain I didn't slap her. Not that I would, although she might slap me.

"Oh." She steps back and gives a nervous laugh. "They told you I said that?"

Having regained some of my personal space, my shoulders unbind. "Out of the mouths of babes."

"Uh, yeah. I didn't realize they were listenin'. They had their earphones in and were singing along with their iPods." She frowns. "Or so I thought."

I pull a hand down my face. It's a good thing I never took to makeup. "It's all right. I know you didn't mean it to hurt me."

She raises her hands palms up. "I needed to talk it out with Claude. You know how I worry about you."

Not really, but we live a ways from each other, averaging two visits a year when she and her family drive through on their way to elsewhere. However, that pattern will be broken when my sister and her husband leave the twins with their grandparents for eight weeks while they're in the Ukraine to study the development of children awaiting adoption. My mother will have her hands full, but I'll help however I can.

"I really am sorry for what I said to Birdie and Miles. It won't happen again."

Once more, Bonnie invades my space, and this time I'm the one who startles when she lays a hand on my cheek. "Oh, Bridget, how are you going to keep that promise when you're still wrapped up in all those widow's weeds?"

Don't pull back. It's your sister, not a widow sniffer trying to get a hook into the lonely little widow.

Pressing my dry lips, I long for my Burt's Bees lip balm. "I've accepted my loss. It's just taking me longer than some to adjust. But I am adjustin'."

Her eyes snap to slits. "Really?"

"Yes."

"No, if you were adjusting, you wouldn't still be clinging to your wedding ring."

I catch my breath. "There's nothing wrong with wearing it."

"Yes, there is." She grabs my hand and lifts it before my face. "It's time. *Past* time. You have to let him go."

I do *not* like this. "I have. I accept he's gone—"

"No, not gone. That implies he can come back. He's dead. And you have to call it what it is and get on with your life. Not yours and Easton's life. *Your* life."

I pull my hand free. "I'm getting there."

"Well, at this rate, you'll be in your own grave before you arrive."

My own grave. I feel cold. At thirty-three, if I live to see my body stoop and shrivel, that will be a very long time. Like one big unending yawn.

Bonnie tilts her chin forward. "That makes me plain sad, so take off the ring."

Now? That's asking too much. "I will when—"

"Take it off."

"But—"

"You made my little girl cry!"

I did. And though I don't care to look too deeply into myself, here I am, still holding tight to my interrupted life with Easton.

"Give me your hand."

I don't want to, and yet I raise my arm.

With surprising gentleness, Bonnie cups my fingers in hers. "It's for the best. I promise."

I hold my breath, and she tugs. And tugs. Then wrenches.

"Ow!" I try to pull free, but she sets her jaw and lifts her foot, as if to brace it against me for leverage.

"Stop it!" As I push her away, the ring comes free.

"Got it!"

Staring at it between her thumb and forefinger, I feel the air go out of me. How long before my deflated self pools on the floor? It doesn't happen. I miss the constriction around my finger, and I may be a bit numb, but that's it. Am I in shock?

"You okay, Bridge?"

"I think so."

She presses the ring into my palm. "Put that in a good place where you won't be looking at it every day."

I close my fingers around it. How's that for a good place?

She smooths her blouse. "Now let's go outside so everyone will see I didn't yank out those ugly dreadlocks of yours."

"They aren't ugly."

"They aren't beautiful. Just"—she waves at my head—"more widow's weeds."

She's not the first to call them that, seeing as Easton had dreads and always wanted me to try them. Unfortunately, God didn't give him a chance to see how well I wear them. No, God had other plans for my man, and they didn't include me. If ever there was a reason not to talk to Him or His Son, there it is.

"Those are next," Bonnie says.

"What?"

"The dreads have to go."

I want to argue, but I don't have the energy. Besides, maybe she's right. Since that night on the mansion's roof months ago when a dread caught in the telescope and I had to cut it free, I've considered returning to my formerly undreaded locks that once fell soft and fluid down my back.

"Bridget?" She worries her bottom lip. "I know you have a business to run, but when Miles and Birdie come to stay in September, you will help Mama, won't you?"

"Of course."

Her gaze intensifies. "I mean really help—take them off her hands overnight and some weekends."

Overnight? Weekends? Visits to the park, nature walks, and occasional lunches out are what I had in mind. Though Maggie's daughter, Devyn, sometimes sleeps over, she's the only one I've allowed to do so since I lost Easton. And she either shares the bed in the guest room with me or crashes on the couch. There's no way Birdie, Miles, and I will fit into the guest room's full-sized bed.

"It's going to be a long eight weeks for"—Bonnie's voice cracks—"everyone."

I can't remember the last time I saw her so sorrowful. Was she ever? I have a sudden impulse to give her a hug, but she's not a hugger, and since Easton's death, I've related to this side of her.

"So?" she prompts.

She's not asking much. And it's not as if she even knows what she's asking.

Or does she? Keeping Birdie and Miles overnight fits nicely with her demand that I remove my wedding ring.

Which is only a problem if you plan to live the rest of your life in mourning and persist in making little girls cry.

"Bridget!"

Out of my mouth pops, "I'd be happy to keep them overnight."

Bonnie's body eases. "Thank you."

I can handle it—once I get used to my bare left hand. And it is six weeks before my niece and nephew return to Pickwick. Surely between now and then I can…well, reset my life.

"Eight weeks didn't seem long when we started planning the study a year ago, but now…" Bonnie sniffs, only to snort. "My period must be coming. We won't be gone that long, for goodness' sake! And this *is* our last opportunity to conduct a full-fledged study abroad before the children start school."

Is the study the reason Miles and Birdie aren't enrolled in school this year? The newly minted five-year-olds certainly seem bright enough to start kindergarten.

Bonnie points a finger at me. "No more tales of heroes dying."

"I won't make that mistake again."

"Good. Let's get back to the party."

Over the next two hours, I stand on the sidelines, watching happily married couples as my finger silently mourns the loss of its constant companion. Time and again, I touch it through the dress's crisscrossed top where I slipped the ring into my bra. I know it's just a symbol of the love Easton and I shared, but on *my* wedding day, I'd believed I would wear it to the grave after years and years with the man I loved. I didn't even come close. And as I watch Trinity with her Bart, Piper with her Axel, and

Bonnie with her Claude, I force myself to put a name to what earlier made me retreat inside the big house.

Envy.

An ache opens at the center of me and radiates out to the ends. I want what they have—one another. All I have is *one*. My *another* is gone, and every time I think about opening my eyes to other men, I'm set upon by guilt and uncertainty. After all, it may have been four years, but Easton wasn't a coffeepot that needs replacing every so often. He was my love. How could I ever have another? And yet...

My cousin Maggie puts her head on the shoulder of what's-his-name. I frown. What *is* his name? Since it looks like he plans on being a major part of her life, I ought to make more of an effort to—

Reece! That's his name. Reece, who runs his fingers through her red curls, tilts her chin up, and kisses her.

My hand goes to my ring, but the feel of it does little to ease my longing for a shoulder on which to lay my head, a mouth to make mine flush, a heart to make mine jump.

CHAPTER TWO

She did not do that. Oh yes, she did—chucked her gum out the window, which landed on my windshield after she crossed a double yellow line into the oncoming lane and flew past me, after she honked at my unavoidable deceleration up a particularly steep rise on Pickwick Pike. If that doesn't beat all, according to her magnetic door sign, she's a real-estate agent.

Let it go, Bridget.

"I know," I mutter, doing my best to reduce the gum in the corner of my windshield to a blur, "but..." It's been one of those days, and so near a total loss I don't see how anything I do can make it much worse.

Bringing the gum back into focus, I put the pedal to the

metal, causing Buchanan's Nursery truck to lurch and growl. Fortunately, with a bit of prodding and flattery—and now that I'm on the other side of the incline—I can always count on my trusty Ford to pick up speed. "You can do it. You're strong. And not bad lookin' either." Beauty is in the eye of the beholder.

Before long I'm riding the bumper of the sporty little Cadillac, honking and blinking my lights and motioning for the litterbug to pull over. But she pays me no mind, just keeps yakking at her passenger—probably a client, and it looks to be a man.

Time to take it to the next level.

Far better you get home to Reggie and let this day wash itself away.

As the pike curves to the right, the sinking sunlight zings off the roof of the car ahead, nearly blinding me, but I flip my sunglasses on and I'm good to go.

Gaining momentum, I swerve into the opposite lane that is empty as far as the eye can see and roar past the Caddy. I'm not rash, so I give the woman plenty of warning, gradually decelerating as I straddle the two lanes so she can't get around me on the narrow road. When I stop, she has no choice but to brake or mess up that shiny grill of hers.

I push open the moan-and-groan door, swing my legs out, and drop to the asphalt, only to remember I'm barefoot—and still wearing Maggie's dress that poofs up around me like an open umbrella. I whack it down as I approach the car.

When I'm twenty feet out, the driver's door swings open and the woman says, "Gracious no, it's just one of those good ol' girls I told you about. I can handle her."

Oh yeah?

"Besides, I know how important it is we maintain your anonymity."

Obviously, someone full up on himself. As the asphalt heats up my feet, almost making me wish for Piper's pointy shoes, I attempt to make out the man on the other side of the windshield. However, he's mostly in shadow.

The woman, jacked up on three-inch heels, steps from the car, closes the door with a swat, and saunters forward to meet me at her front fender. She cants her glossy head to the side, revealing a talkie thing in her ear. "What is your problem?"

Man, the asphalt is hot! I pull off my sunglasses, the better for her to read my eyes. "That would be the gum you tossed out the window a ways back. It's called litterin'. And it's illegal."

Her copper-colored lips part as she stares at me. "All this because of a little piece of gum?"

"That and your reckless driving."

Shifting her gaze past me to my truck, she drawls, "Right, and there's nothing at all reckless about parking in the middle of a two-way road, hmm?"

I open my mouth to remind her there's good line of sight in both directions, that I'm not the one who crossed a double yellow line, and Pickwick Pike is rarely traveled since the new highway exit went in, but she does have something of a point. So I close my mouth and raise my eyebrows.

She plants her manicured hands on her hips. "Look, I have a very important client in the car, and people like you, putting on displays like this, make people like him think Pickwick is uncivilized and unfit to live in."

"I'm okay with that."

She looks me up and down. "Well, of course you are, darlin'."

My imagination momentarily transports me out of my body, and I see myself as I appear before this professional woman and her client—barefoot, wearing a fancy dress a bit too long, a bit too wide, and way too stiff, no makeup, and dreads hanging down my back. And mustn't forget the backdrop of my battered Ford.

Oh, to be in a pair of jeans, not too long, not too wide, and soft as peach fuzz. And my Crocs. If I don't get off this asphalt soon, I'm gonna be blistered.

The woman checks her watch. "I need to get back to Asheville."

I shift my weight to my right foot to give my left a break. "Just as soon as you take care of the gum."

With a chicken bob of her head, she says, "You expect me to go back and scrape it off the road?"

"You're in luck. It's stuck to my windshield." I hitch a thumb over my shoulder.

She rolls her eyes. "Honestly!"

"I have all day." I fold my arms over my chest.

She peers beyond me, as if to calculate the likelihood of squeezing past my truck without scraping the guardrail on one side and the chiseled-out mountain on the other. Of course, if she waits long enough, eventually a car will come down the pike and I'll be forced to move out of the way.

She huffs. "Fine."

As I start to follow her to my truck, I glance through the Caddy's windshield and catch sight of reflective sunglasses. And a wedge of white teeth.

Yes, this is a peculiar situation, and I might find humor in it if my feet weren't blistering, two five-year-olds hadn't manipulated me into saying *H.E.A.*, and my wedding band wasn't burning a hole in my bra.

I hurry after the woman. "You know, if your gum hadn't landed there, it could have become a deathtrap for some critter that got it caught in its craw."

"Uh-huh." She reaches to my windshield only to snatch her hand back, whip around, and splay that same hand in my approaching face. "Oh. My. Word. Hold it!"

I do, ensuring her white-tipped fingernails don't come within a foot of my face. "What?"

"I know you."

I look closer at her. "No, you don't." Unless she knows *of* me, what with me being a scandalous Pickwick, more specifically, she of The Great Crop Circle Hoax that gained worldwide attention years ago before I exposed my creation for what it was.

With a satisfied smile, she drops her hand. "You're Bridget Pickwick—"

Buchanan.

"—tree huggin', animal lovin' prankster."

"Your point?"

"Cotillion."

Oh. That. "Yes, that was me."

"And your skunk—was it Stripe?"

I'm surprised she knows his name. But then it was in the Asheville newspaper, along with the headline: *Pickwicks Raise a Stink at Cotillion.* More accurately, Bridget Pickwick, who foiled her mother's attempts to transform her into a Southern lady by loosing her skunk on the ballroom.

I reconsider my once-fellow debutante—her wide mouth, narrow nose, and heavily lashed eyes. "I suppose you were there."

"I was. Sprained my big toe and tore my new dress in the stampede."

"Sorry about that. He was deskunked, you know."

"Found that out after the fact." She narrows her lids. "You haven't changed much, have you?"

Not a compliment. "Thankfully, no." I point at the windshield. "Do you mind?"

She gives a throaty laugh. "If you ask me, we're more than even."

But— Oh, all right! "Even we are."

She sidesteps. "Thank you for the lesson in environmental stewardship. I can't tell you how it's impacted me." She walks past. "Oh, here's a little something for you."

When I turn, she's holding out a business card. "Wesley Trousdale, Premier Real-Estate Agent." Her smile turns sly. "I have a feelin' we'll meet again soon."

The Pickwick estate. That's probably why she's here all the way from Asheville. The day just gets heavier. "Not likely." Still, I take the card.

As she sways back to her car, I peel the gum from my windshield and climb into my truck. After wrapping the sticky offender in an old paper napkin, I press the accelerator with a foot destined for blisters and pull into the right lane. Not unexpectedly, Wesley Trousdale draws alongside. As she accelerates past, I glimpse the sunglassed face of her anonymous client.

"No, you are not getting your hands on my family's estate," I mutter. Though how in the world I'm going to stop him, I haven't the foggiest.

Ten minutes later, I halt at the end of my long driveway and lower my forehead to the steering wheel. What a day—my brother married to a female version of himself, that whole *H.E.A.* business, the argument with Bonnie, happy couples all around…

I tug a dread—a comfort, especially when I'm missing Easton—then dig my wedding ring out of my bra and stare at its out-of-place shape between my thumb and forefinger. How's Bonnie to know? I start to slide it on, but the pale circle at the base of my finger that contrasts with the tanned length above and below makes me hesitate. It's as if I'm wearing an invisible ring and, actually, I can still feel it there.

Goose bumps rising, I turn the simple band around, reading the words inscribed on the inside: *You and me. Forever.*

"About as make believe as *H.E.A.*" However, once more I position the ring to slide it on.

Don't do it. Bonnie's right. When you make little girls cry, it's time to say good-bye. Time to stopper the big yawn between now and the grave and get on with your life. Your life, Bridget. Easton is dead. Dead.

I try to say the four-letter word, but I can only mouth it. Yes, Easton is. Not just gone as Bonnie pointed out. He's... Yes, he is.

In the next instant, anger stomps me up one side and down the other. What is my problem? "Easton is dead. D-E-A-D." I curl my fingers around the ring. "And I can say..."

A mental door behind which I haven't looked in a long while creaks open, and I see Easton on our wedding day. It's the first dance. A slow dance. He's so near I can feel the beat of his heart. "And they lived," he lowers his forehead to mine, "happily ever after."

I swallow hard. "No, they didn't." But I can say it. "Happily..." I draw a breath. "...ever after."

Now all I have to do is figure out how to live happily *after* ever after.

Dear Reader, if you enjoyed this excerpt of RESTLESS IN CAROLINA, *the book is available at your online retailer.*

ALSO BY TAMARA LEIGH

INSPIRATIONAL HISTORICAL ROMANCE

AGE OF FAITH: A Medieval Romance Series

The Unveiling: Book One

The Yielding: Book Two

The Redeeming: Book Three

The Kindling: Book Four

The Longing: Book Five

The Vexing: Book Six

The Awakening: Book Seven

The Raveling: Book Eight

AGE OF CONQUEST: A Medieval Romance Series

Merciless: Book One

Fearless: Book Two

Nameless: Book Three

Heartless: Book Four (Spring 2020)

❧

CLEAN READ HISTORICAL ROMANCE

THE FEUD: A Medieval Romance Series

Baron Of Godsmere: Book One

Baron Of Emberly: Book Two

Baron of Blackwood: Book Three

LADY: A Medieval Romance Series

Lady At Arms: Book One

Lady Of Eve: Book Two

BEYOND TIME: A Medieval Time Travel Romance Series

Dreamspell: Book One

Lady Ever After: Book Two

STAND-ALONE Medieval Romance Novels

Lady Of Fire

Lady Of Conquest

Lady Undaunted

Lady Betrayed

❧

INSPIRATIONAL CONTEMPORARY ROMANCE

HEAD OVER HEELS: Stand-Alone Romance Collection

Stealing Adda

Perfecting Kate

Splitting Harriet

Faking Grace

SOUTHERN DISCOMFORT: A Contemporary Romance Series

Leaving Carolina: Book One

Nowhere, Carolina: Book Two

Restless in Carolina: Book Three

cover artwork Sarah Hansen, Okay Creations

❧

OUT-OF-PRINT GENERAL MARKET REWRITES

Warrior Bride 1994: Bantam Books (Lady At Arms)

*****Virgin Bride*** 1994: Bantam Books (Lady Of Eve)

Pagan Bride 1995: Bantam Books (Lady Of Fire)

Saxon Bride 1995: Bantam Books (Lady Of Conquest)

Misbegotten 1996: HarperCollins (Lady Undaunted)

Unforgotten 1997: HarperCollins (Lady Ever After)

Blackheart 2001: Dorchester Leisure (Lady Betrayed)

For new releases and special promotions, subscribe to Tamara Leigh's mailing list: www.TamaraLeigh.com

ABOUT THE AUTHOR

Tamara Leigh signed a 4-book contract with Bantam Books in 1993, her debut medieval romance was nominated for a RITA award, and successive books with Bantam, HarperCollins, and Dorchester earned awards and appeared on national bestseller lists.

In 2006, the first of Tamara's inspirational contemporary romances was published, followed by six more with Multnomah and RandomHouse. Perfecting Kate was optioned for a movie, Splitting Harriet won an ACFW Book of the Year award, and Faking Grace was nominated for a RITA award.

In 2012, Tamara returned to writing historical romance with the release of Dreamspell and the bestselling Age of Faith and The Feud series. Among her #1 bestsellers are her general market romances rewritten as clean and inspirational reads, including Lady at Arms and Lady of Conquest. In late 2018, she released Merciless, the first book in the new AGE OF CONQUEST series, followed by Fearless and Nameless, unveiling the origins of the Wulfrith family. Psst!—It all began with a woman. Watch for Heartless in Spring 2020.

Tamara lives near Nashville with her husband, a German Shepherd who has never met a squeaky toy she can't destroy, and a feisty Morkie who keeps her company during long writing stints.

Connect with Tamara at her website www.tamaraleigh.com, Facebook, Twitter and tamaraleightenn@gmail.com.

For new releases and special promotions, subscribe to Tamara Leigh's mailing list: www.tamaraleigh.com

Made in United States
Troutdale, OR
01/09/2025

27754373R00189